Johnny One-Eye

Johnny One-Eye

A Tale of the American Revolution

Jerome Charyn

W. W. Norton & Company
New York • London

Printed in the United States of America
First Edition

For information about permission to reproduce selections from this book, write to Permissions, W. W. Norton & Company, Inc., 500 Fifth Avenue, New York, NY 10110

For information about special discounts for bulk purchases, please contact W. W. Norton Special Sales at specialsales@wwnorton.com or 800-233-4830

Manufacturing by RR Donnelley, Harrisonburg
Book design by Charlotte Staub
Production manager: Julia Druskin

Library of Congress Cataloging-in-Publication Data

Charyn, Jerome.
Johnny One-Eye : a tale of the American Revolution / Jerome Charyn. — 1st ed.
p. cm.
ISBN 978-0-393-06497-1
1. Spies—Fiction. 2. Prostitutes—Fiction. 3. Brothels—Fiction.
4. New York (N.Y.)—History—Revolution, 1775–1783—Fiction.
I. Title.
PS3553.H33J64 2008
813'.54—dc22

2007034343

W. W. Norton & Company, Inc.
500 Fifth Avenue, New York, N.Y. 10110
www.wwnorton.com

W. W. Norton & Company Ltd.
Castle House, 75/76 Wells Street, London W1T 3QT

1 2 3 4 5 6 7 8 9 0

This book is for Bob Weil.

And for the late Jim Shenton,
who loved American history
more than anyone I know.

Contents

List of Illustrations

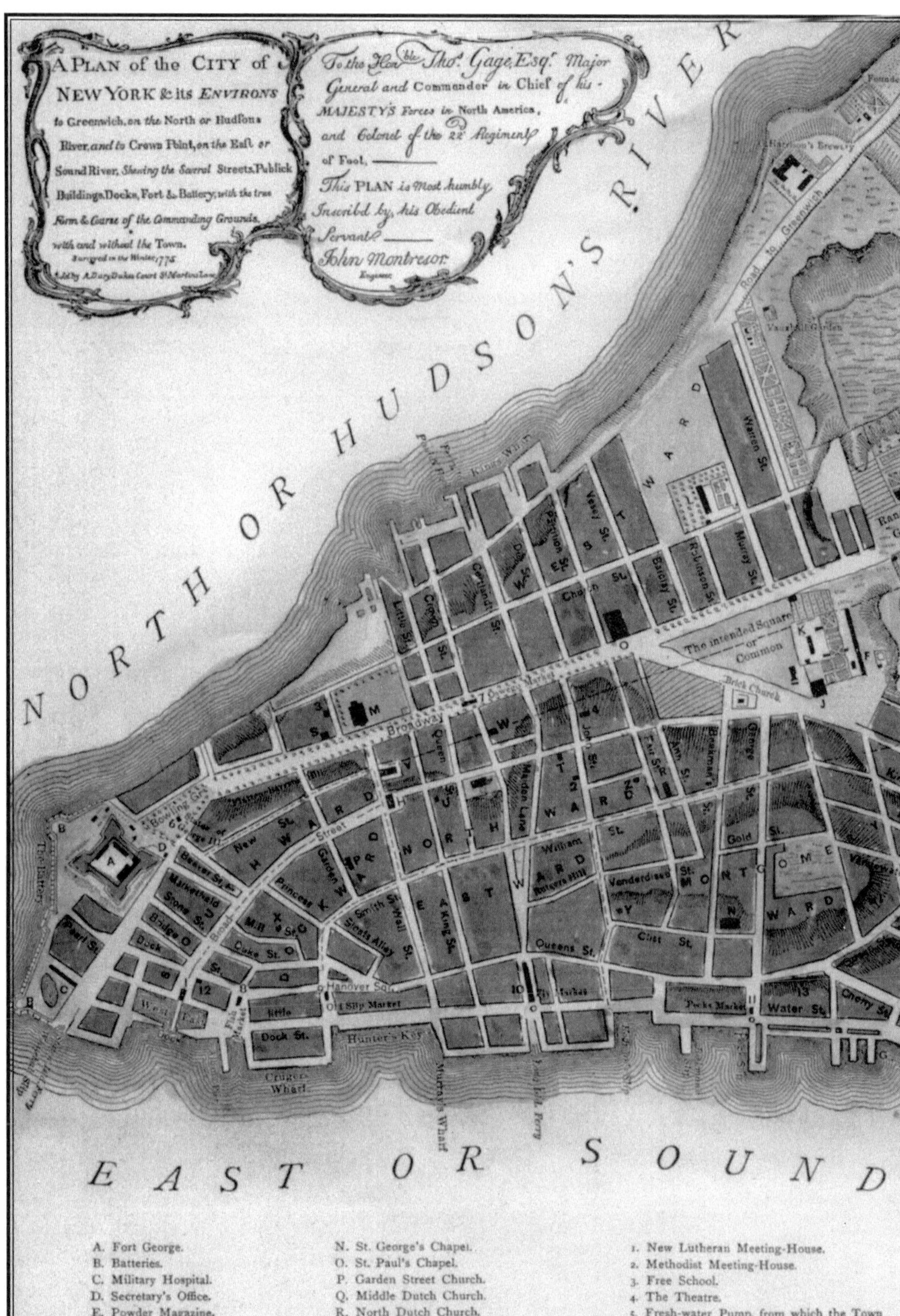

A. Fort George.
B. Batteries.
C. Military Hospital.
D. Secretary's Office.
E. Powder Magazine.
F. Soldiers' Barracks.
G. Ship-Yards.
H. City Hall.
I. Exchange.
J. Jail.
K. Work-House.
L. College.
M. Trinity Church.

N. St. George's Chapel.
O. St. Paul's Chapel.
P. Garden Street Church.
Q. Middle Dutch Church.
R. North Dutch Church.
S. Lutheran Church.
T. German Reformed Church.
U. French Protestant Church.
V. First Presbyterian Church.
W. Quaker Meeting-House.
X. Jews' Synagogue.
Y. Baptists' Meeting-House.
Z. Moravian Meeting-House.

1. New Lutheran Meeting-House.
2. Methodist Meeting-House.
3. Free School.
4. The Theatre.
5. Fresh-water Pump, from which the Town is supplied.
6. Statue of George III.
7. Oswego Market.
8. Fish Market.
9. Old Slip Market.
10. Fly Market.
11. Peck's Market.
12. Fraunce's Tavern.
13. Walton Mansion.

The City of New York 1776

Dramatis Personae

PRINCIPAL PLAYERS

JOHN STOCKING, *alias* JOHNNY ONE-EYE, *a man-child of uncertain birth*

MRS. GERTRUDE JENNINGS, *proprietress of the Queen's Yard, a bordello in Manhattan*

CLARA, *an octoroon from Dominica, in the West Indies, and a "nun" at the Queen's Yard*

GEORGE WASHINGTON, *commander in chief of the Continental Army*

BENEDICT ARNOLD, *American general and turncoat*

PEGGY SHIPPEN, *later* PEGGY SHIPPEN ARNOLD, *the daughter of a Philadelphia merchant with Loyalist sympathies*

SECONDARY PLAYERS

GERTRUDE'S NUNS, *omnipresent at the Queen's Yard, who serve as a silent chorus*

"BLACK DICK," *viz., Admiral Lord Richard Howe, commander in chief of the British fleet in North America*

GENERAL SIR WILLIAM HOWE, *alias* SIR BILLY, *commander in chief of the British army and Black Dick's younger brother*

MRS. (ELIZABETH) LORING, *concubine and "war wife" of General Howe*

JOSHUA LORING, *husband of Mrs. Loring*

MRS. ANNE HARDING, *wife of a Massachusetts farmer*

PRINCE PAUL, *leader of Little Africa, Manhattan's impoverished black quarter*

JOHN ANDRÉ, *British officer, aide-de-camp to General Henry Clinton and head of Clinton's secret service*

HENRY CLINTON, *British general and commander in chief*

SIR HAROLD MORSE, *a resident of the Queen's Yard and mentor to Johnny One-Eye*

SPARKS, *Washington's military valet*

ALEXANDER HAMILTON, *illegitimate son of James Hamilton and Rachel Lavien, Washington's chief aide and former fellow student of Johnny One-Eye*

JASON JENNINGS, *a pirate and assassin*

FELTRINELLI, *or the* ANGEL OF BOLOGNA, *a castrato noted for his sexual prowess and his interpretation of Handel's oratorios*

MORTIMER, *General Howe's valet and bodyguard*

MAJOR MALCOLM TREAT, *Washington's chief of intelligence*

✳ TERTIARY PLAYERS ✳

HARVEY HILL, *or the* TOWN CRIER, *a member of Washington's secret service*

CORPORAL MARTIN JAGGERS, *a member of Benedict Arnold's expeditionary force to Canada in 1775*

SERGEANT JOHN CHAMPE, *a member of Washington's Life Guard*

HERCULES, *Washington's mulatto cook*

MARTHA CUSTIS WASHINGTON, *wife of George Washington*

ELIZABETH SCHUYLER, *later* ELIZABETH SCHUYLER HAMILTON, *daughter of Philip Schuyler, Continental general and Hudson Valley baron*

FAT TOBIAS, *a jailor on the* Jersey

REDMUND, *Manhattan's mulatto hangman*

CAPTAIN KIDD, *high sheriff of Manhattan*

THE COMTE DE ROCHAMBEAU, *commander of the French Army in North America*

THE MARQUIS DE LAFAYETTE, *a French nobleman who in 1777 will become Washington's youngest general*

LORD CHARLES CORNWALLIS, *British general and Clinton's second-in-command*

MATTHEW PIN, *former president of King's College*

"BLACK SAM" FRAUNCES, *proprietor of Fraunces' Tavern*

Ambrose Serle, *Admiral Howe's civilian aide*

Ned Stark, *a British captain and frequent reveler at the Queen's Yard*

Simon, *the royal chimney sweep*

Assassin *in a red wig*

✳ CHARACTERS MENTIONED ✳ BUT NEVER SEEN

George III, *the farmer-king who ruled Great Britain from 1760 to 1820*

John Burgoyne, *British general*

Charles Lee, *flamboyant American general who always went around with a pack of dogs*

Jack Custis, *Washington's stepson*

Tall Water, *an Algonquin chief*

Anno Domini 1776

THE CARETAKER OF KING'S

Manhattan

April 1776

It was the very mask of war. General Sir William Howe, the British commander in chief, had disappeared with his armada of men and battleships. There was not a redcoat to be found in all the colonies, not even a drummer boy. And so there was a strange calm, a profound and disturbing silence instead of cannon fire.

George Washington had arrived in Manhattan but a few weeks ago on his white horse. Both rebels and Loyalists were in awe of the Continental Army's commander in chief, who sat in his saddle with the insouciance of a king. He was the tallest man on our island, and seemed everywhere at once, inspecting the works near Fort George, crossing with his horse on the barge to Brooklyn so that he could inspect our works at Brooklyn Heights.

Every street of Manhattan had been turned into a ditch—our island was now an armed camp. Black stevedores dug beside militiamen. Women and children could not be found. We waited in a kind of fractured peace for the sound of a squall—the wind that would bring the British. General Howe could have but one objective: to drive Washington out of Manhattan, or better still, to break him and his army on the island itself and thus bring a quick death to the rebellion.

The rebels' hopes hinged on this very man, the farmer-soldier from Virginia. And the only time he ever appeared without his horse was when he visited Holy Ground, a street of brothels so named because of its proximity to St. Paul's Chapel; hence its whores were known as nuns. The commander in chief was not a whoremonger. But he did have a secret vice—he loved to gamble. He would come to Holy Ground and its most celebrated brothel, the Queen's Yard, when he was mortally tired and could not sleep. He would play vingt-et-un—Manhattan blackjack—a game that might have been born at this brothel. He would lose his britches every third or fourth night, but the nuns who presided over vingt-et-un always returned his coins and his britches to the commander in chief. And since he never sat at the table with a single bodyguard, the nuns themselves would often drive him back to headquarters, a little north of Holy Ground.

One

WHERE SHALL I BEGIN MY UNREMARKABLE LIFE? My hands were bound with hangman's rope. A rifle dug into my ribs. My accomplices were slobbering at my side, a pair of yobs from Westchester who didn't comprehend the ways of York Island. "It's him," they said, pointing to me with their snouts, since their hands were tied as tight as mine.

"It's him, Your Worship. He's the Divil. He made us do it."

"'Tis true," said the second scoundrel. "We're innocent as lambs, Your Worthy. He hissed evil things in our ears. Offered us pieces of silver to poison your soup. We're cooks, I swear we are. Attached to your rebel army."

The first scoundrel corrected him. "Don't say rebel, Charles. Say the Continentals. He's their king . . . and commander."

He was a giant, this commander and king, with reddish hair and a long nose. I liked him, truly liked him. The lord of all the rebels was an erstwhile land surveyor from Virginia, not a professional soldier and assassin, like King George's generals. He had far more power than any monarch, even with a piddling army that could not stand in formation or fight in an open field. His pigtail was tied with a piece of fine silk. He was a gentleman with a farmer's rough hands.

"Please don't hang us, Your Worship," begged the scoundrels, slobbering again. They were stinking Cowboys who worried the hills of Westchester and shouldn't have come to our waterfront. I'd paid them handsomely, but they were counting on more. They would have slaughtered me and disappeared with my purse once the poison had taken hold and the general sat with his young aides, all of them puking out their guts.

"George Washington, bless that name!" the first yob said.

"I'll repent, Your Worship, I will. Save us, Sir George," said the second.

The general was no longer looking at these yobs. His bodyguards blindfolded them with their own neckcloths and took them out to the gibbet, an ordinary hanging tree. He dismissed his aides and sat down at his portable writing desk with a glass of Madeira and a piece of mutton. But his youngest aide wouldn't leave.

"Excellency, what about *him*? He's a desperate character," meaning your humble servant. "He might be hiding a knife somewhere on his person . . . or under his patch. I don't believe in that impertinent eye patch."

And then the young aide flicked his riding crop perilously close to my one good eye. He was hot to blind me. "Shall I undress his eye, sir?"

The general wouldn't answer him. He must have been sick with fatigue. I've seen it before, in soldiers and clergymen who have a bit of the colic and bad teeth. Grudgingly, with murder in his own grim gray eyes—murder for me—the young man left. And now the giant and I were alone. He got up from his desk (it could barely contain his knees) and cut my cords with a scalping knife. He'd been an Indian fighter long before he was a general, and some chief might have rewarded him with such a knife out of fear and trembling.

"What's your name, boy?"

"You heard those lads. I'm the Divil." I had to rub my hands, because they'd gone to sleep. "And John Stocking some of the time, Sir John to my friends, or Professor John."

"How old are you, Professor?"

"Seventeen, Your Excellency, seventeen years and eleven days."

"And you go around poisoning people's soup."

I had to be twice as clever as this rebel king. I didn't want him to guess my grand design. The poison was but a mix of magnesia and castor oil—a powerful purge. It couldn't have killed a flea.

"Well?" he asked, impatient to rid himself of me.

"A ruse, sir. I knew it wouldn't work. I was hoping it would get me into your camp . . . for a tête-à-tête."

He laughed. He didn't have a tooth I could find, but some device that served as teeth.

"Give me one good reason why I shouldn't hang you?"

"I could lend you a dozen. I'm attached to Sir William in a tinkering sort of way." Sir William Howe had sailed out of Boston with the entire British fleet and fell off the face of the earth. No one could find him, not George Washington, not King George.

"Tinkerer, are you soldier or civilian?"

"Both. I'm a secret agent."

The general offered me some Madeira in a cup that wasn't entirely clean. "You're blunt enough, I'll give you that. Lost you an eye in Sir William's service?"

"No, sir. I lost it while I was with General Arnold in Quebec."

Benedict Arnold had tried to steal Quebec from the British by scampering across the wilderness of Maine. That wilderness was uncrossable to anyone but a madman or a brilliant soldier. And Arnold was both.

But the giant didn't believe I'd been with Arnold. His face filled with fury. He began to scold me like a father to a wayward son. "Rude little boy, didst thou trek with Arnold across the wild lands?"

And I answered him with all the Divil's wile. "Arnold doth not have much of a hand. I had to write his letters and read his dispatches . . . as a confidential secretary. He was but a colonel then. I would parry with my sword and read to him from the Holy Book. I was foolish and wanton. We were in the midst of war, and whilst I prattled, a redcoat stole up and stabbed me in the eye."

"Hang me, boy, if I haven't heard about a one-eyed parson over at the King's College."

King's sat like a citadel on our highest hill. I'd been a student there before I joined up with Arnold. The college was a rookery for Loyalists until Washington shut it down and turned it into an army barracks.

"I am not a parson, sir. I am the caretaker at King's. No one else is around. We haven't a single scholar. The president ran away to London and abandoned us to our misery."

"And from your perch in the bell tower you signal to the British fleet, I fancy."

"The fleet is gone. But I have infiltrated your secret service to the last man," says I, fibbing like a drunken brigadier. "I can sing every name."

"I have no such service," he said, his pale blue eyes narrowing to merciless points. I'd offended the giant, talked about his precious secret service. And I knew I'd have to play him in gentle fashion.

"Excellency, can you not recall? We have met before . . . at King's. Ere three years ago. You brought your stepson up from Virginia to have a little taste of the college. 'Tis a pity he didn't last very long. I was fond of young Jack."

Jack Custis was no scholar. He gambled, kept spiders in his

closet, bullied some of the other lads, but he had a strange fondness for me. I was useful to Jack. I fed him Aristotle, tho' he cared not a fig about philosophy. He eloped after a month or two of classes, bequeathing his soiled neckcloths and shirts to me. He never spoke of the woman he meant to marry. She might have been a tart or a rich widow, like his mum. But I couldn't forget the giant who accompanied him to King's, his stepfather in long white stockings and a cocked hat, a ribbon in his red hair. He remained with me as the giant who looked after Jack, manly and tender with him, whilst I ate my heart out wishing I had such a giant as my dear old dad.

"Stocking," he said, "I can recall every other man and boy I met at the college, not you."

"That's because I was in the president's black book. I had to live in the shadows, like some dark thing. But I did kiss your hand, sir, I swear. I asked your blessing . . . as an orphan at the mercy of the college. And you the father of my only friend."

His ruddy face softened a bit. "I will not hang you, boy."

"Sir, 't would give me much pleasure to kiss your hand again."

He had a very long hand. The joints were gigantic, and his knuckles as large and various as the gold crowns on the gates at King's. I kissed Georgey's hand. It was like brushing against a porcupine with its quills removed, harmless and scratchy. I was immortal at that moment, an angler playing with his worms.

Washington's young aide returned, led me into the officers' mess without so much as a look at me. And that's when I realized who was the angler and who was the worm. The two yobs hadn't been brought out to the gibbet tree in their blindfolds. They weren't blindfolded at all. They sat with the officers, grease on their lips, chewing mutton and leering at your unfortunate friend.

Two

A PAIR OF SERGEANTS OPENED A TRAPDOOR AND kicked me down into a cellar that must have belonged to the cook. I fell against a mountain of potatoes. Then the sergeants pummeled me, and I was left without human companionship.

I began to rot beside that moldy mountain, sprouting carbuncles like a potato. I'm not sure how long I lingered underground. No one bothered to look after my wants. I went unwashed for days, wondering if their plan was to starve me to death or have me die from mental injury. But I wasn't starved, sirrah. I had my own imaginings. And this mountain became my universe. The stars tasted of salt. I had wings with talons on them, such as some perverse angel might use as a weapon.

And then a crack of light appeared in the roof of my little firmament. A man climbed down the stairs with a dish of dried peas . . . and a lantern swinging from his belt like a coxcomb on fire. He wore the buff and blue of Washington's military family, with their cocked hats and epaulettes and pigtails all wrapped in silk. But this was no young aide with an aristocratic brow, the son of some merchant prince who sided with the rebels. He had an eyepatch like myself, and runnels that ran along his cheek, souvenirs of the Indian wars. I recognized Major Malcolm Treat of Washington's secret service.

"I wouldn't have fed you. The peas are from His Excellency's own ration. He's awful fond of peas."

The major hadn't come with cutlery. I had to dig my face into the dish.

"We took a vote. I was for hanging ye without the bother of a tribunal. But His Excellency kept saying how you might have been the companion of young Jack, tho' Jack never mentioned a John Stocking. And I practically raised that lad. I also sent dispatches to General Arnold, hoping he would verify your existence, but he doesn't seem in much of a hurry to confirm or deny that you were with him at Quebec. So far, we have proof of nothing, Sir John. And I can't even grant that you were at King's. The registry has disappeared. And some maudlin hermit has declared himself as keeper of College Hall, giving lectures from time to time, but anyone could have wandered into King's during all the chaos. You didn't go to grammar school in the colony, I'll wager that."

"I went to Parson Smiley's Free School for colored people. I was the one white boy in the class."

"Never heard of Parson Smiley's."

"That's because the school no longer exists."

"Then I can't examine the parson's ledgers, can I? And what would I have found? A pack of pickaninnies, without a pinch of pedigree. Where were you raised, Mr. Stocking?"

"Right on Robinson Street."

He pulled his cocked hat over his eye patch and chortled like a fiend. "In a nunnery? Then your mama must be a whore on Holy Ground."

Treat wasn't so wrong, alas. The Holy Ground was a pig-pen and a paradise rolled into one, with gilded carriages and sailors slobbering their guts. I'd seen Major Treat many a time at the Queen's Yard, the nunnery that ruled York Island. I'd seen royal governors enter and leave by a private porch. In truth, I'd seen Giant George and his aides at poker and whist in the Yard's main parlor, tho' he'd never spotted me. But it wasn't poker that drew these men, or wine, or the mulatto mistresses that a general or governor might keep in an upstairs patio with its own secret garden. It was the royal mistress of the house, Mrs. Gertrude Jennings, with the beauty marks on her shoulder, the headdress that was like a castle of burnt red hair, the outrageously long neck, a bodice made of silver and bone, legs and arms that moved like machines with their own indescribable musk, a face as strong as it was beautiful, with gray eyes and an intelligence that could have been found nowhere else on the island. I can't swear that Gentle George took Gertrude to bed. But he played cards with her, watched her bosoms breathe under a certain layer of silk, talked about rebels, plantations, and kings. The nuns tell me that Gert reminded George of his own lost love, some married harlot who haunted his youth and could still disturb his dreams.

I'd grown up at the Queen's Yard, as Treat surmised. Can't even say who my mother was. Perhaps she was a nun who died of yellow fever, perhaps a chambermaid. I was told my father was a forger who escaped the death penalty by smuggling himself out of Leeds and had spent half his life in one nunnery or another, hiding from the Crown. He was a drunkard who attached himself to Queen Gertrude as her confidant and pet. He understood her, was her mime and storyteller. She would beat him, then toss him a mutton chop. He died before I was ten, but Gertrude did not rid herself of me. I warmed the nuns' blankets with a brazier, delivered messages to the queen's suitors. I wasn't her jester the way my father had been. But I did have a roof until I moved across the road to King's.

Treat squinted at me. "That's how you got so thick and easy with the king's men. You fed them wine and wormwood."

He was shrewder than he could have imagined, this handler of spies.

"Who was your patron, boy?"

"Queen Gertrude."

"Monster," he muttered. "You got close to some Brit in Gert's bed. And he sent you to His Excellency with a fantastic tale."

"I came of my own accord."

He slapped humble John, and the dish clattered to the ground with my precious peas.

"I have broken grander liars than yourself. Confess, you are an adventurer in the employ of the Crown, hoping to wedge yourself into our good graces."

"And why, Major Treat, would the Crown trust me?"

"Because you were clever enough to sneak into our camp with two Cowboys and impertinent enough to poison His Excellency's soup."

"Soup that you would feed to your dog before it ever arrived at His Excellency's lips."

He kicked me with his boot, drowned me in potato dust until I was blind.

I rotted another two days with that dust in my eye before he returned with a second dish of peas, the lantern swinging like an obscene engine between his legs.

"His Excellency seems worried about ye. But I've already dressed the hanging tree. The gibbet, that's your reward."

And this lovely major beat me harder than before. I wasn't much of a stranger to blows. I'd been crowned with broken bottles, bitten and beaten by Gert's suitors, those frustrated and forlorn sons of the gentry who could not please Her Highness or ply favors from her. She was particular about the lads she would let kiss her beauty marks. Gold or silver wasn't much on her mind. She had generals in her kitchen and merchants who could have bought and sold Robinson Street. She demanded conversation and wit. The poorest philosopher could have won her to bed as long as the queen could bathe him first. I'd seen Madame with pirates, peddlers, paupers, and drill sergeants, while she scorned captains, chevaliers, and the president of King's, who stole from the college's endowment to pay for his afternoons in her parlor.

But my hunger in this infernal hole must have given me palpitations. I saw a vision in the potato pile, a ghost with green eyes and an uncanny resemblance to one of Gertrude's girls, Mistress Clara, an octoroon from the Windwards. I was in love with the wench, tho' Clara never bothered to notice me. I was as unremarkable to her as a dish of hardened peas. And the greatest torment of my life occurred when I was still at college. I thought that Washington's stepson, young Jack, had run away with Clara. He would visit with her all the time at the Queen's Yard. He would buy her little baubles. And when I heard that he'd eloped, I fell into a melancholy that near devoured me. I couldn't find Clara. I mourned her with a stinking candle. But she hadn't gone with Jack. She'd cruised Manhattan Island with some nabob or another—a pirate, a general, or an aristocrat with holes in his britches. I cared not a nonce. I was jealous only of Jack.

Treat visited me six more times, prattled on and on about his hanging tree. But he was near to desperation, so he kicked and kicked, and turned my peas to porridge. Finally, after a month meseems, he said, "You're free to go, Mr. Leapfrog."

"I am not a frog."

"You are. The frog who leaps back and forth between the royals and us. You ain't worth a sack of shit."

And he rose up through the trapdoor with his lantern, taking with him the last wrinkle of light and my ghost with green eyes.

Three

THE YOBS RELEASED ME AT LAST, EVEN MADE some pretense of brushing off potato dust. But I looked like a pickaninny. My complection had changed in the dark. I was kicked out of the American camp, manhandled, called Blackie and Son of Ham.

I marched all alone from Montgomerie Ward, where Washington was, at the northern edge of Manhattan, to West Ward and Robinson Street, with its caravan of sailors. Once upon a time, there had been college boys and redcoats with their allowance from the king. But the nunneries weren't accustomed to this new American way of life, where silver was scarce. The nunneries had to reflect Manhattan's patriotic mood. They couldn't even hold onto their names—Royal Court, Piccadilly Palace, King's Road, or Rotten Borough—not in the spring of 1776. The Piccadilly was now Emma's Roost. The Royal Court had become Patriot Hall; Rotten Borough was Island Inn. Only the Queen's Yard remained. Gert was much too powerful a force to be whittled down by the radical committees that governed the island; these governors and sheriffs were Gertrude's clients and supplicants. "Hark," sang the high sheriff of Manhattan, "ain't Gert an American queen? The one and only queen of Queen's Yard."

The lamplighter had come to light the lamps on Robinson Street, change the wicks, and fill their reservoirs with sperm oil; every sixth house was furnished with a lamp, but the nunneries were allowed extra lamps, and Holy Ground was lit up like a bazaar. Children were urged to avoid the route, since it was cluttered with highwaymen and sailors who might seize a lad and press him upon some privateer that patrolled the waters, looking for British bounty. Last year, when fighting broke out between rebels and the king's men, certain sailors saw their chance and seized my own skin. Queen Gertrude had to descend into the bowels of some miserable ship to rescue me. She poked the pirate captain with her parasol, threatened to banish him from the island if he didn't return poor John Stocking. The captain laughed and considered waylaying Gertrude and setting up a brothel on board his ship when the high sheriff suddenly appeared with his constables, struck the captain, and denied him a license to land in our waters. The high sheriff hadn't the right to strip a privateer who had been chartered by Congress, but no one dared question his rank and authority on York Island. He's been a highwayman himself, this grandson of Captain Kidd, who had ungodly rages where he might chew off a man's leg, but was devoted to Gertrude and would permit no harm to her customers or her kin.

And now he was in the parlor at Gert's place, wearing a ridiculous wig that might have been in fashion in 1750, during the reign of George II; but George III, our George, barely wore a wig at all. And the captain sat snoring with one leg propped over the arm of Gert's prize chair. He weighed three hundred pounds, and the chair would rock under him.

I flew right past Captain Kidd. But the queen had her spies, those nuns who waited on her hand and foot, and they captured me, smacked the dust off my coat with their brooms, stripped me naked, carried my carcass to the queen's porcelain tub, their hands on my privates, as if they were fondling their favorite sheep. They sat me down in Madame's perfumed water and kept bringing fresh pails like some mischievous fire company. They washed behind my ears, their open bodices rising above me. They cackled and smoked their pipes, since the nuns of Robinson Street were addicted to tobacco and would rather smoke than please a man or welcome a prince into their beds. They never ate tobacco or scooped it into their nostrils, but not even Madame could cure them of sucking on a pipe. They were fine Christian women who went to the mariners' church, the only one that would have them, and indebted themselves to the tobacco dealers who took advantage of their passion.

I didn't have a pipe of my own. But the nuns would always lend me theirs. And I was puffing on a clay pipe with a tiny bowl and a stem that was almost as long as my arm. It was Clara's pipe, Clara of the Windward Islands, the nun who loved me not.

She claimed that the pipe belonged to a British planter who had married her mother and then wanted to take Clara as his second wife. But Clara had come to Manhattan instead, and the queen found her living on the docks like a wild animal, with lice on her eyelashes. She brought her to Robinson Street, bathed her, and never insisted that she sleep with a man. There wasn't a captain or a merchant on York Island who hadn't considered buying Clara from the queen or renting her as a concubine with woolly blond hair. But Clara wouldn't remove herself from Robinson Street with just any man, no matter how rich he was. Within a month the Queen's Yard had become her home. And she would only share her pipe with someone who took her fancy.

She still shared it with me, humble John, who had never received a single kiss from Clara. Her green eyes didn't dwell on me for very long. She had her own recipe for tobacco, with cured leaves from Jamestown, and petals called blue fire from the private stock of an Algonquin chief named Tall Water. This said chief had sought to buy Clara from the queen. And Clara must have been smitten by this strange man who was much less of a savage than the high sheriff or the king's soldier-assassins.

She left the convent, and I was terrified never to see her again. I'd already been accepted at King's, had my rooms in College Hall, but I'd wander into the Queen's Yard looking for Clara, suffering her absence like a fit of fever. And then, one afternoon, Mistress Clara was back sitting in the parlor, smoking her long clay pipe, as if she'd never been gone. The queen hadn't given Clara's closet to another girl. It still had her blankets and her dolls from Dominica, the dolls she'd carried with her across the ocean, that had been covered with lice when the queen first found her on the docks. Not a living soul dared ask her about Tall Water. She smoked blue fire from a different chief. It was cannabis or some other flower that got your brains to float . . .

Now I sat in the parlor in a fresh suit of clothes that the nuns had extracted from my closet at King's. I had a shirt with a ruffled collar and britches with tiny tassels that the best Englishmen wore. The nuns brushed my hair, tied my tail with a piece of silk. I stared in the mirror and saw only one girl. Clara. We took turns puffing on her long pipe, Clara and I. Her green eyes had begun to spin.

"Johnny," she said, to torture me, "have you been stealing my slippers again?"

She was like some prophetic black *and* blond witch with a complection that was half coffee, half cream. I had pilfered her slippers and shoes from time to time. They were marvelous talismans. I'd never had so propitious a good-luck charm as one of Clara's silk and leather beauties with a silver buckle and a broken heel. I'd kept it on my person all the while I was in Maine with Arnold. I would have drowned in the Dead River were it not for that shoe. But the shoe had begun to unravel of late and I hid it in my new quarters at the college.

"Mistress," says I, in as formal a tone as I could muster. "I have but one of your shoes, a pathetic thing I found in the trash barrel. I use it as a memento."

"Memento of what?"

"Of my better days."

It was pure twaddle. I'd had no better days. There was only one heaven on earth: to watch Clara as her bodice went up and down ever so slightly with each of her breaths. And while I pondered, a hand knocked the pipe from my mouth, spilling a fiery dust across the parlor.

Four

I DIDN'T HAVE TO GUESS WHOSE HAND IT WAS.

"Majesty," I said, with a bow that could have been spectacular at court. "I would be forever grateful if you introduced yourself with less passion."

She was in her morning gown, a peignoir from Paris. She was nowhere as tall as Clara, and couldn't glide across a room the way Clara could. Madame was plump, with a few islands of gray hair, but she had a fire that rose from her belly. And she was fearless.

"John Stocking, you will not use your education against me, all your fancy talk."

"How have I offended you?"

"You disappear like a wisp of smoke and return with such nonchalance that you can bury yourself in Clara's pipe without greeting me."

"Madam, you rarely wake before five of an afternoon. And if I am not mistaken, the clock struck five but a minute ago."

"Impostor," she said. "You could have knocked once and announced yourself."

"What? And disturb your paramour?"

She ripped me right out of my chair, and while I crawled about like a baboon, she kicked and scratched and robbed me of a fistful of hair. The nuns were horrified. Not even Clara, her favorite, had an inkling of what to do. But Gertrude's door opened and Harold Morse marched out, with nothing on but his britches, like a prize fighter—his sinews could have been worms set on fire by some sinister god. He was the only one who could risk the queen's wrath.

"Dearest," he said, "would you murder the boy?"

"Yes. With much glee."

"Fine. Murder him, do. I shan't weep. But it is not quite becoming to watch you nag at the boy like a common chicken plucker. Your legs seem small."

Gert released my scalp. "My legs are not small."

She rose, defeated by Sir Harold's remark.

"May I borrow the boy?" he said, and he grabbed my neckcloth as if it were a wooden collar, navigated me into the queen's boudoir, and locked the door. The queen had mirrors everywhere, mirrors from the quarters of sea captains, from harlots' houses in New Orleans, from the mansions of Loyalists who had to flee our island, from the bedchamber of some marquesa along the Spanish Main. A clever thief could have found a market for himself in Madame's mirrors, but he wouldn't have survived his pillage. Harold would have chopped him off at the legs and fed him to Madame's cats, limb by limb. He was no ordinary soldier-assassin. He traveled incognito, without epaulettes. He was a knight of the realm, but no one was privy to this information except myself and the king who had knighted him.

I was waiting for Sir Harold to congratulate me. But a minute after he closed Gert's door, he gave me a hiding such as I have never had. It was much worse than what Washington's little major had inflicted upon my body and soul. I didn't bleed. But my kidneys were so sore, I lay curled up like some homunculus.

"Sir Harold, I followed your plans to the letter. And we won. That half-blind major will welcome me into Washington's secret service. I swear on my life."

"They were readying to hang you, Johnny. And don't call me Sir Harold. Someone might hear you."

"But Major Treat said—"

"Quiet. Wasn't Arnold meant to be our rescuer? All he had to do was swear that you had lost an eye fighting for him. Wouldn't have cost him a farthing. 'T was his silence that convicted you. Johnny, they'd prepared the tree."

"Then who is my savior?" says I.

"Gert. She met with the major, convinced him that the nunnery was now a patriotic nest."

"And he believed her?"

"After a little grog and a lot of kisses," said Sir Harold. "And you forgot to thank her, to let her know you're still alive."

"And that's why you bruised my kidneys? Best sleep with both eyes open. I mean to kill you."

"What, and lose your only anchor?" And he turned poetic in that false inflection of his. "Dost thou still love me, boy?"

But I wouldn't play his game and mouth the expected remark. *I love thee not.*

I loved him the way you could love a poisonous spider that you lived with. And he loved no one but a king for whom he would commit any crime. He would have cut all our throats in a single night, dispatched the entire nunnery, if it could have given him America.

I WALKED OUT OF THE BOUDOIR, licking my wounds. The nuns weren't about. They must have gone to their own rooms. The sheriff was gone. Gertrude sat alone in the parlor. She was sucking on a pipe without a lick of tobacco and contemplating the known and the unknown. A wrinkle appeared on her brow.

I kissed the back of her neck. Her body stiffened.

"Madam, why do you cringe whenever I touch you?"

"Habit," she said. "I remember how handsome you were as a little boy. I could have swallowed you entire."

"Then you should have."

"You weren't my child. And your father occupied my bed if I'm not mistaken."

"But I'm a grown man, at the college now. Couldn't we inhabit some neutral ground?"

"There is no neutral ground. We are like warriors, you and I, in a battle I can barely comprehend. I love you and hate you in the same instant, as if lightning struck."

"I must be perilous for you, madam."

No matter. I kissed her again. It wasn't impudence. And she did not cringe. I walked out of the Queen's Yard. The far end of Robinson Street had been turned into a ditch. Patriots were building their barricades, turning York Island into an armed camp, waiting for Howe's warships to appear on the horizon. Those warships would come. 'T was as certain as Satan himself. The rebels had no navy, nothing but raw recruits and Washington's white horse. He would ride along the roads, rallying his boys, but he must have realized that Manhattan could not be defended, that the thirteen forts his little boys had built wouldn't stop redcoats and royal marines.

I caught Clara smoking in the shadows, her green eyes lit by the embers in the bowl of her pipe. Her mouth was hidden and I couldn't tell if she was in a somber mood.

"Clara, what will ye do when the redcoats come?"

"Harold will welcome them, I won't. I'm not in love with the Brits. I had enough of their royal ways in Dominica. My stepfather wanted to crawl into me when I was twelve. He beat my mama. She helped me run to Manhattan. Sometimes I wish I had stayed long enough to kill him."

"But the British can't be all bad. They taught ye to read."

"Oh, yeah, Stepfather Steven was a learned man. He sat me on his hip and poked a finger in my cunt while he turned the page."

"I'm awful sorry," I said.

She laughed, the embers giving her eyes a devilish hint. "Ain't you Gentleman Johnny? But in your heart of hearts I'll bet you're as brutal as the Brits. You'd love to diddle me with your finger, only you're too scared."

And she went back inside the convent, to her very own closet that no man or boy could enter without Gertrude's permission. Clara was the only nun who had so private a deal. Gert would laugh and say that she was protecting her property, that Clara would become the new queen and mother superior once Gert retired. But it had nothing to do with business. Gertrude loved her with a love that had no limits. Clara could have been the Queen of Sheba if she didn't have blond hair. Or perhaps Gert was the Queen of Sheba, the white Sheba. Clara was her princess, and I some Solomon who fell under their sway, a Solomon without wives or gold or the least bit of sense.

Five

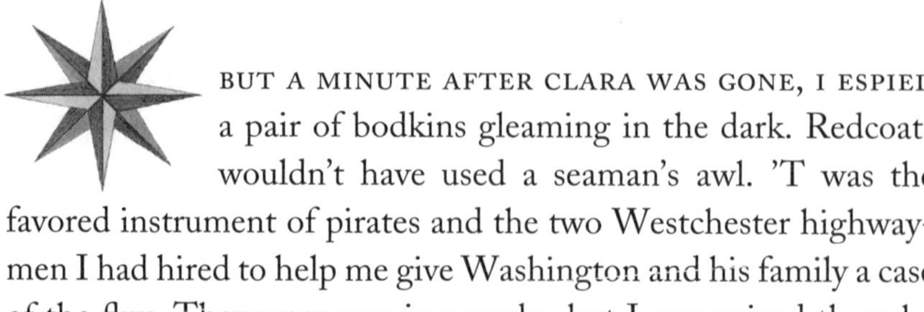

BUT A MINUTE AFTER CLARA WAS GONE, I ESPIED a pair of bodkins gleaming in the dark. Redcoats wouldn't have used a seaman's awl. 'T was the favored instrument of pirates and the two Westchester highwaymen I had hired to help me give Washington and his family a case of the flux. They were wearing masks, but I recognized them by their miserable slouch.

"How are ye, me lovely?" said the fatter of the yobs. "We'll have your purse, since you paid us a pittance."

They'd have punctured my throat no matter what I gave them. All I could think about was Clara. I still had the ribbon I stole from her when I was a little scholar at King's. I would knot the ribbon round my neck and swear to the other little scholars that Clara was my sweetheart. Faith, I intended to marry her, but first I had to survive.

I didn't have a rat's chance. A bodkin was next my throat. Its handle grazed my ear. But then I heard a mooing from the harbor that could have been a ship's horn, or the massacre of a dozen women and men.

"The redcoats, the redcoats," these Cowboys sang. They dropped their bodkins and ran for their lives.

DEPRIVED OF CLARA's face to dwell upon, I had me a bout of melancholia, and I knew of only one tonic that could lift a lad out of his own dark water. Clara's shoe closet. All the nuns kept their shoes and winter boots in the same closet, but Clara had the most spectacular shelf. And when the blackness descended upon my shoulders, I would unlock the closet with a key I'd swiped from Madame and fondle Clara's slippers and shoes. 'T wasn't the shoes themselves, mind you, not their physical trappings, but their proximity to the mistress I adored.

I wasn't always alone in that closet. Seems it was the meeting ground of Clara's suitors; the richest of them would bribe the nuns, paying a handsome price to sniff Clara's shoes. I never felt superior to these nabobs. Shoes were the closest they would ever get to possessing Clara. They might have wormed their way into Clara's bed with their gold coins. But they could not penetrate her green eyes. It was Clara's remoteness that aroused them, Clara's indifference to anything but her dolls.

I caught a wavering light under the closet door. I wasn't in any mood to commiserate with Clara's suitors. But I didn't hear a sound from within the closet. And that infernal silence troubled me. I clutched a handle in the form of a swan's head and sallied inside.

An oil lamp sat on the floor. Near the lamp was Sir Harold Morse, a cape around his shoulders. 'T was most singular, since Harold and a couple of mice in Madame's yard were the only ones on the planet immune to Clara. Yet here he was, contemplating in a shoe closet as if this little island of heels and toes were part of his treasure. He did not budge when I moved betwixt him and the light.

"Harold, have you put a red mark on Madame's gate?"

"What the Devil for?"

"To alert the redcoats . . . that they shouldn't slaughter us in our sleep."

"Imbecile, who would dare slaughter us? I have credentials from the king."

"But credentials do not count for much in the thick of battle."

He did not take prettily to that retort. "Yes, you are the seasoned warrior."

"Hardly. I lost my eye within ten minutes of entering the walls of Quebec."

He softened for a moment, as was his wont. "I do not mean to scold you. I come here often in the middle of night, when the nuns pay no mind to their shoes. I think about the years before I arrived in your wretched colony."

Harold's childhood was almost as perilous as mine. He was the bastard son of a British lord, kicked and beaten by his older brothers. He might have died were it not for King George. The king had discovered him on the road to Windsor Castle. He was riding his horse in the rain, and he stopped for Harold, hoisted him onto his saddle, brought him to Windsor.

Harold grew up at the king's side, learned to fence and fire a brace of pistols. And when George began to feud with his American colonies, he sent over his secret knight to assess the damage and recruit lads who would remain forever loyal to their king. Sir Harold landed in New York, recognized the enormous treasure of King's College, where wellborn lads of the colonies went to school on a hill in Manhattan. But these lads were loyal to no one but themselves. And Sir Harold decided to manufacture his own college boy. I was the only candidate. I'd had no schooling. I was a scavenger and a scamp. Must have reminded Harold of himself when the king found him near Windsor woods. So while I delivered messages and served ale for Madame, Sir Harold insisted on sending me to the parson's school for colored boys.

"Johnny," he said, "'T will be an excellent masquerade. Who would ever suspect a spy among the human trash of Out Ward?"

Out Ward contained the gallows, a hovel called Little Africa, a home and hospital for paupers, and the parson's school, where I sat for a whole year, while Sir Harold supplemented my learning with lessons of his own. And one day a letter arrived on the desk of Matthew Pin, president of King's. The letter bore His Majesty's seal. It nominated John Stocking, age fourteen, as the first king's scholar, with a stipend to the college of three hundred pounds. Matthew Pin was avaricious, but he was no fool. He recognized me as the lad who delivered his beer. He kept the three hundred pounds, but refused to enter me in the college register.

"Stocking," he said, "go away. We do not, and never will, groom beer boys at King's."

And that's when Sir Harold pounced. He appeared at the college with cape and scabbard.

"You're his sponsor," Matthew said, his mouth moving contemptuously. "Any idiot can see that. But there isn't the slightest chance that he could ever pass our entrance exam."

Sir Harold stared into the president's face. "Young John is the king's ward."

And he took a letter out of his wallet. It contained one sentence:

Whoever despises this boy, despises me.

—GEORGE REX

Pin grew apoplectic, but I was guaranteed a place in College Hall.

That was three years ago. And in those three years I studied at King's, went with Arnold to Quebec, lost an eye, and nearly rotted in George Washington's dungeon.

"Sir Harold, will I ever have an audience with the king himself?"

"Once we hang the farmer-general and his family."

The picture of Giant George suspended from a tree pained the king's little scholar.

"Does he mention me in his letters?"

"He's a king, damn you. He has an empire to run . . . but we will go to England, I promise, and get you a knighthood."

"I do not want to be the first American knight. I would like to meet him, that's all. To feel his kindness and his modesty."

I ABANDONED CLARA'S CLOSET, crossed Robinson Street, and went into College Yard. The front gate was open—'t was ethereal, with College Hall on its hill, a stone castle awash in moonlight. I was expecting to meet a multitude of angels or murderous redcoats. But there were only Washington's militiamen and a fistful of students, stragglers who had nowhere else to live. Matthew Pin had left them in the lurch, run away to England with the college's strongbox, and I had to fill the void.

Six

FIVE MONTHS AGO HAROLD AND THE NUNS HAD brought me home from the hospital in Albany, where I had been lying in my bed like a lonely dog with a black hole for an eye. 'T was in December of 1775. I had to walk with a crutch, since both my heels had been singed in Quebec. And how could I avoid a college that was but a street away?

Several tutors and clergymen pranced across College Yard in their black robes to give the impression that there still was a college. But King's was in a state of anarchy. The few firebrands we'd had at the college attached themselves to the ragged tail of George Washington's army. And the others—rich young Loyalists—smoked their pipes, drank wine near the harbor, and sent their servants on scouting missions to buy marmalade on Manhattan's little black market. This marmalade was for the nuns of Robinson Street, who liked nothing better than to lounge in bed with a pot of jelly from the British Isles. With young scholars braying at their feet.

Yet these scholars were more than whoremongers, I'll grant them that. They organized themselves, wouldn't permit the revolution's own watchdog committee onto the premises. This committee of lugubrious men, mechanics and merchants mostly—some of them the very speculators who had sold marmalade to the King's scholars—decided they would rather torch the college than have it exist as a Loyalist house of learning.

They were led on by their wives, women dressed in homespun. These wives had little use for high fashion, for gowns with a pannier underneath, a panoply of wire and whalebone that ballooned out like a basket. They did not wear painted feathers or silks. They looked like ghosts that harangued their misters and helped them light their torches. They meant to smoke the young scholars out of their barricade in College Hall, or see them burned alive.

"Loyalist filth," said their leader, a woman in a white bonnet. "Give up allegiance to your king, or die."

And the scholars replied from their window, "Hurray for George, hurray for George, the kindest king ever to wear a crown."

This only inflamed the women, who hurled torches at the window like bowlers on Bowling Green. The lads would have perished, but some other party wouldn't let these patriotic wives have their bonfire. That party wasn't the sheriff or Manhattan's militia. 'T was the nuns of Robinson Street, Gertrude's nuns in particular, who marched out of the Queen's Yard in their panniers and embroidered boots, carrying cakes, tea, and marmalade on long silver serving dishes. The men of the committee gawked at the nuns and would have given them a laissez-passer into College Hall, but it was their wives who stood in the nuns' way.

From my perch in College Yard, I could catch the glint in Clara's eyes, the craze that would come over her whenever she was thwarted. She did not have the art of politicking that was peculiar to our colony. Perhaps politicking played no part in the Windward Isles. I knew little of her people or how she had been schooled, or whether she had been schooled at all. Still, she had her own strange aristocracy. Other waifs had appeared on our docks with lice all over them, but Gertrude had only welcomed one.

Clara stood perilously close to a torch.

Gertrude pulled on her sleeve to calm her down, and it was like calming an Arabian horse, an Arabian with green eyes. Smoke was coming out the window while the nuns stood face-to-face with wives who wanted to set fire to the panniers.

And that's when I catapulted myself, shot onto the lawn with my crutch, like some coxcomb at Windsor Castle, or my own dad, who had been Madame's personal slave. I did half a somersault on my singed heels, flaunted my eye patch, so that the patriotic men and women could peek at the hole in my head.

The women took a marked interest in me.

"Johnny One-Eye," they said, and whilst they all laughed, I led the nuns into College Hall with my gambols and somersaults. The scholars were glad to welcome Clara and the other nuns, to feast on marmalade after managing to smother bits of fire and smoke in College Hall with their own wet blankets, but they did not have much use for me. I had no place in their little calendar of highborn souls. They didn't offer me the least snippet of cake. I cared not. 'T was Clara's frowns that hurt, the coldness and condemnation in her eyes.

"Always the clown, ain't you, John?" she sang, while the scholars pawed at Clara and fed her cake.

It was Gertrude who defended me of a sudden. "Quiet, Clara. He saved these lads, saved their lives."

"Couldn't he have charged into those committee women with his crutch? I was gettin' hungry for a battle royal."

"While the college burned? Johnny did what he had to do."

"Then can't he eat in a corner?" asked a scholar. "Where clowns are supposed to sit while their betters amuse themselves."

Gertrude slapped the scholar. His mouth quivered, but he

took the slap. Clara would have scratched his eyes out had he ever moved on Madame. He smoldered and stuffed his face with food from a silver dish whilst Gertrude took out her gold windup watch, a bibelot she'd won in a card game at the Queen's Yard.

"Eat your tea," she said. "You have five more minutes of fun."

"But Gert," another scholar said, "we're making our stand. No rebel will drive us out of King's."

"The rebels aren't driving you out. You're leaving of your own volition."

"And why is that?" said the same scholar. "We have our books and our desks."

"Desks fated to be firewood."

"We'd soon as die than surrender to a band of smelly mechanics and their smelly wives."

Gert slapped him too.

"Never malign your enemies," she said. "That's the first lesson of war." She ripped the shirt off a scholar's back, draped it upon a stick, and manufactured her own flag of truce.

"Aw, can't we stay?" said yet another scholar.

"And have my girls roasted as harpies and witches? Because that's what will happen."

The scholars turned gallant. "Madam, we would be mortified to watch fingers of smoke crawling out of Clara's hair, like some perverse picture of the Medusa. We could not—nay, would not—ever allow this to happen."

And they marched out of College Hall with Clara holding the flag. I limped behind them, like some one-eyed animal. Neither the committee men nor their wives molested us. But I could sense the hatred in each woman's eye. Had the mechanics and merchants not been present, their wives would have set us all on fire.

The scholars followed Gert into the nunnery. They sported with the girls, guzzled our best sparkling wine. I would have wandered into the shoe closet, had my own champagne, but I might have been noticed in the hurly-burly of scholars, and I did not relish being spied upon.

Gert stood apart, seemed to look at me, as if to imply: *We will have our own party, John.* And I never felt closer to Madame than on that day, six little months ago, when I gamboled on a lawn and kept my college from burning to the ground.

Seven

FIVE MONTHS LATER AND I'M THE HERMIT OF King's. I'd moved out of the Queen's Yard. I could neither be near Clara nor apart.

I had no right to a room at the college. Washington had turned King's into a hospital and hotel for his militia. But no one seemed in charge, and I could slip in and out at my leisure. Since our former president had fled to England, I lived in Matthew Pin's old rooms. The militiamen had seized the furniture, tore whatever wealth Pin had on the walls. I had nothing but a narrow bed and scraps of clothing that the militia hadn't bothered to steal. The college no longer had a cook, and I had to grab whatever vittles I could. The nuns fed me. They brought soup and bread and wine from Robinson Street. Gert was the instrument. I probably would have starved without the queen. But she wouldn't send the nun I wanted most.

I wasn't a minister, as Matthew had been before he assumed the presidency. But I did lecture once or twice a week inside the chapel that was no longer a chapel, since Matthew Pin had stolen all the artifacts, including the college Bible embroidered in gold.

The militiamen had ripped out half the pews, deposited them in the dining hall that was now their barracks, and I was left with nothing, nothing at all. But the yobs crowded into the chapel to hear me speak. Sailors, militiamen, mechanics and their wives, half the nuns of Holy Ground. "Domine Johnny," they called me, and I didn't even have a churchman's hat or robe. But they longed for a preacher in such precarious times, and preachers were hard to get. York Island was like a lost world, waiting for the redcoats to come. The town was near to madness, and I had to soothe a sorry lot of souls.

I lectured to a band of unwashed patriots, posed as the college's last remaining moral philosopher. I had few credentials but the lies I'd picked up from Harold and the balderdash of my drunken tutors, who were ridden out of town, pelted with stones, pissed upon, because they had ranted against General Washington, had even sentenced him to death in their diatribes. Careful I was. And also confused. I loved a king I'd never met and couldn't seem to hate the rebel commander in chief. I was a Yorker, lads, a child of Holy Ground, but sometimes I couldn't tell the difference between God and the Divil. So I removed myself from the here and now, retreated from the territory of rebels and Loyalists, from Howe's armada and Washington's breastworks and redoubts, the chains he sank in the Hudson to trap the British fleet, the surgeons he'd brought to King's to assuage the certain slaughter of his men. He had neither the arms nor the maneuverability nor the skill to fight the strongest armada in the world—a phantom armada that was hiding somewhere, waiting to pounce, like a monstrous sea lion in a floating field of mice; and it was the palpable aura of General Howe and his invisible brother, Admiral Lord Richard Howe, that poisoned our tranquility.

My subject that day was King Saul, the unfortunate pilgrim who couldn't please God because he was a man without a voice.

Saul was one of us, isolated, alone, stuck inside the island of his own skin. "God isn't fond of silence," I said. "God preferred David and his lyre." But the mechanics interrupted me. I knew what was on their mind. The profound shortage of available black bodies. Blacks had run to the British, both slaves and free men, and the mechanics could find no one to toil for them. The British had been freeing slaves by the dozen, offering them jobs as stevedores or baggage handlers. And the mechanics were frozen up with fury.

"Domine, why do ye waste our time with shepherd boys and kings? Instruct us. Do black men have a soul? The blacks are signing up with King George. If we find one nigger in a red coat, we'll burn him in hot oil. And we'll burn Little Africa. So what is your belief? Do blackies have a soul?"

"They're the children of Ham, and Ham had a soul."

"That's sedition," they said. "Prove to us, Domine, that a black man can reason?"

They were looking for an excuse to rush into Out Ward and capture as many blacks as they could, harness them as packhorses, and pay them a pittance. Thus Little Africa would become one more colony of mechanics. I couldn't stop them. What militia could?

A tall woman strode across that sea of broken pews in a cardinal that obscured her face. She removed her hood when she arrived at the table that served as my lectern. It was Clara, here at King's again, her green eyes blazing at the rabble. Perhaps she'd been to all my lectures in that cardinal of hers and didn't want to give a lad the satisfaction of knowing she was around. I'd never seen her so angry. She brushed me away like a useless fly, but not before she hissed in my ear. "I can't believe a college boy would listen to such trash."

And she turned on the rabble. "I ought to spit. Sailors philosophizing about the human soul. A bunch of devils with light skin."

"Aw, Clara, sit yeself down. We didn't mean you. Whoever heard of a nigger with blond hair?"

"I'll nigger you," she said, and rushed right into the rabble. There was pandemonium.

"Order," I shouted, "order," while the sailors and militiamen surrounded Clara with colossal planks of wood they tore out of the pews. I stood beside her, covering Clara's flank and waiting for a massacre when the high sheriff appeared without a single constable.

"John, are you insane? Encouraging this crowd."

He didn't have a cudgel. He swatted at the sailors with a corner of his hat. "Out, out," he said, and invited the whole mob of women and men to depart from the chapel.

I couldn't find Clara. She must have fled in secret and returned to Holy Ground.

Eight

WENT BACK TO MY ROOMS TRYING TO CONSOLE myself with the one hero I'd ever had. Benedict Arnold. I first came across him during the summer of '75. I'd enlisted with the rebels right out of King's. 'T was the brainchild of my mentor, Sir Harold Morse. His great plan was to have me join up with Manhattan's own regiment of rapscallions and disgraced Sons of Liberty, the Irregulars, because it was much easier to hide within such a chaotic little kernel of men. How could he have known I would lose an eye at Quebec?

"Attach yourself to a general," my mentor told me.

But there were no generals or colonels even close to Fresh Water Pond, north of Robinson Street and the Negroes Burial Ground, where we trained in our britches, just madmen and Sons of Liberty looking for battle. We marched to Massachusetts in fifteen days, and would have arrived sooner if some of the madmen and Sons hadn't stopped to steal from farmers and chase the farmers' wives into the woods, calling them King George's harlots while they ripped off their clothes. I'd have lost my reason had I not reminded myself that I was Harold's homunculus, robbed of all human warmth, put there to join up with some general. But it troubled me to hear such madmen blame my benefactor, George, a king who wouldn't have run after farmers' wives in the fields or helped himself to vittles that ne'er belonged to him. Only once did I lose control and betray the trust that Harold had in me. A yob was chasing after a farmer's wife who looked like a mere child. "Johnny," he said, "will ye have this here harlot first or last?"

I hit him over the head with a rock, told myself that I was taking care of the king's business, that George wouldn't allow one of his American colonists to be ravished in so rough a fashion.

We didn't find much comfort in Cambridge, a town of tents filled with ratty rebels hovering over Boston and a British army in brilliant red uniforms and a barracks with stovepipes and beautiful white tents on Boston's big green. And there wasn't a mound of dust left to billet the Manhattan Irregulars. We had to forage for ourselves like Gypsies. I lived inside a blanket with holes in every corner. And it was the holes that kept me alive. I could watch for thieves who would cut your throat to acquire a powder horn or a colored neckerchief.

A colonel rode in front of us, sitting on a huge chestnut with an arse as wide as a hill. He was searching for volunteers. And I told myself that he was as near a general as I'd ever get. He intended to grab Canada from the British with a single regiment. He wouldn't go by water. He would follow an old Indian trail in the wilds of Maine, catch Quebec by surprise, seize the city while it slept on its rampart, tranquil in the belief that no one would be crazy enough to cross an impenetrable forest, no one but Benedict Arnold. He was not a giant, like George Washington, but rather a smallish man with thick fingers and a bearish chest, tons of silver and gold on his tunic.

The colonel received me in a tent made of the finest sailcloth.

He wore a scarf at his throat, sucked on a pipe, and sipped at a tankard of rum with a silver beak. The rum was meant to swallow his sorrow, I imagine. He was selecting soldiers while he mourned. He'd lost his wife and was left with three sons.

"Private Stocking, show me your hands."

I did.

"Pah," he said. "You have a girl's hands. And I need woodsmen who can deal with a bateau. What can ye offer?"

"Loyalty."

"I can buy all the loyalty I want with a letter of credit."

"But you can't read too many letters while you're high on a horse," says I.

"I don't like your tongue. Were you a magistrate's assistant before ye started to soldier?"

"I was a college boy."

"At some Tory hellhole. And you've been sent to haunt me and my men."

I'd heard that the Indians of the north had named him Dark Eagle. He did have an eagle's black glare. And he must have told fortunes with his blue-gray eyes; he could already read me as a homunculus.

"Can ye spell? Are ye good at grammar? Then I'll attach ye to my person."

"As your bodyguard?"

"Not on your life. As my scribble boy."

He looked at me once with his fortune-teller's eyes, started to swoon, and fell right into my arms. "It's my new mistress," he said, "mistress rum . . . shouldn't let a man drink when he has the gout. I'm raising ye one rank, Corporal Stocking. And you'll be a sergeant come midnight, if ye can restore me to my table, so I can interview the next lad."

And that's how my short career began at Arnold's side in tent town, in the wilderness, under the walls of Quebec, where I lost me an eye and Arnold was shot in the leg, and at the little Catholic hospital where both of us lay wounded. Congress named him a brigadier right from his hospital bed, and I, who was an acting lieutenant by now, fell back into anonymity. He resumed his command without a word of goodbye to his scribble boy. He was hotheaded, mercurial, and must have found another scribe. But he never seized Quebec. And I had to get out of that little hospital in a nonce or become a prisoner of war.

It was Madame and the nuns who nursed me back to whatever health a one-eyed man can have. And I reclaimed my territory at King's, tho' in truth I was nothing more than a watchman who presided over the dismantlement of College Hall.

I HAD A DREAM the very night that Clara had appeared in her cardinal to chastise our mechanics for their woeful disregard of black men. In my dream I could see a one-eyed general wearing a long winter coat, the very coat that Arnold wore when he attacked the Lower Town of Quebec, and plunged, sword in hand, into the heart of a blizzard. "Rush on, brave boys! Rush on!" But Holy Ground was on the far side of the blizzard, not Quebec.

I didn't realize how pregnant my dream was, how ripe with unfortunate meaning. A one-eyed man moved in right across from me at College Hall—Washington's own little major, Malcolm Treat, who guided America's secret service and liked to lock a lad in a potato bin. Treat inherited the apartment that had been set aside for King George himself should His Majesty ever have the whim to cross an ocean and visit the college of kings. This apartment-palace was situated in a corner that looked out upon Robinson Street. The king could have watched all of whoredom from his window.

But I was forlorn when I heard a familiar laugh coming from the king's bedroom. Major Treat had a visitor I longed to know very little about. The laugh was unmistakable. A nun had arrived in full regalia, with a pinched waist and a wide skirt of so many hoops it could have hid a small army. Clara, *my* Clara, was wearing a wig piled high in the lush manner of Madame de Pompadour, she who could terrorize the entire French court until the day she died.

Clara had always been independent, a nun who picked her own clients, who puffed on her pipe and remained aloof from the traffic at the Queen's Yard, and here she was painted up like a harlot. Gertrude's hand was behind it all. Madame had sent her to this truculent little major, and I had to know why. I suffered her cooing for a week, and then I pounced. She was on the way to Treat in her hoops and her tower of hair when I opened my door and kidnapped Clara, one hand over her mouth.

"I'm desperate," I said. "If you promise not to scream, I'll let you go."

Her green eyes were like mirrors to my own terror. I unclasped her mouth. We were lying on my barren floor. I'd never been so near her beauty. Her heart palpitated under my fist, like the bald head of a bird.

"Dear John," she purred. "I will visit you in your sleep and unman you with Harold's razor. I will parade your prick along the harbor and leave the bloodiest of trails. You will not have one morning or afternoon of peace."

"It will be worth the pain if you tell me why you are with such a man."

"Ah," she said, "my poet, the little gentleman who was raised in a brothel and never thought to sample our wares . . . the American major is more of a man than you'll ever be."

Clara must have seen an infernal color pass in front of my face. "Child," she said, "I am simply an ambassadress for Gertrude's brothel. It seems that General Washington is like to close us down. And I have to remind the major what he might miss."

"But you have put too much gusto into being an ambassadress."

"It's a labor of love. Now climb off unless you have some real business."

Clara kicked at me, rose up, and glided her hands across the bumps in her skirt until the line of each hoop was perfect. She looked for but a second in my mirror and calibrated her wig like a gunnery sergeant. And then she was off to her American major.

Nine

IT WAS THE ONE TIME IN MY LIFE I WAS GLAD TO be a spy. A spy could preach moral philosophy, could appear lovable and gay, yet have murder on his mind. I meant to visit Malcolm Treat while he slept and crack his skull with a spade.

Imagining Clara with Treat made me cunning and cruel. I would borrow a spade from Gertrude's garden, carry a pillow to pull over Treat's head, so his brains wouldn't splatter on my one good eye.

But I never visited the major in King George's boudoir; the major visited me, with a spade in his hand, and for a moment I thought he'd come to crown me before I could crown him.

But he thrust the spade into my arms. "Sir John, you'll head a battalion of diggers."

"Diggers? I don't understand."

"I've put together a parcel of slaves and free blacks to build a redoubt at the foot of King's. You and the Africans will dig up the lawn. And if you betray me, Sir John, I'll bury you under the redoubt and rattle your bones at the British."

"But I've never been in charge of a detail of men."

"The Africans will obey you. I've put the fear of God in them, insisted you were as brave as General Arnold's horse."

And so I went out to meet the blacks, all twenty of them. They had a leader, Prince Paul, a slave who'd been let go by a master who couldn't afford to keep him. He lived in Out Ward with a concubine and a flood of nieces and aunts who were under his protection. He'd become a potentate, the king of Little Africa, and was very loyal to His Majesty, King George. Harold was counting on Prince Paul to lead a rebellion against the rebels when the time was ripe, and here he was lending himself to that other George as a digger of ditches.

The Africans were already at work when I found them on the lawn. Paul was a very humble king. He didn't bark orders at the blacks and stand in the shade while one of his brood hovered over him with a fan made of ostrich feathers. He dug with the others and stood up to his neck in a ditch.

I climbed down to be with him in an ignominious hole that snaked across the lawn like an obscene necklace hanging from College Hall. The prince was no stranger to me. We'd both gone to Parson Smiley's school. He was the parson's prodigy, and in a braver world he would have been the president of King's. He was forty years old, but like most of the coloreds in the colony of New York, he'd had to remain a "boy," and couldn't educate himself until Parson Smiley came along. No one else in the colony had thought of schooling slaves and vagabonds like me. And even then, wearing the rags of his master, while Gertrude had dressed me like a little lord, he would recite odes to King George and our mother country. We'd been rivals, but Prince Paul never abused his power as the oldest, tallest, and wisest "boy" in the class. Parson Smiley had instructed us to be as formal and devious and gallant as the courtiers at St. James's.

He'd also told us about Paul's tragedy. His father had been burnt to death during the Great Negro Plot of 1741. The little prince was five or six at the time and had seen his own pa set on fire by officers of the Common Council. A hundred black slaves or so had been accused of plotting to burn the town and kill white women and men. I'd call it balderdash, or worse. There'd been suspicious fires, the parson said. And blacks had already rebelled in Charleston. The winter had been harsh. The black population was growing on York Island, was near one in five. And the Divil was doing his own dirty work. Blacks were hung on a gibbet and left to rot. Blacks were burnt. Blacks were stretched on chains 'til their bodies broke. The luckier ones were banished from the colony.

"Prince Paul," I said from my place in the hole, "dost thou remember me?"

He rubbed the wet earth in his hands. "How could I forget the little grammarian? I couldn't keep up with you. My learning stopped at the parson's door. And you've had King's College."

"But war has leveled us, Paul. We're both standing in a ditch."

"A ditch at your college. And you're the captain of this expedition . . . shouldn't be down here, cap'n. You'll dirty your britches."

And he shoveled a deeper and wider hole with his men, refugees from Little Africa. But I wouldn't let Prince Paul leave me behind in a ditch—I dug like the Divil and still couldn't keep up with Paul's army of slaves. I lost them as the ditch snaked toward Robinson Street. And then I found Paul resting on a rock above the trenches, smoking a pipe and palavering with his men, who carried long strings of rock candy. The men would play at the strings like puppeteers and jump at each other's candy with their jaws. I joined them in their sport.

But our play was interrupted. The strings flew into my face, and I was pelted with rock candy. It wasn't the Africans. It was the little major, Treat, who'd come down from the college with his sword. He hacked away at our candy, tho' the Africans had done nothing illegal with the strings in their hands.

"Stocking, you're building a fort, or did you forget? I could throw you all into jail for loitering."

"Major, the lads were about to build another ditch and stopped for a moment of rest."

"On whose authority?"

"Yours, Sir. Since you made me master of this detail."

"Don't banter with me, boy. Back to work."

But Paul continued to sit and puff on his pipe, while Treat menaced him with the sword. "America does not recognize colored kings in sailor pants. You'd best move before I carve my initials in your bum."

I could see in a flash that Paul would never move from his rock, that he'd either kill the major or get killed, and so I bowed like a fop at the Court of St. James's and said, "Sir, I put him there as my counter. A good counter is worth a dozen men."

"Then let me hear him count."

I waited for destruction, but damn if Prince Paul didn't start counting, as if he'd been born to it. "Nigras and Cap'n John," he said in that dialect he employed to confound white majors. "Into the ditch."

We climbed into that fetid earth with our spades, found ourselves immediately invisible, and Paul imitated every drill sergeant who'd once commandeered the Commons across from the old British barracks. "Prepare to shovel—shovel."

We finished the redoubt in three days, and Paul returned to Little Africa with his men and their cotton candy. The lamplighters had to cross a maze of streets with their ladders and oil cans. The carcasses of carriages and horses rotted on Broadway until the sheriff and his constables carted them to some burial ground behind the colored cemetery.

We were a curious island of forts, waiting for the British to appear. Meanwhile, General Washington rounded up women and children and had them delivered to the mainland. The paupers were gone, removed from the almshouse. There were soldiers, militiamen, sailors, pickaninnies, slaves, and prostitutes. The general had decided not to tamper with Holy Ground. No garrison, not even a rebel one, could thrive without a street of brothels. Besides, Washington loved to play cards, and Gertrude had the best game in town.

She couldn't celebrate the king's birthday with Washington and his family on the premises. She couldn't have fireworks and free ale, roast a pig in the garden, and recite "God Save the King." Sir Harold had to hide in the cellar, or Washington's aides might grow suspicious and start to question him. But I couldn't sit idle on June the 4th and turn my back on King George. I drank a dipper of rum, the way Arnold would do before he went into battle. No man could sit on a horse like Benedict Arnold after a dipper of rum.

I clutched a candle and strode into the barricaded streets near midnight. 'T was an unsettling time, since one of His Majesty's warships, the *Asia*, sat poised in the East River, at the foot of Wall Street—a ghostly galleon with gun ports lined up like a little sea of sightless eyes. The last British soldiers on York Island had marched aboard a month before Washington arrived. Merchants had continued selling supplies to the *Asia* until the Sons of Liberty destroyed their shops, stripped them naked, fitted them with feathered caps, like the king's clowns, and had them parade across Manhattan with candles in their fists to mock George's birthday. The *Asia* flourished for a while without the merchants' wares and would deliver an occasional broadside, knocking off the roofs of taverns and sugarhouses and preventing militiamen from maneuvering in a field. But it seemed to fall into a period of complete silence. Its supply barge lay moored near the docks. It no longer delivered broadsides. Not a single lantern was lit. Yet no one dared board the *Asia*. It was a permanent memorial to the king.

I passed the sentinel boxes where the sheriff's lads were supposed to watch for thieves. But thieves couldn't prosper on such a poor island. And the boxes were unmanned. I approached the harbor, saluted His Majesty's warship with my candle. And that's when I saw the sheriff, Captain Kidd. Gert had sent him. She was playing cards with Washington and couldn't come herself.

"Scribbler, it's past the curfew. And what are you doing with a candle?"

"It's the king's birthday," I said.

"Ah, I didn't catch that, you cretinous boy. You're alive and well because Gert wants you alive and well. But there's a limit to my patience."

He knocked the candle out of my hand and cuffed me behind the ear. Then he dragged me home to King's. I must have slept in a miraculous manner. I woke after a week, near the middle of June, with molasses and corn cakes on my bed. Had Clara brought me the corn cakes? I could almost smell the delight of her skin that was like its own molasses and did not require the trenchant sting of perfume. I wondered if she had kept watch over me.

I climbed up to the roof with the spyglass Sir Harold had lent this lad. King's was the highest point in town, and I was looking for signs of the fleet. The harbor was as smooth and solitary as glass. I would sit in my crow's nest for hours, eating corncakes that kept arriving on my bed.

And then His Majesty's ships did appear on the horizon. It was the very end of June. I was on the roof, and I started to sing and dance—and worry about the coming cannonades. I did not want Gert and Clara to be hit, or Washington to tumble from his white horse, his brains bashed in. I would have been mortified. But I was Harold's homunculus. I belonged to him and the king. And so I kept me good eye screwed into the eyepiece.

I watched a hundred ships sail into the Narrows while I devoured my allotment of corn cakes—the sea itself was like a series of little islands made of wood and cloth, islands flush with drums and fifes and scarlet coats that could have been the Divil's own dream works. Such phantom ships didn't have to fire a shot. Sir William Howe could have won his war with drums—and drums alone.

Ten

I DIDN'T HAVE LONG TO REJOICE. SOME YOBS FROM the Manhattan Irregulars had climbed up onto the roof, frightened to death of the British fleet. I could read the terror on their wrinkled faces. They were the walking wounded, like myself, lads who barely survived the Maine woods with Benedict Arnold. They had little love for me, because of my proximity to Arnold as his scribe. And I had a special feud with Corporal Martin Jaggers, whom I had to crown with a rock after he tried to force himself on a farmer's wife during our march to Boston as Irregulars. Jaggers never recovered from the braining he got. He lived off the slops of George Washington's kitchen table. But his eyes lit with ferocious fever when he saw me come down from the cupola.

"Signalin' to His Majesty, I suppose."

His rotten gang seized the spyglass.

"Tell us about that birthday party you made for the king. It's worse than treason, considerin' that you was once a lieutenant and all, with an officer's sash and a sword betwixt your legs."

"Acting lieutenant," I said. "I had that sword but a single night."

"Pity, Lieutenant John. But you shouldn't have made yourself conspicuous, not while the Brits are menacin' our island."

They kicked me down the stairs, clawed at me, ripped off my clothes, and carried me onto the lawn, where a whole barrel of pine tar was brewing in a caldron that sat above a bonfire. Jaggers himself mixed the tar with a painter's stick, let some of it bubble right onto his hand.

"'T just ain't hot enough, boys . . . Officer John, do you repent? Do you give up your allegiance to Britain's Satanic Majesty?"

"King and country," I said. "King and country."

They tied me to a pole, took paintbrushes out of their britches, dipped the brushes into the caldron, and started slabbering me with tar. I was like a hog that had to be basted on a hot spit. The tar went into my eyelashes, into my hair, into my armpits, into the webs of my fingers, into the fork between my legs, covered my member with a black well. I hollered holy murder. My body was an island of burning skin. The yobs had a mattress they must have stolen from some mansion. They tore into its belly with a knife, reached inside, grabbed clumps of feathers and christened me with them; the hot tar ignited half the feathers until I was nothing but a feathery man on fire. I had to wiggle on the pole to keep the feathers from burning me alive.

The yobs practiced being firemen and pissed on the pieces of flame. I was nearly grateful.

They picked up the pole and drove me down the hill. A mob of mean-looking men had formed, so it seemed, since my head hung upside down and I had to endure my own stinking flesh. I kept falling asleep and waking from the hurt of it all.

Voices kept nagging at me. "Is that King George's nigger?"

King George had brought his unholy ships back to our shores, and someone had to be sacrificed, someone had to be roasted on a rail. Should have gone mad with pain had I not started to reminisce. I'd maligned Jaggers, slandered him a little. He hadn't attacked more than one farmer's wife. He might even have been in love with her. She wore a bonnet, and her eyes were blue. She had blond pigtails that could have belonged on a child. We'd eaten at her farmhouse, the whole rough gang of us, raw recruits. She was half her husband's age. The farmer looked bewildered the more and more we devoured. He slapped his wife, sent her out to the well. Jaggers whispered to his mates and followed her. I slipped away from the farmhouse, found him in a field, warbling at her in some crazy music that was frightening in its devotion. That's why I hit him with the rock.

"I won't hurt you," I said to the farmer's wife, feeling so superior to Corporal Jaggers. "I'm not like him."

Her name was Anne Harding, Mrs. Anne Harding to be exact. She was all of sixteen, and she couldn't bear to have that farmer lie on top of her.

"Sir," she said, "please take me with you. I won't be a bother. And if you don't take me, I'll die."

"I can't. We're Irregulars, joining up with General Washington."

She kept pleading out of that expanse of blue eyes.

"Sir, I'll follow you into battle. I'll wash your drawers."

But I was scared, angry at my own ignorance. I grew up in a brothel, as Clara loved to remind me; I'd slept in the same bed with a whole gallery of nuns. I'd watched them parade with and without their clothes, but I might just as well have been a eunuch. I was frightened to death of this child-woman's proposal, of her bluntness, of her want. And Jaggers wouldn't have suffered from my mistake. He would have claimed Anne Harding as his camp wife. But I hoped to hell that she wouldn't have gone with him.

Now these sons of bitches meant to carry me across the entire village of Manhattan. Folks spat at us.

"He's the rector of King's College," Jaggers shouted. "We caught him signalin' to the fleet."

I wondered where the sheriff and his constables were. He could have broken up any mob, but not on the same afternoon that the British were spotted in the bay. I looked for Gertrude and the nuns as I rode through Robinson Street. I looked for Benedict Arnold, but he was practicing his generalship somewhere far from Manhattan. I looked for any mate who would halt this caravan, but no mates were to be had, except for these Irregulars. They dropped me to the ground, and I thought the journey was over, that I could hide under a hill and lick my wounds.

And then the yobs untied me, covered me in a robe that was like a long napkin. They put a paper crown on my head and a candle in my hand, sat me down in a sedan chair, and here I was, king of the harbor.

Jaggers bowed to me and laughed. "Sire, are you pleased with your throne?"

They hoisted me onto their shoulders and raced across the Commons to old King George Street that the rebels loved to call Liberty Lane.

"A king on the king's road," they shouted, their spittle flying above my head. "A king for a king."

A little mob of men formed in front of my chair, a ragtag army with muskets and fifes and an aging drummer boy.

"Come meet the tar king, with a soul as black as the Divil."

They stopped for free beer and rum at a sailor's tavern on Cherry Street, parking me near the door. The lads pissed on my paper crown, spat in my face, poured beer on my tar and feather coat, handled humble John without a notch of kindness or civility. My skin began to crack with blisters. My throat was parched, but not a single lad offered me a drop of ale. I was the pariah who had to be paraded around, the village idiot in his sedan chair, the effigy of a colored King George who happened to be made of flesh.

I grew delirious. I began to consider Clara and her corn cakes, imagined being married to that missy from Dominica. No matter how I tried, I couldn't seem to find another abode for us than Gertrude's convent. I loved my king, but I had no country. I was the renegade sheriff of Robinson Street.

Surly, drunken mechanics arrived from our disused shipyards and attacked me with their tinderboxes; I was nearly blinded from the sparks. One mechanic seized the candle and set my robe on fire. Jaggers rushed out of the tavern and roared, "That's Majesty's candle. Give it back."

Only after the candle was returned to my fist did he douse the robe in a tankard of ale and rip it right off my back. "Mustn't harm him. He's precious. The coloreds will worship him, I'm willin' to wager."

Eleven

DIRTY, FILTHY JAGGERS HAD FOUR MECHANICS pick up the sedan chair and charge across our old Palisade—the Indian wall of 1745—built by ambitious town fathers to free us forever from the curse of hostile Indians, and we entered Out Ward, home to the public slaughterhouse and tanneries that stank to heaven. Out Ward was where the highborns fought their duels over something they liked to call honor, tho' this honor was often about a lady or a bill that went unpaid. The gallows was here and a potter's field, the final home of paupers, convicts, slaves, and Indians who weren't lucky enough to lie in sacred ground. There were no mansions or gardens or drinking wells. There wasn't a single cobblestone or paved street. The lamplighter never visited Out Ward; there was no reason for him to come; he had nothing to light in a district without lamps. The shanties and hovels sat in the dark at the mercy of pirates and thieves and drunken armies like the one that was wielding me.

The yobs had found what they were looking for—Little Africa, land of outcasts, paupers, and slaves. The high sheriff never bothered about a man once he was on the far side of our Indian wall.

But it wasn't a lawless region, even if it was lacking in lamps. Prince Paul was his own constabulary. He broke heads when he had to. He protected his nieces from drunken soldiers and pirates. He cut off the hand of more than one thief, but there weren't all that many highwaymen in a ward that had so few highways, and where the proudest pirate might get lost in a maze of unlit streets.

But Jaggers hadn't led his caravan into Little Africa by any accident. He'd brought Prince Paul a black king. He was making fun of the district's most important holiday, "Pinkster," or black Pentecost, when Little Africa elected its own king and paraded him around the ward in a sedan chair like mine.

His lads had lit half a dozen torches. "Blackies," he shouted, "I brung you your king." He was edging for a fight. He had to take his mind off the Brits in our bay. He had to destroy. And who would have held him accountable if he ran amok in Little Africa among a black rabble that sided with King George?

Prince Paul appeared in the fickle light of the torches. He was much more noble than any of these men. He wore a satin coat and britches with a waistband. He had to use all his cunning to save the women and children of Little Africa. He got down on one knee. I could read the quivers under his eye. I knew how much it cost him to be civil to such a gang.

"Prince," Jaggers said, "how do you like your Johnny boy?"

"Very well. He's a most sensible king."

"I figured the feathers was a nice touch. I mean, if you're goin' to tar a man, you might as well have a deeper purpose, like the Lord's design. Black Easter may be months away. But heck, if we ain't manufactured a fine king with feathers and frills. I'd be obliged if you'd kiss Majesty John on the mouth and wipe his feet."

He expected Prince Paul to rant and rave. Then Jaggers could pounce and set fire to every hovel, ravish as many African princesses as his heart desired. But Paul stood up and approached my chair. I could feel his rage even in my delirium, but there was something else in his eyes, compassion for a white man who'd been turned into a forest of feathers. And I started to cry, because it was the only tender look I'd had since these yobs had dragged me off the roof. No one else on Manhattan Island had looked at me with anything but hate.

"Paul," I whispered. "I'm sorry. I—"

"Cottonhead," he hissed in that African dialect of his. "You want to get both of us kilt?"

Paul didn't hesitate. He kissed me on the mouth. His lips were as rough and thorny as mine. Then he unwound his waistband and wiped my feet with that splendid piece of silk.

Jaggers was horrified. And he didn't like what he found in the shadows. Colored boys with bayonets.

"Paul, I'd lend Johnny to you and your kin, but the rest of the island would like to have a look at him."

Jaggers knocked on my chair and led the caravan back across the Indian wall. He had a terrible fury in his face. A black prince had outsmarted him. And he wanted to seek some revenge. There was an outpost of poor whites in Montgomerie Ward, and he could menace this outpost, steal some women, and put the blame on me. "His Majesty encouraged us," he'd sing to some magistrate. But he couldn't control his anger. He and his men began to pillage on the way to Montgomerie Ward.

We were still in some no-man's-land near the Indian wall when I heard the rhythmic clap of hoofs that could only have belonged to a blooded horse. A very tall man in a three-cornered hat was coming toward us on a white charger. Jaggers froze in his tracks. I wished it was my general, but no amount of wishing could bring me Benedict Arnold. Arnold was a robust man, a compact man, and this man was lean and tall. He rode like an aristocrat.

It was the commander in chief himself. I wondered if he'd gone to exercise his horse and heard all the hullabaloo. He drove right into that mob, spilling muskets and men, and walloped Jaggers with the flat of his sword. And Jaggers still hadn't moved. He trembled and took the blows.

"Excellency, we couldn't sit idle while the British fleet was upon us. And we caught this here lieutenant signalin' to soldiers and sailors."

"Knave, to what end? Shall he repeat to Sir William Howe what Sir William already knows? That we are a vile band of men who tar and feather people for our own amusement."

General Washington knocked Jaggers to the ground and then he reached low and plucked me out of the chair. I landed on his saddle like a lad swinging from a magic trapeze.

Twelve

I WOKE UP ON A NARROW COT WITHOUT MY TAR and feathers. I wore a nightshirt. George Washington sat on a bench nearby with a black orderly who brushed his hair. He was eating a dish of peas, always peas, and drinking Madeira. They started a game of whist and decided not to notice me.

The orderly's name was Sparks. He'd been Washington's valet in Virginia.

I was astonished to learn that the general loved to cheat at cards. Sparks had to fine him a guinea every game.

"Sir, you keep signing notes, but soon you will be a bankrupt. I will own your farms and all your land reaching to the Ohio."

"I cannot concentrate if you jabber about money. A pox on all my bad luck!"

"It has nothing to do with luck. You are a poor player. And you deceive me with your tricks."

"I will send you to the hangman. Mark my words."

"You're a candidate for the hangman, I should think. A general who leads a revolt. They will draw and quarter you, send your handkerchiefs to the king as a memento of America's biggest barbarian."

"They will not catch me alive. I will fold my tent and move to the wilderness."

"And who will brush your hair?" Sparks asked.

"You will."

"And if I side with the British?"

"I'll hound you into hell."

"Sir, you will give this sick boy a rather poor impression of us."

"He's a varlet. He tried to poison my soup," said the giant.

"Yet you allow the poisoner into your very own quarters for the second time. You sleep beside him. Admit. You're fond of the boy."

"As I'm fond of snakes. I intend to turn him into my best viper . . . are you listening, child?"

I tried to sit up. My back burned and my arms ached. But I had to answer the general. I couldn't just lie there in silence while he slandered me.

"I am not your child. I was bloodied in the war. I lost me an eye."

"Sparks, look how he whimpers. He's a nanny goat, not a viper."

"A nanny goat who went through Maine, fought at Arnold's side," I said.

"That's odd. Arnold disremembers you. He has not mentioned your name in a single dispatch. And I described you to a whisker. 'Dear Arnold, dost thou recall a little snotty-nose who went by the name of John Stocking? This said Stocking swears he was your secretary.' And not a word from Arnold. . . . Sparks, tend to the child. He makes me ill."

The general abandoned his cards and his Madeira and his peas and strolled out of the bald little room that served as his private quarters. Sparks rubbed me down with wool grease. That white concoction soothed all the blisters.

"Pay no attention to the general, Mr. John. He's a worrier. And when he worries, he cheats and says what he ought not say. He's a melancholy man until the action starts."

The general returned after midnight, and Sparks had to put him to bed. He must have been out drinking ale and wine with the young officers of his family. The general had the longest arms and legs I'd ever seen. That's why he could pick me out of a sedan chair. It took Sparks half an hour to fit all of him into a nightshirt. The three of us slept on narrow cots in a room that was no bigger than that closet on Holy Ground where the nuns stored their shoes.

My blisters got worse, and I had such a high fever that the general himself helped carry me on a stretcher to the hospital that had been set up at King's. Washington warned the surgeons: "Gentlemen, I brought him here alive and see to it that he comes back alive."

These surgeons were scared to death about dealing with me, but they did administer laxatives and leeches and a liquid that made me vomit, piss, and sweat. The leeches sucked my blood until my ears and lips were blue. But I didn't feel faint, or delirious. I was as lucid as a clock.

There was lots of howling on my ward, lots of unrest. More British supply ships and men-o'-war appeared on the horizon this same July, under the command of General Howe's older brother, Admiral Lord Richard Howe, alias "Black Dick," master of His Majesty's North American fleet. The New World had never seen such a pair of military masterminds as the two brothers. Black Dick was rumored to be dark as a Gypsy, while Sir William was a tall, reddish man, like George Washington. Black Dick had brought a secret weapon from England: Hessian troops with brass helmets, hired by King George. Our surgeons had watched them with their telescopes from the college's bell tower. The Hessians swaggered on board Black Dick's tubs with fixed bayonets, while rebel volunteers on York Island or inside Washington's Brooklyn works had no bayonets and wouldn't have known how to stab a man with one—I wasn't a Loyalist, lads, and I wasn't a rebel, but faith, I did not want Black Dick's bayonets to win.

The British slept on Staten Island with their fleet, and it looked like a long, brutal slumber. The whole world could have been asleep. Black Dick fired a few of the guns on his flagship, but it wasn't to menace us. He was saluting his fellow officers, or something as harmless as that. And we were in suspended animation all the while, somewhere betwixt the living and the dead. Manhattan and Brooklyn braced for a war that only Sir William and Black Dick had the power to commence. Washington's lads dug deeper and deeper ditches and lugged their cannons closer to the Battery, but they were like feeble dancing masters with nowhere left to dance, and Washington himself scuttled between Brooklyn Heights and the Manhattan docks on a ferry that was always about to sink.

My own high fever made me tremble like a dog. My doctors preferred their telescopes to me. In their eyes I was nothing but a sick puppy who belonged to the commander in chief.

Thirteen

I WAS IN A WARD WITH NINETEEN OTHER BEDS, with soldiers who screamed in the night and suffered from malaria and the shits. But there was a sudden hush on my ward when a man entered in a tricorn, a cape, a powdered wig, a gorgeous neckcloth, and one gold epaulette. In my fever I thought at first it was Black Dick, or the Divil pretendin' to be Dick. Had the commander of the British fleet come to kill me? Black Dick's marines must have established their own beachhead near Peck Slip or the Battery. Yet I wasn't convinced. Admirals of the line didn't run around in a rebel uniform. And this rebel was limping from that bullet he took in Quebec.

I was happy as a harlot to see him, but I did not reveal my affection. He had a poke of bonbons in his hand.

"How are ye, Johnny boy?"

"Is that Arnold?" I asked with as much wickedness as I could muster. "Or is it but a shadow of him?"

"That's unkind. I brought ye bonbons."

"They say Arnold does not recognize the existence of those who served under him, not even his own secretary."

"Ye gods, I had no choice. You shouldn't have told His Excellency that I had a punctuation problem. Congress will never promote a general who cannot spell. I didn't deny ye, Johnny. I was protecting my flank."

"Always the soldier," I said, but I grabbed the bonbons. And we chewed on them like a couple of conspirators. I admired his dark complection, that hawk's nose of his. He was still wearing a black ribbon, his widower's weeds, tho' his wife had died before we'd ever gone into the Maine woods.

He removed a packet from under his scarf. It was a letter folded into four parts. "John, there's a certain Miss Betsy Deblois of Boston, an angel, a heavenly gal, seventeen if a day, and I mean to marry her."

"But General, you're still wearing your weeds."

"I have three children, John. They would profit greatly from a new mother. Come. I've started a letter. 'Twenty times have I taken my pen to write you, and twenty times has . . .' "

I couldn't leave him hanging in midair.

". . . and twenty times has my trembling hand refused to obey the dictates of my heart."

"That's delicious, John. But here, you scribble it for me."

I scribbled the entire letter with the pen and ink Arnold removed from his pocket. We finished the bonbons. My general signed his name, folded up the letter into the same neat packet, and thrust it under his scarf.

"Bless ye, Johnny. Wish I could dally, but I have to beat the Brits to Lake Champlain."

"Take me with you. I won't be a nuisance. I'll carry your spyglass and write to a hundred Betsy Debloises."

"But I can only marry one . . . I'll send for ye, John. When you're up and about."

"General, couldn't you tell Mr. Washington that I was with you in Quebec?"

"Ah, I will, I will."

And he darted out of the ward on that limping leg of his, strapped into a high boot. I missed him sorely the moment he was gone. I'd been less of a homunculus in Maine. None of our lads was lost. We had Arnold's hot blood in us, Arnold's love of the impossible, of finding Canada through some Indian trail that might not be there. For a minute I wasn't Harold's creation. I had no secret meetings in the woods. There was nobody to meet with, unless a wild pig that had strayed down from Acadia. I kept no memorandum book, nothing but the notes that Arnold demanded of me. He would dictate while our stomachs growled.

November the fifth, 1775. We slaughtered our last dog. I'm filled with heartbreak. It was a Newfoundland I admired. We'd dubbed him Hercules. He belonged to the entire troop. He'd followed us into the wilderness, and we could only thank Hercules by turning his bones into broth. But it strengthened the lads who were ill. They would not drink of Hercules until I commanded them. I hid my tears. I was not mourning our brave Newfoundland. Nor was I pitying myself. I was decrying our circumstances, the sadness of soldiers.

I saw the forest and the revolution through Arnold's eyes, and I was never so bold as I had been then.

I looked up from my bed. It was the middle of the night. And I wasn't in the Maine woods with Arnold. I was in a hospital ward at King's, and another general now sat beside me, the commander in chief, with his raw red face and reddish hair. His wig was awry. He looked exhausted. He must have come from Brooklyn, crossed over on the ferry long after dark. No one could predict with much clarity where the man-killers and their Hessian mercenaries would strike. Washington couldn't be in Brooklyn and Manhattan at the same time to catch the Howe brothers, with their bayonets and their battleships.

"We'll lose New York," he said in a whisper. "'Tis a matter of hours, days, or minutes—not more. The Howes will move their armada. It makes no difference where or when. Our forts will not hold. And I will need a man on this island. John Stocking, are you that man?"

He would have me killed, kill me himself, right here in the hospital, had I said no. I could read that much in his pale blue eyes. George Washington was his very own secret service.

"Are you that man?"

"Yes," I said, and not out of fear.

"And if I asked you to burn this village to the ground, would you accomplish such a mission?"

"Yes."

"You will sit here on York Island until we have need of you. And should you betray us, even once, I will weave a path of destruction around you that will feel much worse than a plague of feathers. You'll be kept alive, but not your loved ones."

Washington gripped my hand. Then he was gone.

Fourteen

I SAT ON MY BED IN THE HOSPITAL AT KING'S, wondering when the cannonade would begin. But I heard no cannons. Sir William's warships didn't bombard our shores. And our batteries delivered nothing. There was the noise of wagons, of men bustling about. My ward began to empty. Soon I was the only customer.

From my window I could see wagons filled with families and furniture—bedposts and pillows with trails of running thread, and dogs that ate the thread in desperate need of nourishment. Slaves ran behind the wagons, with half a mountain of dry goods tottering on their backs. Other servants and slaves wore silly uniforms: extra hats and fur cloaks, as if a man might turn himself into a dancing clothes tree in the thick of August's infernal heat. 'T was a heartless, sickening sight.

Despite the mayhem in the rest of Manhattan, I had a visitor on my deserted ward. Madame in her summer cape, her hair like a beehive. She'd brought me vittles from Robinson Street and chocolate from France.

"Child, no one would tell me where you were. Harold bribed

all the sheriff's men. But they're useless in time of war. I had to beg the commander in chief."

"He loves you, Your Highness. You seem to remind him of a certain lady. Why won't you tell me her name?"

"I cannot—will not—betray his confidence."

But I knew she was dying to tell. She was fond of the general. Washington was her cavalier, her North American knight, tho' the Brits were about to be Gert's main business.

"He was but a boy when he met her," Madame finally volunteered, "and she the wife of a neighbor and a friend. Sarah Fairfax, the good Sally, a bride of eighteen, and he could not cease to look at her. She flirted with him."

"A harlot," I said.

"Hold your tongue. She was not a harlot, child. I'm the nun, not Sally Fairfax."

"And you should be proud of it. Nobility need not come at birth, madam. You are queen of the finest nunnery in North America."

She laughed, and the skin around her neck rippled with small explosions. I was jealous of George. He could lead a revolt, while I was stuck in a hospital ward, a lad without a lady, unless you counted Clara, who wasn't my lady at all.

"The commander in chief insists that all civilians must leave the island. We're being sent to Albany like cattle, Johnny."

"Not Clara, I trust. She belongs to Major Treat. She's his bitch."

"Clara's a saint. She kept Robinson Street alive as long as she could by visiting that reptile."

"Methinks the reptile made her groan, madam. Groan with pleasure."

"Child, you do not have the littlest notion of a woman's pleasure. Clara vomited into the slop barrel after each visit."

I was calm. *Clara loves him not.*

"And where's His Lordship?"

"Harold's disappeared, as of yesterday. Without a note, without a pat on my bum."

"Sounds like him. Perhaps he joined the rebels under a different name. He'll return when the colors are more to his liking."

"You shouldn't malign your tutor. You'd never have grown into a gentleman without Sir Harry."

"Gentleman? I'm the king's scholar in a new little country of regicides. I now live by what I learn from the Town Crier," I told Madame.

My new mentor was Harvey Hill. He was the one who sang out the declaration of independence to Washington's entire troop. 'T was on the 9th of July, in the Year of Our Lord 1776, whilst I was still here at the hospital. The Crier had stood on the Commons with mechanics and soldiers, and rang his bell. Most of the Loyalists did not hear him. They'd already fled. We lived in a village of deserted houses, with soldiers bivouacking wherever they pleased.

"The Crier's a besotted fool," Gert said. "He invents half of what he hears. He's been barred from the nunneries on account of his lies. But I've struck a bargain with him. He will bring you your vittles. I've promised him a handsome sum."

"Mother, when will you be back?"

The color collapsed from her eyes. I had not meant to wound Madame.

"I didn't raise you. The Divil did."

And she was gone without sampling a sweet. The biscuits she brought lasted eleven days. I was lucky, because the Town Crier hadn't come to feed me, no matter what his arrangements were with Madame. But he would prance onto the ward like a wolf, wearing a coat with long skirts, his long hair tied in several knots, and I had to furnish him with my biscuits. He couldn't be fastidious about his person in all the fury of waiting, waiting for war. He had holes in his stockings, and his britches weren't very pure. It was hard to fathom where his voice came from. He had no neck and was cursed with a narrow chest that protruded in a pair of sharp points. But when he rang his bell and shouted "Oyez, oyez," half the island seemed to wake to his call. The redcoats might have listened to Harvey from across the bay.

There were no more gazettes on the island. The rebels had destroyed all the Tory printing presses and ran the last printers out of Manhattan or drove them into the sea. But Harvey had become a walking gazette. He had a spyglass and a notebook and would climb from roof to roof to discover the best angle, the most unfettered vision. Harvey would hallucinate whatever he couldn't see.

"Sir William's on Staten Island, frying eggs on a rock."

"Preposterous. I will not believe another word."

Suddenly we could hear the cannons roar right in the middle of August. The planks of the college shook under our feet.

"The Divil take Sir William Howe!" Harvey screamed.

But there were no royal marines on our doorstep, no British admirals landing near Whitehall Slip, no Union flags flying under our window. The cannons were our own, from little batteries on both sides of the Hudson. The *Rose* and the *Phoenix*, two British warships, broke from the fleet anchored off Staten Island, entered the Narrows, and sailed up the Hudson like a pair of tarts put there to tease the American guns. They cruised the length of Manhattan unchallenged and unscathed, cannonballs sinking all around them. Not a piece of timber was sullied or scratched, not a flag was touched. The warships could have been on a picnic; their captains toasted one another while our cannoneers miscalculated and shot our own men.

It was a terrible taste of battle. The British seamen sang to themselves, and in the midst of their morning serenade they fired once or twice into the heart of Manhattan, ruining a house on Partition Street and leaving holes in the cemetery behind St. Paul's.

I shuddered to think what would come next. But why should Sir William take Manhattan one house or street at a time? He hoped to have us as his prize jewel, and a jewel couldn't be littered with dead men and burning wharves. He moved half his army across the Narrows. He meant to capture Washington and surround his military camp on Brooklyn Heights.

The invasion began in earnest but a week later, on August 22nd, when barges and longboats, accompanied by six men-o'-war, ferried a swarm of man-killers to Gravesend, with the sound of drums and fifes. Several of the barges contained a whole sea of Hessian bronze hats.

That's what Harve the Crier sang to me. I'm not sure how much of the story came from his spyglass or his intuition or the tidbits he'd gathered from some officers near the Brooklyn ferry. But we began to hear the dull plock of musket fire across the East River, and then Washington's surgeons reappeared, and the ward began to fill. I saw mutilated men, blinded men, but I could not assist them. The surgeons wouldn't allow me to remain on the ward, and I moved back to Robinson Street, to the nunneries that had been my childhood home. They were deserted now, and I had the Queen's Yard to myself.

My hands were trembling as I entered the Yard. I did not want to live around Sir William and his brother, Black Dick. Perhaps the king had paid for my tuition, but I was no bloody Englishman and would never be.

I claimed Gert's boudoir with its gigantic bed. I searched the closets for her clothes. Faith, I found a pot of rouge and a swatch of silver hair on her wig stand, but not a single garment. I sat in front of her mirror, put on the wig, and painted my cheeks. Was it madness or my own sly need to evade the Brits?

A pinched face peered at me from the glass. I wondered if Beelzebub had followed me into the Queen's Yard.

"Spirit," I said, "speak, or you'll wish you'd never spied on John Stocking."

I tossed Gert's pot of rouge into the glass, which cracked and multiplied the spirit, made it look more and more like Beelzebub.

"It's me, the Crier. And I have malignant news. The redcoats have seized Brooklyn, captured three generals and fifteen hundred men, and the commander in chief barely escaped with his life. He would have lost his army but for a regiment of black fishermen from Marblehead, brave lads all, who found the means to row the rebels across the river in a fog. Lord knows how many men drowned or vanished into another world."

"Crier, there is no other world."

"I will not listen to a nonbeliever. But I admire your ruby complection."

"Take one more step and I'll throttle you."

"Throttle me later. We don't have time. The Continentals are still coming across. We have to help the commander in chief."

I wiped off the paint and got free of the wig. Harvey took out his tinderbox, lit a torch, and we scrambled down Robinson Street to the East River docks. The light from Harvey's torch danced off broken buildings, little hurried forts, and streets pocked with holes. The Crier was a marvel at disentangling himself from snares on the ground, but I tripped twice and banged my shins against a disused water pump.

There was pandemonium at the docks. Men would rise out of the water from battered canoes, rowboats, and barges, and stumble ashore, moving into the fog like creatures born in wind and rain. Some of them were carrying tents and small artillery pieces.

They seemed stranded in the dream of war. The tents were useless, ripped from corner to corner, but they continued to clutch them, as if such fabric had become the last comfort they had in the world.

I held a lantern up to their eyes, wanted to give them a hand, but they drifted past the Crier and me. We kept seeing black sailors, the men from Marblehead, bundling wounded soldiers out of barges and skiffs. They'd crawl along the edge of a barge in bare feet, the only people who weren't stunned or petrified. They soared like powerful acrobats, and created their own cohesion among such a bamboozled army.

I saw no officers. The black sailors could have been in command. They talked very little. Upon landing their boats, they formed a human chain, pulled soldiers and other sailors onto dry ground. They struggled until dawn when the last soldier was pulled from a boat. And then the commander in chief came out of the water in a wet cape, his hat low upon his forehead, his pale eyes brimming with alertness and a will to fight as he progressed along the human chain.

"Your Excellency," the sailors said.

His sword belt hung by a hair. His boots were without heels. His gaze turned from the Crier to me, but he wouldn't acknowledge Harvey Hill.

"Young John, are you here to collect trophies for the British?"

But he didn't wait for an answer. He trod into town in his boots without heels, vanished into the darkness of Golden Hill Street, and not the Crier or myself could even guess where he was going.

Fifteen

I TALKED TO SOLDIERS THE FOLLOWING AFTERnoon as they collected near the Battery to share what they didn't want to remember. They'd been routed by Brits who landed on the beaches of Gravesend and fell upon Washington's raw recruits with thousands of bayonets and Hessians in bronze hats, two regiments of Loyalists from Long Island, and hundreds of slaves who had deserted the American cause and carried King George's supplies on their backs. The rebels could do little against this swarm of men and matériel, and a slaughter ensued during the last terrible days of August. The king's soldier-assassins pinned Americans to tree after tree with their bayonets. Other Americans wandered in some forlorn field holding their guts in their hands. You could not fight these soldier-assassins. They never once broke their line. An entire company could turn like the spokes of a wheel and capture rebels before they had a chance to flee. Washington's riflemen and musketeers had never encountered such precision. The enemy was like a musical clock with bayonets and musket balls. And the rebels could only tap out the pathetic little tunes of individual men.

No one had bothered to teach them the art of stabbing with a bayonet. They didn't even have bayonets.

Sir William Howe could have captured the whole kit and caboodle, but he hesitated. He sat in the rain, a few hundred yards from the rebel works on Brooklyn Heights, hoping that Washington would deliver his sword and surrender these new United States. But Washington would not surrender. A monstrous fog shielded him and his men as they trundled without a word to the ferry landing. He got the remnants of his army across the river, both the walking and the wounded.

And now he had an army adrift in the streets of Manhattan, with useless tents and other paraphernalia propped in front of houses like the signals of his defeat. He let the paraphernalia lie there. He wasn't concerned with signals and signs. He had to regroup and rebuild. He didn't have the luxury of warships to deliver his men to some battleground. Sir William could land his assassins at the far edge of Out Ward, cut off Washington's routes, and trap him behind the old Indian wall. He would have had to fight from the rooftops, and Sir William could finish him a soldier boy at a time. He left behind one general and a few thousand men and moved his army out of town. Sir William's warships cruised along the East River in mid-September and bombarded the Americans wherever they were. The fire of British cannons flashed across the hills of upper Manhattan. And then our lone general abandoned us to the Brits, skulking out of town with his troops.

Suddenly the *Asia*, that ghostly galleon at the foot of Wall Street, was lit up with its own lanterns. British soldiers in brilliant red uniforms marched down the gangplank. With them was the late president of King's, Matthew Pin, who hadn't fled to London, as he had wanted us to believe. He'd been closeted aboard the *Asia* like the rattler he always was. He wore a fresh coat, shoes with silver buckles, and bright green stockings that emphasized his spindly calves.

"Gentlemen," he said to no one in particular, "until Sir William arrives to take command, I'm declaring myself military governor of Manhattan."

I could have lived with his foolishness, but another man rode down the plank with a lot more muscle in his calves. He wore the uniform of an admiral, with a pointy hat that seemed as long as the *Asia*'s bow. It was Sir Harold himself, my late mentor at the Queen's Yard. I couldn't hide my disappointment and dismay. An attack of the shivers told hold of me. I ran to Robinson Street.

Sir Harold followed me right into Gert's boudoir.

"The king's little orphan, are we not?" I growled at him. "Raised at Windsor like a royal Gypsy. It was the baldest of lies. Does Gert know you're an admiral?"

"Yes," he said. "She's known for years. The king made me an admiral before I landed in America."

"I shall never talk to that woman again."

"How pretty, how full of flavor, you little bitch. You wouldn't have arrived at seventeen without Gert's ministrations, without her invisible hand. I will not thrash you whilst I wear the king's clothes. But mark me, little one, if I catch you when I'm not in uniform . . ."

"You might start, milord, by getting out of your ridiculous hat. Faith, I'll do it for you."

And I knocked the royal battleship off Sir Harold's head.

He came at me, the whole of him aquiver, and I calculated to myself—if die I must, Lord, let it be now. But not a hair of me was touched. We heard the brouhaha of an army outside Madame's bedchamber. I imagined it was Sir William and his brother, Black Dick. But it was not the Howes. It was Madame herself, fresh from Albany with all her nuns in their finest capes and hats, and a contingent of redcoats behind them carrying their luggage.

I bowed à la française, a full sweep, with my head as low as my bum. But I didn't see Clara, and my heart began to race. Had she gone off with Washington's one-eyed toad, Malcolm Treat?

"How stunning, madam, that you should arrive on the very day Sir Harold disembarks from the ghost ship in our harbor. Did he communicate via carrier pigeon?"

She slapped me and twisted my ear in front of the girls.

"I worry about you and all I get is venom."

"Madam, you shouldn't molest me in public."

"My closet is not open to the public. It's for my family. And it's my misfortune that you are part of this family."

I no longer listened, or felt the ignominy of a crippled ear. I saw Clara in a hat and veil, redcoats buzzing around her. I didn't know whether to kill her or kiss her feet. The nuns went into the parlor to smoke their pipes, and I had to watch Clara's skirts disappear a hoop at a time. And while Madame's maids unpacked her clothes, commandeered water from the Tea Water Pump, the only well in town that still had potable water, and delivered Madame's room from the mess I had made, Sir Harold and I shared a pipe in a closet near her boudoir. He told me about the *Asia*, how it sat in the harbor without one lantern lit. It was Harold who'd arranged Matthew Pin's flight from King's College, while an angry mob prepared to feed him tar and feathers. Harold had put his name in the manifest of a merchantman leaving for London, and then sneaked him aboard the *Asia*, which could survey Manhattan while the rebels ruled the island.

And when the rebels grew suspicious, he cut off all signs of life, and let the *Asia* drift in place inside the harbor. He could no longer use his supply barge. It was the nuns who serviced Harold's ship, the nuns who managed to bring him his supplies, while Harold himself flitted between the *Asia* and Robinson Street. And when Washington's secret service prepared to pounce, it was Clara who sucked certain plans out of Major Malcolm Treat, and Harold withdrew into the belly of the boat. I had to wonder if Clara was a British spy, or was only following Gert's instructions. It rubbed me wrong. I could not comprehend the maneuverings of womankind. But then I had to recall that I had been raised around the nuns, and perhaps I was as devious as them all.

I could no longer return to the college. It was full of redcoats who took the wounded lads Washington had left behind, loaded then into the sugarhouse on Cortlandt Street, and placed their own wounded in the wards. And I had to occupy my old quarters at the nunnery, an alcove behind the kitchen. I earned my keep, sirrah. I shoehorned myself into this new world of the Brits. I wrote letters to British merchants for the nuns, who had a habit of not paying their bills. They had to have the latest London fashions, and since they bought so much tobacco for their pipes, they were penniless by the middle of the month.

The nuns began to worry that they would lose out during the British conquest. Generals might import ladies from London with stylish hats, ladies who could threaten the prestige of Holy Ground. The nuns could ill afford to anger their cloak-makers and boot-makers. And so I had to write letters to these distinguished men, outlining the nuns' difficulties, with promises to pay.

It startled me when Clara appeared in my alcove. She required a letter, like the other nuns. She could read Aristotle but never learned to write save with a childish scrawl. I didn't lord it over her, request a ransom for the use of my pen.

"Clara, was it you that fed me corn cakes while I was lying in a fever after the king's birthday?"

"That was my duty, child, my obligation to Gertrude. You might have starved in your sleep."

She puffed on her pipe and sat down on my bed, knocking her knees together like some mysterious musical instrument. It pained me to see her next to my pillow. 'T was where I had first met Mistress Clara five or six years ago, but she was hardly a mistress then. I could summon up Clara bald as an egg, with no eyelashes to speak of, and still laden with lice. She had the body of a girl, ye gods, but she might as well have been a boy. Gertrude had to shave every piece and parcel of her—her maiden hair too, tho' I'd have blushed like the Divil had I been obliged to look between her legs. She shivered, cried, slept with a doll. Gertrude wanted to keep her away from the customers while she was in such deplorable condition. And what better accomplice could she have had than little John? I was twelve at the time. I couldn't have ruined her. I didn't know how. We played in that alcove when I wasn't at school. I brought her kites and lip rouge I stole from the nuns. She'd hug me in the middle of the night whenever there was a storm. That's what killed me, lads. Breathing skin that smelled like spring water. And after a couple of months, as blond hair sprouted on her skull and her eyelashes returned, Gert gave her a closet of her own, with mirrors and a bed as broad as a battle cruiser, so she could be far away from her suitors when she had to lie down with them. And I disappeared from her own line of sight—until she needed the little scribe.

Now she wanted the latest fashion from London's best bootery—leopard-skin inlays, needlelike toes, heels that could eat a man's heart out. I thought to lose my senses dreaming of Clara's boots. She lent me a drawing of her own foot and Madame's (to instruct the boot-maker), clapped her knees for the last time, and catapulted off my bed without the littlest goodbye, while I had to live with her sweet musk in my mind.

The king's officers began to monopolize Clara's time. I heard them boast about their exploits in the fields of Brooklyn. "Combatants? They were nothing but niggers and old men. We could have killed them all with our eyes closed."

But Clara let these assassins into her closet, and I could not bear it. They lost money to Madame at her card tables. They guzzled wine and champagne from Tory cellars and shops, those same Tories who had come rushing back to town with a passion to rid the foul odor of rebels from their private gardens. The slave market and the coffee houses flourished again. English officers had to have servants and stable hands. More and more of them arrived with their mistresses and wives. Manhattan had gone from an American to a British camp within a month.

But it wasn't clear who governed the island while Sir William was with his men, pursuing the rebels across some wheat field in Harlem Heights. He couldn't seem to capture the commander in chief. Washington would appear like a phantom on his white horse, bemoaning the louts he had instead of an army, but when the assassins closed in on him, he vanished inside the wheat.

"I cannot fight a man who vaporizes himself," Sir William revealed to his officers. So said Harvey Hill.

"The commander stood in the corn," continued the Crier.

"Wheat, I thought it was wheat."

"He stood in the corn. His troops ran right past him, fleeing from the Brits. It was north of us, near the Bloomingdale Road. The sun beat down upon him. He couldn't halt the retreat. He trampled his own hat. Such was his despair at the sight of his men. 'Ye gods! How shall we ever win?' He wouldn't move from the spot. His aides had to shield him from enemy fire. And when he saw them drop around him, he could not control his tears. 'Good fellows,' he said, 'we must hasten from here, or all is lost.' "

"Crier," I said, "that's no song you're singing. You were with the commander in chief."

"Blood sickens me. I bandy news, not bullets."

"But news is your bullet. I'll wager you're with Washington's secret service."

He began to throttle me with my own neckcloth.

Suddenly all his crying made sense. The commander in chief had used him as a codebook. He could cry out his own keys, emphasize whatever he wanted as he delivered the news.

"Didn't a certain general visit you while you recovered from a lot of feathers? Didn't that same general carry you in his own arms to hospital? Didn't he demand something of you?"

"He did."

"And could it have been about burning York Island to the ground?"

"But hundreds will die in the fire," I said.

"Ah, do I detect a moral note from the philosopher of King's? We will not give Sir William a free hand to use our island as his headquarters and his whore. Or should we not speak of whores, since you belong to that fictitious admiral, Sir Harold Morse. He bribed you to poison my general's soup. Did you suppose we were ignorant of little John Stocking?"

"You must have been. General Washington did not know of me."

Harvey chortled into his sleeve. I hated him and the power he had. He was like a succubus who could rip the real from the unreal. Had I visited George Washington at his headquarters, or had Washington visited me?

"Ye gods, we could have stopped you at the picket line, dangled you from a tree, let the buzzards eat your eyes."

"I have but one eye, sir. You would have done well to notice."

"One eye, two eyes, our general wanted to see you. That's why you got through the pickets. Your route was rehearsed."

"See me for what reason?" says I.

"To have you as his changeling."

"A turncoat, you mean."

"A changeling. A fickle spy who finds his romance by serving two masters, a general and a king."

"And I serve neither. The king pays for my tuition, or did pay until the college collapsed."

The Crier throttled me again. "Did you not offer your services to my general? You were a changeling before you ever arrived at our camp. It is in your nature to be a spy who spies on other spies. Your final allegiance is to yourself. I will burn Manhattan, and you, dear John, will keep out of my way."

Sixteen

I WAS NOT IGNORANT OF FIRES. PARSON SMILEY had taught us about London's own Great Fire. It was of a Sunday morning in September 1666, when the town was asleep, more than a century ago. Not a dog or cat was astir. The fire started in a bakery on Pudding Lane. Some embers in an oven might have heated up and turned the bakery into a bomb. It could have been the malice of a boy who was brooding over a kick in the arse he'd received from the boss baker. Or perhaps it was God's work. But a high wind shoved the fire beyond Pudding Lane. And still the night watchmen couldn't rouse themselves from their slumber and attack the flames with the pathetic water bottles they had to carry by hand to a fire. The skies over London reversed themselves. There was no night for three days. London sat in the constant glow of wood and metal until the wind shifted and revealed an empty village. The entire population had moved outside the walls.

I shivered to imagine the same fiery wrath on our island. I wandered the streets, went down to the slave market above Albany

Pier. Prince Paul stood in irons with half his kingdom. The assassins must have gone into Out Ward looking for labor. It mattered but little that Paul was a free man and a prince. Our occupiers had seized upon Little Africa as a source of revenue.

It swelled my spleen to see him thus. I was filled with bile. Paul could have received a magnificent bounty to join up with the redcoats. Slaves and freed blacks had come crawling into town to serve King George. 'T was Sir William Howe's own idea. He promised freedom to every slave who was willing to fight against the rebels. And he promised a bounty to freed blacks, such as Prince Paul. But the "military life" Sir William had in mind was that of a baggage handler. He wasn't offering a musket and a bayonet. Paul would rather have been forced into a labor gang than accept a bounty. He loved the king as much as I did. The king had never harmed him. But the Yorkers had burnt his father at the stake in the bonfire of 1741, had separated him from his sisters and brothers, had banished him to Little Africa in the Out Ward, because every five or six years there would be a few suspicious fires, and the nabobs of Manhattan would shout, "The Negroes are rising, the Negroes are rising!"

Blacks had to have their own burial ground, six putrid acres near the gallows and the swamps. They had no lamplighter because there weren't any lamps to light. But Paul had made Little Africa his home, and neither the redcoats nor the rebels could tempt him. Only a numbskull would have offered a bounty to a black prince.

I went up to Paul with a cup of sweet water I'd purchased from one of the water boys.

"Scat," Paul said. "We're not supposed to put our blue lips near a white man's cup."

"Balderdash. Your lips aren't any bluer than mine."

A soldier-assassin knocked the cup out of my hand with his

bayonet. "Move on, old son. This here is king's property, and I'll feed it water when it's time to feed."

I ran to Harvey Hill. 'T was near dusk on the twenty-first of September, three weeks after Washington had disappeared from Manhattan, and the Crier stood in front of a coffeehouse retailing General Washington's latest defeat. Merchants showered him with coins.

"George Washington is to be carried in irons to Windsor Castle, where the king will question him before burying his bones."

"They say his capture is imminent, a matter of hours," said the merchants.

"He's running for his life. Sir William's redcoats will surely track him down," said Harvey, picking up the coins and signaling to me with his eye. I followed him away from the coffeehouse.

"John, you shouldn't dog me like that. The Britishers will get ideas. The Town Crier mingling with a lusty lad like you. They'll call it sedition. What do ye want?"

"Membership in your arson ring. I don't care for the way those assassins smell."

"Skittish, ain't we? Like a colt. Well, if I had it in me to manufacture a fire, I'd start somewhere in Out Ward, close upon the gallows or the Hebrew cemetery."

I could see that the Crier didn't trust me at all. A fire in Out Ward would mean nothing to the British. They'd let it burn while they dug trenches on the near side of the old Indian Palisade. They could hug each other and sing goodbye to Little Africa and its hundred hovels. No, Harvey would attack the foot of the island, where the assassins felt utterly safe. They had their fort and their Battery and a night watch that began at the Bowling Green.

And so I followed Harvey Hill. He favored the taverns near Whitehall Slip—the Sea Horse and the Fighting Cocks—where he would dance on a table or huddle with privateers that the British hadn't gotten around to arrest. And I could feel in my bones where the fire would start.

I returned to Robinson Street. A tall man in a powdered wig, with painted eyes, half his face hidden in a scarf, lurched past me like a drunken sailor. But sailors didn't wear a general's fine boots. It was George Washington, or the ghost of him.

I dared not call out his name in British New York. I would have compromised his mission, might even have caused his death. But why would the commander in chief enter Holy Ground in greasepaint?

I ran inside to Gert.

"The commander was here. And don't bother to lie."

She said nothing.

"What could be so important that he would risk capture and the very ruin of his career?"

She wouldn't speak.

"I'm a babe," I said, "a babe in a wilderness of spies . . . you don't remind him of some lost love. You are that love."

She took a pistol out of her pocket no bigger than a rat's head.

"One more syllable, John, one more syllable . . ."

"And you'll do what? Rid me of my brains? I'm the injured party. I'm tossed about, tilted in the wind. I enter his camp with two ruffians when I should have been stopped at the outer gate. He pretends I'm a stranger when he has my complete story. And who could have told him that story, madam? No one but yourself."

She fired the gun. The explosion rocked in my head. The chandelier swayed above us like God's own pendulum. Blood splattered on the wall. And for an instant I thought Gert had indeed brained me, and I was only a vapor that hadn't yet floated down to hell. And then I started to howl. Madame had nicked my ear. She didn't show the slightest remorse.

The nuns brought towels and rags and an unguent with which

to swab my ear. It was only Clara who had the courage to take the gun out of Gert's hand. But Clara chastised me, not Madame.

"You fool," she said. "You jackanapes."

"Like my father. Wasn't he Gert's clown?"

"Monkey, that was before my time."

And so I walked about with a bandaged ear, and not one person pitied me. I sat on the wall of the old French church and could catch pieces of fire in the vicinity of Whitehall, as if a small party of men was moving about with chunks of burning wood. And then the Fighting Cocks exploded into a wall of flame.

I ran back toward the Queen's Yard. "Poor Lawrence," I muttered. The late Lawrence was my father, the queen's clown. Lawrence Stocking, Esq., the original jackanapes. A forger who lived in the queen's bed. She was always hiding men, first my father, and then Harold, the clandestine knight. But Harold didn't entertain her, didn't wear a coxcomb, didn't do somersaults in the parlor, didn't carry pails of slop like a common donkey. I missed the old man.

He taught me grammar before Harold and the parson ever did. I received my penmanship from him. But he never mentioned a "Mrs. Stocking." Who could my mother be but Gert? *Gert, Gert, Gert.* She'd passed me off as a changeling, a transient in her parlor, saving me from the orphan asylum. I would have preferred the poorhouse, with runaway slaves. I'd have forged certificates of freedom for them. Wasn't I a runaway? A motherless, fatherless lad.

The fire had already climbed to Beaver Street, and God knows when the wind would carry it to Holy Ground. I had no fire bell to ring, no trumpet to rally the nuns. But when I arrived at the Yard, I received a rude surprise. The nuns had rallied themselves. They'd collected in the parlor, save for Clara and Madame. They'd bundled up their very best hats. I grabbed a knife from the kitchen and went into the queen's boudoir.

Seventeen

SHE SAT ON HER CARAVAN OF A BED WITH A SMALL valise that must have contained her treasury, but the mad and vacant look in her eye had nothing to do with treasure.

"Mother," I said, with as much malice as I could summon. "*Mother.*"

She didn't protest.

"Why did you keep my father as a boy? Couldn't he satisfy you, madam? Was he not built in a manly way?"

"I'll kill you," she said, coming out of her trance.

"Mr. Washington calls me his changeling. How apt, madam, how appropriate. What crib did you steal me from? None but your own. I was born into obscurity on account of you. George Washington's changeling."

"I forbid you to pronounce that name," she said.

And my heart shivered with its own unbearable knowledge. "Bitch, whore, foul fox. Lawrence wasn't my father at all."

She sought to scratch my eyes, but I clutched both her wrists in one hand and held the knife to her throat. Then I dragged her out of the boudoir and let her bristle in front of her own girls.

"How would you like your mistress? With or without a scalp?"

The nuns circled around me, shrieking, clutching at their bodices, but they didn't dare approach. My knife was too close to Madame. Then Clara came out of her closet with a British officer, a young captain with a brutish face.

"What's this?" he said. "A colonial who likes to play with knives?"

"I will puncture her, monsieur," I said, like some wild courtier.

"What's this? I arrest you in the name of the king. I will haul you in front of a magistrate, even if we have none at the moment." He turned to Clara. "Darling, I will declare myself a magistrate. That is brilliant." Then he turned to honest John. "We are civilized, sir. We don't molest ladies with a knife. Captain Ned Stark of the Royal Fusiliers at your service. I'm unarmed, man. Go at me. Not Gert."

And he danced around me like a royal rooster. I was bewildered. I had mothers and fathers on my mind, not this musketeer. But his rapid movements put me in a trance.

"Come on, go at me, you monster of the New World, spawned from the seed of a billy goat. You Americans."

I lunged at him with the knife, not to wound him, but to stop his patter. I couldn't. There was a continent between us. I never got near his skin nor his coat. "Lovely," he would say at the end of each lunge. "That's lovely." And when I was tired enough from my thrusts, he slapped the knife out of my hand, knocked me to the floor, and began to kick with all the savagery of a soldier-assassin. The nuns threw themselves at him, but he flung them away.

Clara was as tenacious as the musketeer. "Ned Stark," she told him, "Captain Ned, you have lost me forever."

He pondered that remark, mumbled "Blazes to all of you," and continued his kicking until Sir Harold arrived covered in soot, his long admiral's hat bent in the middle, with two broken bows.

The musketeer saluted him. "Sir, I have decided to arrest this man. He's been behaving like a beast to the proprietress of this inn."

"This inn is a bawdy house, *my* bawdy house, and its inhabitants —man, woman, and beast—are under my protection. Wake up. Manhattan is burning under your very nose. Can you not smell a fire?"

"Fire," the captain repeated, and ran out of the nunnery.

Harold brushed the soot off his cape and assembled the nuns. "The fire is traveling north by northwest. I don't believe it will swallow the island, but one can never be sure. I recommend that we go to the green. The fire cannot feed on dead grass."

"Harry," Gert insisted, "I'm staying here."

"That's grand. Then we'll all stay and have a picnic under the boiling lead . . . dearest, this is your house, but I'm the master in time of war. We'll go to the green."

The nuns wrapped themselves in their hooded cloaks like a gang of ecclesiastics and went off to the Fields with Harold. Tory merchants and their wives, who had shunned Holy Ground and its street of whores, drifted out of the smoke and flying debris and into the arms of the nuns, Manhattan's newest nurses. Clara and the queen comforted other husbands and wives, while these same husbands were held in thrall by Clara's green eyes.

Yet I did not see much lust in their own weary eyes. They had never encountered such singular angels of mercy. I'd misjudged Madame and the girls, who did not politick, wave banners or flags. Madame felt superior to these merchants, 'tis true, but her contempt for their narrow ways could not cut into her compassion.

I watched Clara feed water to a merchant's wife, but I could not dally.

The smoke mounted and seemed to obscure half the village in

wave after wave of oppressive heat. Horses and children wandered out of that shimmering black hole. Harold had to smother men who were on fire, smother them with his arms and his admiral's cape. He sang songs to frantic children. He thrust a cloak into my hands. "Come, Johnny."

And I followed him into the black hole, where the heat hit our faces like the heaviest of gloves. He improvised a path for us with a poleax, probing the remains of a wall, picking at a dead horse whose eyes glowed in the blackness like hot jewels. We found children, sobbing children, and I couldn't point them to the Fields. I had no sense of north or south. So I let the children clutch at my clothes, and we composed a curious animal with many heads.

The smoke began to clear. I could see the fiery walls of Trinity, its roof gone. It was hard to imagine how a church could be scalped. But the fire had scalped building after building in its wake. Whole streets were gone, ripped by some strange Providence. And I wondered if we too would sit in a fearsome glow of wood and metal, like London and Pudding Lane.

Harold and I had escaped all the flying debris. At dawn the town rose in front of our eyes and offered us a panorama of the fire. I could trace the fire's route with one of my fingers. It had moved westward from Whitehall, rode up through South Ward, flirted with Broadway, crossed into West Ward, and stopped dead at Barclay Street, just before King's College and the nunneries. The fire had respected Holy Ground, but Trinity Church was now an ashen pit with one surviving wall. And then, idiot that I am, I remembered the sugarhouse on Cortlandt Street, where the Crown was holding American prisoners of war.

"Harry, we have to break into the sugarhouse."

"Where's the rush?"

"Some of those men might still be alive."

I walked into the smoldering ruins. I couldn't find the trace of a prisoner, not a hat, not leg irons, not a charred shirt, or a skeleton.

"Have they gone to heaven, Harold?"

"Hardly. The commander in chief set them free just before the fire started."

"Washington was here? At the sugarhouse?"

"Ah, I thought you'd noticed him. A tall chap wearing mascara as his only disguise."

"Then why did you not capture him?" says I.

"Come, come, can't capture a general like that. Wouldn't be up to snuff. I mean, we had to allow him a primitive laissez-passer."

"Who authorized it?" I had to ask.

"I did. By George, we knew the rebels would burn the town. I had to contain the damage. They could have had three gangs of arsonists. I allowed one. A fire at three separate points would mean no more Manhattan."

"And so you fiddled up a fire like some virtuoso of the violin . . . Harold, I do not understand your canons of war and I never will. What was the general doing on Robinson Street?"

"Having tea with his true love."

"Then you're familiar with Madame's attachment to the general."

"She has spoken of little else these past ten years. He has weighed much on her mind. She worries that he will not survive the insurrection. The Queen's Yard was always a British bordello. You Americans have ostracized Madame and her nuns, but she will not wean herself away from the general."

"And in all your conversations, did she ever speak of her own lost son? You sent me to George Washington, knowing that he could not evict me from his camp, that he would divine who I was and who I am. That was your trump card, the card you hoped to play."

"He has divined nothing, except that you once lived with Madame," said Harold.

"Milord, you lie, you cheat—"

"I'm not a churchman, John. I'm a harvester of secret agents."

"'Tis much the same thing," says I.

"I promise you. George Washington is not privy to the particulars of your birth. He has no awareness that Madame ever had a child."

"Neither has Madame."

"Reconsider. A young impoverished aristocrat falls in love with a tavern girl. Would you have them wed?"

"Yes."

"Then you are ignorant of your own America. Here men have to marry, and marry well."

I had to listen to my mother's romance. I could not imagine that Sir Harold, the king's own homunculus, would be such a storyteller. I shook with emotion, lads. 'T was like having a magical show flicker in front of your eyes.

Eighteen

PICTURE A YOUNG COLONEL WHO'D COME HOME from the Indian wars without a penny in 1758. He had his own farm, this tall and handsome rider of white horses. He was already engaged to a young widow, the good little Martha who only came up to the giant's waist, but was the richest woman in the commonwealth. "He loved her not," according to Harold. The young colonel was in love with his married neighbor, Sally Fairfax, a terrible flirt. Sally's father-in-law, Colonel William Fairfax, had been George's benefactor. The boy had little schooling, nothing beyond the age of eleven. He'd learned the art of manners and war at Colonel Will's estate. He'd gone hunting with Will. And he could not bear to philander and steal Sally away. Yet he would write her letters, demanding that she burn them. He grew ill, nearly died—he would suffer from dysentery and the flux right up to the moment he lost Manhattan to the British. He had even considered suicide.

'T was during this terrible state of unrest that he stopped at a tavern in Tidewater country, on the Chesapeake, near the end of a hunting trip. Plagued with the flux, he had to lie abed for a week. He could not even pay for his room. But he was a celebrated soldier who'd saved Virginia from the Indians and the French. And at this tavern in the middle of nowhere, he discovered a beautiful woman reading a book. She was radiant, with red hair, and reminded him of Sally Fairfax. She was not a guest like George. Young women did not travel alone unless they were whores. She worked at the tavern. It touched the giant, her voracious appetite for reading. She could discuss Plato and Pliny, talk about philosophers and writers of romance with a constant warble in her throat.

The giant recovered. But he did not want to continue his journey home.

"Child," he said—she was a year older than George—"you shall instruct me. I'll steal you from this inn and take you with me to Mount Vernon."

"And what will I do? Feed you lemon tarts in front of your bride?"

"I will not marry, least not Martha Custis. You shall be my bride."

The young colonel was in deep dilemma. Nothing he'd discovered at the frontier could help him now. He was trained to be a Virginia gentleman, a soldier, and a planter with an arsenal of slaves and his own crops. He could not maintain Mount Vernon on his own. He would be reduced to penury, would have to sell parcels of his estate, or manage another man's estate. But he'd court a thousand disasters if that could keep him in Gertrude's company. He rode to her tavern in the tidelands once a week, considered running off with her to the Ohio territories, becoming a trapper or some wild man with a farm.

And then one day he arrived at the tavern, and Gertrude was gone. He nearly went blind with rage, rage against himself. His white horse had to lead him back to Mount Vernon. He was like a dead man. He would not eat. His estate fell apart. Then he roused himself from his solitude, rallied his slaves, and mended every single fence within a hundred miles of Mount Vernon. Fierce, mindless activity seemed to cure him of his melancholia. He had no more wars to fight.

"Confound you," I said to Harold, "what happened to my ma?"

She'd fled to Manhattan without realizing that she was already big with child. She had to break with her George in brutal fashion or he would not have let her go. She had little means and the town fathers would never have permitted a tavern girl from the tidelands of Virginia to teach school. Most school mistresses were the wives of church wardens. And so Gertrude gravitated to Robinson Street. Her intelligence, her beauty, and her wit helped her on Holy Ground. She had her own nunnery before the little boy was born.

"Little boy, little boy. Milord, that was no anonymous creature. You're discussing my own nativity. Shouldn't the giant have been informed?"

"Not while Gertrude breathed. She knew how ferocious he would have been as a father, that he would have come for her at all cost, would have abandoned Mount Vernon, mother, bride, and stepchildren to keep his son."

"Would that he had."

She never let the little boy out of her sight. And she began to weave the fiction of a boy born out of intrigue in a brothel.

"'T was no fiction, milord. How ironic it is, how just, that George Washington should call me his changeling."

"I cannot follow you, boy."

"I thought it was a common term among spymasters. Are you naïve of a sudden? I'm Washington's changeling, the son who was torn from his life and the spy who tears himself from one enemy camp to the other."

Harold bowed to me and laughed. "Bravo! You can call yourself a double agent."

And he disappeared into some dwindling curtain of smoke.

I THOUGHT TO GO INSANE with the incertitude of who I was and what I'd become. Luckily there was the fire. I still had children clutching at me, children who were discombobulated by all the pieces of ash that crept into their eyes. I took this dragon's tail of lost children to the Fields, which had filled with Tories who carried whatever valuables they could on their backs—strongboxes, brocaded cloth, chairs and tables with gold filigree—and didn't seem very mindful of their own lost sons.

The cloud of soot had completely lifted; Harold reappeared with five "fireflies"—river rats clad in irons—and a packet of armed men. As the island's provost marshal, Harold was entitled to his own police.

"Hang 'em, but not him," he said, pointing to Harvey Hill, who was also in irons. And I understood the latitude of a provost marshal. Harvey was still valuable to him, Harvey was as much of a changeling as honest John. But I couldn't bear to look at the Crier, or consider myself as his twin.

I watched Gert and the nuns administer to men and women who had swallowed too much smoke. I could not even pretend to hate her. She'd loved a man, loved him unto madness, and I was born into her very own whirlwind. And that left me more of a child than a changeling.

And I wondered how the giant ever did find her again. He'd come to Manhattan in March with his ragged army and his secret service, had camped a little north of the Fields, near the old British barracks. He knew that he could never hold the town, but his presence served as a country in itself, proof that the Continentals had more than a flag, a fife, and notes of rebellion. He had no uniforms for half his men; there was a dearth of flint and powder too. For a while he lived at No. 2 Broadway, more like a nabob than a general recovering from dysentery. But he abandoned Broadway and moved in with his men, strolled among them, let them look at his linen and his long hair. His captains must have told him that Gert's was the place to gamble, that he couldn't come to New York and not visit the Queen's Yard. Would her very name—*Gertrude*—have sent him running to the latrine? Filled him with anticipation and dread? And when he walked the few scant blocks from the old barracks to Robinson Street, with his bodyguards and members of his family, what could he have been thinking? And that first sight of her, red hair blazing, freckles like spotted fruit—didn't it negate and nullify the last eighteen years, as if he were that boy colonel again, with the flux, mending in a tavern on the Chesapeake, while a redhead recited Plato to him, something about a cave, and men who could only see the image of an image on a dark wall? Didn't he have the urge to abandon the new nation, the whole military apparatus, tents and manuals of warfare, and do what he should always have done, disappear with this redhead into the far country and never be heard of again?

Anno Domini 1777

VINGT-ET-UN

Morristown

MARCH 1777

He'd been encamped in Morristown since the 6th of January—his winter quarters a tavern right on the village green. He ate and slept with the stink of beer in his nostrils. He had his surgeons "prick" his men against that dreaded poison, the small-pox, by scratching their arms with a tiny portion of the pox. This infernal scratching was supposed to protect them, but his troops resisted, and the commander in chief had to travel on his white charger to each log hut. Not a single lad withstood being pricked once Washington entered these huts on Thimble Mountain.

He also sent out raiding parties that robbed the Brits of their precious forage. Armies were not supposed to skirmish in winter, General Howe complained to his own officers. "For the past two months, or nearly, we have been boxed about as if we had no feelings—our cantonments attacked, and the forage carried off from us, our troops harassed beyond measure."

But Washington's own intelligence chiefs considered this com-plaint a mere subterfuge. Sir William Howe was up to mischief, hatching plots to dispose of His Excellency, and sending out assas-

sins in one guise or another. They begged Washington to remain within the tavern's walls.

"Sir, our spies say Howe is filled with folly—win or lose, he will have your head," insisted one of the chiefs. But Washington would rather risk Sir William's assassins than breathe the smell of beer. Damn the British and their rules of war! They were like aristocratic rabbits who wouldn't come out of their holes 'til mid-May, whilst the rebels preferred to fight in February and March.

He thought of Gertrude ceaselessly in this dreadful solitude. He did not even have the war to contain him, nothing but the fear of smallpox, forage for his horses, and winter coats for his men. He wondered if a kind of lunacy had descended upon him—ten times a day he plotted and planned how he might smuggle Gertrude into Morristown. He had enough spies to accomplish such a mission. Yet he could not count on his ablest spymasters. The camp itself had been compromised. A lunatic had come at him with a hatchet but a week ago. He could not say how much gold Sir William had offered such a desperate lad. Hence he would have to plot all alone.

And while he was at his planning table, with a cup of Spanish wine to sweeten his solitude, a woman arrived at headquarters with a surfeit of red hair beneath her scarf. Even under duress he realized: How clever Sir William is to hire a redheaded assassin. He cared not whether she carried a dagger or pistols under her cloak. He invited her to sit down and drink Madeira with him from the very same cup, tho' she was rude enough not to reveal the least part of her visage.

"Gen'ral," she said in a voice that was much rougher than Gertrude's, "I do not see your spectacles."

"I wear none," he answered, tho' it was a little bit of a lie. His vision had gone blurry of a sudden, and he might or might not borrow Sparks' spectacles to read a dispatch in the middle of the night.

"Would you care to kiss me?" Howe's assassin asked.

Washington smiled for the first time in a week. Bold he was but not a fool—a kiss could only mean a knife in the neck. He sipped wine with the redhead, reached across the table, and shoved aside the hood of her cloak. Washington could not hide his disappointment. Britain had sent a man in a red wig.

The assassin laughed and lunged with his knife, but had never bothered to scrutinize the commander in chief, or calculate how long he was in the leg.

Washington kicked him brutally under the table, kicked him again. The assassin lay writhing on the floor when a pair of pickets burst into headquarters with bayonets. "Excellency, this monster has left a trail of blood a mile long . . ."

He was no longer listening. For a moment the madman's company had lent him the smallest piece of Gertrude. But the moment was gone. And he would not involve himself in whether his pickets should double or treble their numbers this side of Thimble Mountain.

Nineteen

THE KING CAST A PALL OVER MANHATTAN FROM his palace at Windsor, while we sat in a welter of ice, like children waiting to be spanked, and thereby cured of our rebellious nature. But how could the king spank us from across the sea? And so we lived with his agents—the king's own men—in constant unease. They were conquerors who pretended to be our guests. But a guest does not steal the fire from your hearth, a guest does not abandon you to your own wintry cocoon.

In my idleness I prepared a little portrait of our two main antagonists—Sir William Howe and Black Dick—a silhouette cut with venom.

They were the lions of the Western world, a general and an admiral who had joint command over the mightiest armada of munitions and men that had ever been seen on an American shore. These brave and bonny brothers hadn't come to conquer, it seems, but to mollify brutal American farmers, bring them back inside Britannia—peace commissioners, they called themselves. Both were swarthy men, but Black Dick was shorter and darker than his younger brother. Their grandma had been the favorite whore of George I, and hence the Howe brothers were heirs to a bumpy royal line—their own mama was a bitch, a king's illegitimate daughter, making them the two most prominent bastards of the realm.

Black Dick, I'm told, was a monkish man with three daughters and had never been unfaithful to his wife. He'd gone to sea at thirteen. According to Harold, he had a very long nose, yet not one of his features ever moved. He could barely deliver a smile; his face was stiff and brown as leather after thirty years of wind and rain on a battle ship. His brother was a much prettier man.

While Washington froze his arse at Morristown, Sir William sat in Manhattan and seized whatever pleasure he could find. He had his own secret weapon—a certain Mrs. Loring, who was better endowed than any flying bomb or cannonball. Mrs. Loring could leave a hundred men and boys in her wake. Howe's whore, the rebels loved to call her. He'd met Mrs. Loring while he was military dictator of Massachusetts. Now she was duchess of Manhattan, with her own carriage and a brace of mean little lapdogs. Her husband, Joshua Loring, a Tory toad who had lent his wife to Sir William, was rewarded with a remarkable sinecure: commissary of prisons. The toad grew filthy rich starving American prisoners, while Mrs. Loring lived with her knight near the Battery and dictated what every other woman had to wear.

Gert was furious. She had no wish for a female commandant of cosmetics and clothes. Yet she made a conquest—Admiral Lord Richard Howe. He'd become less of a monk on our island. He had his own private closet at the Queen's Yard. He'd never been unfaithful to his wife before, not even once. Perhaps the winter clime had quickened his blood. Or was it the miraculous aroma of the nuns? But Black Dick was not dictator of Manhattan. Sir William was, with his assassins in red coats who could rape and murder without the slightest redress. The military tribunals would never dare sentence a soldier. And I, faith, was a small part of William's infernal machine, connected to Sir Harold Morse.

General Howe was deeply suspicious of a former page at Windsor Castle who wanted to establish a secret service on behalf of the king. And so he buried Harold, put him in charge of recruiting a brigade of Africans—slaves and freemen who could be trained as army butchers, baggage handlers, couriers, and carpenters.

Harold's first measure was to appoint me as his amanuensis with my old rebel rank of acting lieutenant. I was now in charge of gathering the Blues, as African men were often called with a mingling of fear and contempt. I could have declined Harold's offer. But his brigade of Blues would be better off than most whites in wartime Manhattan—we would never starve.

Sir William heaped Harold with honors, made him provost marshal of all Africans on our island. 'T was a bitter task. Harold was responsible for every slave and free black. Even Clara had to report to him. And I had to keep his ledgers, like some unholy scrivener for the Crown. He had a closet inside our fort, and we'd sit above the ramparts, smoking little cigars from the Indies that had come into style long before the revolution.

The British hangman, a mulatto from Canada named Redmund, reported to us. A cultivated fellow with frilled cuffs, he served as the public whipper when he wasn't hanging people. The Loyalists on our island objected to him, wondering if he had the nerve to hang rebellious blacks. That's all they ever muttered about. Rebellious Blues.

Redmund liked to wear a mask, tho' it wasn't included in his contract with the king. No one thwarted Redmund, not even the Howes. He alone decided on the route when a man had to be whipped. He would never whip a woman, preferring to brand her with an iron.

Redmund was like a magistrate. "Elizabeth," he might sing or say, branding the king's initials—GR for George Rex—on a woman's buttocks. "Pray you never steal again." Said Elizabeth would roll her eyes as if she'd been ravished by a kiss of fire. And the hangman would arrive at our office, weeping under his mask.

"Harold, I should like to resign my commission."

"You serve by sufferance of the king. I cannot release you. And neither can those two bastard brothers, Sir Billy and Black Dick. But do us the honor of shedding your mask."

He removed his sheath of black velvet that made his eyes into a hangman's merciless slits. I understood why Redmund wore a mask. He had the eyes of a sufferer, a saint bound to his victims by some invisible thread.

"I'll run away. I'll hide in Out Ward."

"We'll only hunt you down."

"I'll go on a rampage. I'll molest a dozen merchants, I'll brand their wives."

"A pity, that. To hang such an excellent hangman. Where will we find another?"

But how could we hang him? The nuns were delirious over Redmund. I prayed that Clara wouldn't fall in love with the fellow. But she of all the nuns seemed superstitious about the mask. And why should Clara have mingled with a hangman when she had every British officer at her feet?

Yet something else rubbed at me. Sir William could lie abed with Mrs. Loring and her lapdogs for the rest of his life, but I'll wager he thought of one thing only: the quick demise of George Washington. He meant to kill my putative father in whatever devious and dastardly way he could. And he hid his machinations behind the grandiose mask of a peace commissioner. Ye gods! Peace for Sir William was nothing less than Washington's burial ground.

Twenty

FAITH, THERE WAS LITTLE TO DO ON A WINTRY night without one of Gert's supper parties, when extra lanterns illuminated the length of Robinson Street, and Holy Ground blazed like a burning barn. Madame's soirées were the envy of British Manhattan, with nabobs and high commissioners sitting next to the nuns. But suddenly there wasn't a single nabob or commissioner at Gert's. Sir William had invited his whore instead, and she's the one who insisted that the hangman appear at Madame's table with Harold and myself. She was curious about us, this Mrs. Loring with her beehive of blond hair and a bosom that lurked like a live animal under her silk scarf. She was of a rare beauty and refinement, with but a little paint and a lorgnette that she held to her left eye whenever she engaged us in talk. 'T was a sign of her singular interest. I cannot tell if she dyed her hair. But she was the blondest lady in the room.

Gert was gracious, but I could feel her anger rise. Mrs. Loring had robbed my mother of her role as reigning queen. 'T was hard to fight such a formidable foe as Mrs. Loring. Sir William's own officers took to calling her "the Sultana," and a sultana she was, spying on one and all with her lorgnette.

Clara was with us, and Lord Howe, alias Black Dick. He might have had the palsy—that's how his hands trembled at the sight of Mistress Clara, tho' there was not a single sign on his leather face.

"Ah," Sir William said to Harold as we sat down. "The king's very rascal. How are you, Harry boy? Letting George Washington through the lines again?"

Black Dick took his eyes off Clara for an instant. "Little Brother, what are you talking about?"

"Sir Harold, admiral as he is, has his own novel ideas about a secret service. He encourages Washington to slink into town, set us afire, and sit with some doxy, all of an evening. And we, poor lads, our hands were tied. Would that I had been there. Then I could have promised you a show."

"But Will," said Black Dick, "who is the doxy?"

"That, I fear, we shall never learn. It's beyond the powers of his secret service. My own lads trailed the big oaf to Robinson Street and lost him again. But should he grace us with a second visit, he'll be shot on sight, or hung by his long hair. Is that plain enough, Sir Harold?"

William the Conqueror scrutinized the table. I dared not look at Gertrude. And I thought it odd that of all the people in Madame's parlor, it was General Howe himself who most resembled George Washington. Both were giants, both had long hair, both were handsome men.

"Dick," said the general, "did you not hear that His Majesty had to teach Harold how to eat with knife and fork? And now he plays the military man. I should think he's Colonel Washington's greatest ally."

I could read their British strategy like the Bible. Sir William was longing to goad Harold into a duel. Black Dick might serve as his second. They would venture far beyond the Fields, into the no-man's-land of Out Ward, where even a general could duel. Harold had to hold his tongue if he meant to stay alive.

"Milord," I said, "Colonel Washington bears your rank. He's America's commander in chief."

"Who's that?" Sir William asked.

"Harold's little subaltern, Johnny One-Eye," said Black Dick, whose closet at the Queen's Yard was close to mine.

"None other," says I, bowing to Sir William.

"Dick, the boy's game, I'll give you that, more game than Silent Hal."

"Sir," I said, "you should not misinterpret Admiral Morse's silence. He dare not contradict you. But were you not commander in chief, he would rip out your throat."

"Enough," Harold shouted, his entire head aflame, as if Redmund had branded him with a hundred irons. "You must desist. I command you."

"And I command you to speak," Sir William said. "He's a saucy lad. I like him. Continue, Johnny One-Eye. Please."

"Not until the admiral instructs me to do so."

"All right, all right. Admiral Morse, may I have the honor of conversing with your subaltern?"

There was a madness in Harold, a rage I had never seen before, but he still nodded yes, as if all his history had come down to nothing, and he the little boy again that His Majesty had found in a forest. I loved him at this moment when he was as naked as I, with no more merit than his own skin. And I decided to duel with this tall bully, Sir William, who could relieve me of my other eye with but a nod, could pin my carcass to a tree, yet was no match for the tongue in my mouth, in spite of his schooling and his proximity to the king.

"Milord, George Washington is a general."

"I think not. A colonel he was and a colonel he will always be," said our William.

"More to your shame, sir, that you let him elude you. And my admiral was right to allow him into our village. He controlled him thus, like a supreme symphonist. He made music with that man, limited his diabolical damage. Had there been three fires, sir, and not one, you would have no Manhattan on which to build your headquarters. You would have a mountain of dust."

"I like this boy," Sir William said, breathing through his nostrils. "Let's steal him. He should be in my family, Dick. Or yours. A true captain of the secret service."

"I'm not your whore," I said, looking Sir William full in the eye.

"No, I am," said Mrs. Loring, who was a greater diplomat than I. "There will be no more quarreling at this table. I am mistress of all conversation, even if I am not mistress of this house."

She bade me sit beside her, and I did. I had never seen my mother look so forlorn, or remain so silent. She had been superseded in her own nunnery by a woman as voluptuous as herself. Mrs. Loring had seized the music and the tempo of our meal. She did not have to flirt. She was the consort of America's most powerful man.

"I wonder who Washington's doxy could be," said Mrs. Loring, looking around the table at Gertrude and the nuns. But Gert wouldn't lower her eyes while Mrs. Loring glanced through her lorgnette.

"Perhaps some goddess of the moon," Gert said.

"I should doubt that. I'm told his linen isn't very clean. And what goddess could ever fall in love with a man in a shoddy shirt?"

I watched the two women duel way beyond Sir William's head. He did not have the imagination to connect George Washington with Madame. Yet Mrs. Loring must have intuited it in a moment. I admired her intelligence and wit. I feared Mrs. Loring and longed to bite her neck. 'T was not akin to that tenderness I had toward Clara, a tenderness that kept me shy and irresolute, without the will to woo her.

I should add that while Mrs. Loring presided over us, she probed under the table with one hand like a salient, live canoe. I was not the least ashamed. I was my own secret service in regard to Mrs. Loring.

She began to parley with the hangman, who dined without his mask.

"Redmund, how unfortunate that you should have to dispatch murderers, spies, and thieves, and punish women who have done no more than steal to keep from starving."

"Dearest one," said Sir William, "you mustn't upset the boy. Had I known your interest in crime and capital punishment, I could have named you a counselor to our chief justice. Confound it, I would have given you his seat. What can they do to us, Dick? We are weary of battlegrounds."

"Yet you bombard and bayonet with much flourish and finesse," says I.

"As a soldier must. But we are warriors who never believed in this war, Dick and I. Did we not organize a peace commission at our own expense? Did we not meet with the rebel commissioners wherever we could, empowered by His Majesty to make peace? I love this land of yours, Johnny One-Eye. I did not long to come here as a man-killer. I was ordered to do so. I should rather have been on a fox hunt with that long colonel from Virginia who calls himself commander in chief. And if I sit here and sup with you, it is out of affection."

"Will, dear," said Mrs. Loring, "that's almost a declaration of surrender. And what will happen to a Tory princess like me?"

"There's the thrust of it. That's why I fight. To keep your husband busy so that he will forget he ever had a wife. Ain't that my policy, Dick?"

Black Dick had lost the little string of our table talk, tho' I could not read much into his leather face. He excused himself, bowed to Mrs. Loring and Madame, and went off with Clara. He'd abandoned the *Eagle*, his flagship, abandoned his charts, his telescope, and his staff, and made his headquarters at Madame's.

Sir William sang bawdy songs about a subaltern and a French maid. And my mother? She had to endure him and Mrs. Loring in her house. She was protecting George Washington with her silence. She could not show her pique, or Sir William might have woken from his mental slumber to realize that George Washington's moon goddess was Madame.

Gert left the table, and I followed her up to the roof, where she had her own little verandah that was like a crow's nest. We could still hear Sir William's songs, the stamping of his feet. My mother, who seldom smoked, began to puff on Clara's long-stemmed pipe. She was much too unsettled to offer a draught to her only son.

"Mother," I said, "we must leave this place. We must pack our belongings before those assassins suck on our liver."

Finally she looked up and offered me the pipe. "And where will we go, John?"

"Anywhere," I said, "but not a Manhattan where men have become vultures."

"Child," she said, "we would only find other vultures."

"Indeed, but General Howe is not the half-wit you think he is. He will connect you to Washington, and then he will tighten the noose, lure him to Robinson Street with false signals and false reports. Go to your general, Madame, with all the girls."

I could catch a faint smile under all the puff clouds from her pipe.

"And sit with him at Morristown? He does not need a camp wife. And he would not have one. He has America on his mind."

"Mother," I said, "you are that America."

But she'd gone back inside her reverie with that infernal pipe, and there was no point in trying to reason with her. She was not reasonable on the subject of General Washington, and why should she have been? Her own life had been wound up with his in a most unreasonable way.

I went out into the winter, exhausted by our talk. The stars seemed to align right over Robinson Street. Little bonfires crackled, delivering curlicues of smoke. The crackling got into my blood. I was haunted of a sudden by Black Dick and his leathery look. I pictured him as some leper king luxuriating in all the mystery of a mask. But he was far from a leper—him with a navy at his beck and call. It drove me to despair to consider this: Clara and only Clara had enough magic to crawl under that bark he had for skin. *I* was the leper. And I'd have to use all my cunning to steal her away from the man in a leather mask.

Twenty-One

FIVE MONTHS AFTER THE GREAT FIRE OF '76, AND our island still sat in its own ruin. I bundled up against the bitter cold of February, while the wind howled off the Hudson, and I scrutinized Canvas Town, the tent city that was springing up in the charred remains near the river. Blacks from Westchester who began to pour into our streets, believing that Sir William would save them, now had nowhere to live. Prince Paul, the lord of Little Africa, had to accommodate them. No one else would. Wasn't an empty room to be found in all of Manhattan. Soldiers and their wives, sweethearts, and children were swallowing the town. Their barracks could appear on any street, their canteens in some widow's yard. The provisioners had no provisions. Farmers would cross over from Brooklyn and have nothing left but a few weevils in their potato bins five minutes after they landed. A biblical plague could have been upon us.

But I didn't starve. Madame relied on Black Dick, using Clara as her bait. While the admiral was around, we feasted off his flagship. And when he was aboard the *Eagle*, Madame had her own suppliers, delirious men—Loyalists all—who abandoned their wives for a week and plowed their profits into a "honeymoon" with a particular nun. It would have mattered but little had that nun not been my Clara. I brooded that a stinking pirate could buy Clara's affection or afford to keep her in chains, but not Johnny One-Eye, who found it impossible to bribe her with licorice she could get from Black Dick. All I could do was feed my own belly.

I had chestnuts and licorice and cones of rock candy that I would share with urchins along the road. But I had to be careful lest I cause a riot. And it was while feeding a small army of waifs on Little Queen Street, at the very edge of Canvas Town, that I heard the furious rumble of wheels. I was nearly run down. A chariot with golden doors and an insolent black driver stopped but a hair from my head.

"Boy, I'll have you whipped."

The driver laughed. And then I noticed who was inside his livery—Prince Paul himself, lately of Little Africa.

"Sorry, Paul."

The gilded door opened, and it all made sense. 'T was Mrs. Loring in her winter boots and a hood of white fur that lent a paleness to her cheeks. Hadn't seen her since Gert's supper party this past week. She'd picked Paul as her coachman, and she could ride unmolested through the darkest street or the sinister ruins of Canvas Town. Africans were not allowed to wear a pistol, but Paul could have injured any party with his coachman's whip.

I climbed up into the chariot. And one little detail kept rubbing at me. I was curious as the Divil. "Mrs. Loring, ma'am, might I press you to ask if you own a Christian name?"

"Does it matter so much? You might call me Liz, Betsey, or Elizabeth, if you like."

"And what does Sir William call you?"

"Cunny when he's sober and Mrs. Loring when he's drunk. But it's of little interest to us right now."

She started to fondle me, tho' I was still thinking of Clara and the fact that Black Dick could feed her licorice wholesale. Suddenly I felt the softness of Mrs. Loring's white hood against my ear.

I could talk of passion and light any lamp on the island with a bounty of words. But 't was not at all like that. We did not sigh or groan or sweat in that dark chariot with the turmoil of acrobats. Never mind that the chariot did not have the proportions of a proper bed. And it had little need of a stove. Neither of us undressed. She parted her skirts, sat on my thighs, and unbuttoned my britches, while the wind rattled against the chariot's walls. And when she grew warm, she knocked against the ceiling with her hood and pronounced my name in her Boston lilt as if it were the line of some melody. Then she twisted around and sat sidesaddle as we rode along. She had her fingers in my scalp. "What thinks my brooding boy?"

"I could kidnap you."

"I'm not much of a prize. You might consider a merchant's daughter who'd never slept with a man. Or find yourself a rich widow, like the general from Virginia."

"Mrs. Loring, you dishonor me by offering yourself as my matrimonial agent. Manhattan is small, ma'am, and my interest is uncommonly large. I will chase your chariot."

"And if you found another inside?"

"I'd sample her wares while dreaming of you."

Liar that I am, I thought only of making a fortune and marrying Clara. But I could not silence that rascal tongue of mine.

"I surrender," she said. "You're shameful. You wear a woman out."

The chariot stopped. Milady slid off my lap. The general must have given Mrs. Loring her very own birdcage, a lovely little yellow house on Dock Street. Or perhaps the birdcage belonged to someone else. She went inside without looking back once.

I wondered where the chariot would bring me next. I should have liked to share a pint with Paul. But the chariot swerved about and delivered me to the general's mansion on Broadway.

"Coachman," I said to Paul, "methinks you have missed your mark." But when I climbed down the chariot's single step, I didn't discover Paul in the coachman's box. He must have been discarded while I was with Mrs. Loring. Instead, one of the king's assassins sat in the box. A great big brute with black holes in his mouth instead of teeth, Mortimer his name, and he was the general's very own bodyguard and valet, I would soon learn. He'd been a prizefighter who enlisted in the army and followed Sir William to America, just as he followed me into the house.

Sir William waited in the parlor, drowning himself in port. He seemed rather melancholy for someone in a jealous rage. He stood in his bare feet, a nightshirt over his military tunic. He really did remind me of General Washington. Sir William had his own tall elegance, even in a nightshirt. I wondered if he'd hang me for having knocked about with Mrs. Loring.

"Milord," I said, "it wasn't her fault. I waylaid her chariot, forced myself upon her."

"Mortimer, he prattles on and on, when I'm sick to death about my brother. We couldn't find you, Johnny One-Eye, and I said to Mort, 'Do you suppose he's with Cunny in her carriage? Should we hazard a guess? Him with a classical education. And my brother suffering so.' It seems the nuns at Gertrude's shop are also classicists. That is, a particular nun. Clara by name. Gorgeous girl. Never saw a Negress with such blond hair."

Mortimer corrected him. "An octoroon, Master Will. With a surprising mix of blood."

"We thought of killing her, hiding her body in a swamp behind the Fields. But I can't have my brother mourn. Of what good will he be to us? He's insane about the blond apparition, he who prayed from morning to night and never looked at a woman outside his marriage. It was like a thunderclap, Mort, even worse. And she mocks him, quotes Aristotle, and he's lost. I won't have it. I lack the manpower to help Dick. His own officers have been serving since they were fourteen or younger. They can't put Aristotle between their compasses and themselves. Confound it, Johnny One-Eye, I've come to your country to punish and bring fear, to startle you Americans into a state of submission, not to recite songs."

"But I am not a songster, General."

"Mort, will you knock him on the head if he doesn't listen?"

"He'll listen. Wouldn't want to cripple your only candidate. Do I have your permission to convey him to your brother, Master Will?"

"Yes, but quickly, or I will not be responsible for that Negress's loss of life or limb."

WE TOOK THE SAME CHARIOT, Mortimer and I, and I sat upstairs with him in the coachman's box, but I was worried about Paul, since the general had talked so much about murder and mayhem. But "Cunny's coachman" had not been harmed. And I could see that there was a logic to Mortimer's murderings. He wasn't like King George's own mercenaries, the Hessians, who plundered friend and foe. He'd been a boxer from the time he was eleven, traveling from fair to fair. He could neither read nor write, but he'd fought at Sir William's side, tho' a manservant shouldn't have been on the field of battle. He was with William on Long Island and in Harlem, where he almost captured George Washington with his own hands.

"I was ten feet away," Mortimer said. "In the buckwheat. He was on his horse. I confess, he was even fiercer than my William. I looked him in the eye. And he held my gaze like a bloody magnet. I might have shivered on another occasion. But I went for his stirrups with a roar in my throat. And his lieutenants poked at him, pulled him out of harm's way. Johnny, you mustn't tell Will. But you can't win against a warrior like that. I'll wager he pisses ice for breakfast."

Mortimer gave me a scarf to wear as we rode into the wind. I wrapped the scarf under my eyes, and the two of us must have looked like avengers out of hell. I could see over the ruins of Trinity, over the sailcloth stitched to the blackened chimneys and walls of Canvas Town. No constable, no marauder, no drunken soldier, stood in our way. We arrived on Robinson Street with grit under our wheels.

"I'll not go in with you, John. The admiral dislikes me. Says I have an undue influence over his brother. But he's a babe in the woods, that man is. Wants to run away with his Clara, and I'm not so sure she'll have him. Had to tell my master. 'Black Dick ought to beat her silly.' I offered to strangle her myself."

"Then you would have me as an enemy for life. I'm attached to Clara . . . to all the nuns."

"Right. Wouldn't want a brainy lad like yourself on my bad side. Give us a kiss. To seal our reconciliation."

I kissed the brute. I'd grown fond of him in such a short time, in spite of his absent teeth. Still, I couldn't rely on Mortimer. These Brits, meseems, were great hunters of women and men. And I worried over Mr. Washington most of all. Sir William and his brute were looking for ways to murder him—that was foremost in Sir William's mind. Such a man had nothing but mayhem in his heart.

We were near Canvas Town again, and I could see the path

where the fire had leapt and raged. I remembered the horses I had found with charred manes, their eyes filled with wild fluid. They didn't bolt, but stood like sentries in the infernal black wind. I led them out of the fire, feeling the heat of their hides, clucking at them as you might sing to a baby.

Twenty-Two

I JUMPED DOWN FROM THE COACHMAN'S BOX AND went inside to Gert's. The lamps were dying, and I found the admiral all alone in the parlor with as much melancholy as I'd ever seen on a man with a leather face. He wasn't drinking port, like his brother. He was beyond drink, beyond war and the weather.

I helped him out of his boots, yet I had the urge to flay him, to find whatever blood could breathe underneath that somber carapace. He had the money and the peerage to have his own nun, while I had a changeling's bitter, broken line. But I pitied him and the sullen mask he had to wear for life.

"Are you an orderly?" he said. "I cannot see your puss in this light."

"'Tis Johnny One-Eye."

"The boy who bastinadoed my brother, cut him to the quick. I admire that. I have no such way with words."

"An admiral must dream of the sea, milord, and nothing else. You have a grave disadvantage on land."

"Then should I carry Mistress Clara aboard the *Eagle*? Is that what you're hinting at? I ought to break your neck . . . where's my secretary? Where's Serle? I keep forgetting. Can't invite him to a bordello. He's on familiar terms with my wife . . . who sent you here?"

"Your brother, milord."

"He's a meddler, my Will." The admiral began to pick at his fingernails with an enormous knife. For a moment I thought he'd gone mad. It wouldn't be the first time it had happened to a tenant at the Queen's Yard.

"Clara mocks me, licks my ear with Aristotle. And I can't go to Serle. 'Tis a pity 'cause Ambrose has the gift. Do you know what he said about Mr. Washington? 'A paltry little colonel of militia at the head of loathsome banditti.' I'm rather fond of that."

"They aren't banditti. They're farmers and mechanics who became militiamen."

"Shut your mouth. She mocks me. 'What must a theatre piece have?' Mistress Clara asks."

"A beginning, a middle, and an end."

The admiral stared at me, his eyes murderous under the mask. "Not more than that? And what is the most necessary ingredient?"

"Suffering," I said.

"And it must imitate actions that excite . . . excite what?"

"Pity and fear."

The rage had gone out of him. He stopped picking at his nails with a knife. "I'm still confused about the order of impossible possibilities in Aristotle's art."

"Think of it like a navy battle, milord. Poets and admirals should prefer probable impossibilities to improbable possibilities . . . the probable is what matters, or you couldn't wage war."

"Correct. The enemy cannot manufacture an improbable fleet, nor should I have to chase down an improbable ship of the line. Have I mastered Aristotle?"

"In a nutshell."

"And will you teach me Plato and Plotinus? I'll pay you a shilling per philosopher. And will you guide my hand in a letter to Clara? Confound it, Ambrose Serle does all my drafts. And I daren't ask him to plead my case to a whore, delightful and cultivated tho' she be. Besides, the little shit might fall in love with her. And I'd have to feed him to the sharks."

"But I should warn you, milord. I'm already in love with Clara."

"I'll risk that. I'm not worried about her American admirers. But I cannot cobble. The words do not meet. I am like a joiner without his joints. Johnny, I have not composed a decent letter in all my life. I've always had someone to help me."

Dolt that I am, I pictured myself as a knight of the realm entombed in a leather mask and crazily in love with Clara. It wasn't that far from the truth. We were in the same careening boat, Black Dick and I, about to plunge into a waterfall.

"How shall we begin?" the admiral asked. "*Dear Mistress Clara*, or . . ."

"*My Lady with the Green Eyes.*"

"Ah, that will wake her for me. *Dost thou love thy admiral in the parlor?*"

"Too direct, milord. You must feint like the fastest cruiser in your fleet. She must not be able to divine your purpose until you are prepared to pounce."

"Then what do you favor?"

"A strict neutrality. Perhaps a note about Aristotle, something not so very large. *My Lady with the Green Eyes. Brutes may mimic a man, but not his music. I come to you with all the fear and pity of a poet, a poet of the seas who cannot find comfort on land save to look into your green eyes.*"

"A miracle. You must write it down."

DIDN'T HAVE TO WRITE A LINE. I rode the admiral's waterfall and its music tumbled out of my head. The force of it frightened me. I went into my opium den, the shoe closet, where I could live in war and peace with Clara's slippers and shoes. I picked at the rhinestones on a slipper, smashed the silken toe of her favorite mule with meanness in my heart. I would ruin her whole collection.

Never got the chance.

Gert had arrived. She didn't come at me with a broom or her pocket pistols. She didn't even grab my hand. She must have seen my madness, seen my hell as she looked at me with her lantern.

"Child, Clara will have to go barefoot among the Brits if you destroy all her shoes."

"I wish she would."

"But you will defeat your purpose. It will inflame them to see a nun's bare toes."

"Then I will cut off their noses."

"And have the British hang you and make a widow of me?"

"Madame, I am not your husband. I am your son."

I saw her in the lantern light. Her mouth twisted into a gargoyle's grimace. "You must keep away from Clara. You must not interfere with Clara's work."

"Work," says I. "Mixing her spittle with a man whose face is so worn it resembles a mask."

"The admiral has been kind to us, or do you forget?"

"Not at all. I savor his licorice, but beware. Let Clara wiggle her toes at the Brits. I will break every last one of her shoes."

"She will delight in your folly," Gert said, and vacated the closet with her lamp.

Twenty-Three

AS FEBRUARY YIELDED TO MARCH, SIR WILLIAM continued in his sloth, while soldiers, sailors, starving blacks, Loyalist merchants and their wives swelled the island's population six months after the British arrived in their longboats. Not even Sir William's war marshal could contain the Hessian mercenaries, who robbed everyone in sight until a drunken gang of dockers battled them on the Commons. The Brits were much too busy playing golf on the heathlands of Long Island to bother about Hessian highwaymen. Cricket matches appeared on the Bowling Green. Sir William's senior officers hunted wild pigs in Canarsie. Prices rose like rockets hurtling in the winter sky.

The poor had to come to Holy Ground, where nuns let them have the leftovers that always seemed to drop from their baskets by Divine accident. Clara was most prominent among these nuns. Black Dick must have given her extra rations. She could have attended cricket matches, but she remained on the ramparts of Robinson Street—the same ramparts the rebels had built—and led her own platoon of nuns whenever she wasn't with Black

Dick, platoons that fed the poor. The heels of her precious shoes wore down, but she cared not a whit; rhinestones fell into the mud. I could do nothing but dream about Clara. I'd watch her for hours—and she knew I was watching—until she called to me without turning her head of woolly blond hair.

"Mr. One-Eye, ain't you gonna lend us a hand?"

I worked beside her half the night. Other nuns would bring us water. Clara lent me her silk handkerchief to wipe my brow, and once she even wiped it herself. I shivered at her simplest touch. This was the Clara I remembered from the time I was twelve and would sing her to sleep—the first and last honeymoon I'd ever had, when Clara shared my closet after Gert shaved all her hair. And now I was on the ramparts of Robinson Street feeding poor souls—black and white—that the Brits had left out of their family circle. Clara started to laugh while she swilled water in her mouth, and I had to fight the desire to lick the droplets off her chin.

"Master John, have you been visiting the closet lately? How doth my shoes appeal to your nose?"

I could have answered anyone else, parried with the Divil, but not with Clara. I dropped the nuns' water ladle and decided to disappear.

BLACK DICK FOUND ME skulking on Gert's verandah. He'd come with a hanger at his side, the short sword admirals were supposed to wear into battle. Sir William might have held to his winter home, unwilling to campaign, but Black Dick would not discontinue his naval maneuvers. He insisted that I accompany him.

We drove to the harbor in his carriage and boarded the *Eagle* in one great swoop. I'd never been near such a seabird, with masts as tall as most skies. I'd been on a boat with Benedict Arnold, a tiny skiff of sorts that leaked and nearly destroyed us, delivered all our souls to the bottom of the Dead River had we not followed Arnold's instructions and bailed with our hats. But the admiral's flagship was mysterious to me. It had objects and things I could not name, booms and gaffs and little nests within that endless universe of rope. We went down to the admiral's quarters. I could not have imagined so many tunnels in the belly of a boat.

Serle presided in the cabin, Black Dick's little secretary. He wore no uniform, no hanger at his side. He was a minor aristocrat, a married man. He'd come to America as Black Dick's civilian secretary and saw the whole United States as a bunch of banditti.

"Ah," he said, "this is the vagabond who serenades your high-yellow slut."

"Careful," Black Dick said, "or I'll let the vagabond loose, and he'll bite your nose off. His name is Johnny One-Eye."

"How picturesque. A pirate of the lower depths. Does he prime the whore before you mount her?"

The admiral slapped his secretary. But I found little anger there. It was part of his naval maneuvers.

"I beg your pardon, Lord Howe. I've had the dysentery. And it's sucked the life out of me."

"I'm told General Washington has the flux night and day, and he commands an army, Serle."

"Not an army, sir, a mob. The rebels have their own irregular nation. Why, it's naught but an ochlocracy—rule by mob and mob alone. They shall never win against us, these noisome fellows, cowards one and all."

I was boiling hot, but I had to hold my hands in my britches to keep from pummeling him.

"Shut up, Serle," said Black Dick. "The boy has lost an eye fighting against our Canadians on the walls of Quebec."

Who had told him that? Was it Clara who'd given up my secrets while she labored over Aristotle?

"I am sorry," Serle said. "I'm homesick, you see. I miss my wife and it makes my bile run . . . where are we going, milord?"

"To Montresor Island. It's been reoccupied. The rebels have planted a flag on their own former works. And their young major has taunted me and my brother, says if Black Dick can have Manhattan, he'll have Montresor."

'T was a worthless little island off Manhattan's east coast, just south of Harlem.

"Milord," I asked, "what is the name of this officer?"

"Malcolm Treat."

I felt sorry for the Brits. That one-eyed major was still in charge of Washington's secret service, and he wasn't wintering in Morristown with the commander in chief. Malcolm Treat had found the means to get back onto Manhattan Island. He would make his stand on Montresor and have a poor lovesick admiral capture him.

Equipped with long coats, we went up to the quarterdeck, stared at the cozy little fortress on Montresor that looked like crooked teeth on a wall.

"Milord," Serle asked in his long coat, "are we not pulling too close? They could lob a shell into our hull and ground the *Eagle*."

"With their paltry guns? I could catch their cannonballs with my fists. Do shut up."

Black Dick signaled to an officer I could not see, and the *Eagle* delivered a ferocious broadside that tore up the island and roiled the water to such a degree that I thought the ship would sink. We'd come to Hell Gate, a maelstrom, a vortex that we locals liked to call the Pot, because at high or half tide it could capture *anything*—soldiers, horses on a barge, sailors in their ships. There was a mountain right below the Pot, rocky crags that had already caused a pair of frigates carrying paymaster's silver and gold to sink without a sign. And here was Black Dick with his *Eagle*, willing to risk us all in a whirlpool, on account of Aristotle. If Clara had not crawled under his skin, would a sane man have entered this ungodly channel when he could have rowed across from Manhattan to Montresor?

A second broadside seemed to level most of the island's works and leave Montresor a patch of smoldering ruins. And while the *Eagle* rocked to and fro, we got into a little landing boat—ten marines, the admiral, Serle, and myself—and we rode the currents until we found somewhere to make purchase on the island. The rebels could have shot us to pieces had there been five of them behind a wall, five with flintlocks. The admiral wore his ceremonial hat, but the hat was wet, and his cape was furled around him, so that he resembled some lunatic washed ashore by the tide.

He handed me the white flag that he'd kept all the time under his cape.

"Johnny One-Eye, tell your compatriots that we mean them no harm. Should they surrender without a shot, we shan't harm a hair on their heads. But His Majesty will not countenance rebels in control of Montresor."

"Yes, yes," Serle said, "tell these unhappy men what you must."

The admiral glared at him under the enormous prow of his hat. "Serle, you are confusing the boy."

I wasn't confused. I was the receptacle of a mad mission.

I thought to find broken bodies everywhere, men wounded or killed by the *Eagle*'s shattering force and firepower. But I heard not a single human sound, not a groan, not a hiss, not a battle cry. I walked on top of the works, the crumbling walls that the Brits had cannonaded so well. No party of men could have survived it, large or small.

Then a face leapt out at me like a sinister lantern from what might have been a man-made crevice in the wall. The face belonged to Malcolm Treat. He wore mud and grease as camouflage.

His complaint broke the silence.

"If it isn't the king's little reptile. Do you know how many your cannon have killed?"

"None," I said. "You overran the island with twenty ruffians like yourself, took no prisoners, slaughtered whoever was here, buried them under the works, got your lads off the island, and waited for the fools to come."

"Divil," he said, "assassin, you're one of Black Dick's agents now."

I did what I always wanted to do ever since Treat had held me prisoner in a potato bin. I thrashed him, first with my fist, and then with the flagpole. Why should the likes of him have ever ruled over me? He was nothing but a puny one-eyed parasite who'd attached himself to Washington's waistcoat. I'd have finished him there, on Montresor, among the ruins and those missiles off the *Eagle* that sat like pocked pumpkin heads on the rough soil.

But my pleasure was short. Little Serle came upon me, in advance of the admiral and the marines. And I had to put down the flagpole. But I was a shiver from almost murdering a man. And then I caught Black Dick's man-o'-war through the mist. It was a seabird, by God, with its own enormous tilted beak and wings of cloth, its gun decks like row upon row of hollowed eyes hung with feathers of smoke, feathers that didn't seem to fade. I could understand now why the admiral was so vulnerable away from the sea, prone to folly. He had no need of Aristotle aboard the *Eagle*.

He tilted his head and looked upon Treat, who lay within the crumbling works, a spent cannonball inches from his ear. "Major, I am moved by your heroic stand. To hold your little island against a battleship. You are my prisoner, and you'll dine with me on board the *Eagle*."

He put his cape around the major, got him to his feet, and had his marines carry him to our landing boat. Treat had triumphed, not I. He would be put on parole with the admiral's approval. And Black Dick would recommend him to the players of John Street, who called themselves Howe's Thespians, in honor of Sir William. Little Treat could assume the women's roles, like the Empress of China or the Old Maid.

I furled up my white flag and walked through the mist, watching the *Eagle*'s many eyes. I dreaded returning to dry land. I liked it here. There were no ambiguities, viz., my curious relationship with Clara, which had started as a honeymoon, albeit chaste, and was now but a battlefield.

Twenty-Four

THERE WAS MUCH BRUIT IN MY OWN FRONT YARD. A gang of British sappers arrived in mid-March and reduced our rampart to the tiniest of hills. Next they built a guardhouse, a little hut, and we had redcoats stationed right on Robinson Street. Had Sir William stumbled upon George Washington's own secret history with Gert? Redcoats on our lawn wouldn't have been the way to lure him into the Queen's Yard—yet it troubled the soul. Sir William meant to trap George Washington within Gertrude's garden.

And what if I were wrong? Perhaps Sir William worried that some rebel sharpshooter might take a potshot at his brother, who wandered about the nunnery unless he was on board the *Eagle*—or was politicking for Malcolm Treat's parole in front of the king's tribunal.

Black Dick had given his word that the little major would not flee the confines of Manhattan and shouldn't be locked up in a barn, a church, a sugarhouse, or one of the prison ships moored in Wallabout Bay, across the East River. "Wallabout is for common criminals, for dubious rebel soldiers and seamen," said Black Dick, "not for men of Malcolm Treat's heroic mold."

The admiral was a lonely man in love with Clara. He must have longed to welcome Malcolm One-Eye as his own lost prodigal son, a son he'd never had, and display him like some tamed brute, viz., a model American. He offered to let him live on board the *Eagle*, but a man-o'-war was not considered part of Manhattan, and might expose a rebel major to certain military secrets. Black Dick was willing to defy the Barrack Board, steal housing from a British colonel to make room for Treat, but Treat was twice as clever as his captors and asked to live at Gert's.

"Agreed," said the admiral. "We'll have grog together."

Black Dick could not see the perfidy of that little man. Treat meant to diddle with Clara while Black Dick was on board the *Eagle*, or was busy with some maritime matter. And it seemed unheroic of him to hurt his very sponsor—'tis a lie. I wasn't thinking of Black Dick. I was jealous of that little major, jealous beyond words or reason, jealous of yet another shit-in-the-pants who cut off my own path to Clara.

So I trapped him at Madame's table, eating mutton pie. He could recall the thrashing he got on Montresor. He flinched, held the mutton pie over his jowls.

"Keep away from Clara if you value your life. She's with the admiral now."

"She is not. And how dare you intrude. I'm an adjutant in the Continental Army."

"On parole. And if I tell the admiral of your interest in Clara, he'll kick you as far as Wallabout."

Treat shivered. His Majesty warehoused American prisoners at this notorious Brooklyn bay, with its stinking, rotten ships.

"You gadfly," he said, "you unconscionable pest. I'm innocent. It's Clara who's interested in me."

I counted the gunports on some imagined man-o'-war to keep from strangling him. But I stole his mutton pie, devoured it in front of his eyes, and kicked him like a dog. He vanished into a closet. I sat with my heels on the table, whistled a song, and waited. I didn't have to budge.

Clara appeared, her eyes ablaze, as bountiful as a hundred men-o'-war, real or imagined, in brocaded boots with buckles and pointed toes, her bodice shimmering with gold filigree. I would have surrendered without a fight on any other day.

"Are you the procurer of Robinson Street, Johnny One-Eye? No one tells me what man I will or will not see. And have the grace to stop writing letters for Admiral Dick. He's not a child."

"Yet you treat him like one."

"Perhaps this is what he wants, to become a child in Clara's arms."

"So you can read him Aristotle and unman him."

"Are you not an expert on that subject? Perhaps you might teach him a few tricks. On how to live amongst whores and be woefully ignorant of their ways."

She knew how to bathe a boy in her own venom.

"Clara," I said, "do you remember how it was when we lived together?"

Her green eyes covered me like a pair of suspicious patrol boats. "We never did."

"You were bald as an egg."

"I wasn't," she said, caressing her own mountain of hair.

"Clara, how can you forget but five years ago, five little years?"

"Child," she said, "I don't keep such a strict calendar. But I do recall a kind little boy who delivered drinks to Gert's customers.

And then he put on airs. He traveled across the road to King's College, took to wearin' a black gown. And I prefer a soldier any day to an educated crow."

Had to tell her for the hundredth time how I went to war and served under Benedict Arnold.

"Why ain't you with Arnold right now? Ah, but you're still a boy. And if I ever lived in your bed, as you love to boast, why didn't you keep me there?"

"I couldn't."

Only Clara could make me cry—not Gert, not that horseman, General Washington, not the Howes, and not the king himself. When Clara saw the first tears settle on my nose, she seemed satisfied, as if a duel had been won. She wiped my tears with one of her long fingers. I could not stop marveling at the natural grace of that digit—like a serpent that had decided not to sting.

"Johnny, did you tell me stories in that cradle of ours?"

"Every night."

"About snowmen and orphans and African kings—"

"And birds with impossible mouths that could swallow a live pig."

She laughed, and I was struck with a pernicious pain. I would never arrive at that far territory—my own Ohio—where I might possess the magic of other men and make Clara love me.

"And toads in feathered hats," she said, rubbing my hair with a rhythmic concentration that was close to a caress.

"Then you do remember?"

I clutched her hand and Clara pulled away.

"Child, I'm only singin' whatever it is you want to hear." And I could not hold back my hate.

"I can have you banished from this island," I said.

"The little provost of all the colored people. Banish me, then."

And she left me with the remains of my mutton pie.

I SOON HAD other worries. Sir William was plotting in the parlor, and I could learn nothing. Mortimer, his brute, kept me out of reach. William and his brother had their ships and their men. Washington had to maneuver without a navy. He never had the guns of the *Isis* or the *Eagle*. He had to maraud and run. But he did not lack fiery young officers, one of them being my classmate, Hamilton, a West Indian orphan who was older than I when he entered King's. He'd been a pamphleteer at my college—a writer of revolutionary tracts—and a captain at nineteen.

We all knew that Washington had delivered a lightning raid last Christmas, crossing the Delaware on a wet and windy night, falling upon Trenton and its hundred houses, capturing or killing a whole garrison of Hessians. And Hamilton—a veritable runt, two inches shorter than I—distinguished himself chasing Hessians from house to house. Their colonel, Johann Rall, had called the Continentals "country clowns." Yet Rall was the clown, a drunken sod who would not build any works. "We want no trenches," he said. "We will go at them with the bayonet." But his men could barely get him onto his horse. Their muskets were wet and would not hold flint. Washington's lads fired at them like flies. Johann fell from his horse and died the next day. Harvey Hill, the Crier, sang Johann's story across our little island. The Hessian colonel who wandered through Trenton's hundred houses and died in his own excrement.

Loyalist merchants and British soldiers in Manhattan could afford to laugh. The Hessians were hirelings, after all, and didn't really belong to the Crown. The entire garrison had fallen into a drunken stupor and had fought the rebels in winter underwear. And Sir William met with his aides in secret, clearing all of Gertrude's guests out of the Queen's Yard. He was in a foul mood. Poems began to appear on the walls of army barracks, inside coffeehouses and clubs, and on the cannons at Fort George.

Awake, arouse, Sir Billy
There's forage in the plain.
Leave your little filly
And open the campaign.

I wondered if the Crier himself had penned that piffle. Harvey Hill should not have attacked Mrs. Loring. And while Sir William brooded with his aides, he sent Mortimer out to me.

"General would like you to visit with Mrs. L.," said Mortimer. "She's having a crisis, John."

The brute himself drove me to Mrs. Loring's little yellow birdcage on Dock Street. "She's expecting you. Needn't bother to knock."

I went to milady, who was lounging upstairs in bed. "Do you hear what the rebels are saying about me and Will? I shall leave this wretched country."

"Where will you go?"

"That's the problem. I'm a pariah everywhere. They can think of nothing better than to write folderol about Mrs. Loring. I have become the great amusement of this war. Whatever William does, they will blame me. Would they have been so savage to a good little wife?"

"But you are his wife, milady, his war wife. And it's the war that maddens them, makes them cruel. They laugh at your expense because they have so little else to laugh about."

"You are the kindest sort of philosopher. Sit beside me."

I was reluctant, lads. I thought of Clara, of my next battle with her, wherever and whenever that would be. But Mrs. Loring was persistent.

"Sit beside me."

I did not venture to ask why Cunny was naked under her quilt; I simply shucked off my clothes. I have to admit—the beauty of her skin astonished me. Her silken body moved against mine with its own tender truth. And she did not have to sit on my thighs the way she had done in her carriage. Clara fled from my mind for a moment as I pinned milady's arms to the wall; her lapdogs watched us with much curiosity and then devoured my stockings.

Mortimer came for me in the middle of the night, while Mrs. Loring slept against my shoulder. He bade me to get dressed, and I had to leave the yellow house.

"You may visit Mrs. L. so long as it pleases her, but you must not wake up with her. The last lad who insisted upon it is no longer alive."

"Did Sir Billy run him through with his hanger?"

"Hardly, boy. I broke his neck. But I wasn't as fond of him as I am of you. General can imagine many things, but he'd rather not 'magine her waking up with another man. That's his privilege, and his alone."

It had started to snow, and the flakes fell on Dock Street like some sudden enchantment—pieces of powder, crystalline and pure, and I was the only witness. Mortimer had wrapped his head in a scarf.

Twenty-Five

Sir William's entire army fell asleep and would continue to snore until May, when the summer campaign was scheduled to begin. But the general had another campaign. You could not find him conferring with his family. He was playing vingt-et-un. It had become the rage of wartime Manhattan, at least on Holy Ground. The nuns played among themselves, or with guests, always scalping them. But no one scalped Sir William. He acted as the bank, always as the bank, and dealt cards from a little ivory holder smooth as glass. He had a paymaster's box that he called the Bank of England, and it was filled with the currencies you might find in a pirate's chest. I committed them all to memory: the London pound (safe as the Lord), the New York pound (worth half as much as a Londoner), the Portuguese johannes, called "joe" (worth sixteen pounds), and the much more popular "half-joe," the Spanish silver dollar, or piece of eight (as valuable as a London pound), the Spanish gold dollar, or doubloon (worth sixteen pieces of eight), the thaler, or German dollar (worth a little less than a Londoner), the French Guinea, or louis d'or (the value of which went up and down), the gold ducat, first coined in Sicily, the caroline of Württemberg, etc., etc. It was a mystification of money. But the Bank of England never failed. It was Mortimer who was in charge of the box—the brute could count as fast as ten government clerks. He had a wooden claw that scooped up cash and cards. The general was like an invalid without him. He'd been dealing and handling the claw until Mortimer returned to the table.

There was an empty seat, and the general invited me into the game. I sat between two Loyalist merchants.

"Sir William," I said, "I shouldn't. I'm short of silver."

"Mortimer, I asked for a cardplayer, not a baboon. He may bet as he wishes. He is my guest. I will cover him, win or lose."

And Mortimer shoved thalers and doubloons at me with his wooden claw.

Madame and all her nuns were at the table, including Clara, and even nuns from other establishments, loath to miss a game of vingt-et-un with Sir William. The general had to use five decks. But his concentration was fierce.

"Touch me," the players would cry, asking for another card while the brute collected their bets.

And in the middle of dealing, the general turned to me.

"Did you ride my filly, John?"

"Master," the brute said, "'tis not appropriate for the table."

"Haven't lost my charm, Mort. I'm keeping count. Did he ride the filly or not?"

It was only Mortimer who could answer him, not his aides, not the merchants, not Madame.

"There is no such filly, such filly does not exist. It's the invention of your enemies, which have grown numerous around New York. The boy kept Mrs. L. company at the general's request."

"That's better. We're gaining momentum, Mort. Did he ride her?"

The nuns kept watching Sir William and Mortimer, their mouths agape. They had to be careful of Sir William's ire. This dictator of Manhattan had the power to sentence them all to death.

"Well, Mort? I'm waiting."

The brute stopped shoving his claw. He'd lost the momentum of the bank. The general had shoved him outside the realm of cards. He had his own sense of fairness and decorum, tho' he was willing to crack skulls and worse for Master Will. He'd smelled an injustice. He'd murder, but he wouldn't lie, not when that lie would betray Mrs. Loring, who trusted him.

"Did he mount her, Mort? Answer me."

"I did," says I with a chirp.

"Bravo," the general said. "The baboon speaks."

I was a marked man, no matter what I said. He looked at me like some falconer preparing to hunt his prey. He was a falconer, and I'd become half his hunting season. The cards trembled in his hand. He could have squashed my temples with his thumbs. But Gertrude got up from the table.

"You're my guest here, Billy. And if you can't behave, you'll remove yourself with your vingt-et-un."

"Madame," he said, "I could turn your whorehouse into a barracks for drummer boys."

"I wouldn't mind, Billy. I could relocate. I'm told the climate in Newport is soothing for the female skin. You poor sod, you'll miss us the moment we're gone."

"Mort," he said, "remind Gertrude that she's talking to the commander in chief. I'm not in the mood for insolence."

"Then, dear Mortimer, have him arrest me and my girls. That prick will die of loneliness. Where else would he play vingt-et-un? There's not another oak table large enough in the colony."

Madame vanished with all her nuns, while Sir William fumed. He thrust every merchant out of the game, but wouldn't permit me to withdraw. I had to sit with Billy and the brute.

"Mort, who are the finest strategists ever? Some say that Johnny Burgoyne should sit at the top of the list."

"Posh," said the brute.

Gentleman Johnny Burgoyne was the handsomest and most notorious general in the entire British war machine—a playwright, a gambler, an actor, and a whoremaster, he'd also been the first captain of light horse the Brits had ever had, according to Sir Harold. Burgoyne invented the whole idea of lightning cavalry in Portugal, during the Seven Years' War. And he hoped to use much of the same "lightning" against us, to pounce upon George Washington from Britain's own perch in Canada.

"Burgoyne a strategist?" continued the brute. "He can deliver naught but the pox."

"Yet his lads love him so. He'd nary whip a one. No corporal punishment under his command."

"What?" asked the brute, more riled than ever. "Not whip a man who behaves like a dog? That's not an army, sir. That's some foul kennel unfit for humankind."

"Then who, Mortimer, would be high on your list?"

"Alexander the Great and yourself, Master Will."

"No, no, I am middling, but I had a plan. I followed the king's orders. 'Drive them not to despair,' he said, 'but to submission. These are my children.' Ye gods, how can a general fight with such a handicap? Dick and I as commanders and peace commissioners. Yet we were doing well, indeed, with those bellicose farmers on the run. Winter came, and the farmer boys did not have a pair of shoes amongst them. Shoes, Mortimer, that's how a battle is won."

"Alexander would have agreed, milord."

"Don't interrupt. The Continental Army was disappearing—there was no army. I have my spies. We crept into Washington's very war tent. I had his shoeless scrubs walled in. I ordered seven garrisons, seven armed camps, built along a line from the Hackensack to the Delaware, like a chain that would tighten around an enemy and entrap it. The farmers should have froze to death. But I had a weak link, Colonel Rall. I never wanted the man. A drunken sod who built no works. He buggered himself on Christmas night. Washington crosses the Delaware, and not a single scout in sight. It's lucky the little colonel got out of bed . . . lads, face it, the Hessians can't fight. I asked for Cossacks, and I got men with mustachios who plunder and rape. Mort, how many Hessians have I hanged?"

"Three."

"And Rall would have been the fourth had he lived."

"A colonel with his own regiment?" the brute asked, a bit bewildered.

"I'd have kept the hangman busy day and night . . . the farmer in chief resurrects himself, and I'm the butt of every rebel joke. Sir Billy who can't lift his arse from Manhattan's latrine . . . Johnny One-Eye, you can tell the Town Crier that if he ever writes another poem about Mrs. Loring again, I will hack off his ears. He's Washington's spy. I tolerate him because I'd rather have a spy where I can see his face. But one more bit of doggerel and—Johnny, I want the farmer in chief, to capture and to kill him. And the insurrection is over. But if we should pack up our ships and leave America while he lives, there will be anarchy and civil war. I will not disappoint the king."

And he looked at me with the Divil's own grin.

"The farmer in chief loves vingt-et-un as much as I do. He plays it with little Hamilton and all his other lads. Perhaps it was Hamilton himself who scribbled the poem and passed it on to the Crier. He's brilliant, I hear. Was he not with you at King's?"

"A pompous fellow with a fierce temper. I did not know him well. Yet we had one thing in common. We were the poorest students at the college. But I doubt he could have written that doggerel. He has not the least feeling for humor."

"And you consider those wretched four lines humorful?"

"In a cutting, inconsequential way," I told him.

"And you yourself might have been capable of scribbling them?"

"Not about Mrs. Loring, milord."

"Then whom, pray?"

"The farmer in chief," I said, dancing with Sir William. I had to dance, or I would have fallen into the Divil's own dark well. "The farmer in chief," I said again.

He smiled like the master of vingt-et-un.

"And you'll help us capture our George? We'll announce a colossal game, a tournament of champions . . . at the Queen's Yard. My spies tell me that he won't be able to resist. I'll declare a day and night of truce. We'll lure him out of the forests and woods."

"And you mean to capture him thus?"

"It will end the war, Johnny, it will end the war. You'll repeat to the Crier that General Howe offers Mr. Washington twenty-four hours of amnesty, a furlough from fighting, to settle once and for all the question of who is the master of vingt-et-un in North America."

"And Mortimer will be waiting behind the curtain, I suppose, with his very fists as a hammer."

"I need him not. I'm enough of a soldier to dispatch one farmer in chief. And if you don't talk to the Crier, I will."

I nodded to give him the illusion of both yes and no. But I couldn't have him grab Harvey Hill, not yet. I needed Harvey to warn the farmer in chief not to accept Sir William's venomous offer—vingt-et-un was an invitation to a kill.

Now I understood why Sir William sent his sappers to Holy

Ground. They'd leveled the rampart so that George Washington couldn't arrive unnoticed. But there was a bit of complexity, I'd wager, tho' I didn't have a London pound to my name. I was tormented by the notion that George Washington had made a recent visit to Robinson Street, much too recent, else those sappers would not have been digging here.

I WENT TO GERT, who sat with several nuns, puffing on their pipes, redcoats all around. "Madam," I whispered, "you have tricked me."

The nuns tossed pieces of tobacco at my brains, but I would not be deterred.

"Madam, I do believe that General Washington has visited these very premises of late. I alone am ignorant of that fact."

"Idiot," she said, "hold your tongue. The Brits are about."

She wagged her head and the nuns disappeared with their pipes. Madame had a look in her eye that was like a mingling of contempt and sorrow for her bastard boy.

Twenty-Six

WHILE SIR WILLIAM PLAYED VINGT-ET-UN IN THE parlor, Gert and I talked through the night. She told me a tale about the commander in chief, a March tale, full of wind and rain.

"Johnny," she said, "I could not swallow food or a lick of wine. My general but thirty miles away, on his mountain, and he forbids me to see him. *'I would die, Gertrude, if ever you were caught.'* "

"But you could have disguised yourself, mum, dressed as a drummer boy. The Brits are half blind."

"Shush," says Madame. "He was able to sneak one letter through the lines, beggin' me to tear it up after I finished perusing it and all."

I could not keep from trembling. "Do you still have the letter, mum?"

"Idiot, I tore it up and cried for a week, like some silly strumpet. But I knew his words by heart. '*Dearest, your general is in a desperate state. His languor is like some disease he cannot shed. Melancholia always comes when I have to lie abed and cannot lead my boys into battle. Your general attends soirées with his family and their wives, and flirts with the prettiest of them—'tis nothing but a ruse. I would prosper well enough were I able to kiss your eyes.'*"

"More," I said, "much, much more."

"Silence, before you wake up the whole house."

"Let Billy come with his redcoats. He dare not call treasonous the sentences inside your head."

"But his scribes can mark down whatever his torturers pull out of me."

I was a torturer too. I had to pull the tale out of Gert, one thread at a time. *Charles Lee*, she kept talking about Charles Lee, Washington's second-in-command, captured by the Brits this past December. He'd called Washington an amateur, sniped at him, caballed behind his back.

"Madame," I asked, "did you ever meet this Lee?"

"He was a shit-in-the pants. My girls always had to give him a bath."

I shivered at the thought of Clara scrubbing that fellow's balls but said nothing, lest I break Madame's stride.

"He had a fondness for a ripe little widow, a whore with much pretension, called the Widow White, with her own tavern in New Jersey. And Lee was wont to visit her with his pack of dogs. Well, a British patrol heard the dogs howl and arrested General Lee in the widow's bedchamber."

"Capital," I said, until Madame told me that Lee had been Washington's supreme strategist.

"My general thought to drown himself in the Raritan without Lee. '*Child*,' he wrote, '*I have had not one day of rest since the rebellion began*.' And it was perilous, John."

"How so, madam?"

"He thought to take a holiday in Manhattan, among the Howes . . . 't was Clara who discovered him, more dead than alive, in the mud outside my window. God knows how he got across the Hudson."

And I had to imagine for myself, with Madame's lovely voice in mind. Clara rushing downstairs, past Sir William's officers. She had to pull on his gold buttons to waken him. "Widow White," he repeated, "Widow White," according to Madame.

"Must have been a delusion, John. My general had not eaten in twenty hours."

Clara led him into the house half a step at a time, his arms flailing like a straw man. She walked among Howe's own bodyguard, advertising this straw man as a drunken suitor. The bodyguards laughed. They couldn't quite imagine George Washington under the same roof with General Howe.

Clara hid Washington under Madame's massive bed and went into the parlor, where Gert was having a heated game of vingt-et-un with Howe. And the two women employed their own language of little signs while Sir William hovered over his aces or whatever else he had in his hand. Madame didn't say, and I'm not sure if Clara rolled one eye or bent her palm all the way back in a trick she learnt in Dominica, but Madame knew that Washington was in the house. She bowed to Sir William, sat Clara down in her place—"Billy, I think I have the flux"—and rushed to her other general.

She stationed a nun outside her door, fetched Washington from under the bed, propped him on a pillow. He was still delusional—"Damn the Widow White." Then he smiled. "Worth it," he muttered. "The wind and the brackish water. I had to look at your face."

His head dropped onto the pillow and he dozed for an hour. He had a meal in front of him when he opened his eyes. Kippered herring and hot toast, marmalade, coffee from the admiral's flagship. She had already brushed his uniform.

"Child," he said, the way he had addressed her nineteen years ago, and it pleased Madame. "They will dredge the Raritan, thinking I have drowned. I must return."

She had to keep him here for a few more hours, so that he would find his strength and would not fall dizzy in front of Sir William's bodyguard. And she did what New York's most illustrious "abbess" had been taught to do. She played vingt-et-un with the commander in chief while Sir William was into his cups and his cards but two doors away.

Washington was silent during most of the game, didn't bluster, didn't bully, didn't cheat, as Sir William would. Then Clara knocked thrice, and it meant that she'd been able to contact a rebel spy who would spirit Washington away. Madame was not fearful of this return trip. He had the good fortune that generals seemed to have. His face had been like a death mask in repose, robbed of blood—yet the blood returned the moment he smiled.

"'Tis my first wartime holiday. A ride across the river, a roll in the mud. But I wouldn't trade it for a world of royal cushions and crowns."

Then there was another knock, with the loud thump of an Englishman.

"Gert, Gert, lemme in."

Sir William had left his cards and come to her door.

Washington did not hide his epaulettes. And Gert had to pirouette in order to save him. Her heart pounded, but she couldn't ignore William's knock. She undid the latch, and the British commander in chief stood on Gert's doorsill like some trapeze artist who might balance himself forever without really entering the room.

"I was worried about your flux," he said.

He had that blinding discretion of an aristocrat. He wouldn't condescend to notice George Washington or any other man in her boudoir. And she almost loved him for it. He had the rank and the privilege to walk wherever he pleased in a bordello. But Gert's was sacred ground. And that is why he amused himself so.

"Billy," she said, like a buxom moon goddess coming out of her garden just to whisper in Sir William's ear. "Billy, deal me a hand. I'll be right back."

And he was gone. *British New York could go to the Divil,* she sang to herself soon as she fell into Washington's arms.

MADAME WOULD TELL ME nothing more. And now I understood why Sir William had turned the nunnery into an armed camp after the phantom's visit in March. He was expecting an encore from Madame's gentleman caller, but the caller didn't come. And then the guardhouse and the redcoats disappeared from Madame's front lawn. That worried me more. William was enticing—nay, daring—George Washington to visit Gert again. And this time there would be no balancing acts on a doorsill.

"Madam," I said, "you must warn General Washington."

"Do you think I haven't tried? Billy watches me like a hawk."

"But you could send Clara to look for another one of Washington's spies."

"He will hang her or chop off her head if she moves ten paces from the Queen's Yard. Have you not noticed? No nun is allowed to leave the premises."

"But I am still free," I said.

"Are you, Johnny? He has cast you into his net. He will allow you to roam, but will arrest whatsoever you happen upon."

"Madam," I said, "then I am nothing more than Billy's secret agent."

And I ran from Holy Ground.

Twenty-Seven

IT WAS JUST AFTER APRIL FOOL'S, AND THE APRIL fool himself, some British jester, would scamper across our village in his coat of many colors, with children clinging to his ragged tails. The jester looked like Harvey Hill. Harve did not have a charmed life, what with his family gone. His wife and little daughter had died in a fire set by drunken redcoats but five years before. The redcoats were not even punished. And that's when Harve began his career as our Crier. He would never talk about his wife and daughter. But I could feel their presence in his fevered eyes. He was like a man on a haunted mission, wearing the tattered clothes of our April fool.

I cared not a fig or a fart about Sir William and his spies. I had to find Harvey Hill. But he must have realized that the Brits wanted his blood for having scribbled that poem about William's concubine. He went into hiding, and we had no one to cry out the peculiar weather of war, not with his artistry. We lived in limbo, while Sir William defied all his critics. He went with his filly on long carriage rides, gave balls in her honor, balls where she danced the minuet with merchants and admirals, and presided over mountains of food. But Mrs. Loring was no wild-eyed glutton; she didn't gorge herself on some dish the general's own caterers had prepared, didn't excuse herself and belch at the back of the ball. She saved as much food as she could, hoarded it, and begged me to accompany her in her chariot to Canvas Town, to the charity house, and to the hovels of Little Africa.

Highwaymen roamed the streets, but we had Mortimer aloft in the coachman's box, and if they were foolish enough to try and molest us, Mortimer would knock them to the side of the road, leave them lying there for the sheriff and his constables.

I could not ask Mort to be disloyal to Sir William and help me warn General Washington. But I could enlist milady. She was William's consort, 'tis true, but I had the right to ask her not to be neutral toward his bloody designs.

"Your Will means to murder Washington," I said. "To trick him into a game of vingt-et-un and hack him to pieces."

Mrs. Loring looked at me with her blue eyes. "Nothing obliges Washington to play vingt-et-un in the Queen's Yard."

"But Sir William masks his perfidy, talks of a truce."

"Then it would be unworthy of me not to help you."

"How can—"

"Shhh," says she. "My seamstress is married to a rebel. She sends messages to Morristown once a week."

"And you haven't offered her carcass to Sir William?"

"Lord, no. I would not ruin the poor girl. She has promised never to read Will's dispatches that are scattered about my bedroom. We are fair with one another, and the girl trusts me."

I near bit my knuckles in disbelief—I'd found a route to General Washington. I scribbled a note to the seamstress. *The giant is saved*, I sang to myself. But I sang too soon.

Mortimer came up to me with my note crumpled inside his fist.

"I would wallop any other lad but you, report him to Master Will. You must not involve Mrs. Loring in your schemes. It might disturb my master, upset the tranquility of his household."

"I will never understand you," I said. "You would be a willing accomplice in a murder?"

"Yes."

"I will not ride in your carriage."

"Then you'd hurt Mrs. Loring and I'd have to break your bones."

"You are a brute, Mortimer, and a noxious blackmailer. I love thee not."

"Still, you will ride in the carriage."

I'd upset Mort. I could tell. I'd become his little brother on our carriage rides, and it cost him dearly to be deprived of my affection. I crept into the carriage, but 't was not much of a chore. I was moved by milady. She was never frivolous or wanton in her ways. She fed the poor, found them clothing and fuel for winter. She was much like Clara and Gert in this regard. Mrs. Loring might have been a nun in another world. She would not have felt like a pariah on Holy Ground. The German baronesses who had accompanied their highborn captains to America looked down upon her, called her the general's whore behind her back. I wouldn't have traded ten baronesses for milady. They were vile, inbred creatures, the daughters of mad, syphilitic men; they had no color in their cheeks. And still, the general had to please them while he presented Mrs. Loring at the concerts and soirées where Hessian orchestras played a sinfonia of Haydn and a certain Mrs. Hyde sang "If 'tis joy to wound a lover" or "The rapture at battle's end."

I did not enjoy the sounds. Perhaps it was because I was as much a miscreant as Mrs. Loring. I preferred our rides in the chariot, with the brute above us, unless he was involved with the general in vingt-et-un.

MRS. LORING WASN'T utterly free of her husband, tho' Sir William paid him plenty to leave her alone. Still, he was a mountebank and a toad. Sir William's commissary of prisoners had his own manor house in Harlem, his own carriage, his own brutes, who must have told him about our travels to Little Africa in milady's chariot. He could not abide that we were wasting pickled salmon, Russian tongue, and French olives on the poor of Out Ward. He was in the habit of hoarding whatever food he could find or stealing it for one of the five inns he and his partners ran.

The good Joshua was a greedy, grasping fellow. He dressed in British fashion—high-buckle shoes and silky sleeves. But he had one disadvantage. He couldn't cross paths with Sir William too often, since his presence would remind Manhattan's aristocratic ladies of Mrs. Loring's "baggage," a husband in Harlem with an expensive peruke. And he could not bear the signs of her new life. The chariot inflamed him. He fell upon us with his own band of robbers but a week after April Fool's. And even if Mortimer was with us, he had instructions not to interfere with Joshua Loring's banditry.

Loring hung from the side of his horse, poked his head into our window, doffed his London hat. He stank of perfume and powder. He was bewigged like some lord of the high court. He wore a dab of lip rouge, which must have been a rage I had yet to hear about. He'd darkened the moles on his face. He looked like an effeminate pirate, mean beyond imagination. He'd become the richest man on the island now that he fed off every rebel prisoner in the sugarhouses and on Wallabout Bay. He couldn't show his pique to the general, but he could show his distemper to me.

"Who's the infant, dear? Is it the same Johnny One-Eye who has a trove of missing parents? Why is a changeling inside your carriage?"

"Ride on, Joshua. You have no business here."

"I have a lot of business, including your cunny, which rents at an exorbitant rate."

"You will not insult Mrs. Loring," I said.

"I will, particularly when I'm her mister."

"We'll see about that."

I opened the carriage door, climbed down the single step, and stood near five horsemen, including Mr. L. They all had pistols in their pockets.

"Look, me lads, the little prince of Robinson Street. I'm told he was born in a brothel, survived on whores' milk. Mrs. Jennings, the good Gertrude, is his protectress. I wonder what it is she protects."

"Sir, I will meet you in Out Ward, behind the black soldiers' cemetery."

"A cemetery for black soldiers! There's no such place."

"There is," I said. "On the far side of Fresh Water Pond. You may come with seconds, or without. It matters little to me. But you will not bandy Madame Gertrude's name. Pistols or swords, monsieur?"

"A bold little rascal. A born duelist. But why should we wait? I'll crack you right here, on the spot, break every bone in your body."

Mrs. Loring peered out of the chariot. "The Howes would love that, Joshua. They'll mend him on their own, considering that he's Black Dick's confidential secretary."

"If he's a scribe, wifey, I'll spare him his fingers."

"Loring, I am not your wife," she said.

"Then why is it your name is Mrs. Loring?"

"Camouflage. I thought to resemble a snake."

"That's insulting," said the heaviest of the horsemen. "I'd call it a capital crime. She ought to be slapped. Methinks I'll slap her myself. If you'll allow me the liberty, Mr. L."

Mortimer was still in the box above us, like a silent referee. As the heavy horseman got down from his horse, Mortimer said, "Be so kind as to depart from here."

"Mr. L., since when is a rotten, stinking driver allowed to address a landed gentleman like myself?" the horseman asked.

He reached for his pistols, and the brute, without any warning, tossed a horseshoe at his head. I'd never seen horseshoes in the coachman's box. The horseman sank, his skull shattered, his brains leaking on the ground. Only one of God's angels could have pitched a horseshoe like that. I was really taken with the brute, and I had no pity for the horseman with the broken head.

Mr. Loring rode away with the robbers and their extra horse.

His wife was shivering. I covered her with my coat and held her hand like a lad who'd just been betrothed.

"Mortimer," I said, "ought we not bury the man, or summon the sheriff?"

"I'd rather he rots where he lies," Mortimer said, and he drove us out of this wild land where a horseman would soon become carrion.

Twenty-Eight

THE RAINS WERE FIERCE IN APRIL AND 'T WAS bitter cold as I ran round and round in circles like a demented cat and wasn't a hair closer to warning General Washington. Meanwhile, Sir William pumped up his enterprise. His nights at the Yard were famous. All sorts of gamblers would come, and William would give them a moratorium, take their money, and then his brute would escort them to the harbor, where they had to get on the next available ship, whether it was bound for Halifax or the Windward Islands. And pretty soon gamblers stopped coming to the games, but the myth of vingt-et-un grew and grew.

A pig would be roasted in the parlor, and Gertrude found herself feeding an army; the general paid her for every head of hair that held cards and feasted on the pig, but she wasn't interested in his thalers and London pounds. She thought only of Washington and how she might signal to him, but she and the nuns had to live under a pernicious form of house arrest. Redcoats were stationed on every floor.

Sir William now had an enormous establishment to uphold—

his headquarters, Mrs. Loring's yellow house, his tailor in London town, paupers and indigent Loyalists, his various clubs, etc., etc., but he did not gamble to grow rich or bring himself glory. He gambled in order to look into the whites of an opponent's eye at vingt-et-un. It was a battlefield for Billy, and he tossed cards on the table like a commander in chief. He earned his victories by sheer will, and if an opponent got lucky and called out "vingt-et-un," his luck rarely remained for long. The bank would win in the end, all across the table.

And he kept laying down challenges to the farmer in chief. "I'll wager his army against mine in a toss of cards."

I was plagued with a nervous fit. I would hiccough every five minutes as I watched Sir William's money box fill and could feel Washington's doom. Sir William would lure him back to the nunnery one way or another. And it made me hurtful to my very own kin, or whatever kin I had. I went through the Queen's Yard like some heartless angel who wanted to impose his will on the nuns—they were mystified when I bit their necks. I paid them in doubloons, my reward for educating Black Dick to Aristotle and writing his love letters to Clara. It was Mortimer who brought me money on behalf of Dick. The doubloons were as heavy as a pocket pistol and tore right through my purse.

I DID NOT RELISH IT when I strode into Clara's closet. She wore a flimsy gown while she smoked her pipe. "Child, what could you possibly want with me?"

"Your cunny," I said. "Your tits."

I had never talked in so crude a manner. The nuns had raised me. I discovered philosophy at their feet.

Clara put my hand between her legs.

I was mortified. I had no engine within myself that could respond to Clara. I longed to bite off my own hand, like some wolf or wild pig or a madman. I was not a wild pig. I cried with shame as she held my hand on her sex. I felt neither flesh nor fire, but a rigor mortis in all my limbs.

She must have taken pity, because she released my hand, and I was more in love than I had ever been.

"Clara, could you consider marrying me if I made my fortune?"

"Child," she said, "I have as much fortune as I'll ever need in my own closet."

"But I would sing you to sleep every night."

She studied my remark. "Then why wait for a wedding march? Sing to me right now."

"I cannot," I said. "The words will not come."

"Then what are ye good for, Johnny One-Eye?"

'T was my incapacity that pleased her, and the dominion she held over me. She could have had any man on our island—generals, merchants, pirates, and married ministers—but she stayed at Gert's. My mother must have soothed Clara's wild streak. She'd run from the Windwards to escape a lewd stepfather. But she'd confessed to me while we were still bedmates, with but a few patches of blond fur on her bald head, confessed that she had inflamed her stepfather to devil him, that men and boys had wanted her since she was nine. "I must have been born tall," she'd said. And when she came to our island, she must have dreamt that she'd live in a bordello. Gert had never obliged her to rut with a man. She watched the men watching her and wasn't indifferent to the longing in their eyes. She quickly learned to love leather shoes and jeweled slippers and panniers, but this was the armor she chose to wear—the encasings of Clara that could not cloud her mirror. She saw herself without clothes and shoes in the silver glare that shot back at her. She had her dolls and her marmalade and Madame's deep affection. And if such things should ever fail, she still had her tobacco.

I could not compete with that right now. I was readying to disappear from her closet when Clara began to tease me about having touched her sex. "Should I tell the admiral you've been wandering in his waters?"

'T was like a murderous game of vingt-et-un. I had to give back what I got.

"He might not mind. At least I could tell him what his waters look like."

She cracked me on the head with the bowl of her pipe. And my mother arrived, my mother, wielding a broom.

"John Stocking, you have brought havoc to this house."

I'd abused the nuns in my own fashion. But shame only filled me with spite.

"Madame, doth havoc weigh as much as a doubloon?"

She smacked me as she would a bilious boy. I skulked out of the nuns' quarters and discovered Black Dick in the parlor. The admiral was beside himself.

"Clara says I am not pretty enough. She can only fall in love with a pretty man, or a learned man, and I am neither. She cares not a pish for my wealth. A castle in Ireland would bore her . . . John, John, our letters have failed. She saw through the thin veil, recognized your hand, and says the thing she abhors most in this world is a dishonest admiral . . . I think it best that both of us take to the sea tonight, or a reasonable proximity. We'll sleep aboard the *Eagle*. That tub will not betray us. She's a worthy man-o'-war."

We dined together at some little inn for admirals. Beautiful women couldn't take their eyes off Black Dick. He could have bedded down a whole harem of mothers and daughters. He could have taken a consort like his brother did. But he was a quiet, almost religious man, who didn't care for concerts and soirées, didn't indulge in vingt-et-un or other vices, and might have lived a monk's life aboard his flagship, traveling between Manhattan and Newport, had he not come across Clara. She was outside his vocabulary of ropes and waterlines, outside the hundred little obligations of a peer of the realm. He'd never had a doxy in his cabin, though he wasn't blind to the fact that his sailors sneaked women on board. A wise commander didn't count every single soul on his ship—a man-o'-war was filled with devils, doxies, and dogs. He had not been prepared for Clara, who spoke the king's English better than he did, was never grasping, wouldn't have dared ask him for money, and took her own delight no matter whom she was with. Her sense of exchange was profounder than the admiral's. She had few worldly goods, yet she was much more elegant than any mistress of a manor house. She wanted nothing from Black Dick, not his influence, not his titles, not his sex, nor his nearness to the king.

"Johnny," the admiral said, "I cannot breathe."

Neither could I, in love as we were with the very same wench.

We lasted three nights on board the *Eagle*, and then we hurried to Holy Ground like a couple of penitents. The flagship had given us freedom and an appalling appetite—I gobbled sausages and eggs, sausages and eggs—but a loneliness had crept between the rigging and the ratlines, the unnaturalness of constant male company, even if tarts were permitted on board. Both of us needed that strange comfort of the nuns, women who asked nothing of us, gave very little, and allowed us to fit within their own empty space.

But the space wasn't empty any longer. The general had swollen the Queen's Yard with all the fixtures and furniture of vingt-et-un. The Yard was more a grog shop, an inn, and a gambling house than a nunnery. People crowded the closets, flocked to the game. The nuns held cards, smoked their pipes, slept with a couple of stragglers who'd never heard of vingt-et-un, and remained Billy's prisoners of war. But Madame began to wear a smile behind Billy's back. She'd gotten through to Washington—no, 't was her green-eyed protégé who'd gotten through. Clara had seduced a merchant while Black Dick was on board the *Eagle*. This merchant was no spy—he traded with the redcoats and the rebels. Clara bribed him with all the lucre Gert had gotten from Sir William—and bribed him with her own body. She would perform tricks for him that no other suitor had ever seen—but not until he smuggled a note to Washington and got a receipt.

Washington did send a receipt; nothing scratched with a pen—Hamilton wrote all his notes—but a ribbon from Gert, a frayed, disfigured piece of silk that she'd let him have years and years ago.

"Johnny," she said, "he's safe, he's safe."

Gert touched the talisman at her throat, confident that her general would never fall into Sir William's trap. But I stopped looking at Gert. Clara was the real sorceress at the table, and Clara had no souvenirs from Morristown. Her green eyes burnt with premonition, as if she could sense the nearness of General Washington—nay, could will it into being.

Twenty-Nine

ONE NIGHT, NEAR THE END OF APRIL, AS THE RAIN racked our roof and flooded Gertrude's little garden, Sir William's own bodyguards arrived at the card table with a wild look, their mouths opening and shutting in some strange awe. They were about to speak when George Washington appeared in a long cloak, accompanied by a much smaller man with the features of a girl, both of them like bandits with scarves covering their mouths.

I recognized the small man in a flash, even with the scarf. It was the same Alexander Hamilton whom I would espy every morning inside the chapel at King's.

He had always been the firebrand, always first, with a temerity that would allow him to stop a mob that was tarring and feathering the wrong man. He was the orator of our class, the most patrician, tho' he didn't have a New York pound in his pocket and was but a bastard like myself. He would wander about College Hall and sing: "My blood, dear John, is as good as any of those who plume themselves upon their ancestry. I shall make my own."

And he did. Scarce twenty years old, he was a lieutenant colonel with the Continentals and Washington's chief secretary. There'd been all sorts of rumors running about—that his mother had a dollop of black blood, that he himself was an octoroon—'t was the secret of his life—and that his father was a Hebrew. The other little scholars chortled behind his back, but I did not. He said that he'd come from a slave island in the Indies, that Manhattan was another island of slaves, and that he himself had been tutored by a Jewess and was mightily proud of it.

I cannot explain why Hamilton's Jewess reminded me of Madame—perhaps 't was because a nunnery was like a college, an abbess like a tutor. But I was never able to get along with little Hamilton. He saw me as a lout who loved the king and whose life would go to wreck. Was he so wrong? My classmate now fought at Washington's side and was chief among his aides, and I was a scuttlebutt, a conjurer without a single trick.

That's not what ate at me. I was frightened to death that Clara would fall in love with a fellow octoroon, that she'd covet his azure eyes and elope with him to her closet. But Clara did not make a move. She was magnetized, like the rest of us.

Hamilton and Washington removed their scarves. They hadn't come in civilian clothes. Indeed, they wore their uniforms under the long cloaks. Petrified, Sir William's officers prepared to arrest the general and his secretary. But William waved them off. He bowed once, pulled out his hanger, and clanked it on the table, like a useless load of iron. He would conceal no weapons from Washington. And Mortimer did the same. He dug into his pockets and put three pistols on the table.

Washington smiled. "Sir," he said to William while glancing at Mortimer. "I do admire your man. He nearly ripped my head off during a skirmish in the Harlem Heights. Had I ten or twenty like him, I could have recaptured York Island ages ago . . . Hamilton, why do you wear such a long face?"

"I was frowning at this contemptible fellow, John Stocking, whom I had the distinct displeasure of knowing at King's. He sits with the British of late."

"Hamilton, you are a prig. I like the lad. I can vouch for him . . . now introduce us, will you?"

"'Tis not necessary, sir," said British Billy. "I assure you."

"I think it is, or you might start calling me Colonel Washington, or the rebel farmer in chief, as your aides were fond of doing."

"It was unpardonable, yet may I ask you to forgive them, General?"

"Done," said the farmer, putting his own hanger on the table and asking little Hamilton for his hanger too. It was only then that he sat down on the chair allotted to him, across from Sir William.

I stared in amazement, mortified. Gertrude was in the room, the woman with whom he'd longed to hide in Ohio, wearing a love knot round her neck, a ribbon. But he would not glance at her, not even long enough to offer the flimsiest of hellos. Yet he'd come for her, I'll wager, as much as vingt-et-un. He was reckless as only a principled man can be. His officers had begged for furloughs, had gone to visit their families, while he walked through camp, visiting with whatever little army he had left. And if he couldn't be cavalier in risking his own men, men he didn't have, might he not gamble himself, accept Sir William's challenge by materializing once more on the wild side of Manhattan?

Poor Billy. He hadn't counted on a general who would turn vingt-et-un into a metaphysical maneuver. Yet I feared for Washington's life. The British assassins meant to break his neck. Hadn't Mortimer almost accomplished it at Harlem Heights?

Wouldn't have been much of an effort for him to reach across the table and finish the job. And where in hell was that spy on parole, Major Malcolm Treat? The farmer could have used pistols behind him, but Treat was nowhere in sight.

Sir William must have given his officers some secret sign. They tossed in their cards and left the table. He had an unhealthy squint in his eye, imagining the farmer as flesh for the crows. I liked it not. Gert couldn't intervene. Washington would not have allowed her to do so. And not even Clara's sorcery could quiet this war between the generals. Billy manipulated the last nuns out of the game. The nuns could not sit on their cards and they constantly overdrew, while Billy nursed a nine or ten in the hole, doubled and tripled bets until the nuns didn't have a New York pound in their pockets.

Vingt-e-un had come down to the farmer and him.

"General," he said, "'tis quite noisy out here. I cannot concentrate on the cards. I fear I will lose my wig and my drawers to the Americans if we continue in this atmosphere. I suggest we play in quieter circumstances . . . Gertrude, am I correct? Is there not quite a wide closet behind that door?"

I could read the terror on my mother's face. She was pondering how to answer the British war machine.

And I stepped in. "Sir William, methinks the general and little Hamilton have had a long journey, and—"

"Who is little Hamilton?" little Hamilton asked. "I am a lieutenant colonel attached to the commander in chief."

"But you must both be famished. Could we not—"

"Thank you, Johnny One-Eye, but we'll feast in private, commander in chief to commander in chief," said Billy. "Mortimer will look after our wants."

"Sir," little Hamilton said to the farmer, fearing that he might be left out. "I ought to take notes."

Washington smiled. "Later, Hamilton. Britain is not in the mood for notes tonight."

He left his hanger on the table and was about to enter the back room with Sir Billy and the brute. I could not tell whether he was the biggest fool in Manhattan or the real master of vingt-et-un. Perhaps he was both. And finally he did acknowledge Gert.

"Madam," he said, "might I borrow your ribbon?"

My mother reached beyond William's snares and sported with her general, in spite of the danger.

"Your Excellency," she said, "'tis a very old thing. I doubt it has much value."

"But it has great value to me."

Billy was aboil, red hot. He must have considered arresting Madame, charging her with high treason for having sheltered George Washington in her bedchamber, but alas, he couldn't charge her without also charging himself. Washington had appeared during Sir William's watch, while William was playing vingt-et-un under the same roof, in a house filled with redcoats. And so all he could do was look and listen while Gert tied that piece of silk round Washington's neck.

There was such unmerciful intimacy in that little gesture—a tenderness he had never seen in Madame—that it bridled Billy. His jowls went blue, his eyes at the very point of popping out of his head.

Washington bowed to Gert with a sweep of his arm that was like the motion of a duelist or a dancer of the minuet. For a moment he was outside Billy's realm—Billy's headquarters and house of cards—and was only with Madame. He committed the edge of her ribbon to his lips, said, "Now I have the luck I will need," and ducked inside the closet.

I moved toward him out of some instinct of survival, the farmer's survival, but the door shut in my face, and a pair of officers stood guard, almost as big as the brute. Madame whispered to Clara, and Clara took flight, but not fast enough to alarm Sir Billy's guards. She disappeared from the parlor, and I thought for a moment that the nuns themselves might storm into the back room, with the pistols my mother kept in the cupboard. But I did not have my wits about me. Lads, I was too alarmed. I counted off the seconds like some musical clock, wondering how long Washington would last in that room, all alone.

Clara didn't return with an army of nuns. 'T was Black Dick, with a rage that broke through his crust of leather skin. What had she promised him, what had she said? He approached the door. Billy's guards were in a turmoil. They couldn't knock an admiral over the head, an admiral who happened to be Billy's brother.

They saluted him, but held to the door.

"Lads," he said, "do I have to piss on your leg? Get out of my way."

He shoved them aside and knocked on the door.

"It's me, Will. Your bleeding brother, Black Dick."

The door opened from within. The admiral entered, and the door closed behind him.

I could have swallowed my own heart. I'd have felt some improvement had I heard the admiral, heard him once. One little shout. There was nothing. And then the door opened. Washington sallied out like some horseman. He was quite alive. The king had not won his war tonight.

Thirty

NARY A SOUL WOULD REVEAL WHAT HAD TRANSpired in Gert's back room. Sir William wouldn't talk to the likes of me, and I couldn't ask Black Dick—the admiral was far too discreet. That left Mortimer as my only witness, and Mort was reluctant to break the seal of so mysterious a game.

I had to catch him alone after one of our carriage rides. He was more loquacious in the middle of the night. I watched him ponder while he scratched his head. "'T was wickedly warm within that room."

"But did you have instructions to finish off the farmer?"

"That was the plan. But he was fearless."

"The details, Mortimer," I growled. "Can you not recall the moment?"

It had burnt into him like the hangman's hot poker. It scorched his eyes. The two commanders in chief playing vingt-et-un on Billy's tile table. And 't was George Washington—not Billy—who broke the bank. His cards keep coming up twenty-one. No one had ever humiliated Mort's general like that, not even some lord of gamblers. But Sir William looked Washington in the eye and said, "General, will you end the war and go back to Virginia? The king will pay you a handsome price, offer you a peerage. Your line will continue for as long as there are kings. Your people will be remembered past eternity."

"I seek no such remembrance," Washington said.

"Then what if I told you that you will never leave this room alive?"

Mort had put on the face of Death—a face that could frighten a battlefield—and this American madman returned Mort's glare.

"Good," said the madman. "It will inspire my boys, but you will not kill me?"

"And what if I say I will?" said Billy.

The madman smiled. "His Majesty's subjects will say that General Howe is a toad, not a man. He extinguished poor Washington because he could not win at vingt-et-un."

That's when Black Dick came charging through the door, his leather mask of a face on fire. Mortimer hid his delight from his master, but he would have found it indecent to murder a man of Washington's mettle.

Black Dick hopped around Billy and took Washington's hand, warrior to warrior. "You must forgive my brother, sir. He is not himself of late. He shuffles cards so much he has forgotten how to lead an army. But please have the goodness never to visit Gertrude again. It would upset our officers to find the rebel chief in their favorite brothel and not have permission to pluck out his eyes."

Black Dick did not acknowledge Billy until Washington was gone. Then he sat at the tile table with his hanger between his legs and started to weep. "What will become of us, Will? We have landed in a swamp."

BLACK DICK NEVER RETURNED to the Queen's Yard. I assume he said goodbye to Clara, but he left me not a single note. He sailed to Newport with half his fleet. So we heard. He was an upright, honest admiral who didn't lose his dignity even when he was most puzzled by his love for Clara. If noble birth could make a man more humane, then Black Dick was an exemplar of nobility.

Somehow he made me think of Hamilton, who had no coin other than his wish to excel—that was his nobility, nobility in a much newer world.

Washington could have had his pick of the revolution's richest sons, but chose Hamilton as his secretary and aide, the pauper from St. Croix. 'T was hotheads like Hamilton who would shake the continent. There were no such strivers among the Brits, only men who had bought their commissions and had studied the ways and means of bowing to His Majesty.

Washington had not been wanton in coming here. He'd studied the Howes, assessed them, but the Howes had not studied him, had not taken his measure. His men were without shoes, and his one surprise attack had to be himself. He gambled that he would get out of Sir William's little den of vipers alive, and in doing so he would heartily discourage the Howes.

That night of vingt-et-un had doomed Sir Billy, sealed his fate. The fighting season would soon begin, but after Washington's visit he had lost his eagerness to mount campaigns. Gentleman Johnny Burgoyne, Britain's playwright-general, would be coming down from Canada this summer on his way to Albany with his redcoats, his whores, his flunkies, and his baggage cars filled with clothes and copies of his plays. He had five hundred Indians, I hear, the fiercest fighters in the land. And Gentleman Johnny threatened to scalp the whole countryside if we Americans didn't behave. There'd been talk that Sir William would ride up the Hudson with his men and meet General Burgoyne, building an invisible barrier across America that could break the back of the rebellion in a single blow.

Sir William had other plans. He meant to capture Philadelphia, America's largest town, citadel of its wealth, and seat of our new Congress, but still he sat in Manhattan, where he attended cricket matches with his "lads"—officers who loved him and would have gone to the Divil with their Billy and stabbed every rebel in North America with their bayonets; even they had become a part of Billy's *tableau vivant*, artful at striking one pose after the other until they were caught in the final pose of fighting men.

Thirty-One

IT ALL CHANGED IN A NONCE WHEN BURGOYNE swooped down from the north with his noxious army in late June and captured Ticonderoga, Washington's one "impregnable" fort. Our island was ablaze with excitement when word reached us about Gentleman Johnny. We could sense that something was afoot.

There had always been some commotion in the British barracks north of Holy Ground—redcoats marching hither and thither, the sound of drums and fifes, the drunken roil of drill-masters away from their men. But that suddenly changed one morning in July. The redcoats where everywhere, thousands upon thousands, marching in unbroken, endless columns through the cobbled streets, with their drummer boys maintaining a miraculous rhythm that seemed to lend much power to the soldiers themselves.

The redcoats filed down the narrowest of lanes—past churches, the Hebrew synagogue, and the old slave market—toward the docks, where barges were waiting, like lions on a leash, to take them out to battleships in the harbor. I could not recall ever seeing such bounty. 'T was as if Sir William had removed all that was natural in the world, all that was kind, and replaced it with cannons and colored coats. He sailed out of New York harbor with fifteen thousand men, having kissed his consort goodbye. Mrs. Loring perched like a widow in her yellow house, with only myself to comfort her.

"He'll be loyal," I said. I had to lie. "Sir Billy regards your silhouette while he plays vingt-et-un, says it brings him luck."

Billy did keep a silhouette of Mrs. L. near his strongbox, but her likeness had gathered dust. That contest with the farmer had taken the blood out of Sir William. Loyalists in British Manhattan started to panic. Rumors abounded across Broadway. General Howe had left his filly but was still hibernating in July. He's gone to Halifax, agonized our Tory merchants. They were frightened that George Washington would swoop into Manhattan with his ferocious farmers. But Billy wasn't floundering in Canadian waters. Night riders brought the news: Billy's invasion fleet had been spotted in the Chesapeake. He toyed with the Americans at Brandywine, utterly confusing them, and for a moment it seemed as if Sir William would "wash away the rebels," as the Loyalist papers reported. There were bets at the coffeehouses that Washington would sink into the dust and that the war would be over in a matter of days. The Continental Congress had already packed up and dispersed to Lancaster, like dogs on the run.

Billy's captains arrived in Philadelphia in late September without firing a shot. They expected the entire town to greet them as liberators. Beautiful Tory princesses would no longer have to hide from Washington's smelly soldiers. Spies had assured the redcoats that "friends thicker than a forest" would appear. Yet the British drummer boys discovered a town with eerily empty houses along the route of their march and a row of women with wilted flowers in their fists.

But Sir William rejoiced. New York was a barbaric little town compared to Philadelphia, a veritable metropolis with water that a refined person could drink from one of Philadelphia's five hundred pumps. Here London fashions still ruled, in spite of the farmers, and he could find dancing societies and literary clubs that were sophisticated enough to welcome him and his lady. He rented a house on Prince Street for Mrs. Loring and seized the most magnificent house in Philadelphia for himself—the Penn Mansion at Sixth and Market had become his headquarters. Billy's officers built a magnificent playhouse within the old bones of an abandoned building. Howe's Philadelphia Thespians opened on South Street. He was like a king in a new kingdom, but without a countryside. American snipers shot at the king's men a mile from Market Street. Sir William had to surround Philadelphia with a fortified line. He had houses burnt near the no-man's-land to deprive such snipers a hold on Philadelphia. And he made merry as best he could.

Mrs. Loring couldn't join him by carriage. The roads weren't safe. And so she and her chariot, her maid, her furniture, and sixteen trunks of clothes had to sail from our island to Philadelphia on the *Isis*, a man-o'-war. There had been wild stories about Sir William and milady, and their so-called concubinage, how he'd come to Boston two years ago, discovered Mrs. Loring at a regimental ball, bent her over a table and rogered her in full view of his officers. But Mrs. Loring had a different tale to tell. She'd first met Billy during the Indian wars, when she was a child of seven—the daughter of a prominent Boston doctor—and he a young captain or lieutenant colonel in the colonies. She would ride with him and her family in her father's carriage, and he so gentle and gallant that her own mother took to calling him "the savior of Massachusetts." Mrs. Loring confessed she could never love another man after meeting Billy, tho' he was not quite so gentle now.

She cried when I saw her for the last time in her yellow birdcage. "Johnny One-Eye, I am loath to leave Manhattan."

"But the citizens have not been kind to you here. They have been most rude. 'Tis almost as if they had banished you to Out Ward and Little Africa."

"Worse, Johnny, far worse. I feel I've been living in a lazaretto, but you have been kind. And now your mother will have you all to herself."

"My mother?"

I had not informed her of my curious standing as Gertrude's lost son.

"'Tis not such a fast secret, child."

I was eighteen or nineteen, perhaps twenty, since my mother's calendar was not to be trusted in matters of my birth. But I did not mind milady calling me *her* child.

"You are Gertrude's boy, however hard she hides it. I would take you from her if I could, keep you on board the *Isis*. I'd have my Will find a place for you at headquarters."

"Your Will does not like me."

"He's a soldier. He considers what can be useful to him and what cannot."

"Useful?" I said. "I won't be his spy."

"Spies he has aplenty. But no one to converse with save Mortimer."

"He has his brother, by God."

"He does not get along with Dick. Dick never gambles. Dick prefers to dine on board a battleship."

"But this war cannot go on forever. One side will win."

"I am not so certain. Both sides might also lose."

How prescient she was. Perhaps both sides had already lost—with killing and plunder as a permanent language. But I sought to calm milady.

"You can still take to the wind in your chariot, like the night riders."

"You have no heart," she said. "You tease, while I am in earnest. You are almost as cruel as my Will."

Crueler perhaps, because I was not a general who could shove his army into ships, but a lad without much material, who had to live his life at a slant. I loved Clara but could never get beneath her skin. It was different with milady, who had but little hold over me. I did not have to mourn her yellow house. A changeling like myself did not belong to any house or farm, village, country, or continent. A duelist, as her husband had described me, a man who hid beneath a madrigal of words.

Mortimer had come from Philadelphia to accompany Mrs. Loring and help her pack. He would not stop crying.

"I've grown attached to ye, boy."

I kissed him with as much passion as I could muster for a brute with a blackened mouth.

"Speak of Philadelphia," I said. "There the water is sweet. That is what I am told."

"Too sweet. A man could die of sweet water."

"How, pray?"

"By overdrinking," said the brute.

"Mortimer, that is a monstrous tale."

"Monstrous or not, I have seen men die at the wells, keel over and die in the middle of pumping water. And there are nunneries, but not an entire street, nothing that could hold a candle to Holy Ground. My general is sore to find another host for his card game."

"I thought he had given up vingt-et-un."

"Not in Philadelphia. The games are held at headquarters. But they lack a . . . I cannot locate the word. They suffer from an absence of Mrs. Jennings. How many times has my general said, 'Mort, 'tis mere trickery without Gertrude.'"

I was loath to say adieu to Mortimer and Mrs. Loring. I took my last carriage ride with her and Mort right down to where the *Isis* was docked.

"Goodbye, Elizabeth," I said, suddenly free to pronounce her Christian name.

AUTUMN BODED ILL for the rebels. George Washington had to skulk about in the woods not far from Philadelphia, survive without sweet water, deal with mutiny. He had yet another danger. Gentleman Johnny Burgoyne was going to build a human bridge between Albany and Philadelphia, capture Washington within a relentless chain of redcoats, supplied by Sir William and himself—and the rebels would have to surrender without their farmer in chief. But Burgoyne never got to Albany. He had to abandon his baggage train, and his Indians abandoned him, those scalpers who had terrified the whole Hudson Valley. He crossed the Hudson in mid-September with five thousand men. His camp followers had devoured most of the food, and the men were starving. He still dreamed that Sir William would join him soon, and felt he had no need of extra rations. His own messengers had misled him, or at least the message he wanted to hear never arrived. He was stopped at Saratoga, with General Arnold leading a charge that cost him the use of his left leg, a leg that had already been bent in battle. Benedict Arnold had to be carried from *this* battlefield in a wheelbarrow.

Burgoyne surrendered whatever men he had and was allowed to sail home to England with a couple of his aides. And Sir William fortified himself in Philadelphia without Gentleman Johnny, shot quail with his officers, rode around with Mrs. Loring. "Sir Billy shut his eyes," sang several critics, "drank his bottle, had his little whore"—I did not like this wanton caricature of Mrs. Loring—"and never read a single letter that he signed."

But he did read one, a letter of resignation that he wrote near the end of October, while the oaks on Market Street began to turn a startling red that defied the war itself, and all of Philadelphia was like a momentary magic festival, despite Washington's sharpshooters and the little fires that burnt at the edge of town. And since it would take his letter a month to cross the Atlantic and another month to be opened by the king, Billy had all the time in the world to plan a party at his mansion to welcome the New Year. I could sense that Saratoga spelled the end of British North America—Billy knew that Burgoyne's debacle would embolden France to recognize this runt of a republic, and with France came the French fleet. King George would have to protect his own interests in the Caribbean, and thirteen rebellious colonies did not seem quite so valuable as sugar plantations. The king's sugar islands brought in more revenue than a hundred Manhattans. "Sugar was God, sugar was gold," Billy loved to blaspheme.

Hence, he turned his mansion into a gambling den for his little soirée, with a whole floor devoted to vingt-et-un. He dressed Mortimer in silver and gold trim, had him lug a mountain of specie from his own Philadelphia coffers. But he didn't have Gert or the other nuns of Holy Ground to mingle with his honored guests. Nor did he have Gert's splendid octoroon, the lass with the green eyes who had nearly wrecked Black Dick. He thought to kidnap Clara, I would imagine, but he did not want a scandal to mark his last months as commander in chief.

The reports that Gert got back from William's own officers are proof that his end-of-year party flumped. Mrs. Loring served punch and purple champagne. She wore a dress of silver lamé that occupied a whole battalion of women's tailors for nine weeks. But she moved like a ghost in silver lining—she must have realized that Billy would never take her to England, that he could not, considering his own entanglements with family, king, and court. And perhaps Billy himself began to feel like an apparition. He drank his purple champagne, toasted 1777 and the New Year, but with little enchantment in his eyes, little delight. That is what his captains swore to Gert.

But I had other news—a note that Elizabeth Loring's Philadelphia seamstress had smuggled into Manhattan somehow. It contradicted the reports of Will's own captains.

Johnny, I do not much enjoy the riches of Philadelphia while Mr. Washington and his army are close to starvation and cannot leave their tents and little huts in the wilderness for want of coats and shoes. Will's whore I may be, but I won't rejoice at their misfortune. These men are not my enemy. Some have wandered into Philadelphia like half-crazed horses. I have commandeered Mortimer, who has much the same pity, tho' he is at war with these men. I use my rights and privileges as William's war wife (you once described me thus) to ride into no-man's-land and deliver food and clothes to rebel pickets. I pray such pickets are not scoundrels and will bring the provisions to Valley Forge.

My angel, Mortimer, encourages me to declare how much we miss you. He curses the gods of his childhood that he was never taught to spell properly, even during his tenure with Will. And so I bid you adieu from both of us.

Yr. Obedient and Loving Servants,
Elizabeth and Mortimer.

The Divil himself could have pulled tears from an epistle such as that. I now read William's end-of-year party in a different light. Neither Mort nor Elizabeth Loring must have enjoyed the splendor of purple champagne. They had simply gone through the motions for their William. Mort couldn't have been content in silver sleeves while Washington's lads lived without shoes. Mort was a civilian warrior who would gladly kill a man, but he was not a demon.

And Elizabeth? Did she pretend to stuff herself at the soirée all the while she was storing up provisions in some secret basket? William's cold cuts must have helped provide nourishment in the wilderness. I like to think that Elizabeth was radiant at the party, not a ghost, but a warm-blooded woman who glided across William's waxed floor in her slippers, knowing there would be less hunger at Valley Forge for the next few nights.

Anno Domini 1778

SILVER BULLETS AND THE BLACK BRIGADE

Valley Forge
January 1778

His new winter quarters were twenty miles northwest of Philadelphia as the crow flies. Valley Forge was not a town with a town's provisions. 'T was "a cold, bleak hill," where men were obliged to sleep "under frost and snow without clothes or blankets," his own officers would complain. He could have occupied some village near Philadelphia, but he would also have had to scatter its inhabitants and create a horde of vagabonds and refugees. And so he set about to build a city of tents for an army that was itself a little nation of vagabonds.

His men were starving and he had to maraud—but he'd not attack neighboring towns. He would harass and alarm General Howe in his Philadelphia haven, and pillage Howe's supply trains. He had in truth become the robber in chief.

So long as his men slept in tents, he too would sleep in a tent. He helped them hammer and saw at their huts, shared whatever scraps of food he had. Horses seemed to starve faster than men—his camp was littered with rotting carcasses. There was blood in the snow from the naked feet of his men. And as he moved about

Valley Forge, with icicles in his hat, he could hear the boys chant, "No pay, no clothes, no provisions, no rum."

The robber in chief pondered to himself—where the Divil could he scare up some rum? He returned to his own tent, slapped the icicles off his hat, lay down without taking off his boots, weary as he was, like some worn-out strumpet. And he started to dream without shutting his eyes, could feel his own fingers in a tangle of red hair, as if Gertrude sat right beside him. The palpability of it frightened Washington, conjuring up an apparition with a heartbeat he could hear. But this apparition soon vanished with all her freckled skin. Perhaps he should only cavort with creatures of solid flesh. He could have found a wench but wanted none—the redhead he craved was in Manhattan, rivers and rivers away.

Thirty-Two

WE HAD FIVE MONTHS OF TRANQUILITY ON OUR little island while Sir William sat in Philadelphia with his high command. Soldiers plundered, bread was scarce, but the Brits did not maraud on Robinson Street. We did have a visit tho' from one of the king's representatives: Simon, the royal chimney sweep, appeared at the Queen's Yard with his little parcel of slaves, and while they crept up the chimneys with their brooms, he drank sassafras tea in the parlor and ogled every nun.

"Simon," Clara asked, "do you ever pay any of your assistants?"

"You don't pay a picanniny," he said. "You give 'em cold tea and a kick in the pants."

I had to keep Clara from strangling him. But she shamed the son of a bitch. She shucked off her clothes and crawled up the chimneys with the little colored sweeps, who could not have been older than nine or ten. Simon realized soon enough that Clara was never lovelier than when she was covered in soot. It made him delirious to watch her lithe form glistening with black dust.

I was equally delirious but could not show it. Clara would have read my rampant desire as a betrayal of her—she was punishing the royal sweep, wanted him to feed on his own heart. He offered her a month of profits, all of which derived from the labor of his little sweeps, if he could accompany Clara into her closet for five minutes.

I waited for Clara to impugn the royal sweep and laugh in his face. But she bartered with him instead.

"I will give you fifteen minutes, Simon, *fifteen*, if you crawl up a chimney with your lads."

"Clara, darling, I am much too fat."

But in his folly he went into the flues and was stuck there for one unholy hour. Clara suggested we saw off his legs, but I applied a tub of lard to his person and we managed to pull him out. Neither Simon nor his little sweeps ever went near the nunnery again.

THUS WE LIVED from January to June, away from the Brits, without a single tax collector or picket coming here to plague Gertrude and the nuns. But our tranquility, our freedom from the British lion, did not last. The French fleet suddenly appeared off Manhattan in the middle of June and blockaded our port. Victuallers from London could not supply the British lords and ladies on our island with tubs of marmalade and wheels of cheese for two entire weeks. And now the panic spread. Pickets arrived on Robinson Street and perused the denizens of Holy Ground as potential spies. Did their commandant imagine we were signaling to the French fleet?

I couldn't even climb to the tower at King's College and have a proper look. King's was now a hospital and rest home for decrepit British officers. I had to sneak upstairs to Gert's verandah with my spyglass and probe the harbor without attracting attention from the pickets. 'T was a most puny fleet, more like tubs than battleships, and utterly removed from the British armada that lay off Staten Island two years ago with its wonder of cloth and wood.

Then one morning the French fleet disappeared, as if it had been but a mirage. And soon we had another mirage, an army that materialized right out of the dust, at the beginning of July. I had never seen soldiers so forlorn, moving like ragamuffins rather than men of the line. Some were without shoes. At first I thought they belonged to one of Washington's ghostly regiments, but within all the hurly-burly I began to hear British fifes and drums; drummer boys themselves emerged from the dust, as bedraggled as the rest.

And then a portly man appeared on a horse—ye gods, he looked like some pony rider from a circus. He had a most comical paunch and smallish eyes. I was astounded to learn that this hatless pony rider was Sir Henry Clinton, the new commander in chief. He no more resembled Sir William than a hare might resemble a hound.

Our William, it seems, had sailed home to Mother England near the end of May. And Clinton abandoned Philadelphia in June, began his march back to York Island, meeting George Washington along the way—'t was Washington who bloodied Clinton at Monmouth, scattered his drummer boys, riding across the battlefield on a white horse. The farmer in chief lacked the matériel to destroy Clinton's army, but his lads did manage to rob a good many redcoats of their shoes.

And here was Sir Henry coming out of the July dust.

My mentor, Sir Harold Morse, would tutor me in the habits of Henry Clinton. His long silences, Harold said, were notorious. His wife had died several years ago, and Clinton became all but a recluse. He was barely civil to his own officers. But he was obsessed with one thing—a secret service.

FOR THIS HE WOULD SOON count on Sir Harold himself, commandant of the Black Brigade, who had remained invisible while Sir William was commander in chief. Clinton was much less suspicious of Harold. Perhaps he was touched that Harold had risen out of nowhere, that the king had found him in a forest. Perhaps the silence of Harold's life succored his own silence. But Harold would meet with him at his headquarters on Broadway, near the Bowling Green. And Harold began to bring me along—'t was a veritable fortress, with pickets stationed every five or six feet. The floor was made of marble that shone like a mirror: I could see my own quizzical face in the mirror, a lad in the lion's den.

We were ushered into the war room, where Clinton was waiting. The only other person at this audience was Clinton's young adjutant, Major John André, a swarthy man-killer with the air of an educated Gypsy. Clinton gazed upon this boy as if he were some miracle. I did not understand at first. Major André was most petulant. He strutted across the room with such a scowl I thought he meant to bite us. His hold on Sir Henry, I would soon discover, was much more insidious than any hold little Hamilton might have had on George Washington. He'd ingratiated himself with Clinton to such a degree that no one else could get near the general. Major André had managed to isolate him utterly from the rest of mankind. He humored Harold and myself, considering us as little more than Clinton's personal clowns.

I'd never seen such a Divil as John André, tho' he often played a cherub with olive skin. He'd crept into Sir William's graces in Philadelphia, put himself in charge of the Meschianza, a farewell party and costume ball that Sir William's officers gave in his honor. It was the most extravagant affair Philadelphia had ever seen. Young officers jousted in mock tilts and tournaments, while Philadelphia's daughters dressed as Turkish maidens. André drew silhouettes of each Tory princess and thrust them under his spell, as he loved to remind us. He meant to convert these princesses into spies, and he would remain their spymaster. I could not imagine using a woman so, Tory princess or not, and I mentioned my chagrin.

"Major André, you were most chivalrous at the Meschianza, lest I am mistaken."

"It was for Sir William," André insisted, "all for Sir William. But he spoiled my Meschianza. He arrived with his whore."

I bowed once, while André sat with his hanger, boots on the table. I did not have even the smallest of swords.

"Elizabeth Loring happens to be a friend of mine. And I do not take your insult lightly."

Harold nudged my knee under the table, but André only laughed. "I dare say, Sir Harold, your lad is trying to entice me into a duel. He is the real knight, defending a lady who has slept with half my dragoons, and I had to joust like a fiend to prevent her from propositioning me."

I would bide my time, kill him in some dark corner, and not disgrace Harold by parrying with André at headquarters. He drank Madeira, while the general sat and said not a word and was soon fast asleep.

"Yes, I designed hats, and helped the misses with their hair. But it was camouflage. I was recruiting, recruiting all the time. And we may do wonders, gentlemen. I am in correspondence with my two favorite Philadelphia misses. Peggy Shippen and Peggy Chew. Might even give them a lesson in invisible ink," he said, winking to Harold.

He claimed to have infiltrated the Queen's Yard, that half the nuns were spies of his. He talked of an American plot to kidnap Clinton from these very headquarters, a house that was guarded all through the night. I was appalled and bewildered by André's remarks. Had not Clara openly declared herself against the Crown? A nun who rousted the royal chimney sweep couldn't have been a spy.

But the little shit mocked Harold and me, said we could assist in the capture and arrest of Washington's agents. André ran the theatre on John Street, Clinton's Thespians, and this preposterous kidnapping sounded like a theatre piece, a play of his. I expected to meet his own thespians—disguised as American agents—on the lawn at the back of Clinton's house and headquarters.

I had small delight in such theatrics. But I was Harold's second-in-command. We shielded Manhattan Negroes, put them in the Black Brigade so they wouldn't have to work as stevedores or be carted off to the Carolinas. And Harold swore we couldn't protect these Africans without the help of Sir Henry Clinton. We had to cajole, come to British headquarters on Broadway and listen to their lies. I was loath to do it, lads, but we lived on an island of redcoats, an island of John Andrés.

Thirty-Three

AS I SAT AND WAITED IN THE WAR ROOM WITH Harold, Sir Henry, and the little shit, there was a knock on the door. "Enter," André rasped, and a short, fat man came into the room wearing Clinton's uniform. André must have found Clinton's double at his playhouse. The double was a sergeant with black teeth. He could not have fooled an infant or a doddering old lady in the almshouse, but here he was trying to outsmart Washington's secret service.

We left the war room while Clinton slept, and we marched downstairs to Clinton's garden, which looked upon the Hudson and had a royal view of the little houses and woods across the river. And within the garden's white pavilion was a magnificent chaise longue upholstered in scarlet, with lion heads carved into its wooden borders. Some British brutes must have carried it from the house whenever Clinton decided to take a nap, and now André deposited Clinton's double in the chair.

We stood behind the pavilion, Harold, André, and I, without another soldier, another guard. André held a pistol to his own head, and I thought he'd gone berserk and meant to blow his brains out. But he was only scratching his ear with the pistol's silver beak. He looked at his timepiece, yawned, and behold!—a man appeared in the grass, as if he'd come right out of the tide. A thespian, I opined to myself, one of André's own. The man drew nearer and nearer. He wore leggings and a black handkerchief round his head, like the river rats on our wharves.

Through the lattice rails I could see the whites of his eyes. He had no other weapon than a knife. The scars on his face could not have been manufactured. André had chosen well. As the man approached the chair, André cocked his pistol and ventured out from behind the pavilion. "Stand," he said. "Stand, or I will give you a ticket to hell."

The man started to run. André did not seem to aim at all, but when I heard the pistol's report—a popping sound that failed to echo across the grass—I could scarcely believe what I saw. The man's brains had begun to fly. Where his scalp had once been, I noticed something raw and red.

RIGHT AFTER THE SHOOTING I raced to Robinson Street. I caught Clara smoking her pipe and reading Jonathan Swift in the parlor. I knocked the book out of her hand. I couldn't even startle Clara—she smiled at so much activity coming out of little John.

"Johnny One-Eye, what in thunder will you do next? Swallow a page of my book?"

"Only if it will displease you," I said. "Tell me, dearest, does André pay you in London pounds?"

She pouted with her eyes. "Darling, that nasty little man has never been near my bed."

"Oh, I didn't mean the rabbit hutch. There is a kind of rogering that requires not a bed but a silver bullet."

Silver bullets were notorious material in both the American and British secret service. Spies could carry messages in their hollowed interior, and if about to be captured, could swallow the bullet. But handlers of the opposite service would make them drink castor oil or some other elixir until the bullet was flushed from their bowels.

And it perturbed me because Clara pretended to be ignorant of spies and spying.

"I have no such bullet," she said.

I slapped her and she must have considered it a caress—she laughed and went with her pipe into a different closet. Perhaps she was not so cavalier as I had imagined, since my mother came flying in a few minutes after Clara was gone.

"Mother, speak plainly to me. Did you inform Major John André that the rebels meant to kidnap General Clinton from his garden?"

"Yes."

"And are you aware that the kidnapper was murdered by André?"

"That was always a risk."

"I cannot—will not—believe that you are in the paid employ of André's secret service."

"I am," she said, and there was not the least bit of shame in her voice. I was the one who sat down, not Gert. I had to ponder all the ramifications of a silver bullet.

"Ye gods, I am the blindest of boys. The nunnery is Washington's secret camp. You carry his silver bullets, and if he came here last winter, came here twice, it's because the bullets didn't get through. And he had to be his very own bullet. He tricked Billy into believing that he came for love, and to accept his challenge of vingt-et-un . . . Mother, I am lost. You fed André a piece of cheese when you might have had Clinton as a prisoner in Washington's camp—why, why?"

"No one wanted the fellow. It would be *our* misfortune to capture him, since the king would never find a commander as lazy and incompetent as Clinton. That is what Hamilton said."

Hamilton, always Hamilton. I had to wonder if that little shit was my mother's spymaster.

"And so 't was a maneuver—"

"To keep André off the track. He has been suspicious of my nuns. He knows that the Queen's Yard is the favorite nest of British officers in New York."

My head was exploding with intrigue, as if I inhabited some mirror land where the world was upside down and nothing could ever remain what it had been before.

Gert took my hand. Was it another of Hamilton's tricks?

"You must not be so harsh with Clara. She is delicate, and this constant British parade confuses her."

"Madam, I was soft as a swan. I caressed Clara."

"You slapped her face," Gert said. "Go to her. She is in her closet. Sing her to sleep. She has nightmares whenever she shuts her eyes."

I WENT TO CLARA on tiptoe, quiet as a mouse. She lay about in her nightgown, tho' it was not yet night.

I sat beside Clara, cradled her head in my arms. She did not resist. And I sang to her the way I would when we were children and she not yet a nun. I sang lullabies that I would invent for Clara, only Clara. I'm not certain that Madame ever listened through the door. Scribbler that I am, I never recorded the lullabies, never wrote them down. They were about forests and all the creatures that inhabited them—slaves who had run from their masters; wolves as black as coal but with pink, slavering tongues;

pirates who all had one eye, and therefore composed a vicious, one-eyed panoply; brown bears who lumbered along in all their bulk, with claws as complicated as a fisherman's knife; and one very tall girl with pyramids of woolly blond hair who fed water to the slaves, took pity on the pirates, went up to the wolves and stroked their wildness away, and danced for the brown bears until they had no more malice, no more desire to eviscerate her with their claws.

And thus I passed the night with Clara, singing to her and wetting her lips with water. I fell asleep, and when I woke, Clara was no longer there; her nightgown sat in one long wrinkle near my legs. And then she burst into the closet wearing lip rouge and a long leather hat that hid her eyes.

"Gracious," she said, "are you still here? I have a merchant to entertain who's rich as Croesus. He sells supplies to the rebels and the king's men."

"But you do not care for rich merchants," I said.

"Then I will have to make an exception. Now will you get out, Johnny One-Eye?"

I seized her, trapped her in my arms, because I was still drunk with the power of my own melodies. She did not fight. She trembled under the leather of her hat. "The siren with his songs," she said, "the siren with his songs . . . I never lived the whole night with a man. I cannot fall asleep in a man's arms."

"But you just slept in my arms."

"Because of your songs. You are my addiction."

And she broke from me, the brim of her hat glancing off my forehead like some leather blade.

Thirty-Four

I KNEW NOT WHICH STEPS TO TAKE. I HAD TO BE careful of Clinton, careful of André, and careful not to put the nuns in danger. I could not bear the thought of Clara and Gert being sent to a prison ship in Wallabout Bay, or going to the gallows. But they would not consider leaving Holy Ground. The nunnery was Washington's outpost in Manhattan, his citadel, Gert said. It mattered naught that Martha Washington often accompanied her general to his winter quarters. Gert had become Washington's incontestable camp wife. She kept Clinton's hyena at bay, fed him scraps from Washington's own table.

But the nuns were no longer under house arrest, as they had been under Billy. Gert and Clara attended Clinton's parties—parties that were closed to Harold and myself. Gert swore that she and Clara threw up into the same bucket after the soirées. Yet how could Clara not have been the beauty of Clinton's balls? She with her marvelous freckles and woolly blond hair? I'd watch young captains and lieutenant colonels escort her to the parties in Clinton's own carriage. Clinton never danced, but his officers kept buying tickets to these charity balls and spent such tickets on capturing Clara. Tory princesses and rich old maids must have watched her dance with malice in their hearts—they couldn't stone Clara, because it might have angered Clinton. So they rallied against Gert, called her the whore of Babylon, and drove her out of the balls.

'T was Clara who suffered most without my mother. She'd return home with her eyes darting in her head like a dervish. My mother would give her honey and hot milk, and this was the only time—after a ball—that Clara invited me into her closet. She had monstrous corns on her heels and had disabled her best dancing slippers.

"Sing me to sleep, will ye, Johnny One-Eye? Be a good boy. I'll pay you a London pound."

A pound for every lullaby, I thought, a pound for every kiss.

I covered her in blankets, cradled her in my arms, sang about that tall girl from lullaby land who calmed animals and men lurking in the forest, but I would not spend the night—I'd only wake to find her mocking me in her full regalia of clothes.

SEPTEMBER HAD COME and gone, and I had to go to headquarters, observe Major André for any sign that he might molest Clara or Gert and close the nunnery. But he couldn't risk Clinton's wrath, not while the British commander sent his coach for Clara. Clinton needed her presence as a souvenir to arouse him from his perpetual slumber. Yet I did not like the manner in which that little major looked at me, as if he were manufacturing silver bullets with my name and Gert's inside the hollow shell.

I walked out of headquarters in a foul mood. There was a cold wind off the Hudson, a wind that could bite like the Divil.

"Milord," I said to Harold, "teach me to kill."

"You're the one who gallivanted with Benedict Arnold. I've never been in battle."

"Battle is easy once you shit your pants," I said. "You close your eyes and imagine your enemy's heart. I do not mean that kind of killing."

"What other kind is there?"

"*Your* kind. With a hanger. Teach me to kill."

"And watch you go after André like a pup . . . have him cut you to ribbons while he is drinking a glass of wine. Don't forget, Johnny, he went to school in Geneva, where he could buy a dozen fencing masters. Do not let his ability to sew or wear women's paint at the theatre fool you. He is the champion of his regiment. I dare not vex him. He would unman me in a minute."

"Then I shall find another way to rid ourselves of the little shit. There must be some blackguard I could hire at the docks. A scalp hunter or pirate in retirement."

"Then I would be obliged to have Prince Paul arrest you."

Harold, in his infinite wisdom, had named Prince Paul captain and commander of the Blue Brigade. "If we have to fight," he'd said, "'tis best the Blues fight under him." The Blues were never sent out on patrol. They had no ammunition. What they did have was a mandate to lock drunkards up in the attic at City Hall. And they had their own prince.

Paul loved King George but not his man-killers in Manhattan. He could have run over to the American side, but that would have meant abandoning Little Africa, and the Brits would have punished Paul's people. Yet the Yorkers themselves had burnt his father at the stake, and Paul lived in an uneasy truce with York Island. He had his own holidays inside Little Africa and an Ethiopian Ball, where black women often dressed up in the style of their white masters and mistresses. The Brits envied such balls but were seldom invited to them—besides, they would have had to arrive with a garrison of redcoats, since they feared for their lives in Little Africa.

Paul valued this fear and used it to prevent the Brits from policing Little Africa. He indulged Sir Harold's Black Brigade, but he was reluctant to arrest paupers, since many of said paupers were black. And so we had to narrow our mandate to wild men who disturbed the peace.

ONE MORNING IN OCTOBER I received a grandiloquent envelope addressed to Squire John Stocking, with an invitation inside to the next Ethiopian Ball. I imagined the prince himself had sent it, inviting a white man to this black soirée.

On the night of the ball a carriage arrived for Squire Stocking, with a black coachman and a bevy of maidens with silver birthmarks painted on their cleavage in the style of Marie Antoinette.

I could not comprehend a word they spoke—it must have been the peculiar mishmash of Little Africa. I listened harder. These Marie Antoinettes were mocking the conversation of their current or former mistresses, but in their very own music. They gossiped about a Tory princess who when squatting on her pot produced urine that could heal a leper's wounds.

"'T was prodigious, Mattie Girl," said the tallest Marie Antoinette. "Magic water that could make flowers bloom in my bum."

On the way to the Ethiopian Ball, we passed the old Indian wall that was meant to keep hostile savages out of Manhattan and blacks inside Little Africa. We passed the High Road to Boston, the Hebrew burial grounds, passed the gallows, the dueling fields, and Fresh Water Pond, and arrived at the old munitions factory near a vacant parcel of land on Winne Street. The factory had blown up twice, sending plumes of black smoke across the island and covering Robinson Street with a cloud that killed the sun for a day and a half, but 't was abandoned now.

Yet I saw carriages and horses in front of the factory. I went inside with the Marie Antoinettes, and I could scarce believe my eyes. This cavern was a replica of the ballroom at headquarters, tho' six or seven times as large. I'd never appreciated the quality of Paul's boldness. The men at his ball were dressed as British officers—generals, colonels, majors, and captains with their regimental colors. Paul alone did not wear a uniform. Paul alone stood outside this extravagant jest. And the women at the ball resembled a tribe of Tory princesses, merchants' wives, and the wives of Hessian officers who had headdresses wired up like the tallest of citadels, powdered pink.

The prince had installed an entire sinfonia, with a harpsichord, violas, and violoncellos, but there was silence while Paul's officers and "Ethiopian" women stood like partners in a frozen minuet. The lighting was sparse, with lanterns placed at long intervals. The munitions factory had no chandeliers. Paul clutched a wooden staff that a dancing master might carry. He struck the staff once against the factory floor—the smack it made had the crispness of a bell. A woman descended the factory's staircase, moving in and out of the somber light. She wore a mask, but I could not mistake her poise or her pyramid of blond hair—my Clara, an octoroon with freckles, was queen of the Ethiopian Ball.

The musicians began to play once Clara arrived at the bottom stair. She moved among the partners, tapping each male on the shoulder; one by one, the couples started to dance, while Paul beat out the tempo of each step with his staff. I hadn't realized how cruel the minuet was—how relentless the rhythm—until I saw his dancers dance. Paul's minuet had all the sad machinations of the civilized world, its clockwork, its precision. But it also had a beauty here in the far reaches of the Out Ward, on Winne Street, a small, forgotten territory without redcoats or royal pudding.

The queen of the ball came up to me while the dancing master continued his magical beat. I shivered hard the moment I understood the purpose of her visit. She meant to pick me as her partner—I had never studied the steps, tho' I had often watched the nuns play-dance among themselves.

She tapped me on the shoulder. I did not bow as I should have done. Her eyes flickered under the velvet mask. She tapped me again.

"Majesty," I said, "I will not dance until you remove your mask."

The flickering stopped. I could detect the trace of a smile at the border of the black velvet. "You are my subject, sir, and will do whatever I ask."

"Remove the mask."

She tapped me a third time. I was the fool of fools. Clara had invited me, not Prince Paul. Clara must have sent the enormous envelope, scratching my name in the largest letters, so she could disguise her scrawl.

I lent her my hand and prayed that I could discover the steps under the tutelage of Paul's dancing stick. And as we twirled about, Clara did remove her mask. The light was wan, but I still had one eye in my head. Verily her face was aglow. The munitions factory was keeping her alive. She couldn't have survived dancing with all those bloody Englishmen at Clinton's balls without her little sojourns to the far side of the Indian Wall. She was Gert's amanuensis in the middle of a revolution, and had to make the British believe that she was their very own plaything, a beautiful informer and double agent who could dance with an army of officers.

"Johnny," she said, "didn't you know? Partners are encouraged to kiss. That's what the rule book says."

I didn't believe there was such a book. But when I reached over to kiss Clara, I lost the dancing master's rhythm and had to prevent myself from falling over my own feet.

Trying to accomplish that kiss was like hoping to find the Minotaur inside a maze.

Clara laughed. I'd pleasured her with my maladroit maneuvers. The Minotaur could eat me alive—I cared not a feather or a fig . . . as long as I continued to dance. But the minuet must have gone into another phase at the factory. Couples broke up near the end of a turn, with men's knees hanging in midair. Clara's hand slipped out of mine and she vanished into the shadows, a queen without a partner.

Thirty-Five

I WOULD HAVE BANKRUPTED ALL THE KING'S MEN and paid a million pounds for another invitation to the Ethiopian Ball. I received none. Perhaps the balls themselves had vanished with the black Marie Antoinettes. Clinton had also closed his shop. The party season must have ended for the British in late October. Clinton sent no more carriages, and Clara seemed to have less need of lullabies. I was not summoned to her closet again. But I trapped Clara in a damp corridor behind Gertrude's kitchen. "Where the Divil is my queen of the night?"

"What manner of queen is that?"

"The mistress of the Ethiopian Ball."

"You are mistaken," she said. "'Tis illegal to have dancing assemblies in the Out Ward. Blacks are not supposed to congregate lest Little Africa rise up against the white king."

And in my chagrin I grew formal with Clara. "Dost thou deny that we ever danced?"

She stunned me to the quick—haughty Clara started to cry. "Major André is gonna shut us down, and Gert doesn't want you implicated with us, not while André is gunnin' to get ye."

I SAW NO GALLOWS being built. I was still invited to the war room at Clinton's headquarters, where André presided with his boot heels on the table. He had a harebrained idea to capture one of Washington's generals.

"We ought to start at the top of the list," Harold said. "Why not the farmer in chief, why not Washington himself?"

And that's when André turned in my direction. "Let us ask our John. He has met the farmer, has seen him in the flesh . . . aren't women Washington's weakness?"

I had to be as artful and devious as that little shit. "I should think so, Major."

"Were you not present at his marathon game of vingt-et-un with Sir William on Holy Ground?"

"Indeed I was. He's daft about the mistress of the house, my own matron, Gertrude Jennings . . . we should pounce on him, using Madame as bait."

Harold looked at me as if I'd gone berserk. But I had to deflect André by going into the lion's mouth. "Arrest Madame, and the farmer might come out of the woods. Hang Madame, and he will grieve for her," says I.

André rolled his eyes in contempt.

"Washington will not come out of the woods for Mrs. Jennings. I cannot believe he loves that creature. She is his spy, and I will hang her when the time is ripe. We can forget the farmer."

"Shall we pick another general?" Harold asked. "What about Benedict Arnold?"

André ruffled his nose and rolled his eyes again. "I am not in the habit of traducing cripples. He has a shattered leg. We will leave Arnold where he is and go after bigger game."

Every child in creation knew that Benedict Arnold had become military governor of Philadelphia after the British left in June. He was no longer a fighting general. He could not even sit on a horse. He'd spent months at a hospital in Albany, immobilized, his body tied to a board, while he screamed at his doctors, who wanted to amputate his leg. "Better take my life. I'll kill you all if I do not walk out of this hospital complete."

Arnold did walk out with both his legs but had to live on crutches. He inherited Sir Billy's old headquarters on Market Street, moved a little army of servants into the mansion, bought the finest carriage in Philadelphia, indulged himself like a duke.

Philadelphia was not for him. He got into trouble with Pennsylvania's revolutionary council, and he'd always been at war with a Continental Congress that had snubbed him, raising mediocre generals over his head. He rode around in his carriage with bodyguards, entertained rich Tories. He began outfitting his own merchant ships and investing in privateers. The council accused him of peculation, of turning war into a business. Sir Billy had had his hand in different pots, had received hard cash from his commissaries, or he would have drowned in debt. But Arnold wasn't an aristocrat. He didn't dance with Billy's grace. He didn't dance at all now that his left leg was three inches shorter than the right.

And then I learned that Arnold had become engaged to the daughter of a Philadelphia nabob—a damsel of eighteen, blindingly blond. She was called the greatest beauty in the metropolis, shy and brilliant, and she'd read as many books as Gertrude's nuns. Her name was Peggy Shippen, she who had her silhouette done by Major André. That little shit had recruited her as one of his spies. She was Salome, and my poor general was John the Baptist, soon to be without a head.

I couldn't even maneuver against the British in my own masked way. André stopped inviting me to headquarters.

"Why have I been disinherited?" I asked Sir Harold.

"Clinton doesn't like you."

"Clinton doesn't know I'm alive."

"Don't be misled. He sees much more than any waking man."

"'Tis that blond bitch. Peggy Shippen. André has found an avenue to her, from the very heart of Manhattan. He will entrap Benedict Arnold, military governor of Philadelphia."

"I dare not say. I am part of the secret service. And you, sir, are neglecting the Black Brigade."

Harold had never been so formal as to call me "sir." And Arnold, whose vanities betrayed him beyond the battlefield, was a doomed man. He was no match for a master spy, even if she was but a girl—Peggy Shippen.

Thirty-Six

WE WERE A TOWN OF INNUENDO AND DIVISION under British rule, of mayhem and civil strife, where the poor suffered in canvas houses, while some high commissioner might have several mansions and a birdcage for his mistress. The rich had their own private parks where madrigals could be heard, and all beggars and Africans were excluded. Bakers could only bake bread for the British army and certain nabobs; everyone else had to find ovens and scraps of stale dough. Women and children did not venture abroad at night without a military escort. Highwaymen lurked in the alleys. And those who were robbed most were Africans, who had no escort but the Black Brigade.

We'd been given a new task, to contain the Skinners, those rebel ruffians who operated in the "Neutral Ground" between British Manhattan and the Highlands of Westchester, where the patriots had their pickets. The Skinners would fight the Cowboys, Tory ruffians, and maim one another. But they also did their own business, and were notorious highwaymen, scalp hunters, and cattle thieves. They would scalp men, molest women, and murder children.

We could have done little about it, but these marauders had been sighted in Harlem and King's Bridge, below Neutral Ground, where they had no business. The Black Brigade wasn't issued live ammunition. The Brits wanted us to fail—we were their jesters, their clowns—but our captain, Prince Paul, had ammunition of his own, enough powder and lead balls to make at least one of our muskets a little less than useless. Now we were fighting men, even if we were only called upon to attack civilian pirates.

I despised the Cowboys and the Skinners and would have been willing to hunt them into hell. But we had to keep within the integrity of our island. We had no permission to wander far afield. And in early November we went in wagons up the Bloomingdale Road, with our captain on a white horse. "Brigade" was a misnomer. We were nine men in gold and green uniforms, the colors that Harold had bequeathed us. I had a cutlass, and pistols in my pocket without a single lead ball. The buttons on our tunics were brass replicas of the king's head.

We followed the tracks of a rampage. The Cowboys had been looting Harlem wholesale, making off with women and cows, battering children into speechlessness. 'T was not a pretty picture.

"There's a complicity to this madness I do not like," said Paul. "These Cowboys aren't running wild. Seems as if they have their own general with a battle plan for desolation."

I had to agree. This roughness was a little too symmetrical in its waywardness. Cowboys and Skinners did not have the imagination to accomplish such deeds.

We fell upon an extravagant farm, the country estate of Joshua Loring. He had barns and horses and cows, and he lived like a bloody Englishman in a manor upon a hill. He'd grown fat off the fare of prisoners, but he served at the pleasure of the Crown. And his protector, Sir Billy, was long gone. I wondered where Mrs. Loring was. I'd had no news of her. Not even the Crier, who poked his nose into everything, could tell me if Mrs. L. had gone to England or was locked up inside the manor house like a madwoman. She vanished once Billy departed from Philadelphia aboard one of his brother's ships six months ago.

But we hadn't come to the manor about Mrs. Loring. Why had the plague not visited this farm? 'T was ripe for plundering. The pirates could have grabbed half a hundred cows. Joshua had a host of servants and slaves, but this host could never have stood up to muskets and stink bombs and bayonets. And then we discovered Loring's secret saviors. A detachment of Hessians in their tall helmets lay on Loring's grass. These lads were cavorting with milkmaids while their horses nibbled grass at their feet. It was like some idyll of northern Manhattan painted by a very sly painter. Something was amiss. As we got close, we could see specks of dried blood on their uniforms.

Suddenly the idyllic landscape turned into a frieze. The soldiers stiffened. The milkmaids ran to a barn. A Hessian officer with a blade of grass in his mouth approached me. His uniform had no blood.

"Yes, yes, how can I help?" he asked without the slightest of accents. He could have stepped out of any court in Europe.

"Captain Paul of the Royal Irregulars," our prince said from his horse. "We're looking for Skinners. They've been attacking farms in the area, making off with women and cows."

"Ah, but we have not seen them, Herr Captain, or heard a single shot, or we would have come down hard on their backs."

"I'm quite sure of it. But I would like permission to search these grounds."

"Permission denied, Herr Captain. This is not my estate."

We did not have enough bullets to put a hole in their helmets. His men could have cut us to pieces and plucked the buttons off our tunics while we lay writhing in the grass. The Hessians did not love this war. Hirelings on foreign soil, they often could not distinguish between rebels and Loyalists. They plundered wherever and whenever they could. Adventurous lads and also lazy, they were still prepared to butcher us. But someone in a velvet waistcoat, silk stockings, and the fashionable tricorn of a gentleman farmer traveled down from the hill with all the power of a British commissary. 'T was Loring himself. And he had no mischievous horsemen around him, no meddlers, like the last time, when he'd tried to waylay me and Mrs. Loring, remove us from her carriage.

He bowed, hat in hand.

"'Tis the changeling again, my wife's little paramour. You are trespassing, sir."

"We're soldiers of the Crown on a military matter."

Loring laughed. I did not like him.

"Soldiers, you say? If you do not leave this minute, I will appropriate every one of you and put you to work as field hands on my farm."

I would have cracked him over the head with my cutlass, but I wasn't captain here. It was the prince who was playing vingt-et-un without a card in his hand.

"Do we have your word that you are not hiding ruffians on your farm?"

Loring turned his back on the prince. Paul signaled to his Blues, and like the finest actors around, our lads rattled their muskets, while the Hessians busied themselves with their powder horns, ramming rods, and live ammunition.

Loring's ears pricked at these sounds of war. Then he smiled and performed a jig in his buckled shoes. He must have been aware that the king's men would never issue ammunition to toy soldiers such as ourselves. That's when Paul seized the one live musket we had and shot a lead ball into the air. Loring froze in his tracks, like a rabbit or red squirrel caught in lantern light. He was petrified. Imagining that he might find himself in some crossfire, he faced the prince again.

"I do not harbor criminals, sir."

And he bolted toward the manor in a palpable rage that tightened his neck under the tricorn.

Mindful of Hessians, the prince and I moved out of earshot.

"Captain Paul," I said. "'Tis plain as day. He's behind the bloodshed. He's a murderous profiteer."

"And who are we? Black men on a mission with one white officer? Not a man, woman, or child in Manhattan would admit that we're soldiers."

"And I am not a genuine officer," says I.

"But they believe you are. And that belief is our only flag . . . come, Johnny, we have Cowboys to catch."

"You mean Hessians posing as Cowboys."

"I mean Cowboys."

We rode off in our wagons, drank from our canteens, dove into our knapsacks for lumps of hard cheese. 'T was a bitter meal, lads. But Paul had the patience of a prince. We passed magnificent farms and pastures, red barns and rolling hills, until I thought we'd come to a domain ruled by horses and cows. And that's when we saw puffs of musket fire and heard the dull crack that accompanied it.

We stole upon the scene. Five or six drunken Hessians were raiding a farm a few miles from Loring's hill. One of the Hessians held a woman by her hair. They ignored us and continued their carnage.

I cared not about the wretched state of our musketry. I had my cutlass. "Captain, permission to murder that man."

"Lieutenant Stocking, you will stand down."

He grabbed the cutlass out of my hand, rode into the Hessians on his horse, and drubbed that Hessian who was holding the woman, drubbed him with the dull edge of his sword until the Hessian's knees buckled, and the woman dropped out of his hands. The prince climbed down from his horse, put his knapsack under the woman's head, and began to feed her water from his canteen. She started to sob, and Paul rocked her like a baby.

"We'll be back for you, ma'am, but first we have to take these butchers to our base."

We had no base, but the prince had gotten used to soldiering, and thought we had.

The five other Hessians were so besotted, they had little resistance left. We dumped them into a wagon, but another batch of helmets arrived from Loring's farm with Loring himself and his own motley crew of marauders that meant to murder us on the spot and leave no witnesses. Loring and his lads rode up to me and Paul with pistols in their hands.

"Negro swine," he said to Prince Paul. "You and your little white slut who calls himself One-Eye. I will relieve you both of your brains."

I couldn't stop thinking of Clara and Gert, how André would get his talons on them once I was dead—saw Clara in my mind's eye, Clara wearing her black velvet mask. Ye gods, I would not go lightly. I'd whack Loring the moment he came near enough. But he pushed his pistol into Paul's cheek.

"Mr. Black Brigade, I will give you one second to say your prayers."

Paul smiled. "One second will not suffice. I need two."

He wasn't a captain now of an uncertain British brigade, but the prince of Little Africa, with a knife that appeared willy-nilly from his sleeve, a knife he held against Loring's neck.

Loring squealed like a pig in a slaughterhouse and started to blubber.

"Don't kill me, please. I have nothing against the Blues. 'Tis John Stocking I want, only John. He hath made himself free with my missus."

Loring's lads cocked their pistols, and Paul dug his knife a bit deeper into Loring's flesh.

"Disarm, disarm . . . he's killing me."

We did disarm the whole lot of them, and they rode off with Loring, a bloody handkerchief tied like a tourniquet round his neck. I was not in the mood to gloat. I helped the Blues pick up their cache of weapons, and then we returned to our "base," a barn for black soldiers near my old college.

Thirty-Seven

I WAS EXHAUSTED AFTER I LEFT THE BARN. I LAY in my closet back at the nunnery and could hear marching on the cobbled streets. There must have been a full company of redcoats. And my first thought was, The farmer in chief is attacking the town! But there was no musket fire, no brouhaha of animals and men—nothing but the merciless drumming of feet.

And then I shuddered at the truth of it. These merry lads weren't going to the Commons. Not even redcoats were diligent enough to drill at three o'clock of a morning, when the witches and succubi were about and lads like me were abed. I ran around in my nightshirt as they kicked open our gate. They'd come to arrest Clara and Gert, and I had nothing to defend the nuns with except a worthless pistol and my cutlass from the Black Brigade.

I would give the redcoats neither girl. I rushed out into the yard, where indeed the nuns were all assembled in their nightgowns—I remember the lace, Clara's lace, and the look of terror in my mother's eyes. But something was amiss. Gert wouldn't have feared her own capture. Major André stood against a tree in his powdered white wig and the regalia he might wear at a ball. He had not arrived on Holy Ground to menace the nuns.

He plucked an apple from my mother's tiny orchard and commenced eating it, while he waved a writ in my face, under the feeble light of an evening lamp.

"Ah, how good of you to rise," André said. He signaled once and his redcoats, who could scarcely fit in our yard, aimed their muskets at me.

"John Stocking, I arrest you in the name of His Britannic Majesty, King George."

THE LITTLE SHIT had a warrant signed by Clinton himself. I was led out of the nunnery with my ankles tied together so that I had to hop in my nightshirt across Robinson Street. I wasn't taken to the king's own jail, because I wasn't even considered a military prisoner. I was hustled off to our own lockup for drunkards in the attic of City Hall.

André manufactured a tiny cell for me, clearing out a handful of drunken men, and stationed two redcoats outside my door.

I had pen and ink, a chamber pot, a straw pallet, and a lantern with a very weak wick so that the redcoats could see me if I tried to burn myself. But I wasn't going to become my own funeral pyre to satisfy Major André. I hadn't visited a magistrate. We had no magistrates in Manhattan. We were under martial law.

I'd have to go before a tribunal that was held together by John André himself. It was André who danced around the provost marshal, André who selected and sat the court. He'd become the entire apparatus of the British army away from the battlefield. He prepared all the books. I assumed that he would have one of his own assistants drill me, tell me how I ought to behave in front of the tribunal.

But I'd misread the little shit. He came with a steward carrying a jug of wine, a chicken leg, and delicacies that only Great Britain could have dreamed of for its Manhattan subjects—mushroom ketchup, blancmange, red and white currants.

André had no bodyguards with him. The steward unlocked the door and fed all the drunken men in the attic, not mushroom ketchup, but little cakes and crumbs of cheese, while André brought me some of his clothes to wear, including a neckcloth. But I wasn't in the mood to be gracious.

"Sir, am I to be charged with trespassing or piracy?"

"Attempted murder, I should imagine. Firing one of the king's own muskets at a British officer. But my secretary hasn't finished copying the bill."

"Hessian," I said. "Not British."

"Still an officer of the Crown. And you needn't play on heroics. If you think you're protecting Captain Paul and his Blues, don't bother. I have an elaborate picture of what occurred, moment by moment."

"From Commissary Loring's mouth, I presume."

Loring was the richest nabob on our little island. He could have bribed the court.

"Stocking, I'm not the fool you think I am. Loring is a bully and a thief. We shall disabuse ourselves of him and, I should add, dismantle his whole enterprise, from the ground up. And you, dear soul, could trespass until time stands still. It would not injure me or the Crown. But you should not have poached."

"Poached, sir?"

"Yes, you are a hunter of the king's men. You had no authority to interfere with the Hessians."

"Who steal cows and molest women," I said.

"They shall be dealt with in due time. I am familiar with their designs. But you are not a soldier, and you cannot stop soldiers, no matter the cause. You were told to discourage civilians. Those dreadful Cowboys."

"And when your Hessians disguise themselves as Cowboys?"

"They wore no disguise, Stocking. They were in uniform."

He gulped wine and offered me a goblet. "From the general's own table," he told me. "Admit, you were leading an insurrection."

I looked at this lunatic. "What insurrection?"

"You were followed to a clandestine meeting but a month ago in Little Africa, a meeting in the guise of a ball, where you and your black devils plotted to overthrow His Majesty's government in North America and create an independent black republic. And Holy Ground was also at this meeting in the person of Mistress Clara."

"I swear to you, Mistress Clara presided over the minuet."

"A cover-up, a mask. Did you not have live ammunition in your search of Loring's estate when you were strictly forbidden to carry loaded guns?"

"We had enough lead balls to furnish a single musket."

"And that, dear boy, is the start of an insurrection. But Clinton says we must not alienate our colored sappers and drummer boys, that we would lose their affection and would not find fresh recruits should we torment them. And so I will pursue the narrower subject of Hessians and Harlem Heights. You have no one on your side, not a flea. The Blues cannot save you. They are but cattle or cargo in a military court and do not exist as men with a heart and soul."

"Is that British custom, sir, or British law?"

"You make light of me. Captain Blue will not appear in your defense. He struck a Hessian—and nearly disgorged Mr. Loring, who is the king's commissary, despite his peculations—but since your captain does not exist, you must be tried in his place."

"That is pretty *and* profound," says I, aware that the major had manufactured his own little quagmire for me, a veritable drowning pool.

"Harold may have hired you as his puppy, but you live in limbo as far as the Crown is concerned. Neither soldier nor civilian. For us you are an injured American combatant on perpetual parole. And you broke that parole once you entered Clinton's headquarters and sat with members of his staff and listened to military secrets."

I smiled, and it unnerved the major.

"'Tis all about Peggy Shippen," I said. "She is your recruit. You mean to entrap my poor, poor Arnold, bring him over to the British with your blond Salome."

He snapped off the bottom joint of my chicken leg, dipped it in the mushroom ketchup, and started to bite while he mumbled, "Good, very good . . . congratulations, John. You shall be hanged as a spy. I will see to that, mark my words. I will sway the court, build such bold arguments as can never be challenged . . . unless you deliver Madame and all her nuns. These harlots take me for an idiot. That's what hurts. And you also think I'm a ninny. The nuns are Washington's slaves, that much I know. I would not be astonished had they slept with half his army, if ever he had an army. But I cannot arrest them. It might interfere with Clinton's parties if Mistress Clara sat in jail."

I smelled a wound somewhere, and 't wasn't only mine. I let him rattle on.

"She will be my agent, she says, sleep with my officers—with Clinton himself—but not with me. I heard what she did to General Howe's brother—Black Dick. Nearly sent him to the asylum. She has the cheek to say that she cannot share a bed with her own spymaster . . . Stocking, I make it a habit to sleep with all my women agents."

The little shit had primed Peggy Shippen, instructed her in the art of seducing Arnold, and now he would have Clara lie down with him *and* seduce the Continental Congress. There was no end to his malefaction. He wasn't some ordinary Divil, hobbled with cloven hooves. André was the Fiend, bred in Great Britain, an aristocrat who danced on air and made life miserable for everyone who did not have his own aristocratic liens. He meant to break Arnold and break me.

"You will deliver Madame and her nuns into my hands. You will sign affidavits at my suggestion, naming the nuns as George Washington's secret agents. And you will deliver Clara, say that it is in her own interest and the interest of the nuns to be much more pliable with me. And if you cannot do as I ask, I will most certainly kill you, John, with or without the hangman's help."

He snapped his finger at the steward, wiped his mouth with *my* napkin, and had the steward lock my cage. I wasn't even his homunculus. I could have delivered the world and it would not have saved me. He must have had his spies at the Ethiopian Ball, spies who caught me dancing with Clara—and it infuriated the Fiend, assuming willy-nilly that I had a certain sway over Clara when I had none. Perhaps Clara and Peggy Shippen had become fused in his head—the Philadelphia princess he'd seduced with one of his silhouettes and the tall octoroon who could not be captured in a silhouette. He meant to kick me into hell like a dog for dancing with Clara at the Ethiopian Ball and stumbling upon the secret of Peggy Shippen.

A chill had entered the attic, and I could not drive it off. Winter had come to Manhattan, and from the tiny opening in the attic wall, a perch near the ceiling no bigger than the "eye" of a telescope, I could see children skating in the frozen pond outside City Hall. I envied not their freedom, but their delight in gliding about a small infinity of ice. *That* I could not recapture in my cell.

Thirty-Eight

SHE LOOKED LIKE A SPINSTER IN HER SHAWL, not the queen of the finest nunnery from here to Newport. The rawness in her eyes disquieted me, turned me cruel. Perhaps André was right, and I was a hunter of men—mothers and men. And like André, she brought me food and clothes in my attic cell.

"Has Sir Harold switched sides?" I asked. "Why is he not here with you?"

"You should not blame him. Harry has gone begging to the British. You are like a son to him."

"Mother, I forbid you to talk about fathers and sons. You have utterly flummoxed my paternity."

Gertrude began to cry, she who never cried. I could not bear it, lads. I took her in my arms.

"Forgive me, Mum. I have no right."

I stroked her hair, and I was caught in a tide I could not comprehend—the brokenness of her was killing me. I kissed her hair, her cheek, her eyes, and she did not shove me away as she was wont to do. However strange my circumstance, or odd my upbringing, she was still my mum.

"I love thee, little John."

I could not help my feelings. I blubbered like a baby boy.

"Mum, you and Clara are dear to me—dearer than the world. You must flee with her from this godforsaken town."

"I cannot, little John."

"André will get Clara in his clutches and never let her go."

"I would still have to stay," she said

"Dost thou love her less than thy revolution?"

Forgive me—I made my mum cry again with my rotten canister of words. But had I been gentler with her, she might not have told me more about Clara—Clara's arrival, she said, had rescued her from months and months of morbidity. 'T was exactly seven years ago. Mum had wrenched me from her mind—the changeling, the secret child, who'd become the sweep and beer boy in her own establishment. And she had not the slightest hope of ever seeing Washington again, the Virginia farmer with his stepson and stepdaughter and a plantation larger and longer than a town. All she had was a pile of silver and a few nabobs in her bed. Then she found Clara at the docks, a runaway from the Windwards with enough lice on her to make a small plantation. The high sheriff would have delivered Clara to the poorhouse, fed her stale meat, and sold her into slavery.

But Gert brought her to Holy Ground. This strange girl—a woman at thirteen, with a woman's tallness, a woman's bones—never whimpered and kept looking at Gert with outlandish green eyes. It must have been fatal for the two of them, a devotion without much history, and they were almost never apart. But Gert couldn't bed her down in her own apartment with so many nabobs about, leaving their coins and their slaver on every pillow.

She gave her to the beer boy, let her sleep in my closet. And it cured Gert of her melancholy. Now she had a daughter, a girl as mysterious as a jungle plant, a girl she did not have to hide. Gert would have gladly given her a subscription to Mrs. Poor's School of Etiquette on Garden Street, near the Old Dutch Church, but Clara did not wish to be subscribed. She preferred to smoke a pipe with the nuns. Gert's customers couldn't keep their eyes off Clara, and pretty soon Clara was returning each customer's stare. She threatened to run away if Gert did not give her a closet of her own. Gert resisted for a week and caved in.

And so, you see, mum did love Clara as much as her revolution, but she could not abandon Washington's one and only "citadel" on York Island, even if guarding it meant her own death. But my death was a different matter.

"John, I've hired a dozen cutthroats, bitter and brazen men. They will fight their way into this hellhole and free you."

"'Tis for naught, mum. I will not leave this tiny closet."

"But the tribunal is a farce. The king's men are rehearsing witnesses."

"Your pirates will have to tear into my hide before I move. I'm a scholar, mum. I shall beat the British and their bloody laws. Promise to recall the pirates."

She would not promise, but I kissed her again.

I was most perturbed. Mum was a spinster, waiting for a man who had Martha Custis, Mount Vernon, and a war that only he could win. I cannot forget that night of vingt-et-un, when George Washington was both David and Goliath, a lone farmer inside a British arsenal, but Goliath nonetheless, larger than any man's life. 'T was Washington who drove his men back into battle with his curses and his war cries and the example of himself when they tried to flee the British, Washington who took the enemy's fire while he was on his horse, with lead balls slapping against the skirts of his war cape like troublesome bees. He should have been unsaddled—shot right off his horse—but he was never maimed, never touched. His own officers would shut their eyes when he rode into battle, fearing they would soon have to mourn their commander in chief. But he would return after chasing redcoats into the woods—Goliath in a wig. And Mum could only sing to him now with silver bullets.

But I had another bullet in mind.

"Mother," I said. "The Fiend is after Clara."

"I know a hundred fiends, a thousand."

"There is but one—Major André. And he will hurt her."

"No more than he hurts me. André makes use of us, pays seventy pounds per season. We are inscribed in his books."

"His books be damned," I said. "He will burn down the nunnery one day, with all the nuns inside."

"We are more valuable to him than he is willing to admit. André believes that if he presses you, I will light Aladdin's lamp and lead him to Washington's treasure—there is no such treasure. And I will not play cat and mouse with him over your life."

"But the game has already begun. And you cannot remove me from it, not with all your pirates."

"They will drug you and your jailers," she said. "They have my instructions."

"Then the first moment I rouse myself from your drug, I will return to my cell. I like it here."

"You are not my son," she said.

"Gert," I told her. "I'm afraid I am."

We kissed like a pair of babbling idiots until the guards knocked on my door.

"Time's up, time's up," they both shouted. "Order of the king."

But the queen of Holy Ground was not about to yield, not yet.

"Johnny, one more kiss . . . for your scapegrace of a mother."

"You will not malign yourself," says I, "not while the king's own clock is ticking. Any lad should count himself lucky to have you for a mum."

"You mock me," Gert said, tho' she was purring like one of her own parlor cats.

"Come on, come on," shouted the two yobs. "Quit the blather before we ruin you, old son."

"What?" says I, leaning into their loutish faces. "And deprive Major André of his prize prisoner? He'll whip you like a pair of whelps."

I'd given them a bit of food for reflection. And whilst they scratched their jaws, I spun Gertrude in my arms 'til I was as dizzy as a kite in the wind.

"I am your very own rascal, the littlest John."

"But I put you aside, hid you for years," says she.

"As you should a rascal."

The guards were suddenly adamant. They must have woken from the little spell I had cast around them.

"We'll kill him, Mum, if you don't scatter quick."

Gert could not bribe them with her silver—that's how frightened they were of the Fiend.

She put on her spinster's shawl. I did not want these two yobs to catch me crying. I hugged her for the last time, watched her tread across the attic, until the guards shoved me back into my closet with their usual sneers. But dumb looks could not defeat Gert's own little rascal. I raced to my spy hole, stood on my toes, until I saw Mum, so diminished now, disappear into the December chill.

Thirty-Nine

WAS IT PROVIDENCE OR THE POWER OF MY OWN want that brought Clara to me on the very afternoon of my mother's visit? The guards let her in, but they would not lock the door. They stood on the sill, their tongues swollen inside their mouths, and observed us. I could not forgive their obscenity, their callousness to Clara. One lad pawed her as she passed through, while the other advanced his bayonet near my sightless eye, like some miserable jokester. I would have rushed him, bayonet and all, had Clara not held me with her own green eyes.

She was as much a thespian as Major André, but I could feel the desolation in her moves. She twirled about like a top, fed the guards some cold meat Gert had brought me from the nuns' kitchen, tore a bit of meat from one guard's mouth, and began to gobble.

"I'm ravenous," she said. "Haven't eaten all day."

She fondled my neckcloth in front of the guards. I told her it was André's.

"Who's his clothier?" she asked.

"God, I should think. But you may certainly have it."

"Johnny, you mustn't give mementos before a trial. 'T will ruin your luck."

I did not care. I wrapped that silk cloth round her neck. I could feel a pulse beating like some trapped bird under the skin. It alarmed me. I could never comprehend what tugged at Clara's heart.

We had to employ a private language in front of these two dolts—a palaver that could pass between us like a silver bullet. I spoke in riddles to disarm the dolts. I concocted a fat fairy tale, full of conceits and an impossible heroine—a rich, rich widow who spent her life on a swing. Her admirers hoped to mend their finances by marrying the widow. Yet the good woman would only give herself and her money to the lad who pushed her on her swing. And said swing was fatal for her suitors—all would die of exhaustion attempting to keep the widow's feet aflight.

The guards yawned. They hadn't bargained on stories. The least they could expect was a glimpse of Clara without her bodice.

"One-Eye, ain't you gonna let us borrow Missy?"

They took to pawing her again, and I readied to plunge between their bayonets when my mother's beer boy arrived with two goblets of champagne. That liquid mollified them. They put down their muskets and began to drink. Mum's beer boy produced more goblets.

The guards imbibed and concentrated less and less on Clara. We were inches away. Their drunken songs resounded in my ears like grapeshot. They sang of king and country, began to sob about their lost homeland.

"You can't have a decent kidney pie or pint of bitters in Ameriky."

I might have pitied them had Clara not been so near. And I took advantage of their slobbering, whispered to Clara under the breath of their songs. They could not see us in our tiny cove beside the door.

"Darling, did André hurt you?" I asked.

My jailers had emboldened me. I'd never have found courage to sing the simplest words of love away from this attic.

"I'll strangle André with his own neckcloth if he ever goes near you."

She licked my ear. "Might be more amusing, Johnny, if you strangled me."

I hear that pirates often half-strangled their sweethearts to bring them a bit closer to ecstasy.

"Clara," I said, "you must leave Manhattan at once, shutter the Queen's Yard, and—"

She thrust her fingers into my mouth, and with her other hand she ripped off her bodice, revealed her charms and every goose bump, with the jailers singing and breaking wind in our ears. Had they leaned a bit and peered over the sill, they would have discovered more than mere goose bumps—indeed, the amazing freckled map of her, the narrow waist that needed no whalebone to pinch into one piece, that sudden, startling curve of her hips—a fluting of flesh that you cannot find even in pictures of the most magnificent nymphs.

We couldn't lie down on my pallet. Drunk as they were, the jailers would have spotted us, would have wandered into the closet and ripped our flesh. Clara stood against the wall, and she bade me to enter.

An eye, a bloody eye, interrupted our paradise. One of the jailers pushed his head through the door and was perusing the landscape. I am not certain what the jailer saw. But Clara commenced to stroke his stinking face, and that very act blinded him to us. He sobbed without control. "Bless you, Missy. No one's ever been that kind to a yob like me."

And ’t was curious—Clara stroking him while my own head lay against her bosom. Then her nostrils quivered and she let out a noise that a child might make—a squeal, piercingly soft—delighting me as it filled me with dread. I could not bear the thought that any other man would ever listen to Clara’s music. I’d have to rush into my own fairy tale and slay a mountain of her admirers.

The jailers were coming out of their coma. Clara quickly dressed. I was mortified. I could no longer feast upon her freckles and goose bumps that were like little heavenly bodies. She forbade me to talk about her own future in Manhattan. She put André’s cloth back on my neck.

“Ain’t we a perfect pair.”

That’s all she said. She ran a finger down my face, smiled at the jailers, and left the attic at City Hall.

Forty

THE CROWN HAD LITTLE TO CROW ABOUT THIS year. France had entered the war in May, as we all knew, and General Clinton had to pull thousands of troops from his command in New York to safeguard the sugar islands, keep these islands out of French hands. Clinton had little purchase on the mainland of America, we soon realized. He controlled Manhattan, much of Long Island, and Newport. Washington could peer down at him from the Jersey Palisades, could camp along the Hudson, and grow stronger, while the British lion ate at its own entrails—the Hessians began to desert a hundred at a time, and Clinton's best officers would rather hunt fox than seek out rebels.

Small wonder that Henry Clinton and the master of his secret service, Major André, settled on me. I was the only circus in town. I met with Clinton's court as Christmas neared, tho' I could scarce call such trappings a court. It was some muster room or mess for British officers with a great chair in the middle that had its own canopy and a crown—the king's chair in America, reserved for princes of state. 'T was, in fact, a symbol of the Crown, with plush velvet curtains that would have befit a royal bedroom. On both sides of the great chair were lesser chairs, made of common wood, without a canopy or a cushion; each lesser chair had its own little table with an inkpot and a quill and writing paper. The table in front of the royal chair had nothing but a bell on it. I couldn't take my eyes off that bell.

I entered the room wearing irons. It was not to keep me from running away, but to make me feel small in front of the king's chair—a throne with all the pomp of Windsor, I imagine. The chair was not occupied. It was the lone orphan among the other chairs, occupied by generals and colonels, with their boots sticking out from under their little tables. Standing next to them, in front of the tables, was André in his gold epaulette, his whiter than white neckcloth, and his reddish riding boots. He was the picture of a prosecuting angel, the ultimate king's man.

Neither Clara nor any other nun was in the audience, which consisted of Manhattan's upper crust in camp chairs, nabobs and their perfumed wives—bloody Loyalists, the women in beehive headdresses and the men in braided coats and buckled shoes. They'd come to Clinton's circus in their Sunday clothes to howl at little John, who was suddenly notorious. I saw an empty row of camp chairs behind them, and could only surmise that André meant to pack the court with other demons. And then there were the witnesses, who sat in their own special dock behind a rope in a corner of the room. I recognized Loring and the Hessian officer from Loring's estate—the little king of the Cowboys.

Loring was part of the circus. André would never punish him for peculation. Commissary Loring was much too valuable as a friend of the Crown. He could bribe a fistful of bailiffs.

I was in for it, lads. The whole bloody circus was against me. It could play at being kind—André bowed with much civility.

"Stocking, would you care for a cup of water?"

I was parched, but I wanted nothing from the Fiend. He meant to launch me with the hangman's rope. It was odd, but the hangman was allowed into the room. Perhaps Redmund served as a sheriff or sergeant-at-arms. He was much admired. The nabobs in the audience doffed their hats to him. Their wives blinked at his beauty. He had branded none of these ladies, just the paupers of Manhattan, and he was, I admit, a beautiful lad, with enormous orbs for eyes. But the hangman seemed to suffer over me.

If not for Redmund, I would have had to pull sympathy from the walls.

The bailiff rocked on the heels of his high-buckled shoes. He might have been an army man in civilian clothes. I was not familiar with the customs of their courts, their hanging courts.

And then the bailiff left off his rocking. A door opened in the far wall and General Clinton entered, his wig awry, his hanger belted very low around his waist, his buttons misaligned, so that he looked more like a vagabond than a commander in chief.

"Hark ye," the bailiff said, "general's here."

He announced this as if he were looking at some invisible man. But the court rose in its entirety—generals, colonels, nabobs and their wives, whispering in anticipation of my undoing. I began to shiver at the sight of all these women and men, and realized I would not escape their wrath.

Clinton occupied his throne, sword between his legs. I'll wager the general had been in his cups and 't was not yet noon. He had a hard time of it in Manhattan, with a war that had melted away. He would ride his pony in the field behind his mansion and dream of his dead wife—that is what my jailers swore.

"Mr. André," he asked, "what have we here?"

"The American spy, Acting Lieutenant John Stocking, formerly of General Arnold's raiders."

Clinton peered at me through a lorgnette.

"I remember him. He was at certain meetings, the volume and purpose of which shall remain unsaid. But military secrets were revealed."

"Precisely," said the major.

He would not mention Sir Harold, I'd gamble on that. Harold might embarrass the court. He was probably on some prison ship bound for England.

"And this boy sneaked into our larder, into our shop," Clinton said. "For what purpose?"

"To wound us, Excellency."

André sang up a storm, charging me with treason and insurrection and the rearing of illegal troops, since no such Blue Brigade existed in His Majesty's books. I let him sing. Clinton was already fast asleep. André had to rouse him from time to time with a word in his ear.

Loring rose in the witness dock and spat out his bile, swearing how I and my gang of colored Cowboys had invaded his farm with the purpose of molesting his milkmaids and his livestock.

"He is a bandit of the worst stripe," Loring said, addressing the throne.

But André grabbed at him. "Did he ask you suspicious questions?"

"Most suspicious. He demanded to know how many Hessians were currently encamped on my farm. I saw him scribble a note for one of his black couriers. I heard him pronounce Washington's name."

"Which Washington?" Clinton asked, rising out of his sleep.

"Excellency, there is only one—George Washington, the rebel commander in chief."

And now 't was the Hessian officer's turn. In the king's best English he told the court how a band of colored ruffians had dragged him from his horse, stepped on him, asked him to draw a picture of the nearest fort.

"Did you draw such a picture?" André asked.

"I did not, Herr Major. I gave them nothing. And then they violated my uniform, stole my buttons, and laughed at the British."

He saluted all the chairs and returned to his dock.

André asked me if I hoped to refute the king's witnesses. I declined—would only have dragged me further into the Fiend's black hole.

He was an extraordinary actor in his rouge and powdered wig, acting for the Crown. The generals and colonels dipped into their inkpots and scratched a volume of lines. There were not sufficient pages for them, and the hangman had to withdraw into a closet and return with fresh writing paper. These members of the tribunal uttered not a word. But André was prepared to weave for Clinton and the court.

I saw the foul beauty of his plan, might even have marveled at it had I not been filled with such bitter bile. First there was the marching of redcoats outside the room, then the nuns arrived without a single soldier and sat themselves down in the empty row of chairs behind the Loyalists—nuns' chairs, I soon realized. Gert was not with them. I could not help but rejoice at the sight of Clara, tho' André meant to pull the nuns into his little circus and did not want my mother to interfere.

But she *had* interfered. She'd dressed them up as dolls and marionettes, with slashes of red paint on their cheeks and in the leather jerkins of river rats and lady pirates. Gert was having the nuns announce their independence of Clinton and his court, that they could wear whatever they wished. Or perhaps it was done out of desperation. I was glad of one thing. As a frequenter of the nuns' shoe closet, I could recognize all the familiar markings and varieties of their paste-encrusted boots.

Clara looked at me not a once.

André had his bailiff escort her to the dock. She was the most vivacious of marionettes. She wore that leather jerkin like a princess *and* a lady pirate. I'm not sure what part Clinton played in André's enterprise, but he was careful about Clara, who had been the chief attraction at his balls.

"Bailiff," he said, "will you look to her wants?"

"Excellency," Clara insisted, "I have no wants."

But Clinton growled at Major André. "Why have you brought this child here? She was not on your lists."

"She is essential to my arguments. And I needed the element of surprise."

André pivoted on his heels and approached the dock. "Witness," he sang, "may I beg you to state your name and your age?"

"I am twenty years and one," she said. "Clara is my name."

"But your surname," André said, "to please the court."

"I have none."

"Ah, then you are a mystery."

"No," she said, looking at Clinton now. "I am a mystery child. My mother married a man who thought so little of marriage he kept it a secret to himself."

"Leave this line of questioning," Clinton said. "She is Mistress Clara. And she ought not be here—she's a colored girl, for God's sake, an octoroon."

"I have the right to call her as a witness should it please the court."

"It doth not please the court, but get on with it."

"Mistress Clara," André said, "what is your relation to the accused?"

Clara pondered inside her dock. "Relation, sir? He did prick me once unless I am mistaken—once, not twice. We were under the roof of a castle called City Hall."

The nabobs and their wives began to gasp; they were confused by Clara, did not know whether to pity her or cover her with vituperation. They did both, while Clinton clutched his head and growled at André.

"You have pressed the girl and made her lose her mind."

"'Tis a ploy," André said. "I know her well."

"Excellency," Clara said to Clinton, "he does not know me at all."

But André stepped between the witness dock and the throne and cut off Clara's view of Clinton. He meant to break her no matter the cost. "You live inside a brothel—a notorious nunnery—with the accused. And what is his occupation?"

"He hath none. His education has put him in a parlous state as 't has done to many a young man."

"He is a silver bullet," André said, "a spy who carries messages to General Washington on his person. And you are in his employ."

I dreaded this moment. He would hit at Clara with his little hammers, knowing I could not bear it. And André was counting on this. That is why he had let her into the attic—to break my heart. Soon he would bring up the Ethiopian Ball, build a case against Clara as the rebel vixen of Little Africa.

"Cease," I said. "I am a spy. And I did not enlist any of the nuns."

Only then did Clara look at me, as if to say I was the biggest dunce in America, that she'd have outlasted André's onslaught. But her eyes could not even hold their gaze on me. They fluttered like that time when Gert had put her in my closet with a bald head. And André wouldn't allow me to serenade her with lullabies.

"Mistress Clara," said the Fiend, "you are dismissed."

The bailiff led every nun out of the room and locked the door. And I stood there, a wounded dog without its master.

Forty-One

HE WAS A BETTER TACTICIAN THAN I. HE'D allowed Gert and Clara to visit me in the attic and then neutered us all. He sent Sir Harold to some other shore, kept Gert out of court, so that she could not comfort Clara, and put Clara into the dock, knowing that however much she might embarrass him, she would wilt under his scrutiny, and her knight with one eye would rescue her and condemn himself in the very same stroke.

"I would sunder your heart," John André said to the throne and the nabobs in camp chairs, "incite you to anger, if I chose to compile every sin of John Stocking, the condemned man in this court."

"The accused," Clinton said, waking up long enough to correct André. "We are not barbarians. 'Tis a British tribunal."

André bowed to the throne. "The accused lost an eye during the Canadian campaign of '75 and has been on parole. But he offered his services to General Washington and used Holy Ground as his headquarters. I beg the court to deliver this self-professed enemy agent to the hangman, who is present, and will watch over him until—"

Clinton opened his other eye. "The court feels that you are

still riding much too fast . . . Mr. Stocking, have you something to say?"

Clara was right. My education had left me in a parlous state. I was but a shipwreck that could still walk. Yet college had also kept me cold and cunning—they were nothing but inkpots, these men of the tribunal.

"Excellency, I was the king's own scholar at my college."

"The king's scholar? André, is this true?"

"All the more to prove his perfidy," André said.

"I did lose an eye in Canada, fighting beside General Arnold. I was his secretary."

Clinton perused me up and down. "A secretary with a sword?"

"Mock heroics," André said. "A wooden soldier."

"Wait, I am intrigued."

"Arnold was a general unlike any other," I said to Clinton. "He would dictate to me in the middle of a charge."

"You carried a quill as you burst into Quebec?"

"No, Your Excellency, I would remember wholesale whatever he wished, line for line."

"André, I like this fellow. He has fine blood for an American."

The Fiend grew nervous, began to twitch.

"Sir," he said, "I most humbly disagree."

"Then I shall query the poor chap . . . Mr. Stocking, you stand accused of treason. How say you to this charge?"

"I am a man most divided, milord. I love my king. I could not have attended college without him. I might have become a wig-maker or a boy who delivers ale. 'T was not any anger at the king that bought me to Arnold's tent in Massachusetts, or deep sympathy with the rebel cause. Quite the contrary. My sponsor, Sir Harold Morse, prodded me. I was to penetrate the American ranks as best I could. That was my mission. And I did.

"Arnold confided in me. He was dreadful as a speller, not very acute with the quill. But kind he was with his men, loath to flog them. And when our rations ran out in the woodlands, he fed the lads with his own food. I saw him starve. I starved with him."

André interrupted. "I beg you, sir, this must stop. He gives us Chinese opera rather than a real defense."

That's when Clinton clutched his bell and rang it with a fury. "Do shut up, man. I'm listening to the boy."

"I could not betray Arnold, Excellency. I would not. Perhaps I was not the best of the king's soldiers."

"You were never one of ours," André hissed.

The nabobs rocked in their camp chairs and made little noises, mousy squeaks, while Clinton clacked his bell until I thought an army of the king's cows might enter this throne room and stampede us all.

"You've had your go at him, André. Shut up, before I have the bailiff gag you."

And I stepped in like the sweetest choirboy. "May I continue, General?"

"Please do," says he.

"I took a bayonet in the eye, but the British never captured me and I was never on parole. I wasn't released from the New York Irregulars. It was Harold who brought me home, plucked me from a poorhouse, and we fled to the Queen's Yard. A nunnery, as Major André says, but General Howe's unofficial headquarters. I saw him there every night. Gambling was his tonic, sir. He could not have gone to war without a good round of vingt-et-un."

"You must not shame us, boy," Clinton said. "Sir William was a bit of a rowdy and a rake."

"I mean not to shame him, but prove his proximity to Sir Harold. 'T was Billy—Sir William—who put Harold in charge of all the blacks on the island. Harold formed a brigade at his own expense, a black brigade, and I was its liaison."

"With what legality?" André asked.

"None."

"There," André said. "We have him, sir."

Ah, how I led him to the dénouement, tricked him with his own tricks.

"But pirates lurked in the city. Women dared not venture abroad without a bodyguard. And we served as the police. We looked for pirates in the upper reaches of Manhattan, for errant Cowboys and Skinners. That is what brought us to Commissary Loring's farm."

And here I was as agile as a London barrister. I lied. I could not refute Loring and the Hessian officer. I had no witnesses.

"Milord," I said, leaning close to Clinton's chair. "We were in our cups. I have a fondness for the beverage. I did not set a good example. And my lads might have been rough with Loring. But they were wild after being cooped up in their barracks."

And I dabbed my one seeing eye with the edge of André's neckcloth, that piece of silk he had given me.

"Sir, I was a ruffian, worse than the Cowboys, and for that you must punish me. But I did not betray the king."

Clinton coughed into his own handkerchief.

"Boy, no man shall hang you. I would go to Hades on your behalf, even if I had to wrestle with the Crown. Yet I am caught in a quandary. You are not a spy or a British soldier. And I judge you with a certain peril. Had there been no rebellion, you would have gone to a different court. But we are where we are. And as much as I like you, Mr. Stocking, and your mettle, you are an impostor, to say the least. You intruded upon me and my headquarters with a false note. Had I known of your late employ as Arnold's amanuensis, I should have exiled you to a far corner. As a rebel soldier who ran from his service, maimed as you were, I have no choice but to treat you as a prisoner of war and confine you for the duration."

I did not rejoice. I thought of Clara climbing the wall, her long legs wrapped around me like a delicious spider, and I watching her green eyes go round and round in her moment of delirium. That noise she made, the sweetest of squeals, as I remained silent.

I wanted to hold her forever with her bum in the air. But the tribunal intruded upon my dream, the one remembrance that mattered to me. I could see Redmund laugh with the knowledge that he wouldn't have to deal with my neck. The choir of generals in front of me kept scratching with their quills, as if the earth might move to their particular music, while the nabobs and their wives humphed at me with great contempt.

Only André was idle, his dark mien devoid of color save for the rouge he wore.

And then Clinton rose, bundled up his sword belt, as the bailiff shouted, "Attention! Court's dismissed," and that fat little general disappeared behind his door.

But my victory was far from complete. André held both the black and red aces. The nuns were in his custody. He could permit them to flourish on Holy Ground, or reduce them to ragamuffins. But he would not forget Clara's little rhapsody in court. He would bide his time, and while Clinton slept, he would slither around and strike with all his virulence. And I was a lad in leg irons, a lad who could be of no help.

Anno Domini 1779

THE *JERSEY*

Philadelphia

JANUARY 1779

He could not encamp his army this winter in one place. His lines of supply were much too thin—'t was simpler to scrounge for food from many smaller camps on both sides of the Hudson. The paper he had was without value—it lost five percent day after day. Continental currency, he would complain to his captains, was now "a rat in the shape of a horse," growing larger as it was worth less and less.

And so he went to Philadelphia, to seek funds and punish peculation. He saw nobody but moneymen—his main suppliers—who fattened themselves while his army dressed in rags. He longed to go into their temples of commerce on Market Street and break their bones.

He would dine in Philadelphia, attend parties, flirt with patriotic widows, and then flee to his own cramped winter quarters. He would not sleep far from his troops. "The army," he told an aide, "requires constant attention—to keep it from crumbling."

And then, perchance, he caught a glimpse of Arnold's chariot—his bravest general riding over Philadelphia like some rajah on an elephant. He'd met with Arnold earlier in the month, but resisted dining with him. He could not bear Arnold's pomp in the midst of so many suffering soldiers. And when he saw that angel in the chariot—Peggy Shippen, with a whole choir of chaperones—his heart leapt. He'd known her as a child, had adored the little blond creature, so flirtatious and full of curiosity.

And he had a most unkind thought—what was Peggy Shippen doing with this dour man? He chided himself for having belittled Benedict Arnold.

He must rid himself of Philadelphia and all its sirens.

Forty-Two

I ENDED 1778 WITH NOTHING TO READ—NOT A book, not a pamphlet, not a letter from Clara or Gert, not even a venomous note from André. From my bird's-eye window in the attic wall—a hole not half as big as my thumb—I could watch the Britishers on our island plunge toward the New Year. Officers and their sweethearts skated on the frozen pond of City Hall. Tory princesses and their beaux gathered whatever firewood was left in the streets of Manhattan. One little lass rubbed against the ice on a rocking horse.

A sudden boom shot across the attic as if to announce the end of the world—the warships in our harbor were saluting 1779 just as they had saluted '78. It had been a rattish year, with the Brits enfeebling us and adding to their dominion over our island. If Washington was across the Hudson, I could not hear him. There were no salutes or salvos from his side of the river.

I still had some resources. I bribed a guard with the last shillings in my purse, convinced him to carry a letter to Holy Ground.

He was rather shy. "Is it treasonable stuff, old son?"

He tore the letter open and glanced at it, his lips moving over each line like some rodent. And I realized that he did not live inside the kingdom of words. "Read it to me."

I wouldn't deceive the rogue. I had to give him something juicy, or my letter was lost. He would not deliver it.

"Dearest Clara, I must be brief. I consider you every moment of my wakeful hours. I consider you in my sleep. Let them deny me ink and pen. I shall pass my whole incarceration imagining letters to you. Please tell Gertrude that I miss her so. Your most humble and adoring servant, John."

The guard seemed disappointed. "What kind of love letter? You never speak of her cunt."

I had to woo him as I'd wooed Sir Henry Clinton in André's court.

"'Tis secret writing, old son. If you could but follow the code, you would find a plethora of cunts."

That seemed to satisfy him, whilst I, without the least hope of a holiday, supped on stale biscuits and a dish of dry peas . . . and thought of Washington in his tent somewhere, half his soldiers without shoes, his orderly, Sparks, without a winter coat, and the farmer forced to play vingt-et-un with peas instead of pounds. New York was a mere river away, but he had neither the men nor the cannons to take it from the Crown. The French fleet would appear and disappear, battling the British in the West Indies or on Narragansett Bay, but even if that fleet had come in full force, it could never dislodge Clinton from our harbor.

I was stirred from my reverie at five in the morning, kicked awake by a pair of André's policemen, redcoats who served as prisoners' police. They bundled my meager belongings into a blanket, clamped me in irons, and carried me down from the attic as if I were their own mischievous child. A wagon was waiting for us, filled with yobs like myself—ragamuffins and misfits, men without a future, sailors who had the misfortune of being captured on some

American ship, pirates who were nabbed inside a British granary, suspicious foreigners found bobbing in American waters.

Our carcasses bumped up and down as the wagon brought us to the docks, where a whaleboat was waiting for us. We were shoved onto the boat, chained together, and carried out to sea, with ourselves as the oarsmen *and* the cargo. Our captors did nothing but smirk and spit and pass morsels of food among themselves. We rowed across the East River to Wallabout Bay, with a nest of ghostly ships moored in the mud flats, ships without masts or sails or rigging, all the beauty gone, so unlike the munificence of flags and guns on board Black Dick's blessèd *Eagle*.

I wasn't blind to the village that receded from our view. The bottom of Manhattan was like a black ball in dark silver water, with specks of light coming off the Battery, until that light was only an illusion and Manhattan fell away with the mist.

We were hauled onto the deck of a retired man-o'-war, with bars placed over the gun ports. But there was barely a soul aboard—a few feral sailors with muskets. The other prisoners were led below, but I was taken to a little makeshift house on the poop deck, with canvas ribs and an awning to occlude the sun. It could have been a tent in Canvas Town, but this tent had a glorious oak chair. Joshua Loring sat preening in the chair with his legs crossed. He had embroidered britches and silk hose that could not hide the feebleness of his calves. With him were those loutish horsemen who had nearly kidnapped Mrs. Loring's chariot. And I realized who these lads were—overseers of a little fleet of prison ships that stole the prisoners' grub and then put on masks to rob the rich and relieve farmers of their cows and milkmaids.

"Well, hello, Johnny One-Eye. Quite the clever scholar to outduel André in his own court and dazzle Clinton with your soliloquies. And then to say that you and your niggers were in your cups and beat old Loring about the ears. Ought to hire you as my solicitor, eh?"

"Where's Mrs. Loring?"

He winked at his brethren. "I was about to ask you that very question. The whore's gone. Methinks she fled to Britannia with Sir Billy. The hottest bitches always follow their knights home from war."

"You slander milady," I said.

"Milady, he calls her," the good Joshua said with a snort. "I'd call her hag—a jade poisoned with the pox."

"I am at a disadvantage, sir, held in irons, or I should slap you silly."

Loring and his henchmen guffawed in my face.

"I am mistaken, Johnny. You're her knight. But know this. You will never leave the *Jersey* alive. I'm commander of this fleet. Tobias," he said to his fattest friend. "What's the mortality rate on my *Jersey*?"

"Six or seven corpses a night."

"And how long will a lad like our Johnny last?"

"A month at the most, milord."

"That's far too kind. I'd like him dead within the week . . . laddy, you can poke fun of the British and their military tribunals. But I'm not the British. I would have had the bailiff squash your head. You shouldn't have meddled with my wife."

I began to cry in front of these yobs. I would not see Clara again.

"Look," said Fat Tobias, "he's bawling like a baby. Soon he'll shit his pants."

My bowels were tight as a fist—'t was my mind that was porous. I couldn't stop thinking of Benedict Arnold. Who would save him from Peggy Shippen? *Thou shouldst not have gone to Philadelphia.* He had a fondness for baubles and decorations on his military coat. His enemies in Congress said he was a horse trader and should not have been given a single command. But I'd rather have been commanded by Arnold than any other officer. Those who had been at his side in battle were spoiled for other commanders and other wars. And so, lads, I had little to lose.

"Loring, I did not ever go to sleep with your wife. Sir Billy's brute shoved me out of her bed in the middle of the night."

He leaped from his chair and meant to pluck out my good eye. Fat Tobias had to stop him.

"He'll only live longer, Sir Joshua. We'll have to take him aboard the hospital ship. And there they give 'em better grub. Leave the lad to us."

"Whatever you do, do it slow. I want it to be the bitterest week he's ever had."

He prepared to go. But I was not without a battle plan, despite my shackles. He passed a little too close to me, like a blind ship in the night. And Johnny the serpent bit him on the cheek. I could taste the blood as my teeth sank in. I wanted to suck the life out of Loring. I wanted to drink him dry and might have done so if the horsemen hadn't kicked at me.

Loring howled in agony. "He's Beelzebub, he's Beelzebub."

And suppose I am.

I thought of Arnold's bastinadoes—he'd oblige a few recreant soldiers to undress and slap their feet with a stave of wood until they promised never to desert again. But Loring's lads had an Oriental touch. They didn't even rob me of my clothes. They leaned honest John over the chair, pulled off my stockings, and attacked the poor soles of my feet with a schoolmaster's cane. I yelped like a cur.

I would have signed a ticket to hell. I cared not about harbors and sailless prison ships, only about Clara with red paint on her cheeks as she stood in André's infernal witness box. *Beautiful is her body*, I sang to myself. But their bastinado began to drive the songs from me. I could not dream or reconsider. I lived in the now, where the pain was like a savagely sharp knife on my sweet skin.

They'd stop and start again, with malignant delight. It was devilish, because as sharp as that knife was, 't did not allow me to swoon. There was no relief from the bastinado of Wallabout Bay.

And then Fat Tobias punched me to sleep with the wind inside his fist, a wind that was like some long sad caress.

Forty-Three

I HAD NEVER SEEN SUCH A BRACKISH YELLOW—colorless as candle drip—a constant inundation of yellow, as if some mischievous god had stamped all men with grim, impossible faces. That's what I woke to, a stinking hold with hundreds of such yellowish men. It was not only the stench of vomit and sour blood and human shit that assaulted me. It was the decay of corpses lying in our midst. The living and the dead were crawling with lice. The only glimmer we had in that hole was the feeble light of a lantern that came through little cracks in the bowels of the *Jersey*. And if that lantern light wavered or pulled off course, we had to lie in the foul blackness.

At dawn a guard would show himself and cry, "Deliver your dead!" And we had to search the hold for dead men, who belonged to us, however much they stank and rotted in our nostrils. But if the guards caught us harboring a dead man, they would open the hatches above us and piss down on our heads, deprive us of the wormy bread and dish water that served as our meal, and wouldn't allow us into the light.

And so we had to surrender the dead, which they didn't bother to drape, and then dumped overboard into the mud flats. It was a burial for dogs, but on the *Jersey* 't was the dogs that had become men. Each little sailor had a poodle, and their masters, the guards and minor commandants, had bulldogs that they reared on deck. The dogs ate liver and drank milk. And when we rose like Lazarus out of the dark, two at a time, and breathed the wondrous air on the quarterdeck, the dogs would gaze at us in deep disgust. These bulls were trained to battle and enjoy bloody meat, not endure the stench of prisoners.

My heart broke during one of our little walks. A woman was rowed aboard from another ship. I recognized her under her shawl, with her rich blond hair and maidenly smile under a pound of paint—'t was Mrs. Anne Harding, that young farmer's wife I'd saved from Jaggers, a demented fool of a man, when I marched with the Manhattan Irregulars. She'd wanted to march with me, become my camp wife, and coward that I was, I'd refused. She'd have been better off with Jaggers.

I knew the heft of things, lads. Loring must have bought her from her husband like a cow. I wondered if there had been a bill of sale. Or perhaps she just ran away and had become another Johnny's camp wife, or the "mum" of an entire regiment. I could speculate like some sage in a skullcap, but the pith of it was that Mrs. Harding had become the whore of Loring's little fleet.

She dared not look at me. She was much too ashamed, ashamed that I should see her as she was, with all the powder and paint of a doxy. I would have groveled at her feet, begged forgiveness for abandoning her, but I'd have frightened the girl, and the dogs would have grown suspicious, seen my groveling as a sign of alarm, all that agitation from a heap of filth, and might have hurt Anne Harding. And so I kept away, didn't even acknowledge that I knew her, as she traipsed to the little canvas poophouse. I could not bare to think what she had to perform for Fat Tobias and his madmen. I felt murderous enough to swallow my own lice.

I was shunted below in my chains. That walk on the deck did me small good. Drinking air couldn't refresh a yob who had to watch Anne Harding's pitiful gait as she prepared herself for her own doom. I moaned in the dark. The other stinking yobs tried to comfort me.

"There, there, soldier, you'll pull through . . . weren't you with Arnold in the Maine woods?"

He was the one general they ever spoke about. We prisoners called ourselves the Jerseys, not out of respect for this vile, pediculous hulk, but because it was our commonality, the glue that held us in its glorious stink. These yobs had been with Arnold in Quebec, at Saratoga, at Ticonderoga, where he captured the cannons that Washington would need to drive the British out of Boston, and at Valcour Island, where Arnold was the commodore of the one little navy America ever had. He did not possess a real gunner aboard his flagship, the *Congress*, and Arnold had to "point" the cannons like the conductor of a sinfonie. It was Arnold who had his own small flotilla of galleys—ships with sails and oars—and paid a bunch of pirates to build such galleys, and when he couldn't pay them in coin, he paid them in cows. At the end of the battle, Arnold beached his broken ships, set them afire, so the British couldn't have them. He'd held his own against the Royal Navy, their admirals, their gunnery officers, their heavier cannonballs. And he flew his colors in defiance as the galleys burned.

It was not a rebel fairy tale. The pirates in the hold had sailed with Arnold, had watched him maneuver against the British. Ye gods, the man loved to fight. But the stories these yobs traded began to sicken me. The commodore sat in Philadelphia with his castle on Market Street and an army of coachmen.

IT WAS DIFFICULT TO SLEEP in this dungeon. And twice fat Tobias had come with his cronies, handkerchiefs under their eyes, not to hide their identity, but to safeguard them from the noisome fumes. And they'd deliver their bastinadoes in some mandarin passageway, each one thwacking me with a cane that was so thin, 't seemed invisible.

I could not have survived a third such thrashing, but fate intervened in a most curious fashion. I was called up to the poophouse in my chains. This time André sat in the pilot's chair, covering his nose with his neckcloth.

"Heavens, man, you stink!"

"These are your accommodations. I did not ask for this particular inn—what will happen to Gert and Clara? Did you close the nunnery, arrest the nuns?"

"Not at all. Good fellow, your imagination grows in much too fertile soil. The nuns will sit in place while I want them to sit. As for Clara? Well, I will punish her when it moves me, and not a moment before."

I knew the Fiend. He would find the nuns a prison ship of their own. But I had to play along with him—Clara's life could depend on it.

"I've found you a spot of work," he said. "You admit that you were Arnold's secretary. Well, the lads on the *Jersey* are as illiterate as mice. You will write their correspondence. Prisoners can't be paid. But I can promise you better food."

"I'd like to eat with the bulldogs. They have the best food of all."

"Stocking, do shut up! You will have an hour a day on deck. You may dine with the bulls if you like. What on earth are those marks on your neck?"

"Loring's lads have been caning me."

He removed the neckcloth from his nose. Was it anger or only playacting that got him to twitch? Who could read into his theatrical soul? André might have you bayoneted or spill your brains, but he also had the maddening British sense of fair play. I'd seen it on those Manhattan lawns the Brits liked to dress up as cricket fields. Warfare was but another game.

"Stocking, you have my word. Those lads will not beat you again."

"I need a grander favor. There's a woman that these reptiles have turned into a harlot. I knew her once upon a time. Mrs. Anne Harding, a farmer's wife she was."

"And an American spy."

"Spy? I can barely believe it. The woman is familiar to you?"

"I banished her to Wallabout Bay," André said. "She whored in George Washington's behalf. 'T was the hangman's knot, or—"

"Becoming the consort to an entire fleet of jailers. I admire your British justice. 'T has a delightful ring."

"You have no say in this matter. I did offer her a choice. She could either become a slop girl or a whore. Like it or not, I think she was already involved in that second trade."

"André, if I had a sword, I . . ."

He smiled and put the neckcloth to his nose again.

"You may have fifteen minutes of time with her every fortnight. And if I have uttered a single untruth, I will release her. Would you care to sleep in another compartment? I can arrange it."

"Wouldn't separate myself from these men. They're my brothers."

"But you will have to wash, or the greatest penmanship in the world won't get you topside long enough to scratch a single letter . . . ah, almost forgot, old son."

André reached into a secret pocket where a spymaster might

have kept his most precious maps, pulled out a piece of parchment paper that held a silhouette, and presented it to me. I recognized André's subject within the dark border—that willful profile, that pyramid of hair. He'd captured my Clara.

"Not to worry, John. Didn't force her to pose. I accomplished it from memory."

And he was gone, this fiendish savior of mine. Why had he come here? To torment me with the one memento I would value most? A portrait of Clara! Did he miss our conversations? Or was he setting a trap for me that included Clara and Anne Harding? And how long would it be before I too turned as yellow as the men around me and disappeared into the mire?

Forty-Four

I DID NOT DISAPPEAR—QUITE THE CONTRARY. I bathed in a barrel. The guards gave me a swabbie's clothes to wear. I wrote love letters for the keepers of the pit dogs. And when the dogs saw how attentive their masters were to me, their own complection changed. The bulls would come prancing and lick my hand. I'd never have thought that these killers would be so sentimental. They'd wag their knobby little tails that had to be bandaged before a fight, because the tail was a bulldog's weakest point. They'd slobber over me. I'd become their mascot. We'd have our daily repast of liver and milk.

I would get to know their names. How could I not? Hunter, like the *Hunter*, our hospital ship, where surgeons practiced the art of the scalpel on prisoners, if a surgeon could ever be found. Eagle, like Lord Howe's flagship. Black Dick, like the admiral himself. Sir Billy. Osiris, god of the underworld and also a ship of the line.

I became devoted to these savage creatures. Once a week a gondola would carry them into some hellhole close to the shore, where they would battle the bulls bred by some ferocious farmer in a pit inside a barn. The guards cared more about the money they might lose than about the dogs themselves. If one dog died, these yobs would train another. Perhaps I am wrong, and they'd hardened themselves against the loss of a favorite bulldog. But I moped for a week when Osiris, *my* favorite, didn't return on the gondola—kept me from thinking of Clara.

The guards would cackle while I wrote love letters to a particular housemaid they hoped to capture with my words.

"Look at him. A regular weeper."

And then they'd cry into the black silk handkerchiefs they wore around their heads like gunners or pirates.

"Cunts and cocks. I miss that lad. No one could bite into a dog's gullet like my Osiris."

They had little interest in the war. But they did talk about that curious sleepwalk of Clinton and Washington—1779 looked to be a war year without much war. Clinton had no time for rebels. Manhattan had become the new capital and command post of the Crown's Caribbean colonies. Clinton had to send his best matériel and men to protect sugar plantations from the French.

I could not consider these guards as my mates. But they would give me extra rations for the Jerseys down below. And they'd let me have a little respite with Anne Harding. She couldn't have been but twenty, yet she was as worn and stooped as a grandmother. Or was it that the paint had hardened into a grim mask?

She would muster the hint of a smile the moment she saw me, could not wait to clutch my hand as if I were the very last delight in the world. We'd stand on deck with little noises coming from the marsh and swampland. Giant frogs, I'd imagine, and their croaks lent a certain music to life on board the *Jersey*. And Anne would enlighten me. Little André hadn't lied. She was a spy, and 't was that spymaster, Major Malcolm Treat, who sent her into a

British officers' brothel while he himself was on parole. There was no goodness in the gods of war.

"Johnny, you shouldn't frown," she said. "The officers were perfect gentlemen. And a vice admiral fell in love with me and asked if he might keep me—tiaras, capes, a maisonette of my own. That was my undoing. He caught me copying some of his papers. But I'm glad. How else would I ever have met you again?"

"Jesus, you could have knocked on my door at the Queen's Yard."

"And ask for a ghost? You came into my life for half a minute five years ago."

"Did you leave you husband?"

"Yes, I came to Manhattan with a highwayman."

That highwayman was Jaggers. He'd kidnapped her, she said, but she did not mind. He'd introduced her to a village that was beyond her ability to calculate and dream. She had never seen such a flurry of people as lived on our island—redcoats and traders and colored men who carried their own chains, beggars and river rats and women in headdresses that could reach a roof. She, a simple country soul, was astounded at the wealth of merchants in their tumbling merchants' streets and at the desolation behind Broadway, where buildings had not been repaired since the Great Fire of '76, their gutted frames poking out like raw, malevolent teeth.

She might have stayed with Jaggers, who drank himself into delirium, but the minute he was sober, Jaggers grew as jealous and overbearing as a husband. She had no wish for another Mr. Harding.

I asked her what she wished for.

"You," she said.

"You play with me, Anne, like the worst coquette."

"I am a coquette."

"Jaggers hit you, I 'magine. And that's when you met Major Treat."

"Yes. And Jaggers couldn't fetch me once I moved inside a brothel."

The logic was as merciless as the laws of gravity. Might have propelled her in another direction had I made her my camp wife when I'd marched to Boston with the Irregulars, and had I allowed her to follow me and Arnold's men to Maine and Quebec. But suppose she had perished in the wilderness, or fought beside her "husband," as some of the camp wives did, and ended up with a bayonet in *her* eye. Lads, not even an Aristotle could play with such certainties and uncertainties and not go mad. I could do nothing but follow history's humble lines and let the future unfold. But I flourished on activity and not on fate.

"Anne, I could lead a rebellion and save you the trip from poophouse to poophouse."

"You dasn't. I'm gathering information."

She was still a spy. And I promised myself that should I ever escape these lads, I would bastinado Major Treat worse, much worse, than Loring's lads had bastinadoed me.

WOULDN'T HAVE KNOWN it was St. Valentine's had Anne not brought me sweets. She fed me caramels from a little bag.

"You're my Valentine, John. I fancy you. I always did. I think of your face when I'm with those other men."

"You mustn't."

I wished to die from the pain. It was like a hundred bastinadoes.

"But we could hide behind the dogs' kennel. There's a space into which we can crawl. You could go under my skirts and have my bum . . . if you want."

I could not even consider such copulations. 'T would have been no ravishment at all. Yet I did have a hunger to hold her.

"I don't have the pox," she said. "I bathe in mercury balls and I . . . don't you fancy me just a little?"

"Not here, Anne, not now, in this infernal place where I have to watch you walk your own terrible station."

"Johnny, ain't I your Valentine?" she asked. And how could I mention Clara, or Clara's silhouette?

"I have no other," I said, as the yobs in the poophouse called her name.

Forty-Five

I HAD THE DIVIL OF A TIME HOLDING ON TO Clara's silhouette and keeping it out of the guards' hands. I tucked it deep inside this blouse of mine that resembled a scabrous cave with many fissures and parenthetical pockets. I'd look at Clara's silhouette and see the outline of Anne Harding. 'Tis not that I coveted Anne more than Clara—the prison ship had unhinged me. I'd die if I didn't escape. I'd have to lead a rebellion on board the *Jersey*, seize Anne from Loring's men, even if I had but the narrowest chance. I was as much a gambler as George Washington or General Howe. I'd have to play vingt-et-un with my own life.

There had been rebellions on other boats. Prisoners had burnt half the *Scorpion*, jumped into the water, but redcoats found them in the swamps of Wallabout Bay, returned them to their wounded ship, where they starved to death or were poisoned by Loring, who put arsenic into their bread. So the pirates say.

"Lad, he wants us to rebel. The money he saves on grub goes into Loring's own pocket."

"What grub?" I growled like my poor dead Osiris.

"The British pay aplenty. We ought to have decent soup and decent bread. But we get the slops from the men-o'-war in the harbor. And Loring divides the profits with whatever admiral or muckamuck is around."

"But we could repair this ship and . . ."

The yobs laughed at me. "Some sailor you are. She's beyond repair, mate. Worms are eatin' her arse. Soon she won't have a bottom, and we'll be sleepin' in mud."

The pirates began to call me Adm'ral America since I was something of a hero—I'd made a mockery of Clinton's court-martial and had thumbed my nose at the hanging tree, according to the pirates, who boasted that if I ever wore a black silk handkerchief about my head, they might mistake me for their leader. How precocious they were. I meant to become a pirate in a black silk handkerchief. But first I had to attend the dogs. I'd convince the guards to let me go into their gondola, but what would I have done with Hunter and Eagle, who only lived to fight?

'T was an idle dream. I had to bring my chains when I climbed out of the hold.

And the guards would have shot me in the face with their muskets had I tried to get near the gondola. And if I jumped ship? I would have drowned with my shackles, even at low water.

But I had my Valentine, even if the sight of her tore into my guts. Anne had become my Town Crier. She arrived with news from abroad, news she'd gathered from different sailors on different poop decks.

Seems Arnold had married Peggy Shippen in April and was fighting Philadelphia. The radicals said he was a thief who enriched himself with profiteering. Congress was baying at his back. And the blond serpent must have whispered in his ear. He could not read his own ruin.

Arnold thought the job of military governor meant he was

some kind of king—he had a gilded coach, twenty horses, stewards, cooks, maids and washerwomen, and rode about Philadelphia with a bodyguard of twenty men. Had the war itself not been in such limbo, he might have volunteered to take his coach into battle (he could not climb onto a horse with his crippled leg). And then we would have seen my Arnold, coach and horses creating havoc within enemy lines. He was the one American general that the British feared, tho' they loved to disparage Arnold, call him "that wild apothecary," because he was not a gentleman soldier like themselves. But he had nothing and no one to fight, except Philadelphia and his own self. Or perhaps I misread him and he'd always dreamt of gilded coaches and a gaggle of cooks, with Peggy but another portion of this dream. No matter. She sealed his doom. I am certain of that.

I HAD ONLY TO WAIT for André's next visit if ever I wanted to learn more about Peggy Shippen. How did I know he would come again to my stinking tub? Because he was wed to me in some strange fashion—I had become his poodle, his pet case. I suspicion he was tormented by Clara but could not wholly admit this to himself, hence I was the instrument that linked him to her.

'T was hard to keep my own calendar on board the *Jersey*. All days were equally grim and I had only the weather to gauge the season. Still, I'd swear it was June or July, with its stinking hot miasma, when André suffered to call on me. I know this much. Loring's lads were frightened of him; their chief, Fat Tobias, went out of his way to please Clinton's young spymaster and offer whatever vittles he had on hand—nuts and peas and a leg of lamb.

André treated Fat Tobias like a mad dog, hurling the peas and nuts in his face and ordering him off the poop deck. My survival depended on André, so it seems, but I had no wish to be servile with him.

"How's the strumpet?" I asked.

He laughed. "Which one?"

"Mrs. General Arnold."

He laughed again. "You are rather cheeky for a lad in your position. I like that."

"But you will like it not when I get word to Washington."

"Word about what? That the cripple has taken a new bride, half his age?"

"A bride you have bamboozled with your tricks," I said, "trained as your spy. You have infiltrated Arnold's very bridal bed. Has he already gone over to the Brits?"

I read his face as a scorpion might read it—John André had little to hide from the lad of Wallabout Bay.

"Not yet," he told me. "The negotiations are decidedly slow. He hath much greed, wants a general's commission and ten thousand pounds—twenty if he himself can capture Farmer George."

"Fiend," I said, "whatever Arnold's perfidy, he would never give up General Washington. I'd wager my life on that. And I will find a silver bullet with which to shout in Washington's ear."

He laughed for the third time. "A bullet such as Mrs. Anne Harding? I could have her neck snapped before she ever reaches dry land. Didn't she tell you her own sordid little tale? She worked at the nunnery for a week after you were gone."

"You lie," I said.

"I swear on Saint George. Gertrude took her in. That pig on parole, Major Malcolm Treat, had groomed Anne. But Treat is a trifler. He cannot harm us. And Gertrude had to feed us something. She is on our payroll, after all. Gertrude gave her up."

"Faker," I said, "'t was a British admiral who unmasked Anne. She told me so."

"That is what she believes. But Gertrude had to give us something—your mother gave her up."

I did not like it. I had not granted him the privilege of calling Gert my mum. But he knew more about me than I wished him to know.

"Washington had a vested interest in Gertrude's house, meseems. You are the farmer's love child. And that is the only reason you're still alive. You, John Stocking, will be our bargaining chip should the war not go well. And do not trouble yourself over Arnold. I doubt Clinton will ever agree to his terms."

"I'm not Washington's," I whispered, more to reassure myself than to refute the Fiend.

"André," I said, "do I have Washington's hair or nose or height?"

"You are his whelp. He hath no other. And you may deny it 'til your face turns blue. Took me months to comprehend. The little collegian with his bed inside the nunnery. What was such a prodigy doing in there? 'T was only after I had you ensconced in this hellhole that my head cleared. I installed you on the *Jersey* because it's Loring's flagship. I asked him to have you killed. I paid him in advance. And then it struck me like some monstrous bell—Gert wasn't protecting you. She let you fly in the wind. She was protecting her farmer."

I tried to throttle him. I had not the strength.

"Careful, old son," he said. "Commissary Loring would love to feed you to the sharks—doth thou enjoy the silhouette I made of Mistress Clara?"

I had such rage against Gertrude and the nuns for having given Anne to André that I longed to toss that piece of parchment into the sea. I did not.

André removed his hanger from its leather scabbard with an enormous flourish, and at first I thought he meant to cut my face.

But he scratched his chin with the pommel of the sword. "Would Clara sleep with me if I threatened to hang Gert? I wonder."

He climbed down the poop deck, sword in hand, and stepped onto the gondola that was awaiting him. I watched him being rowed away, while the very edge of Manhattan broke through the mist like some magic promontory—a veritable green horn that might snare the gondola itself, I prayed, and finish André once and for all. But, alas, I had discovered a false Manhattan, and André's gondola went right past that little illusion of land.

Forty-Six

IT PAINED ME THAT ANNE HAD LIVED ON ROBINSON Street but a little week, and Gert and Clara had fed her to the British like a leg of lamb. I could not toss a message into Wallabout Bay that would bob downriver and arrive at my mother's door. And who else would enlighten me? I had to wait like some wily beer boy until Anne's next visit to the *Jersey*. But Anne did not come, and it was exceeding hard to count the fortnights with my own fickle calendar. 'T began to feel like autumn of a sudden; the swamp had lost much of its bloom. But I could still hear the reptilian music that hovered over the water, strange eructions that might have been a signal from Anne herself.

And then, quite like magic, unholy or not, Anne stepped out of her gondola wearing a flimsy coat and the same pound of paint. I could not question her like some inquisitor. I had neither the heart nor the stomach for it. But while we chewed on some sweetmeats she had purchased from a sailor on another ship, I could not help myself.

"Anne, you lived on Holy Ground, did you not?"

She continued to chew.

There was no point in hiding my nativity, since I would never get off this tub. "And you met a certain Mrs. Jennings—she is my mother."

Anne did not bat an eye or seem to redden under her pound of paint. "Major Treat did tell me so."

Malcolm Treat! Was he bandying my biography about, offering it to perfect strangers? Yet Anne was not a stranger.

"And did you not meet a tall girl, even taller than I, who has a fascination for fancy shoes and fine tobacco?"

"Mistress Clara," Anne said between chews. "She was very kind for a colored girl, told me what might please such and such an admiral or commander of Clinton's light horse."

I thought to swoon. I had such a jealous fit I could have swallowed the *Jersey*. But I would not show it to Anne.

"Johnny, I dasn't speak of my sojourn on Holy Ground for fear it might make you homesick and give you a fever. You must listen. I did not come to the *Jersey* by accident—'t was Divine Will. The *Jersey* was not supposed to be on my route."

Route, her captors called it, this bloody gondola ride from hulk to hulk.

"They house us near the harbor, on an old fighting ship, and our warden happed to mention the notorious malcontent, Johnny One-Eye, who was close to leading a black revolt and had to be put away in the foulest prison, where blacks could not find him. I was not certain that this was the same Johnny who had rescued me in Massachusetts . . . and abandoned me just as quick. Still, I volunteered to add the *Jersey* to my route, and the warden thought me mad."

"But, Anne," I insisted, "surely Gert could have told you all you needed to know about Johnny One-Eye."

"She did not . . . Johnny, I have lived this last year between two majors—André and Malcolm Treat. But I'd never have found you if not for them."

I'D LOOK AT CLARA'S SILHOUETTE, cup it in my hand in that false daylight that often fell through the cracks and filtered down into our hold—some strange sky that even the *Jersey* could not dispel. I had to think like a spy. Mum had given up a girl she must have known would soon be compromised. Abandoning Anne meant she could safeguard someone else. And how could Gert have known that Anne Harding would end up on Wallabout Bay?

But whenever I saw Anne, I could no longer reason like a spy. I now had a blinding anger against Mum. I might have diffused it in a moment had I the chance to talk with her and touch her face. But there was no such chance. And I had no furniture—nothing to hold—but that silhouette crafted under André's own perfidious eye. Perhaps it was the same perfidy that altered the silhouette, so that Clara seemed to have Anne's face from time to time. Or perhaps it was my longing for Clara that I had to withhold.

I knew that the fleet Anne serviced would finally kill her, but no immediate harm would come while André was still alive. I would cling to her, tho' we seldom kissed, and she would render unto me the little gazette she had gathered about Benedict Arnold. He still had not bolted to the British. But meanwhile Arnold borrowed money like a little nation. He bought Peggy a house in the countryside, a house he would never live in. There were odd absences, whole weeks that could not be accounted for, as if Arnold had crossed some invisible line. Anne could not clarify this in her gazette, but I wondered whether Arnold was on a secret hunting trip to discern how he and Clinton might end the war.

Anne was convinced that Peggy Shippen Arnold had sneaked

into Manhattan to confer with her spymaster, John André. I'd call it a tryst. The silver bullet she was carrying was her own warm mouth. Anne had also heard that Peggy was big with child. And out of spite, I hoped she would present Arnold with a changeling—a little bastard brother of mine.

Anne could not smuggle books to me, since Loring's brethren looked under her skirts whenever she arrived. But I would compose books for her—rather, recompose them, since I knew several by heart. She preferred the adventures of Lemuel Gulliver in the Land of the Little People. And it mattered not how many times I repeated the tale to her. She would listen enthralled as I parceled out pieces of Gulliver according to the moments she had with me. The tales seemed to soften the trips she would make to the poophouse. I could not bear it when she had to climb. But she would clutch my hand among all the debris and say, "I think in my head that we're making a child, Johnny, and that you're married to me."

And I'd have to descend into the hold, live in the darkness with corpses at my feet and feel my flesh go to yellow and gray. I'd console myself with the words in my head, smile as much as a desperate lad can smile at the picture of Gulliver wallowing around in Lilliput, where men were less than six inches high, where his testicles hung down as his britches decomposed, and where he had to put out a fire in the Lilliputian queen's apartment with his own piss. Anne loved the particulars of this fire, and how the queen was ungrateful, because Gulliver's piss ruined her sense of propriety.

WE WERE ALL LILLIPUTIANS, surrounded by Gullivers in their British attire, great big men with their hanging testicles and their raw red faces, who could drown every last one of us in their own piss. And yet that wasn't what drew Anne to the tale: she worshiped Gulliver, the Man-Mountain, and the way he could carry half a country in the strands of his hair. Gulliver was her hero, not mine. Gulliver couldn't have rescued a single bulldog on the *Jersey*. These ferocious lads kept dying on me; others came onto the deck. I groomed their ridiculous fighting tails. They did not ask of me more than I could give. That made them excellent companions. I could not save them, but my one task was to keep Anne Harding alive as she went from rotten hulk to rotten hulk, all of them filled with some Fat Tobias, who would beat her brains out one day as part of his afternoon sport. I sang to her whatever stories I knew. She never tired of Lemuel Gulliver. Methinks we had what one might call a marriage.

Anno Domini 1780

ARNOLD

Morristown

MARCH 1780

He railed at the Continental Congress from his winter quarters, railed at those "villains"—the civilian commissaries—who were stealing the lifeblood of his army. One such villain, George Olney, appeared at a dinner party given by an aide to the commander in chief.

Washington's officers wallowed in Madeira and perused Olney with a certain mischief in their eyes—he hid with the officers' wives (and his own dear wife), who had withdrawn to another room.

The drunken officers demanded that these ladies surrender Olney. Washington was also in his cups. And with so little to be light about, he joined the fray. Whilst Olney himself cowered behind a chaise, Mrs. Olney, in a great furor, scuffled with the commander in chief. "Sir," she said, "if you will not let go of my hand, I will tear out your eyes and the hair from your head."

Washington turned ashen. He bowed to Mrs. Olney. The wife of one officer—Mrs. General Green—demanded that Mrs. Olney apologize to the commander in chief. But Mrs. Olney attacked Mrs. General Green. And it took every officer at the soirée to separate the two wives.

Washington couldn't stop trembling. He swore never to drink Madeira again in the company of civilian commissaries and their wives. He returned to the log huts where his men were encamped in a hollow three miles west of Morristown, a place soldiers themselves called "log-house city."

There was little or no food coming from George Olney and the other civilian commissaries, who pocketed whatever coin Washington had and could provide nothing but barrels of flour with beetles inside. He should have hanged Olney from the nearest hook and let the Divil deal with Mrs. Olney.

There would be no more dinner parties in Morristown, no more Madeira while his men froze in log huts and had to survive with beetles in their flour.

And when he arrived at his own log hut, he found a man stirring the fire—his master of intelligence, Malcolm Treat, who was on parole and should not have left Manhattan.

"Major, I would kiss you under another circumstance, but we are soldiers still, and sworn to our parole. Should we lie and cheat and kill, we do so not without peril."

"Lawd," said the major on parole, "are you a gen'ral or a preacher man?"

"Malcolm Treat, you have come to me in a drunken stupor."

"How else would I come?"

And Treat pointed to a corner of the hut. There, in the shadows, Washington saw his redhead. His knees buckled under for an instant. Treat had already gone.

Gertrude ventured out of the dark to greet Washington with her red hair.

"General, he was a crazy man, said that if I did not accom-

pany him, he would burn all my nuns. I think he was looking for an excuse to flee his parole for a few days. He might have jeopardized all of us, and . . ."

The commander in chief was shivering so, Gertrude took him in her arms.

"My darling," she said, "please don't cry. I will have no more weapons I might use to part from thee."

He could not rescue his tongue for an entire two minutes—a warrior without the gift of speech. But he knew his own men. 'T was not drunkenness that had brought his master of intelligence here, tho' drunk he was. Treat had a most ungodly power to anticipate his general's needs and desires. Treat had realized from afar that his general was in mortal danger of losing his mind, that only the wildest flower could revive him.

Gertrude was that flower.

"Child," he said as soon as the shivering had stopped. "I too am on parole, on parole with thee."

But there was a knock on the door.

"Gen'ral," Treat roared, "your whole fuckin' family is coming—Hamilton and the rest of the tribe."

Washington groaned, even as he clung to Gertrude. Was there news of some untoward military strike, or another such calamity? He could not enjoy the smallest of paroles. But he had a devilish idea.

"Child" he said, "I dub thee my aide-de-camp. We shall find you ink and quill. Yet Hamilton will be mortified should another person wield the pen in his place—ah, I have it! You will be my mystery guest."

"But I am no mystery to Mr. Hamilton," she said.

And her general screamed at the door. "Treat, bid Mr. Hamilton that he may enter now."

Washington laughed so hard he nearly pissed his pants. He

was a madman in the middle of a war, a general who had command over everything save his own skin. But they could come howling at him, enemies and all—for this night at least Washington was on parole, and no one, not Hamilton or the British high command, would tear Gertrude away from him.

Forty-Seven

THE SHORES OF MANHATTAN WERE BUT A MILE from our little cove at Wallabout, but we happened to face Out Ward and the hovels of Little Africa, which lived without lamps—so darkness reigned on the *Jersey*. The nabobs of the wealthier wards and their Loyalist wives utterly ignored us; it was only the Africans who cared about prisoners, who acknowledged we were still alive. If they had no lamps, they did have a cache of fireworks—their little rockets and bombs would explode in the sky, much to the annoyance of the Brits, who feared that such illuminations might mask a rebel attack, while we, in the belly of our boat, could not often speak of skies. But the Africans delivered us with music that marked their holidays—fifes, fiddles, and kettledrums broke up a monotony that was meant to kill.

I liked to imagine that Prince Paul was communing with me the only way he could. If not for the Africans, I might never have learned about the New Year. Perhaps General Clinton had saluted 1780 in some secret fashion, without a salvo from a man-o'-war. Or perhaps the natural insulation of our cove had deadened the sound of his salvo. But Paul must have acquired his own cannon, which sat on Little Africa's crumbling dock. Paul's cannon fired several salvos, signaling the end of a most tumultuous decade, before someone silenced it—a British patrol, I suspicion, that confiscated the cannon and might have torn up the dock to prevent future cannonades.

I wondered if that cannon had woken Clinton out of his long sleep, but the general was not even on York Island. I learned from Mrs. Harding that he'd sailed out of our harbor just before the New Year, after weeks of loading horses, men, and matériel onto his battleships—he had gone to capture Charleston from the rebels. According to Anne, he took his spymaster with him—Major André.

And, I reckoned, if both Clinton and André might be spending months in and about Charleston, there couldn't have been much room for Benedict Arnold in their daybooks. I'd reckoned wrong. Alas, my general was never very far from André's mind, I would soon discover. In April, Arnold flirted with treason while his son was born—Edward Shippen Arnold; a spirited lad with Peggy's blond hair and Benedict's big eyes, according to Anne Harding's gazette.

Arnold was but looking for the chance to bolt. He was given that chance in early August when Washington named him commandant of West Point.

"Anne," I said, while Mrs. Harding was still on deck, "you must give this message to Major Treat. George Washington is to avoid West Point at all cost."

I saw a certain terror in her eyes. But she still engaged in pantomime. She threaded a needle and sowed my lips.

"Johnny, I work for the British now."

And she went to the poophouse without another word.

I THOUGHT EITHER TO KISS Anne Harding or crush her skull. But truth is I could not harm her. Her fate was like the fate that might befall America—into madness and a kind of slavery. She'd been a farmer's wife, a country lass who got embroiled in war.

"Did that Divil André threaten to kill me, Anne? Is that why you have become his gatherer?"

"Johnny, I must not speak. I am like a woman who carries a malady more potent than the pox. I will only harm you if I come near."

But she could not give up the habit of bringing me sweets.

I went back down into the hold. "I'm Adm'ral America, I am," I said to my mates. "Lads, if we don't get off this ship right away, the rebels are lost. Washington is coming to West Point, and our Arnold means to betray him."

It pained them to hear Arnold presented in so rude a manner.

"He hath a weakness, our Ben," said one of the pirates. "He could never resist baubles and ladies with blond hair."

They began to weep, and I struck at them with my chains.

"This is not the time for tears."

'T was a miracle, the progress we made. A couple of lads bit off their own chains, like sea wolves, others gathered whatever weaponry was about—the leg of a rotting bench, the buckle of a misbegotten shoe some guard had left behind, rusty nails that might serve as a superb claw. We meant to attack the guards when they brought our slop. Good brawlers they were, these lads of mine, older than I and without teeth.

We waited and waited for the servers to bring us our watery soup, but the servers did not come. I should have seen that something was amiss. But I was hot with desire to sound the alarm and awaken Washington. We rose from the *Jersey*'s bowels, a good dozen of us with sticks and buckles in our hands, some of us dragging our chains. We had our mission—to overwhelm the guards and take command of the tub. We'd cloak ourselves in their miserable uniforms, climb into a landing boat with their muskets and little flags, and row like the Divil until we reached Manhattan. God help any man who got in our way!

But the gates to our hold were not even manacled. Still, we climbed. We shattered the doors of the weaponry closet and had a rude awakening—it housed no muskets, and we could not find the least lead ball in the ship's magazine. Still, we climbed. And when we got to the quarterdeck, we were welcomed by a little company of redcoats and royal marines, muskets aimed at our eyes. Joshua Loring was with the marines, a perfumed handkerchief in his fist.

I was a dolt. Loring had planted a spy among the pirates and given all our secrets away.

The reptile bowed to me. "Adm'ral America, or do I mispronounce your name? André sends his greetings. A pity he could not come himself. But he is occupied with larger matters than a worm who wears the dress of a pirate. He has granted me the honor of delivering the *coup de grâce*. Would you care to pen a farewell note to your whore, Mrs. Anne Harding?"

I grabbed at his perfumed handkerchief out of some mischievous folly. Muskets exploded around me with an horrific din. Strings of flesh slapped my face. My own lads fell at my feet, their brains oozing blood and some pale white fluid.

Loring would not look at me. I was manacled again and led back down into the bowels. Adm'ral America.

Forty-Eight

ANDRÉ MUST HAVE TOLD HIS MAN-KILLERS TO keep me alive. I still had some small value, as Washington's putative love child. I felt like a leper among my own lads—nay, a sorcerer who had bewitched them. But I was free to roam about the tub.

We talked of trifles whenever Anne would come. She did not ask about Gulliver, whose hanging testicles could no longer amuse her. And then she stopped coming at all.

The dogs could sense my gloom. They growled at the lice in my hair, nuzzled my neck, almost as if they'd inherited my gloom. But they did not survive very long. Our greatest champion, Scorpion, was only with us a month. I fell in love with these monsters with bitten ears and scarred eyes, warriors every one. But they couldn't bring me the news. I had to depend on the guards, who were stingy with their stories. And then they were filled with a sudden blaze, as a particular story flooded their hearts.

'T was a tale of early autumn—the farmer in chief had come to West Point on or about September 24, and Arnold meant to trap him, to end the war in one terrifying blow. Clinton must have promised Arnold half the world and half the king's colonies too.

My guards mocked Washington's visit. "He near escaped the noose," they said.

And then they grew somber as they sang to me some folderol that had been sung to them by Clinton's Town Crier. But these guards were not gifted storytellers, and I had to stitch together a narrative from their pieces of chaos, reflect on it all, since I had no Crier of my own.

'T was André who botched the grand design. He was coming from a rendezvous with Arnold, in civilian clothes, with Arnold's own plans for the surrender of West Point hidden inside his stocking, when he was captured by a bunch of patriotic Cowboys.

Washington's own secret service soon learned of the mischief in André's stocking. These men could not have suspicioned Arnold himself—no one could have imagined such evil. They alerted Arnold about a possible plot. And while Washington sat drinking coffee nearby with Hamilton, Arnold bolted to the British.

"Our George was livid when he heard the news," the guards said with a guffaw. "His face was of a purple color." He could not calm himself. I understood—Arnold was the general he had counted on.

Mrs. Arnold feigned madness. She swore that a certain clique of Continentals was going to kill her and little Edward, but six months old. "There are hot irons on my head, and no one but General Washington can take them off." So she raved and sat in bed without the bedcovers, her breasts revealed, her lovely breasts. Ah, the nuns could have learned a trick or two from Peggy Shippen Arnold.

ANDRÉ WAS SENT TO TAPPEN, near Washington's headquarters, and was tried by a board of generals. These generals were a ghostly gray as they sentenced André to death. Washington's hands shook when he signed the execution order.

"He's the Divil," sang my jailers. "Big giant George."

And in the short while of André's capture, Hamilton had become André's friend. He played vingt-et-un with the condemned man, drank Spanish wine, talked of music and modern warfare. Hamilton was enraged that Washington would agree to hang a man of such quality. "He should be shot, like an officer and a gentleman, not sent to the gallows like a common dog." This my jailers had overheard from a drunken courier.

Washington agreed to let André's manservant through the lines. On the morning of his execution the servant began to sob. "Leave," André said, "leave until you can show yourself manly!" But he apologized. His sharpness had not been out of rancor, but out of a deep malaise. And I liked him for it.

His servant shaved him, dressed him in the uniform of an adjutant general, and he walked out with the guards to his own death parade like a dancer, with the lightest of steps. When he arrived at the gallows, he took off his hat. Spectators were amazed at his beautiful long black hair, held with a black ribbon.

The American executioner was a knobby little man covered in grime. He put the rope around André's head. And André tightened the noose. He covered his eyes with a white handkerchief. The hangman climbed the gallows like a paradise monkey and tied the other end of the rope to the top beam. André was standing in a wagon attached to two horses. The wagon had its own little shelf—a coffin—and André stood astride this coffin without wavering once. The hangman had already bound his arms. But this hangman had no dignity. He appalled everyone except André, who could no longer see. The hangman kicked one of the horses, and Major André started to swing.

ANNE HARDING HAD LOST her protector, alas. With André gone, the jailers could do with Anne whatever they pleased. But I did meet her one more time, a week after André's execution. She got off the gondola with enormous welts on her face. Her eyes fluttered.

"Anne," I said.

"Johnny, you must not touch me . . . wanted to say goodbye."

And she slid past me with a demonic grace. Fat Tobias was standing on the poop deck, waiting for her. He doffed his hat to me. I did not like his smile. Anne climbed up to him. I should call it Calvary were I a religious man.

I heard her scream, but I could not climb with my chains.

The guards seized me. "Keep out of it, Johnny-O."

The dogs had sensed my own wildness. They bumped me with their muscular heads, in sadness and sympathy.

Anne screamed again.

"Help her," I pleaded, "help her." And then I pleaded no more.

"I will murder every one of you cockfucks," I said.

The dogs howled in a language that must have been terrible even for them.

The guards socked me about the head. I beat off their blows, while Fat Tobias murdered Anne—I watched her body plummet from the poop deck, watched it rise and fall in the marsh, rise and fall like some miraculous mermaid until it rose for the last time, as the guards knocked me down into the hold.

Forty-Nine

I LEARNED TO SURVIVE WITHOUT LIVER AND MILK. And one autumnal afternoon I was pulled from the bowels of the *Jersey* in my odoriferous rags and carried up to the poophouse.

A general sat in Loring's chair, a British general, and I might have wept were I not swollen with anger. To see him in his British buttons. *My* Benedict Arnold, the most reviled man in America.

But I'll say this much for Arnold. He did not put a handkerchief to his nose. He was still a man of war who didn't feel foreign to any odor or clime.

"You'll come with me," Arnold said.

"And if I refuse?"

"Then I'll drag ye out to the gondola in irons."

Now he was talking like the man who almost took Quebec, not the vulture who ran from West Point, his tail tucked between his legs.

"Ah," I said with a smartness that was meant to hurt. "Then I'll have to capitulate."

He was silent on the boat. I could not keep from looking at

him. He should have clawed out his own heart, held it beating in his hand and died together with it. But he did not. He wasn't a genuine British general. He was a brigadier in the provincial army, like a bulldog the Brits might use to snap at Washington's heels. I had the urge to strangle him, right there on the gondola. To end it all, even if the redcoats on the gondola brought me back to Tobias. But there was such softness in his face, sympathy for me, that I could not attack him.

Why had he come to the *Jersey*? He must have had other items on his calendar than the rescue of a former scribe. Perhaps I reminded him of a different Arnold, before Philadelphia, before his battles with Congress, before Peggy Shippen, when he did not need coachmen, could ride in a canoe, lead an army, and sacrifice his own fortune—ye gods, he had not worn silver buttons in Quebec.

I watched the *Jersey* disappear in the mist. I'd been on that wretched tub twenty months if my calculations were correct, twenty months without a letter from home. Not a scratch from Gertrude or Clara, tho' André had hidden me away, and Fat Tobias did not permit any traffic with the world outside. A river, one little river, had created its own eternity.

We did not dock near Out Ward. The gondola continued south, toward the wealthier wards—the lights of York quickened my blood. The lamps had been lit, and I saw men coming out of the coffeehouses. I had forgotten that people on a cobbled walk had their own particular hum, like the sound of bees in the distance.

Arnold caught me crying. "Forgive me," I said. "I did not dream much on the *Jersey*, didn't think of villages and towns, but I could not have known how much I missed Manhattan."

He stood up in the gondola and wrapped his cape around my shoulders.

"I shall need a secretary."

I did not answer him.

WE LANDED AT HUNTER'S KEY, near Little Dock Street. A carriage was waiting for us, but we did not have a long voyage. We went from the harbor to Hanover Square, from Princess Street to the Bowling Green and Broadway. Arnold had rented a house right next to Clinton's headquarters. I was a bag of bones, but he would not have his coachman carry me. The general scooped me up into his arms, deposited me first into a closet off the kitchen, where he ripped off my tatterdemalion blouse and chopped at my beard with a scalping knife, then bathed me with his own hand in a pungence of lye, and how could I strangle this traitor, lads, after such kindness?

Then he carried me upstairs in a huge white sheet, and I had my own room with a proper bed, a canopy, a mirror, a chest of drawers, paintings of wild horses on the wall—a much better establishment than my hotel on Wallabout Bay, with lice and human flesh as my *furniture*. I closed my eyes and dreamt of horses . . . and woke up to Prince Paul staring into my face.

"Should I dress you, master?"

I hugged Paul, and wanted to float with him right across the room.

"Lieutenant Stocking," he said with that half smile of his. "You'll get me whipped."

"But where's our Blues?"

"In a barn behind the old poorhouse. They've been lent out to the British army—stevedores and such."

"Who lent them?" I had to ask.

"Did you gather dust on Wallabout? The Brits lent us to themselves. That's the beauty of martial law. But I'm bountiful—a Blue that can spell his name and dance the minuet. The gen'ral has put me in charge of your welfare."

"Am I mad, or was it you that fired a cannon from Out Ward to welcome in the year?"

"'T was my greeting to the *Jersey* and its prisoners."

"Ye gods, are you a rebel or one of the king's men?"

"A bit of both," he said. "That's all an African can ever hope to be on this island—Clara was always with us at the dock."

I turned suspicious. "My Clara?"

"She danced for you every day, hoping that you'd watch."

"I was not permitted to have a spyglass."

"She still danced, John, every single day."

My mind was swollen with images of Clara dancing on the dock; my brains might have burst had Paul not shook me out of such imaginings. He dressed me in the most beautiful of shirts with brocaded sleeves and cuffs, a silk neckcloth, silk stockings, shoes with silver buckles. He braided my hair, doused me in French perfume, and put a cocked hat on my head.

"The Duke of Bowling Green."

I WENT DOWNSTAIRS on legs that had had so little exercise, and Clara still in my mind's eye, dancing the minuet with an invisible partner—me. And then another image broke through my idyll, ripped at its edge. I saw a woman in a sea-green morning gown and a honeycomb of blond hair flit across the parlor. Salome herself, she who had enticed her poor husband into treachery, fooled Hamilton and the farmer in chief at West Point. I'd call her Satan's strumpet.

"Will you have cocoa with me? I'm the new Mrs. Arnold. But you must call me Peggy. The general talks about you incessantly. He swore in the strictest confidence that he could never write a love letter until he met you. So I'm indebted to you for my marriage."

She bowed to me in a most playful manner.

Didn't even have a chance to duel with Salome. She'd disarmed me with chatter that sounded like a chickadee.

We drank the cocoa, had little cakes with cream on top.

"You will help him, won't you? He does so much need a friend. He's prideful, and he does not get on with the young British officers."

The lady of the house took my hand, squeezed it ever so slightly, her skin like warm and vital flesh. A current passed through me, the tail of a storm. The serpent had already struck.

"Might I hold you to such a promise?" she asked.

I had promised nothing, but was feeble of a sudden before this strumpet.

"I am your servant, madam."

She ruffled her pert little nose, while her bosoms began to heave under her bodice.

"You make me sound like a grandmama," she said.

"Perhaps I am the grandmama."

She laughed into her cocoa.

"You are a wicked boy. 'Tis no wonder that your letters stole into my heart."

"They were your husband's letters. The thought and passion were his. I merely instructed him how to add a bit of relish." Couldn't tell her I'd helped Arnold practice his craft on an earlier fiancée.

"You make fun of me, treat me like a child. You know as well as I do, John, that relish is all. The shaper of words is as much the author as my Mister."

Help me, Lord, I was no match for Mrs. Arnold. She could have worn a wig and sat in my class at King's, become our valedictorian.

"Where did you study, if I may be so bold to ask?"

"In my father's library, on his lap," she said.

I thought of Clara, and the library her planter father might have had on Dominica, tho' I doubt she'd have enjoyed sitting on this planter's lap. But Peggy had read all the masters, from Lemuel Gulliver's creator, Jonathan Swift, to that libertine Rousseau, with his maniacal belief in natural goodness. And I had to be just to Salome—'t was not her charm alone, not the bounce of her bosoms, but the vigor of her mind that had caressed Arnold and confused him.

I THOUGHT TO VISIT Gert and Clara, but seems I could not. The image of Gert giving up Anne Harding to Major André distressed me. I kept seeing Anne plummet into the marsh, her body rising with some unknown will. I missed Clara in a god-awful way, but I would not carry my bag of bones to the nuns' parlor.

I soon became the hermit of Arnold's house. I would not leave, tho' I longed to march about the village. Perhaps I did not want to find redcoats and Hessians in the street. And then I was invited to the commander's ball at British headquarters.

"There must be a mistake," I said to the general *and* his lady. "I am a pariah. It was General Clinton himself who had me sent to Wallabout Bay."

"But Major André was fond of you," said Mrs. Arnold.

"Then 'tis a strange fondness. He spoke for the Crown at my court-martial."

"But you are still connected to him, and hence, you have inherited his aura."

Aura, says she. Seems André's apparition was multiplying in Manhattan—one day I'll bump into his statue on the Bowling Green.

"Madam," I said, "I will not go to Clinton's ball."

"You must," she said. And she turned to the general. "Ben, enlighten this boy."

Arnold had that old embarrassment in his eagle eyes, the look of a man without much language, and I loved him for it.

He pleaded with his wife. "I cannot force Johnny."

"Then at least tell him the consequences," she said.

"Ah," said Arnold, scratching one ear. "Clinton says that if I do not bring ye, John, I should not bother about coming at all."

MRS. ARNOLD WORE A GOWN of golden silk with a décolleté that would have broken the heart of a decent man, and sent an indecent one to howl at some imaginary moon. The general wore a dark cape. I dressed in his boots and other borrowed clothes.

We had no need of a carriage. We simply marched next door and were received with fire, sulfur, and ice. Clinton's young aristocratic officers shunned Arnold in his shabby uniform while they wore silver brocaded into their collars, silver on their sleeves. They bowed to Arnold and turned their backs on him. But they fawned over Mrs. Arnold, and in a world gone topside-turvy, they fawned over me. I'd become the hero of these little aristocrats, André's own "apogee," the most vivid point of his life, even if 't was based on a bloody court-martial.

Never mind that they hadn't given a thought to me while I lay in the *Jersey*'s hold with a beard I could have used to brush an elephant's back. I had risen from Wallabout, returned from the dead, and now I was their favorite apparition—André's living double, tho' I did not look a jot like him. 'T was the madness of human endeavor, and I was wrapped in its mystery. I could have flung their own ballads into their barbarous British faces: *If boats were on land and churches on sea; if redcoats wore blue and rebels loved their king, then all the world would be upside down.*

Clinton danced and drank and talked with Peggy until gossips began to call her "Lady Clinton." And Arnold stood alone, sipping champagne, satisfied that his wife was caught in the whirlwind of a soldier's ball. He was a man who seemed not to understand his own loss, that these arrogant officers were not half as brave or aristocratic as his own thumb.

'T was Clinton who approached me, looking derelict as he always did, even in decorated sleeves. He longed to capture the whole southland, bombard it as he'd bombarded Charleston in May, and thus put an end to the war, but he could not budge while the French fleet roamed hither and beyond, and George Washington sat in New Jersey, hoping to hector him and reclaim Manhattan. Clinton would send his new bulldog, Benedict Arnold, to burn up Virginia *and* Washington's farm. It must have pleased him to think of Arnold as dictator of Mount Vernon.

"There you are," he said, as if he were continuing a conversation we'd had but yesterday. "Are you prepared?"

"Prepared for what, Excellency?"

"To go along with Arnold when he raids Virginia. He'll need a lad of your worth. I can offer you a captaincy, with the provincials, of course. You would not be able to keep such a rank."

"But I'm a wasteling from your prison ships."

"Right you are. No one but you has ever left Wallabout alive . . . except an occasional madman who decided to swim across the currents and did not drown."

"Milord, do you envision me as a raider because I once raided Commissary Loring's farm?"

"Do not speak of that despicable man. I should have listened to André. Loring's a whoremonger and a thief. He sought to build his own private treasury on the back of the king. But I was late in trying to arrest him. He fled with all the wealth of his farm."

I fell into a sweat. "Have all his henchmen gone with him? One in particular. Calls himself Fat Tobias."

Clinton's sullen eyes had a cruel glaze. "Captain Stocking, I'm commander in chief. You'll have to ask my quartermaster about this Fat Tobias. But I haven't invited you here to haggle. You are, young sir, my honored guest."

And he went back to dancing with Mrs. Arnold, while other officers rushed out of his way like scared rabbits and I prowled the deck of this damned ballroom for another face. Hadn't Clara always been the favored beauty at Clinton's balls? Hadn't she danced his officers into exhaustion?

"Sir," I asked one of Clinton's young aristocrats, "I cannot find the commander's tall protégée. An octoroon who goes by the name of Mistress Clara."

He pondered for a moment. "Clara, of course. She has been replaced, Mr. Stocking."

"Replaced by whom?"

"Mrs. General Arnold. Madame said it was not fitting to have a harlot in the house. His Excellency dared not disagree. She has her way with him. He never used to dance at his own balls. Now he dances with her from beginning to end. She has the perfect height for him—Clara, you see, would have made the Old Man look small."

And as I watched the Old Man do the minuet with Mrs. General Arnold, both with perfect proportions, like dolls in a dollhouse, I could conjure up another dancer, who would have broken the dead calm of this ball.

I MOONED ABOUT ARNOLD'S ABODE LIKE A MADman, banging into furniture. Nearly broke one of Peggy's precious lamps. *If redcoats wore blue and rebels loved their king*. In a world gone upside down, my own spirit seemed to flounder somewhere between a nunnery and a prison ship.

Peggy was in the parlor with her infant, Edward Shippen Arnold. He was a brooder, with her blond hair and Benedict's hawklike profile. The mistress of the house was feeding him porridge a day or two after the ball.

"John," she said, "a woman was here, looking for you."

"Old or young," I asked, "tall or short? Was she an octoroon?"

"Gracious, no. She was rather stout, tho' terribly attractive. Edward's nurse recognized her, said she was from that place called Holy Ground, swears she was even a prostitute, a *poule*."

She started to laugh. "I was worried. At first I thought she was looking for the general. Nurse says she might have been to the house once before. But the woman was rather brazen, coming here to solicit you."

"She never solicits," I said. "She's my mother, ma'am. And it must have cost her to come here and destroy your tranquility."

Peggy's eyes bulged like a startled bird. But she was fast, very fast, and she found her composure. She wouldn't have been caught by Cowboys with secret papers in her stockings.

"You are a rogue, John. Were you really born in a bordello?"

"So I have been told. But the tale gets more complex. I have no concrete knowledge of my father. He might have been a pirate, a former page of the king's . . . or some mysterious American general."

She began to giggle. "You're worse than a rogue," she said. "You're positively wicked. Are you suggesting that my Benedict sired you when he was fourteen or so?"

"'Tis within the boundaries of what is possible."

She clapped her hands. "That's delicious. Then I'm your stepmama, and I shall oblige you to behave and be attentive to your baby brother, Edward Shippen."

"I shall love him like a brother. But did you neglect to notice how disconsolate the general was at the ball?"

"Which general? Clinton or my own?"

"They are both yours, madam—"

"Peggy, *please*. I command you to call me Peggy."

"Madam, I cannot."

I was boiling with rage. I admired the bitch's intellect, but I did not like her Philadelphia airs.

"I told you, John, how the young officers slander him, almost to his face. They blame him for André's death. And my general cannot challenge them. It would destroy the army's morale. That's why you must help him. You promised."

"I will not go to Virginia with him and maraud the countryside. I will not burn farms."

"But you'll come to England with us. You must."

I did not answer Salome but left her with Arnold's little heir, and the princedom she imagined for him in a motherland that was no longer mine.

I MARCHED UP BROADWAY to the cadaver of Trinity Church—'t still hadn't been restored after the fire—and our Canvas Town that had grown bigger and wilder in my absence, as if the British were eating up whatever was valuable and spilling out the waste west of Broadway. The wind howled right off the Hudson, and ice had already appeared, in the first week of December. I could not find a single fence save where the generals lived with or without their wives. Firewood was as scarce as a treasure of doubloons.

I arrived on Holy Ground—'t was derelict, without a lantern lit. There were the same ditches that the rebels had dug five years before to defend Manhattan. I saw no customers floating about, sniffing the wares of some brothel. Half the houses were closed; the nuns did not parade on a porch, enticing sailors with their silken garments, their telltale bosoms, and the curve of a leg. Not a sailor could be found. I wondered if it was André's legacy—to erase Robinson Street, annihilate Holy Ground, to punish Clara and Gert in some diabolical fashion, punish them for their own ambiguity toward him, for their willfulness, for their involvement in the rebel cause, and just for being alive.

The Queen's Yard looked more derelict than most, as if some blight had descended upon the grounds. Gert's tiny orchard lay in ruin, with but one apple tree; her garden was a mound of clotted earth, her front porch a pile of broken sticks, without hammocks and chairs. I entered Gert's with much trepidation, found Clara in the parlor, smoking a pipe all by herself. She did not even glance up at me. Her legs were crossed.

She was reading Aeschylus, out of my library, the library I'd left behind.

She turned the page and condescended to notice me.

"Well," said she, "Gert's lost son, is it not? And in the flesh."

"Clara, I never ceased to dream of you . . . and the time when you visited me in André's jail. Did you forget?"

Suddenly she was all a shiver and could not hold the book in her hands.

"Oh, you men, you marvelous men, to think that my body gives you the right of possession . . . I do remember. 'T was like a sweet tooth. I wanted to make love to a certain Johnny who was about to be hanged. And I might have loved you for ever and ever had you not cheated the hangman—why have you waited so long? You go to balls with the English, you live in a traitor's house, and it's Gert who has to come begging for the bad boy. Who in hell do ye think got you out of that prison ship? She'd gone to Clinton, gone to André, and she went to Arnold."

"I am a lost son. Gertrude went to Benedict Arnold?"

"On her knees."

"I will soon be as mad as Orestes, that prince in your precious book who kills his mother . . . she had no right to grovel before Arnold and discuss my life."

"Pride doth not eat the lion, but the lion cub. She should have left you to rot."

"And rob you of your bliss? I might yet have a gallows built for me."

"Oh," she said, "I wouldn't have much use for a man who's been condemned twice."

I went to shake her, but she had a cutlass under her seat, and she struck me with the flat of her blade. I fell to the floor, and when I dove for her ankles, she struck me on the back. I crouched there, trying to surmise the lay of the land.

Clara loomed over me with the cutlass. "I'll kill you one day, Johnny. I promise."

"Darling," I said from my perch on the floor, "Prince Paul swears you danced for me. At the edge of Little Africa—danced every day."

She did not lower the sword. "Are you wheedlin', John? Begging for your life? Gawd, how skinny you are. It could make a person cry. Paul had no right to swear such things. A girl would have to be a fool to dance on a dock for a man who was a mile away. Do I resemble that girl?"

"Indeed," I whispered, mindful of the cutlass. Clara could have lopped my head off in a flight of angry passion. I had to reroute her storm. And suddenly I too was a shiver—'t was the joy of seeing her after twenty months, watching her flesh breathe, staring at the jewels on her slippers, drinking in the aroma of her arms. Let the cutlass fall. I would risk it.

I rose up right under the arc of her blade. Her very presence had emboldened me.

A prison ship was a far better college than King's—I'd lived on hopelessness and fetid soup, a dead man who could still imagine.

"Darling, you came to that dock because I brought you there."

"How?" she asked. "With the little intelligencer inside your pants? Did your very own rooster start to crow?"

I hit her, slapped her with a knuckle, while she held the cutlass. And then I cried.

Call it exhaustion . . . and my proximity to Clara.

"Mistress," I said, "we did play such games if memory serves."

"Where?"

"On my coverlet, when you were bald and I was but a beer boy."

The fight had gone out of her. "I cannot remember," she said.

"You were a mouse, frightened of the wind, but a willful mouse.

No one could order you where to go. We'd lie abed, and you would complete my thoughts like a mind magician. I'd think of cake, and you would describe that cake to me."

"You did not think of cake, John. It was a kite you had, a kite that some mariner had brought to Gert from Arabia. The nuns would give it names—Zephyr, West Wind, Turtle Dove. But you named it Squall."

I bled for that kite—'t was larger than a man, and of a color I had never seen before, a blue not found in all the colonies, richer than cream, a brightness that could beggar the eye. One of Gert's admirers ripped my kite in a drunken rage, ran it through. I was inconsolable.

"Clara, you could summon my thoughts while they were fomenting inside my skull."

She smiled with the cutlass in her two hands.

"I did dance for you on Paul's dock . . . I could feel the rooster in your pants—my Johnny's prick. It was the sweetest kind of longing. No man had ever dreamed of me that much."

I should have taken her in my arms, cutlass and all, but I could not kill the image of Anne plummeting into the marsh—that image stood between us like some kite with a razored edge.

"Dearest," I sang, "do you recall a woman who was in Gert's employ whilst I was gone? Blond, she was. With fair skin. A sensitive creature. She went by the name of Mrs.—"

"Anne Harding." Clara's nostrils quivered. A bulge appeared above her eye as she edged close. And for the first time with Clara I feared for my life.

"THAT'S ENOUGH," came a voice from Gertrude's open door. My own mum had been spying on Clara and me.

I ducked under Clara's cutlass and wandered into the bedchamber with spots in my eyes as vivid as lion cubs. Gert was in an old peignoir she never would have worn around her admirers. Her arms stood out like sticks. She had lost the better part of her plumpness. And Peggy Arnold had called her stout! The Brits must have set an invisible barrier in front of Robinson Street—another of Clinton's blockades. And my poor mother was under siege.

I hugged Gert, and she did not resist.

"Mother, I cannot remain on this island. I must kill a man."

"But I could have him killed for you."

"'Tis not the same thing . . . you shouldn't have gone to Arnold. Now I am indebted to him. And that's not a debt I care to pay."

"But he would have emptied Wallabout in your behalf. He told me so. He loves you, says you are the boldest of his boys."

"Mother, did you play vingt-et-un with him?"

She almost laughed. "I might have. But I didn't get the chance."

I saw no wood near the fireplace. I could feel the rawness in my mother's bones. The Queen's Yard was caught in a deep chill.

"Mother, have you been allotted no fuel?"

"Fuel is for the nabobs and men who control the *marché noir*. I barely have enough oil to light my lamps. Scavengers stole whatever wood we had in the shed, and then stole the shed. I have had to burn my own chairs, or we'd all freeze to death—John, you should not have troubled Clara about Mrs. Harding."

"Then why did you betray her to the British?"

I saw a look of disappointment in my mother's eyes, as if her lout of a son could not capture the missing pieces of a puzzle.

"We did not betray her," Gert said. "Malcolm Treat sent her to us."

"But Treat is head of Washington's secret service."

"Not whilst he is on parole. He asked us to hide her, not knowing she was already compromised. She came to us from British headquarters, and I simply sent her back."

I could not believe Gert. "Mother, you can't be certain."

"She kept messages in her bodice, little notes about our enterprise, where each of us was at a particular hour."

"And who found the messages?" I asked, dreading the answer.

"Clara did. Clara would have kicked her to oblivion. But I did not want Anne's blood on my hands. And so I returned André's precious little parcel—he must have had small use of her after that. He put her to pasture as his whore at Wallabout."

"And she was killed by one of my jailers."

"You may well mourn her, John. I cannot. Did you know that Clara volunteered for the same post?"

"Mother, my head is aching. What post could that be?"

"Ship's whore. Those imbeciles at Wallabout couldn't have harmed Clara. She could always suffer insufferable men. But André would not hear of it. He knew that Clara had volunteered for one reason—to find her way to you. And that possibility ate up André's heart."

I felt like some miserable hound that had let the fox flee the forest. I kissed my mother and went looking for Clara. I even had the boldness to enter her closet—'t appeared as if a hurricane had swept through. Half the furniture was gone. The nuns were selling their favorite settees as firewood.

I wondered if Clara had gone up to the attic to finish the *Oresteia* and find out what happens when Orestes meets the Furies. But Clara wasn't in the attic with Aeschylus. I heard her laugh coming from the back porch—a soft, seductive sound. She was with a British officer I had seen at Clinton's ball. They sat on a broken chaise like bloody lovebirds.

"Clara, may I press this young officer to allow me a moment with you?"

"You may not," she said without once looking at me.

"Then may I beg your forgiveness? I was imprudent. I should not—"

"Captain One-Eye," she said, "we have nattered enough for one day."

She clutched the officer's hand and led him into the dank interior of the house, leaving me on the porch with my own Furies—the monotonous song of crickets in Gert's back yard.

Fifty-One

I DID NOT SEEK THE CAPTAINCY CLINTON HAD proposed at his ball. I despised the idea of Arnold's rangers. But roaming with the rangers could get me firewood. There was no other coin in Manhattan, no other dream but burning wood, when everybody's arse began to freeze as winter attacked our city. Arnold had been commissioned to raise an army of deserters and Loyalists. As his secretary, I wrote the recruiting pamphlets that were then printed up by His Majesty's own printer to all the colonies. Washington may have been shivering in his drawers, but 't was the rare man who would desert him for Benedict Arnold.

Yet there was one surprise, a burly giant with the appropriate name of Champe, John Champe, who had been a sergeant major in a company of American dragoons and now emerged as our own peerless protector. We wouldn't have done much roaming without Sergeant Champe. Gales pounded York Island and did not leave a signboard standing in front of our shops, and we had to find wood for the nuns. But we couldn't crash into a military depot—we had no papers signed by Clinton. And Arnold's signature couldn't have gotten us any fuel. He was burnt in effigy, even in British Manhattan.

So Arnold's marauders had to maraud. We skulked about in floppy hats with feathers in them, the mark of provincial rangers. And since the town was lawless after dark, we waited until a band of scavengers appeared. We'd knock such scavengers to the ground, with Champe as our enforcer—big, burly Champe—steal their firewood, and march to Holy Ground.

I BEGAN TO FREQUENT certain grog houses on Little Dock Street. The pirates on board the *Jersey* had told me about them. One such, the White Hawk, was still something of a rebel retreat. I wore my uniform, because I didn't want these pirates to think me a spy.

The lads of the White Hawk knew I'd suffered on Wallabout Bay, and they welcomed me. They weren't idle. They scouted for Washington, swept the shores of Brooklyn and Staten Island in gondolas and whaleboats, harassing Loyalists.

They swore that Fat Tobias was still about, but not for very long. I had to make him suffer for what he did to Anne. And while I drank my grog and listened to pirates playing on the mandolin, I overheard a conversation that troubled me. The interlocutors were as pickled as Moses after he parted the Red Sea. I'd have drifted off if they hadn't mentioned "John the Giant"—John Champe. And suddenly the grog was gone from my brain. I was all ears.

They mentioned Weehawken and General Washington, and laughed at a habit Benedict Arnold had—he'd take a walk, return at midnight, and move his bowels in the privy behind his house. And they swore that John the Giant intended to grab Arnold while he was on the privy, but when, lads, when? These pirate-patriots, with all the grog in them, were tight-lipped about the particulars. Washington would be waiting in Weehawken, that much I could gather. Waiting with the hangman. They meant to twist my general on a rope right there, without the bother of a review board. Ninny that I am, I'd never suspicioned John Champe—Washington had lent him to our rangers as his very own spy.

Champe would loosen a picket from Arnold's fence. And while Arnold was on his "throne," Champe would crack him over the head—the yobs said this with a laugh. I had to fit the pieces into the puzzle. Champe would hold him as if he were carrying a drunken sailor, would avoid the night watch, bring him to the wharves, where a gondola would help him cross the Hudson.

I still didn't have the date. I could have struck them with my scabbard, but even if I'd loosened their tongues, I would have revealed my own hidden ace, and Washington could have found another giant to catch Arnold in the privy. But it was all posturing until I learned Champe's particulars. I couldn't abandon Arnold. I was in his debt.

I was like a dustman sifting for clues, collecting old bones, old war plans, old tactics. I could walk freely into British headquarters with the hanger I was given to wear. The generals and colonels bowed and touched my shoulder. Once or twice they called me "André." They even discussed the tactics of my own regiment. Clinton was sending along a lieutenant colonel to Virginia who was prepared to replace Arnold should he falter. Arnold was but a chit in the chain of command. And he couldn't even afford to jump into battle, lead his men, since Washington would use all his wits to capture him, dead or alive. And so he was a back-door brigadier who would have to sit in his tent or stand on a hill with a cane in his hand. Took three men to sit him on a horse.

ARNOLD SUMMONED ME to the house. I assumed he would badger me about Virginia—I wasn't going to ransack Virginia with his regiment.

I found him in his study. He sat with his tobacco jar and a jug of wine and a terror in his eyes that I had never seen in the wilderness. He didn't need me to parley about war. But I still started my preamble.

"Spare me, will ye, John? 'Tis Madame Arnold. I fear for her mind. Go to her. You have the words that might calm her. She likes you. She's locked herself in her sewing room and has abandoned husband and child."

I went upstairs to Peggy, knocked on her door.

"Go away," she rasped from within.

"John Stocking, Mum. May I enter?"

"Are you alone, John Stocking? I will not be tricked."

"Alone, madam, alone before the Lord," says I.

I could hear the patter of her feet, the twist of a lock, feet again, and a slight cooing. "Come in."

I entered the sewing room, but I couldn't find a piece of sewing material. She lay on a divan, with nothing on her shoulders but a nightgown. I could see the fullness of her body. She looked like some sea nymph caught in the cling of silk.

She couldn't fool me, lads, the way she'd fooled George Washington at West Point, with her bravura performance as victim of Arnold's treachery, raving that Washington's own Continentals had come to murder her child. Hysterics belonged to André's Theatre Royal. But she was not hysterical. She was fondling a silver locket. I strained to see what was inside—a snippet of black hair.

"Tell me about John," she said.

"Milady, I—"

"*My* John, John André . . . he was supposed to escort me to the Meschianza. He'd sat with us, helped me and my sisters sew our costumes. He drew my silhouette. I was a Turkish maiden, and he was my knight. But when Papa saw our turbans and our veils, he was furious with John André. He would not let us be part of the Meschianza. I had one of my fits. I didn't get out of bed for nine days. Papa threatened to have the whole British army knock down the door."

She stopped, peered at me. "What is that ridiculous thing with the feather?"

"'Tis a ranger's hat."

"Goodness, where do you range, John Stocking?"

I'd plucked a smile out of the melancholy nymph.

She looked inside the locket. "John gave it to me so that I might remember him. It was just before the British marched out of Philadelphia . . . with my life."

"'Tis only dreams," I said like a reptile. "You married Arnold, and André is dead."

"And I am but the ghost of the girl who couldn't wear her veil at the Meschianza," she sang like an actress who relished her own lines.

"Mum, would you have danced while Americans starved?"

"Yes."

"Would you have watched those silly knights of the Meschianza knock at each other while women and children were without shoes?"

"Yes."

"I have no more words," I said.

"But you do, you most decidedly do—tell me, tell. I'm voracious. You spent more time with André than I ever did. I knew him very little."

Yes, Mum, I thought to say, *knew him as your spymaster*. But I dared not introduce that subject with Arnold in the house. He might kill me before I had the chance to save his life.

"André?" I said. "A fastidious man, always changing his neckcloth."

She moved about on the divan with a certain discomfort and disdain, the silver locket in her hand. "Neckcloths are of no interest to me."

"I'd get rid of that locket were I you."

"But you are not me, dear boy."

I grabbed her by the silk of her gown, shook her twice. She had not considered that I would handle her so. Let her cry for Arnold. I'd have my own game of vingt-et-un.

"Milady, I don't have the time to coddle. Your husband is downstairs, deathly pale. He can think of nothing but you. You will go to him and ease his solitude, or I will come back and break all your bones, fingers first."

The nymph sank deeper into her divan. "You are a monster, John Stocking."

But my threat had put her into a trance. She came off the couch with her bosoms as high as her throat, and 't was clear how she'd enthralled little Hamilton and the commander in chief at West Point, rattling on to them while her breasts were bared.

She put on one of Arnold's robes, her hands hidden inside the sleeves, pulled past me, and went down to her husband in bare feet.

Fifty-Two

I WOULD LIE ABED AND THINK OF ANNE HARDING in Manhattan and how Major Malcolm Treat had seduced her into his services. Perhaps all officers on parole pursued the business of war, but Treat should not have abandoned her to the British, and not to Fat Tobias of Wallabout Bay.

When I wasn't abed, I spied on Sergeant Champe. And the night before Arnold was scheduled to leave for Virginia, with more redcoats than American rangers, I caught Champe pulling up a picket as Arnold went into the outhouse. Prince Paul was with me, and both of us carried pistols and swords, like buccaneers from some Caribbean cove. I'd rehearsed what I'd have to say to Champe, but rehearsals had nothing to do with a December night outside a privy.

We couldn't scuffle, or Arnold would hear us, and how could we have fought with a giant of such prodigious strength? As he pulled closer to the privy, with a horrible sneer on his face, my legs buckled out, and the prince had to hold me.

"John Champe," I said in a whisper.

He looked about, a primitive rage burnt into his brow. Then he recognized me.

"This doesn't concern you, Captain."

"Lower your voice, please."

He laughed. "Are you intending to do me bodily harm?"

"I wouldn't have the way or the will."

"Then what prevents me from walking up to the shitter and crowning Mr. Benedict Arnold?"

"Arnold himself. If I call to him, Champe, he'll cut you to pieces with his sword."

"Didn't see him carrying one."

"He always leaves a sword on the shitter for urgences such as this," says I.

"And if I don't believe you?"

"Then call to him."

But I'd destroyed his confidence. He put the picket back into place, cursed me, and strode off with that lumbering body of his cut in half by the moon.

The prince wanted to raise up a hundred huzzahs, but I had to silence him.

"'Tis but the prelude."

We waited until the candle went out in the privy and Arnold strode across the garden and into his house—the husk of a general.

"Are we counting stars, Master John?"

"No, we're like hens waiting for the first egg to drop."

THREE MEN TRAVELED down Broadway with the wind howling behind them. They wore long capes, scarves, and cocked hats, but I recognized Major Malcolm Treat and that pair of pirates from the White Hawk who'd babbled in their drunkenness about Benedict Arnold.

Paul and I moved upwind to greet them, so that the sentries guarding Clinton's headquarters could not catch sight of us.

Treat's face was red with fury.

"John Stocking, you are under arrest."

"I think not, major. This is the king's village if I'm not mistaken. And you are an American officer who has broken his parole."

"Stocking, I will have a summary court-martial right here on the street. I warned the commander in chief that you were a reptile."

I was no swordsman who could have disappeared with Treat to some clandestine dueling ground in the woods, so I hit him over the head with my scabbard. He sank to his knees, and the pair of pirates ran back into the wind.

"Stocking," the major said, "you will be a criminal for the rest of your life."

"And you, sir, are the reptile. Tell me how you recruited Anne Harding."

"I will tell you nothing."

"Paul, blow his brains out."

The prince hesitated. "But not here on Broadway, Master John."

"We'll drag him into the privy."

We grabbed his arms and feet. The little major befouled himself.

"Did you use all your charms on Anne, play the captured American officer on parole?"

"She was stranded. I . . ."

"And you told Anne to rid herself of Jaggers, that poor simpleton who was in love with her. And did you suggest that she move into a bordello so she could be near British officers?"

"'T was our big chance."

"You pushed her deep into danger, then passed her on to Gert. But 't was a little too late. The British took over where you left off. She was a floating whorehouse that served the warders of

Wallabout Bay. You continued to have her carry messages. But do you know who read your secret correspondence? Major John André."

"I don't believe you."

"He was a little less brutal than you. He had all the graces of a spymaster . . . get on that boat to Weehawken, Major Treat, or I promise you, I'll organize our own little trip to the *Jersey*."

"You wouldn't dare."

"Have you been to British headquarters of late? I'm the new André. I'll ask for a gondola and we'll bring you to the prison tub ourselves."

I kicked him, beat him like a mangy cur, mindful of the sentries outside headquarters, and Malcolm Treat crawled away in his besotted breeches.

I SHIVERED IN THE MOONLIGHT.

We traveled across rows of gateless gardens with their privies and arrived at the docks. It was long past curfew when the British bells had rung, when sailors returned to ships that piped the forbidden hours, but the most popular "royal" taverns were also gambling dens and hardly ever closed. I knocked on enormous oak doors; proprietors peered out at my feathered hat and let me in with my servant. There was nothing strange. Officers would bring their manservants to a gambling den with jars of cocoa. The servants would massage their backs during a game and prepare cups of chocolate.

No one knew I was looking for Fat Tobias. He was clear as crystal in my mind's eye—I could see him on the poop deck, the king of the *Jersey*, waiting to devour Anne.

We didn't find Tobias until the fourth tavern. He was hibernating at the Sign of the Dove. I knocked, we were let in, my hanger unsheathed, under my captain's cape, and Paul with pistols in his pockets. The yobs mocked my hat of a provincial ranger. I laughed with them. Tobias was at the far table, his own table, where he served as the banker of vingt-et-un. His fingers flew with cards and coins and the tavern's chips, little painted wooden owls.

He sneered and measured me with his eyes before inviting me into the game. I sat across from him, feeling the space under the table like a blind man. I knew that Tobias went nowhere without his pistols.

I had no gift for gambling, gambling with cards, but I'd served with the greatest gambler of all, Benedict Arnold running into battle like some immense carrier of death.

I never took my seeing eye off Tobias. I bore into him like a menacing drill. I wanted him to know that I was here to kill him. I was his executioner, not some jackal in the dark. He shouldn't have pawed Anne with his fat fingers, shouldn't have dropped her into the marsh.

He called out the cards. He collected chips, and still I looked.

"Johnny One-Eye, your nigger's too close to the table. He's casting his nigger shadow on my cards."

I wouldn't engage him in talk.

"Do ye miss that stinking whore what worked for André? Can you 'magine how many times I tasted her on the *Jersey*, Johnny-O? I broke her back with my lovin', and left you all the bitter pieces of her heart."

He could only read my one relentless eye.

I saw him twitch, and knew he meant to unman me under the table, blow out the fork between my legs with his pistol, but I shifted in the chair and stabbed him in the lower region of his belly, twisted the blade until he rose up in the chair in confusion and pain and complete surprise.

I never stopped. His mouth opened like a whale with little yellow teeth. His own fat body pushed down on the sword, and his trembling was close to suicide.

He died, lads, with my sword roving in his belly, and 't was as if he'd scared himself into dying.

I left the hanger in him and got up from the table.

Another jailer from the *Jersey* began to claw at my clothes. The prince shot him between the eyes. The jailers and soldiers of the tavern looked at us with fear and disgust frozen into their faces.

Paul and I stood back to back. No one harmed us, no one interfered. Once out the Dove, we ran like the Divil. I wasn't a trained assassin like the Brits. I'd stumbled into killing. But I had to avenge Anne Harding, or I would have remained sleepless until the next revolution.

"You put us in a pickle," Paul said as we ran. "Now the rebels and the Brits have a price on our heads, Master John."

"Cut the fanfare," I said, huffing a little. "The tables are turned. You're the prince and I'm the commoner."

The redcoats would never find him, an African in Little Africa, whereas I had the burden of my pink complection. I had a "history," where Paul had none. I wore a feather in my hat.

And that feather would protect me for a few more hours. I'd cross over to Brooklyn, hide in the marshes near Wallabout, next to Anne's watery grave, and then slip aboard some victualler bound for Canada. But I went at things willy-nilly and was seized by a sudden paroxysm—I had forgotten to say goodbye to Clara and my mum.

I did not have to avoid the British lookout posts. News of Fat Tobias had not traveled far from the tavern. I crossed Crown Street, marched to St. Paul's, and entered Holy Ground with an eerie silence at my back. Not a nun was about, not a sailor boy, not a mouse. The lamps inside the nunnery were not lit.

Two men interrupted me in Gertrude's garden. One was very large. The other had a rodent's feral eyes. I had not counted on this, but they, it seems, had counted on my coming here. The shorter one began to stroke his flint. I could see his face in the little scratches of light, the face of Malcolm Treat, and the colossal mug of Sergeant Champe.

"Not a sound," the sergeant said. "Not a peep. Looking for Mistress Clara, eh? A mangy lad always returns to his whore."

And he socked me so hard it created a stirring—a fury in my ears—that drove all the intrigue out of my head.

Fifty-Three

I WOKE WITH A NOOSE ROUND MY NECK. I WAS ON a wagon, with a coffin under my feet; the wagon was hitched to a couple of mares. And for my gallows I had a hanging tree. There were three witnesses at the side of the wagon—Champe, Treat, and another man, who was not in uniform. This third man wore a handsome neckcloth, a velvet waistcoat, velvet britches, and boots that were polished a deep purple. He had white powder in his hair. I would not learn until later that he'd come to Weehawken in his wedding clothes—he'd left his bride in Albany to plan and control the hanging of Benedict Arnold. Even in his velvet britches, he did not have the air of a civilian, or a copyist and aide-de-camp who sat on his arse and lived behind the lines—no, my former schoolfellow, little Hamilton, had that lean look of war.

Treat began to implore him. "Sir, why wait? He's guilty of treason. He let that traitor slip through our hands."

"Mr. Treat, we came for a hanging and a hanging we shall have. But not until His Excellency appears. I would not deprive him of that pleasure."

I must have reminded Hamilton of a leper or a toad. He would not glance at me, offer me the simplest regard. Champe walked behind the wagon. I liked it not. He could have launched me with one little shove of his hand.

"Colonel Hamilton," he said, "the Chief has better things to do than involve himself with one-eyed vermin."

There was a second of hesitation in Hamilton's eyes, and the sergeant major seized his chance. He shoved the wagon with both hands. The horses did not hesitate. And I swung in the air—be a liar if I said I had a great moral rebirth just before my suffocation. I didn't think of André's hanging, so similar to mine. I imagined Clara with blood in her mouth, licking the wounds of some poor slave in Dominica. I cried as the noose tightened, cried with a rage against the world, a rage that Clara would never lick blood off my broken neck. And just as I started to swoon, I stopped swinging. Little Hamilton had grabbed my legs.

"You will do me the honor, Sergeant Champe, of putting some solid support beneath this man."

Champe was a horseman, alright. He slapped one of the mares on her withers, and the wagon wheeled backwards enough to slacken the rope and put my feet on top of the coffin again.

"Sir," Major Treat said with utmost contempt. "The child weeps. Soon we'll have to wipe his snot."

"Mr. Treat, you will refrain from picking on this lad. He is a prisoner of war."

Hamilton grabbed Champe's canteen and fed me water, wiping my lips with his handsome scarf.

And then the commander in chief arrived on a great big chestnut mare, without a single bodyguard. I had not seen him since his perilous game of vingt-et-un at the nunnery, when he wore my mother's ribbon round his neck—he did not wear a ribbon tonight.

"Excellency," Treat said, "Arnold has got away because of this miserable boy."

Washington looked at me from under his long hat. "Why have you trussed him up to a tree?"

Champe and Treat quivered in front of Washington, but Hamilton would not.

"Sir, you mean to save *this*"—pointing his chin at me—"when you would not offer André a much more decent death . . . in front of a firing squad, as he deserved."

"Hamilton, I will not quarrel. Stocking wasn't caught with suspicious papers on his person."

"He has done worse," Hamilton shouted, his forehead bulging. "He's wearing the uniform of Arnold's wretched rangers."

"But he is not Arnold," Washington said.

"Excellency, shall we lock him in a barn?" Champe asked with a certain shyness.

"Bring him to headquarters. And you, dear Hamilton, may return to your bride."

The commander in chief rode off on his chestnut, her buttocks trembling with a love of movement, while I stood on my coffin and watched him ride into the dark.

WE CROSSED THE HUDSON AGAIN. This time I was awake. We were far above Manhattan, in the precinct of New Windsor. Champe wasn't spiteful while we sat in his wagon. The ferry had a most difficult time holding him and the weight of two horses. I suspicioned we would sink. But the ferryman, himself a soldier, leaned on one knee and dug his pole into the currents like some astounding spear. We did not topple, thanks to him.

I was billeted with George Washington, much to my surprise.

His headquarters was in an old Dutch farmhouse right on the river. His entire military staff lived there, four to a room. Washington liked to have his lads around should he need them in the middle of the night. He occupied a bedchamber on the second floor of the farmhouse, next to his office. It felt like former times, when I'd spent several days and nights with the farmer at the beginning of the rebellion. His orderly, Sparks, occupied a cot, while I slept in the same bed—a four-poster—with the commander in chief.

I knew not what to think. Was this how other prisoners of war were billeted? Sparks seemed joyous to see me again—his hair had gone gray. He walked with a limp. But it was the farmer himself who had aged the most. He was near fifty, and he'd had to cobble together an army for the past five and a half years, provide it with shoes, survive the cabals of congressmen and carping generals under his own command. 'T was Washington who fed the army, clothed it, fought the battles, ran his own stable of spies. Congress was bankrupt. Washington could not pay his soldiers. Some officers had already rebelled. But still he cobbled. His critics could not comprehend this. He was larger than their contradictions, relentless in his desire that the army not melt away, and with it the nation itself.

The British could not wear him down—'t was the little ingratitudes of men who were supposedly on his side. He had to fight a war in front of him and in back. That is why he needed his family of aides—Hamilton and the others had rescued him from chaos. And as he sat in his nightshirt, with biscuits and morning coffee, and without his war cloak, I was dismayed. He had to put on spectacles to read the simplest note or dispatch. His hand would follow each line, like some faltering music master. And his red hair, without its pigtail, seemed dullish at the roots.

"Sparks," he said, while I was still under the covers, "what shall we do with the boy?"

"Dispose of him, I'd imagine. Bury him in the garden."

"I have a better idea. I shall enlist him as my informal secretary. Mr. Hamilton is on his honeymoon. I dare not recall him from his wedding bed just to borrow his hand—Sparks, what have you done with the boy's uniform?"

"Burnt it and buried it, Gen'ral."

"Excellent—Mr. Stocking, will you not join us for some coffee or a dish of tea?"

I climbed out of bed wearing one of the general's nightshirts. I could have swum to China inside of it.

"Sir," Sparks said to the general. "The lad's neck was raw and I took the liberty of layin' on some grease last night."

"He deserves no grease. He ruined the hanging party I had prepared for Arnold—by the by, how is your general, Mr. Stocking?"

The trap was set before I drank my coffee—I was lost whether I damned Arnold or sang his praise. I considered it best not to lie while I was under Washington's roof.

"Excellency, he is but the shell of a man. He wanders about. The British love him not."

"Yet Clinton sends him to Virginia like some bulldog, so he can bite, bite, bite."

"He's been muzzled," I said. "Clinton has his own colonels behind him—'tis not Arnold who should worry you, but Arnold's wife. She's the vixen. She wrote the map of his betrayal. She was John Andre's pet and his spy."

Washington reached across the table with one long arm and delivered a slap that sent me flying—I could not imagine him capable of so ungentlemanly a sting.

"Stocking," he said, with blotches of anger on his very pale skin. "We do not speak of women in such a vile fashion. Not at this table. I shall make myself clear. You have no defined existence at New Windsor—in fact, you do not exist. For if you did, I should have to agree with Hamilton and hang you from the nearest tree."

He abandoned his coffee, flung a cape over his nightshirt, and strode out of the bedroom, leaving Sparks to deal with me.

Fifty-Four

THE GENERAL HAD A FONDNESS FOR FAIRY TALES. I'd recite to him about children lost in a forest, about mischievous wolves, princes turned into monsters by some strange alchemy, princesses who were only beautiful in the eyes of the most unmerciful men. He adored both the children and the monsters in these tales. And I could sense the remorse in him that he'd never had "monsters" of his own—save a bastard or two.

Like little John.

The one place where Washington allowed me any privileges was in the dining room—I took my dinners with his family, I supped with him and his aides, who could make neither hide nor hare of me.

Malcolm Treat had joined us at the table. He was no longer on parole. Washington had exchanged him for a pair of British colonels. He dared not attack me in front of the general. But Treat spread his poison behind the general's back, said I was the whoreson of Holy Ground, that I'd bewitched the general. I could not contradict him. Sergeant Champe was always near the farmhouse. He was a member of Washington's Life Guard, two hundred ferocious lads who surrounded Washington when he wanted to be surrounded.

But headquarters began to empty out close to Christmas—members of his staff requested time with their wives, away from the war; soon his whole military family had come down to Sparks and myself. And only then, in this hiatus, did I become his "second Hamilton." I would offer him a choice of words when he had to chide a general for some particular lapse. And he would hurl maledictions upon my head.

"Damn you, Stocking, I'm not enticed by your familiarity with the pen. There's evil in it! A wordish boy like you should never have been born!"

And Sparks would whisper in my ear. "The gen'ral's warming to you, Mr. John, he really is."

But mostly he was silent—Washington was a very silent man. He would sit and brood over his mutton and ask me for another fairy tale.

THERE WERE RUMBLINGS in the barracks. Soldiers had not been paid. Many of them were farmers, like the general. They'd lost their crops. Their wives had been menaced by British raiders. Their children did not have enough to eat. And then one barrack did rebel—threatened to march to Philadelphia and kidnap the Congress.

Hamilton would have arrested the entire barrack, had its leaders whipped. But Hamilton was not around. And the general, who wouldn't tolerate sedition, took another turn.

A few days after Christmas he visited this barrack without his Life Guard, and he brought me along. I filled our haversacks with hardtack and our canteens with Madeira; Washington loved to "nip" on wine. He wouldn't even lend me a horse. I rode with him on his sorrel, next to her beautiful white mane. We followed the Hudson, heard the sound of ice.

Several pickets saw us, but no one asked for the password of the day. Who could have impersonated this tall man with pale skin? And he was no less authentic, even with a strange civilian soldier sitting on his saddle horn.

An officer met us outside the barrack, next to Newburgh, where the army had its main camp. He was puzzled to find us alone. "Excellency, these men are mean. They shot at my hat."

"Captain, should I turn the place into a slaughter yard? The boy and I will go inside."

The barrack had no windows, just narrow slits in the walls. The soldiers inside could see us, whereas we were blind to them. Washington jumped down from his horse, then seized me right off the saddle. Next he removed his hat and asked me to unwind his pigtail. I was astonished—he would always have Sparks dress his hair whenever he went abroad. But he was coming to these soldiers in a state as wild as theirs.

The soldiers had barricaded the door. He would not bargain with them. We waited until we could hear the rumble of furniture being removed. Then Washington bowed and shoved me inside the barrack.

Meseems 't was but a prison ship on dry land—men living like wolves in a wooden cave. The floor was common earth without the little benefits of a garden. The entire barrack was lit by a lone lantern. And in the near darkness these men did look like wolves, wolves with bayonets. There was a full forest of them.

"Does this barrack have its own commander in chief?" the farmer asked.

First there was silence and then a voice barreled out of the dark. "It doth."

"And who may this commander be?"

Someone as tall as Washington strode into the lantern's narrow light. "Corporal Baines, Adam Baines."

I could not determine his features, whether they were hard and wolfish.

"Are ye a farmer?" Washington asked with a measured gruffness.

"A bit of one," said Baines. "I'm also a schoolmaster."

I had expected farmers and blacksmiths, not a schoolmaster. Yet Washington did have an advantage—he and the corporal could parlay like a couple of tall men.

"I have not come here to pay you. I cannot. Nor have I brought you a Christmas treat. There is none. I can promise you nothing. But my aide and I will share with you whatever is in our sacks . . . we cannot win this war without you."

The general did not speak another word. The soldiers put down their muskets and welcomed us into the barrack's hearth—a bench near a fireplace that breathed no fire. I opened the haversacks and passed around hardtack and cheese . . . and the Madeira in our canteens. We supped together in silence.

One or two soldiers sobbed—their own officers had declared a holiday and deserted them, but Washington had come into their wild land, had risked their wrath. He was clever not to bring Sergeant Champe. I was pitiful as a bodyguard. The barrack wolves could see that.

The general shook Baines' hand and we left the barrack with our canteens and haversacks. He hoisted me onto the horn, and we rode back to New Windsor near nightfall.

Pickets shone lamps in our faces, blinding us. "Who goes there? Speak, or I'll . . ."

Washington did not answer. His soul was still inside that barrack. But every single picket waved our sorrel through.

Anno Domini 1781

YORKTOWN

The Jersey Palisades
March 1781

He would creep along the Hudson, observe Manhattan with his spyglass from the Jersey cliffs. He could glimpse not a single tree in the lower part of the island. The landscape was utterly denuded. He could not attack Manhattan without the French fleet, and waiting for such fleet had become the biggest folly of the war. The French would not risk their battleships in an open conflict with the Crown.

And so the war had become a war of attrition between redcoats paid in silver and Continentals clothed in rags. He would sit on the Palisades when circumstances allowed and muse on what might happen were he ever captured by the Crown. They'd carry him across the sea in some cage, have him dine on fetid water. The king would parade him through London town in manacles—Britons perusing him as they might a Barbary ape. They'd call him George the Insurrectionist, toss offal in his eyes. But at least it would be a terminus, an end to something, and all he could do now was crawl on a cliff and conjure up a battle that would never happen.

He was like a prisoner of war with chains that rattled nowhere but inside his head. Perhaps such fanciful chains were an omen of some battle that was yet to be.

And whilst he mused, he heard a ratcheting sound that tore at him, as if some lost child were running rampant on the cliffs. He had no need of a spyglass to search his own terrain. Quickly he found the source of this commotion—one of his troopers, wearing manacles, wandered from tree to tree. A pair of Washington's pickets fell upon the poor soul and beat him into the ground. They stopped only when they saw the commander in chief.

"Excellency," said one of the pickets, "you must away from here. This madman has destroyed an entire barrack."

"And to what purpose?"

"To get even with our army. He swears that you have killed his son. And we thought not to disturb your leisure with a madman's idle claims."

"Leave," Washington shouted. "I will care for the prisoner."

"But he is a danger to you," said the second picket. "See how his eyes roam."

"Leave," Washington had to shout again.

And the pickets departed, grumbling under their breath.

"I will not thank ye," the madman said in a melodious voice.

Washington stooped and fed him water from his own canteen.

"I am your commander in chief. Yet you have a decided advantage. You know my name, and I know nothing of yours."

"A worthy commander would know the names of all his men."

And this manacled trooper began to weep. "I'm starving," he said between sobs.

Washington was choked with pity. He undid his haversack and shared his own portion of brittle cheese with the trooper. They huddled in the March wind, like field mice. And the commander listened to a most disturbing tale.

The trooper had a twelve-year-old son who worshiped Washington, carried his silhouette with him everywhere. And last winter Washington rode past the trooper's farmhouse near Valley Forge. The boy stood waiting with that silhouette in hand.

"Excellency, what must I do if I am not old enough to fight?"

"Badger the British," Washington shouted from his horse.

"And burn their cantonments," sang one of his aides.

The boy journeyed on his own through wind and sleet to a British cantonment on Long Island, was captured with a torch in his hand, and shot in the rudest fashion.

"But I do not remember meeting your boy," Washington said, benumbed by the tale.

"My wife was present when you rode past. She waved to you . . . and wrote me about Robert months ago. Your censors hid the letter. Did they think I would desert?"

Washington's provost did read every piece of mail. Ye gods, what sort of sedition could have crept between the lines? A fool of a clerk must have tossed that letter into some misbegotten sack.

The commander hid his own tears and commenced to tug at the trooper's manacles until his fingers were raw.

Finally a picket arrived with the keys to every manacle in creation.

Washington shouted into the picket's ear. "Sergeant, this man may destroy any barrack should it pleasure him to do so."

And he strode off into the dark, still waiting for an invisible French fleet.

Fifty-Five

THE NEW YEAR WAS NOT VERY KIND, ALAS. I WAS woken by Washington's Life Guard and tossed out of bed with all my belongings. It puzzled me even more when Sparks' cot was also removed. That little bed was a marvel—six and a half feet long, it served as Washington's own camp cot in the thick of battle. And now it was most rudely carried upstairs to a tiny attic in the eaves of the farmhouse, where Sparks was waiting. I considered it a very rare form of house arrest until Sparks told me otherwise.

"Mrs. Gen'ral Washington has come for a visit," he said. "And on such occasions, Johnny boy, we have to remove our arses from her gen'ral's living quarters."

Washington's missus had indeed arrived in New Windsor. I assumed that I would no longer be welcome at the dinner table, but I had misjudged the general.

Champe himself knocked on my door. "The Chief is vexed you have not appeared. Mr. Washington will not say grace without ye."

Sparks tied the ends of my hair into a pigtail and I rushed down to the farmer. His missus sat next to him in a homespun bonnet and homespun dress. She was short and plump, with the tiniest hands I'd ever seen, but she had enormous brown eyes. She did not look upon me as a ragamuffin, the way the others did. She grabbed my hand when Washington introduced me as his young friend who so recently escaped from Manhattan.

"Mr. Stocking was so eager to join my family, Martha, he tried to poison my soup—it was but a ruse. He is a patriot in his own fashion. He near died on board the *Jersey*."

"I'm delighted that you can share our table," she said to me.

Didn't even have a moment to consider Gert and wonder about the farmer's two *madames*. A pair of other faces had intruded upon my thoughts. Little Hamilton had returned from Albany with his bride, Elizabeth. She was a black-eyed beauty with the same tall hairstyle of Peggy Arnold—it resembled a manicured bush, entwined with twigs. Despite the bitter austerity of our rebellion, she wore the most astounding silk dress, with jewels sewn into the bodice. Her father, Philip Schuyler, was the richest landowner on the Hudson. He must have considered Hamilton a curious catch for his daughter—penniless, without a whit of property, "Ham," as the little colonel was called, did wear the green sash of Washington's aide-de-camp.

How I envied that green color, the boldness of it as it crossed Hamilton's chest. I would have given up everything to be the owner of such a sash. But Ham, it seems, did not have the same regard for it. He wanted a field command, and Washington would not give him one. There was much tension at the table because of the quarrel that was growing between them. And in his pique, Ham decided to prey on me. "Young fellow, might you tell my Elizabeth your impression of Manhattan's invaders?"

I was loath to answer. "I have none."

He turned to Washington. "Excellency, can you not seduce the boy, or put some honey on his tongue?"

I could see the anger build under Washington's eyes. "Hamilton, he is our guest."

"And that is why, sir, you treat him better than your aides—he is naught, a fopling with a ribbon in his hair."

"Mr. Hamilton," Washington said, both his hands trembling, "do not enter the boy in our quarrel. I cannot replace you, and I will not have your head shot off on some fool adventure."

"Fool adventure? I asked for a raiding party so that I might harass the king's men in upper Manhattan. I could accomplish this without straying far from headquarters."

"We will not discuss this at the table," Washington said, standing up in the middle of the meal. He bowed to Elizabeth Hamilton and his own wife, kissed their hands. "Forgive us. We soldiers must repair to our little war room on the second floor. We have urgent matters to discuss."

Washington exited with all his aides, but not until Hamilton said to his bride, "Darling, you must ask Mr. Stocking about his own fool adventures on board a prison ship. He led a most daring escape—seems the Divil delivered him from that inferno."

And I was left alone with Martha and Elizabeth. We drank Madeira and played vingt-et-un, played for buttons rather than doubloons. And now, when the two mums asked me about Manhattan, I chattered like a magpie.

I talked of Canvas Town and the Ethiopian Ball, of the British madness for cricket, but I would not talk of Anne Harding. Still, they pressed me for tales about life on board a prison tub, and I was loath to lie. "I had me a bulldog for a companion. Osiris."

"Did he rise up from the underworld like some godling?" Elizabeth asked.

"A godling, no? My Osiris was trained to kill."

"A demon, then."

"Just a dog who shared liver and milk with me, and was much kinder than my jailers . . . I survived, but Osiris did not."

"Johnny," Elizabeth asked, after much Madeira, "do you have a sweetheart?"

"Yes, Mum," I said, tho' Betsey—that is what Ham called her—was at least a year younger than I. "She is from the Windwards. Her name is Clara. She is very tall and reads Aristotle. Her mother was a princess and her father a planter."

"A princess," Martha said.

"Might we ever meet her?" Betsey asked.

"'T would be my dream, Mum."

That's all I dared say.

I WOULD SPEND LONG WINTER EVENINGS with my two mums, since Washington and Hamilton were constantly at their war table—events had worsened inside Virginia. Clinton's bulldog, Benedict Arnold, ransacked Richmond, and it seemed that he would soon cut a swath across the southland.

The farmer in chief prepared to send his most flamboyant officer, the young Marquis de Lafayette, to stop him. Lafayette was quite slender, had red hair and devilish red eyebrows, wore a powdered wig and long stockings, and had a very quick step.

Whenever he dined with us, Lafayette would charm Martha with his magic tricks and let Betsy borrow a garter that had been given him by the French king. Four years in Washington's service had seasoned him as a soldier. He idolized Martha's Old Man, and learned to speak like a Virginian.

"Mrs. General Washington, ma'am, I love my king, but I'd rather be here with you and Mrs. Hamilton in this little house than in the great, great garden at Versailles."

"I fear you toy with us," Betsey fluttered. "I have been told there is no place on earth like the king's palace—that to look upon it is to look at paradise."

The marquis immediately kissed her hand. "But might one not tire of such constant bliss? I prefer your rough land, and men who wear coats made of squirrel, mesdames. And I would much rather hunt down the British than chase wolves and wild boar in the king's park."

I said not a word. I felt like a creature in one of my own fairy tales, about to vanish forever in the forest.

And then, one afternoon, as I marched up to the attic, I could feel a familiar presence. The aroma was unmistakable. I could sniff Clara and her perfume a mile away. She was playing an odd game with Sparks—must have been something she'd picked up in the Caribbean. She rubbed knuckles with him and sang a song in a language I did not comprehend.

A little pulse beat behind her ear. I thought to capture it in my hand but could not. There was so little of Clara I could capture.

She turned about, knowing that I stood there. And the smile she made, with her freckles, was meant to break my heart. Sparks excused himself. I did not even know he was gone.

How did she get through our pickets? Had she come here with a message for the commander in chief? She did not seem in much of a hurry. Clara insisted that we make love with all our clothes on. She was enthralled by the prodigious size of Washington's camp cot. "Johnny, I could live in it for a week." She said I must take her without a single thrust, that my tumescence alone would rouse her insides, that the very best loving was slow.

I listened and did not listen. We drifted as far as the China Sea. And then, at the very same instant, we cried with a delight that was as melodious as her Caribbean song.

I CARRIED UP FRESH WATER from the well and washed morsels of her with her clothes still on. I did not ask questions. I concentrated on every curve of flesh. And when I scrubbed her privates, she allowed her eyes to flutter.

"Johnny, ain't you gonna ask how come I'm here?"

"No," I said.

"Then you must have figured out that I'm Gert's silver bullet."

My hand started to shake. I did not want to know about silver bullets, or the danger of a mad dash across British territory.

"Damn, you're only alive on account of Gert."

"I'm bewildered," I said.

"You are not. That night when Malcolm Treat and his giant were in our garden, Gert sent me out looking for the gen'ral. I swear, Johnny, I had to kiss three British guards, but no more than kiss, just to get through the lines . . ."

I did not want to imagine those kisses, but I could imagine Gert and Clara putting out all the lights in the nunnery once they saw Malcolm Treat and Sergeant Champe. Gert must have known they'd come for me. And so she launched her silver bullet.

"And the gen'ral had to ride back to Weehawken to save your rump," Clara said.

"Then he knew all the time that I'd be under the hanging tree."

"Course he knew. Wouldn't be much of a commander if he didn't."

SHE HAD TO RETURN to holy ground. I would not let her go. "Clara, you must have supper with me at Washington's table."

"I dasn't, Johnny."

"But Betsey Hamilton would love to meet ye."

I could feel a remoteness return to her body, a remoteness that always marked the beginning of a battle.

"Johnny One-Eye, she has no idea I am alive."

"But I promised I would bring my sweetheart to the table. I talked about you, about Dominica. She was most curious."

I should not have insisted, but insist I did. And it's only then that she decided to undress and stand naked in front of my one good eye. She forbade me to touch her, or fondle her in the least. She wiped the dust off her bodice with a little wet rag, straightened the struts of her pannier, shook the mud off her shoes.

Then she wiggled back into her clothes without breaking the line of her body, lean as a knife. She stood next to Sparks' tiny cracked mirror and redid her hair. She would not paint her eyes or her cheeks—wasn't ladylike, she told me. But my Clara did not require paint.

We went downstairs. Washington's family was assembled—not an eye strayed from Clara. The men rose in their boots and bowed, but Martha and Betsey seemed a bit abashed. I'd brought a colored girl to the table, a tall octoroon, and they'd expected an aristocrat from the Windwards. But they couldn't ignore the wonder of Clara.

"Mum," I said to Betsey Hamilton, "I'm most eager to introduce my fiancée."

"Child," Martha Washington said, "you must sit beside my Old Man. The war has wearied him. And we shall all benefit from your loveliness."

And so my Clara sat down next to Martha's Old Man. But something was amiss. I could see Washington brood, even with Clara beside him. He must have been fighting with Hamilton, who seemed equally grim. An anger, a fierce anger, made his eyes exceedingly narrow.

Washington said grace, and then we lit into the meal—mutton and Madeira, and a small fortune of peas, paid out of Washington's own pocket, since Congress had not supplied sufficient funds to feed his family.

"Mistress Clara," Betsey Hamilton said, "my husband is also a man of the West Indies. You must tell us about Dominica."

I could feel a pain flow through Hamilton. Clara must have sensed it too. She spoke with a prudence I had never seen before.

"I have no fond recollections, ma'am."

But Betsey wanted more. Perhaps she was still seeking an aristocrat—in coffee-colored skin. "Johnny has told us that your father was a planter."

"And a most cruel man," Clara said. "He was not gentle with my mama, and he looked upon me as a little stranger he had been saddled with."

Hamilton's face went purple. "Must we continue this farce? I am not amused that Mr. Stocking has brought his little doxy to sit next to my dear wife."

I rose up like some dreamwalker and struck Hamilton across his purple face. He tumbled out of his chair and fell backward a good five feet.

"Mr. Hamilton," I said, "I await your satisfaction."

I was sorry for one thing. Clara had fled the farmhouse while I was occupied with Ham. And I could not find her.

Fifty-Six

I EXPECTED CHAMPE OR TREAT TO STROLL INTO the attic and negotiate for Hamilton the time and place of our duel. But it was Martha's Old Man who knocked on my door.

"I beg you to enter, Excellency."

He had to stoop in the attic, could barely stand. He was not in his neckcloth, and I had a feeling he'd come direct from his own bed.

"Johnny, you must forgive Hamilton. He cannot sleep since he insulted Clara."

"Sir, Clara did not want to come to your table. 'T was most reckless of me to invite her without—"

"I shall grow colic if you continue," Washington said. "Clara is one of my couriers. She may sit with us every night of the week."

"That is most kind. But, sir, I did slap Mr. Hamilton. And I am at his disposal."

"And I promised Gertrude that I would protect you."

I'd swear my eye patch moved—the farmer had never mentioned Gert 'til now. It must have cost him to speak of my mother.

Buried inside a war, and here he was raking up powerful coals, coals that could stir his spirit, make him question the trajectory of his life. He loved Gert—I could feel that love in the tremor with which he said her name. *Gertrude.* But I could also see that he would not welcome my perusal of such private coals.

"Will you promise not to duel with Hamilton?" he asked, his calm a bit restored.

"I cannot, sir."

"And if I locked you in the cellar?"

"I would only escape."

"Then we are at an impasse."

And he left—for a moment I thought he'd never been there, that I'd conjured him up. But the sound of Gertrude's name still sat in my ears.

Then there was another knock—Hamilton sans neckcloth. I bade him enter. Can't help it, lads. I could not remain in a froth over a man who seemed filled with such despair.

"John," he said—he hadn't called me "John" since our days at college. "You must tell Clara that it was not Hamilton who spoke ill if her, but Hamilton's demon—his worst side. She is a most exotic creature. On another occasion, I might have flirted with her until your own head started to spin."

I laughed, but lightly. "Then we would have had to duel on the spot, dear Alec."

That's what I had called him at King's—*Alec.*

"Then we can be friends," he said. "My Betsey would like that."

"But I did slap your face."

"A trifle," he said, "the bark of a flea."

"A flea that knocked you off your chair."

"And deservedly so."

We hugged as only classmates have the right to do. I did believe Ham—he hadn't meant to harm Clara.

BUT HE COULD NOT RECONCILE himself with the life of a soldier in the rear echelons. He disparaged his own worth to Washington, who needed him now that the French, hunkering off Rhode Island in their scarlet britches and white coats, would not move their royal arses an inch closer to Washington's war. Ham was fluent in French, could speak it like a bird, while Washington knew not a syllable. The French officers delighted in Hamilton, preferred him to Washington's generals. Hamilton wove an elaborate web around Washington, seemed to anticipate his thoughts, and articulate them with a grace and speed the farmer did not himself possess. Hamilton had become the *fluency* of this silent man.

Washington was more and more despondent. He could not feed his couriers and their horses—messages would get lost in the middle of nowhere. "We are at the end of our tether," he told Sparks, and Sparks told me. That was why he wanted to recapture Manhattan, strike while he still had an army, but he couldn't strike without the French. And he would never convince Rochambeau, their commander in chief, without Ham. But he seemed to have his own private duel with Hamilton. They hardly spoke outside the war room. And once, on the stairs, Hamilton kept him waiting longer than he wished, and Washington snapped at him. "Colonel Hamilton, you treat me with disrespect."

Hamilton, who was as gloomy as Washington, snapped back. "I am not conscious of it, sir, but since you have thought it necessary to tell me so, we part."

The duel should have ended over a glass of Madeira, but did not. Washington made entreaties, but Ham would not be reconciled—'t was as if he'd delivered a mortal blow. Washington's face was like a death mask with a little moisture under the mouth.

I was a witness to such sad conversation, since the Life Guard moved Sparks, myself, and the prodigious camp cot out of the attic. Martha had gone to visit friends, while we went back to our old routine in Washington's bedchamber. Sparks would comb Washington's hair and I would read fairy tales to the Old Man. His teeth ached. He dreamed of his own doom.

'T was early in March. Hamilton was still at the farmhouse. He would ride with the commander in chief to Newport, confer with Rochambeau, then leave Washington's family forever. He was too distempered to bid me adieu.

The journey itself began with an ill omen. Washington's favorite sorrel fell through a hole on a rotting Connecticut bridge and plunged headfirst into the Housatonic. Washington had leapt off the sorrel's back just in time to spare his own hide, but the image of a plunging horse tormented him, and he had three of his Life Guard remain behind to look after the sorrel.

He accomplished little in Newport. The French gave him trifles, badges of honor to wear, but would not help him recapture Manhattan while their own main fleet sat in Caribbean waters. "Suicide, *mon cher général*. It should be suicide for your soldiers, I swear to God," said General Rochambeau. Not even Hamilton with all his fancy patter could persuade the French.

WHILE WASHINGTON WAS AWAY, I had my own little cabal. I was wandering near the Hudson in a little mountain of snow, dreaming of Clara, wondering when she would visit me again.

And as I ruminated along the river, with its own firm crust of ice, two men wearing hangman's hoods fell upon me and abused my person with such violent blows I could no longer bear the torment of it. But even in my decrepit state I knew these were not local highwaymen, but the savage sons of Washington's own retinue.

I could recognize Sergeant Champe and Major Malcolm Treat under their hoods—Washington had left both lads behind.

"Divil," Champe said, "ye have bewitched our Old Man—the Chief is caught in one of your webs."

And Malcolm Treat poked me with a pigsticker, a knife with a very narrow point. "Pack your things, you piece of filth. Even Washington can't save you. Breathe a word, and we'll mutilate your bitch. I promise you, I will personally chop off Clara's teats."

I realized in a nonce who was the real head of the household—Ham. These two yobs were frightened to death of him. Hamilton ruled headquarters, and the yobs had decided to pounce once he was gone.

They whispered among themselves and removed their hangman's hoods. 'T was as ill an omen as Washington's plunging horse. They'd decided on a simpler solution—murder me and bury my bones under the ice.

"Major," Champe said, "methinks I'll anchor our lovely boy with a rock."

I'd ruined their chance of immortality by not allowing them to grab Benedict Arnold. But Champe frowned when Treat poked me a second time with the pigsticker. "No need to bloody him, Major. Even after the ice melts, the currents will carry him to Connecticut."

A voice crackled in the silent snow. "Connecticut my arse!"

'T was Sparks with a pistol in either hand. He must have caught sight of us from the window near his cot and hurried down with Washington's own weapons.

"Sergeant Champe, you will pick up Mr. John and brush his clothes."

"And supposin' I didn't?" Champe said.

"Then I will shoot out your eyes and subject both of you to a court-martial."

Champe began to snort. "Who'd believe a nigger and a half-blind scribble boy?"

Sparks struck him across the face with both pistol butts.

"It ain't fair," Champe blubbered. "Johnny wouldn't be alive today if he wasn't our Old Man's rotten little bastard."

"Quiet," Treat said. "Shouldn't noise such tales about—Sparks, I could arrest ye for pointing firearms at an American major."

"And I could arrest you for being a rattlesnake—go on back to the house with Sergeant Shit."

Sparks sat down in the snow and allowed my head to lie in his lap. The silence behaved like a balm—I'd have to leave the farmhouse before that rattlesnake struck again. I could do my own minuet around Champe, but Treat controlled the general's secret service, could harm the nuns, get Clara killed. I could petition the general, but he was brooding over Hamilton, and I did not want to create yet another rift in his family. I'd lick my wounds, fill my haversack with food, and light out for the woods.

Fifty-Seven

DAYS PASSED, A WEEK, BUT I COULD NOT LEAVE the general. When he returned to headquarters without Ham, there seemed to be a black hole in the farmhouse. He had other young aides to accomplish Hamilton's tasks, secretaries who could parse his sentences, give them a melodic ring. But not one had Ham's agility of mind, Ham's flair to be all things at once—soldier, minister, moral philosopher, manager of money. The others were content to sit with Washington, work and dine with him, while Ham wanted to go to war.

I didn't have Ham's gift to pluck at the general, goad him like a gadfly, and draw him out of his melancholy. I did try whenever I wasn't watching my own back. Sergeant Champe seemed to have a single wish—send me to my quietus.

I had to walk with a light step, sniff in all directions, and also tend to Washington, sweeten his load a little. "Child," he said on a bleak afternoon, "tell me about Gertrude—and all the minutes, hours, and days I missed."

He'd had too much Madeira, and I couldn't reckon what he

wanted. I did not mouth a syllable. And he began to reminisce about my mother.

"She had the reddest hair in the world when we met. I could not take my eyes off her hair. I was talking to a maiden whose head was on fire. I did not find it extravagant. I was ill, and Gertrude fed me porridge with a great wooden spoon. I opened my mouth like a babe and listened to every command."

He did not summon up Gert more than twice, but when he did, this silent man had as much language—as much song—as a hundred Hamiltons.

I RECEIVED A PACKAGE from Albany at the end of April, wrapped in the finest paper—from Ham. 'T was the green sash he had worn as an aide-de-camp to the commander in chief. With this sash was a note in Hamilton's hand.

Little Stocking,

You must forgive poor Hamilton for not having bid you a proper au revoir. I was in a most unfortunate condition—estranged from the Commander and encumbered with loathing for myself. I want you to have this sash. It is my proudest possession, but I will feel most fortunate should you wear it one day, or have it simply as a token of my esteem.

Adieu.
Your Alec.

I could not keep from crying. No one had ever given me a gift of such magnitude. Could Ham have sensed how much I coveted the sash? Sometimes I wore it under my blouse where it could not be seen except by Sparks.

ON THE VERY LAST DAY OF JULY, Hamilton was given his own command—a New York light-infantry battalion. He'd been pestering Washington for months. I admired his steadfastness, that absolute faith in knowing what he wanted. I rejoiced with him, but in my heart I could not help but feel it was a demotion. He'd never been as firm a soldier as that soldier in the green sash. At headquarters he was heir to Washington's whole army.

Ham had helped Washington with a plan to recapture York Island, and now Washington watched that plan slip away as Clinton grew stronger and stronger inside his own deepwater base. "We have never seen more parlous a time," bemoaned the commander in chief.

Then, like some conjuration, Rochambeau and his white-clad troops appeared in Peekskill and settled in near Washington's own sprawling army, as if he'd suddenly agreed to grab Manhattan away from King George. The French were bemused by American soldiers, reminding them of brigands—a potpourri of white and black men, either half-naked or in hunting shirts, and without a genuine kettledrum to march with.

Rochambeau's headquarters were now on the Hudson, at Dobbs Ferry. He'd taken over half the village. His whitecoats were not like British or Hessian brutes. These lads bowed to women on the street, played with children, and would descend upon village taverns, where they stood locals to round after round of drinks. They were not just convivial—French army engineers would flatten prodigious bumps in the roads, mend steeples and weather vanes, pluck lost cats off trees with a newfangled machine that consisted of pulleys and ropes attached to a wire basket.

And in mid-August, while frogs went berserk in the heat,

Washington received a summons from Rochambeau—seems Admiral de Grasse and his armada had decided to leave Caribbean waters and would soon arrive in the Chesapeake Bay. And Rochambeau, a squat little man with the build of a bull terrier, hinted that the next theatre of war should be Yorktown, not Manhattan Island. General Cornwallis, Clinton's second in command, had moved his men and war machines to Yorktown, where he was busy constructing a deepwater base. But Rochambeau had realized it was also a deepwater grave—surrounded by water on three sides, Cornwallis' citadel could be overrun the moment a French armada appeared in the Chesapeake and blocked off his escape to the sea.

WASHINGTON AGONIZED OVER THIS STRATEGY, fearing that he couldn't move a French-American army across four hundred miles of terrain and not have Clinton discover his whereabouts. He would fail unless Clinton's spies were utterly convinced that Washington still planned to seize Manhattan. And that's when Rochambeau consulted his engineers, who built magnificent ovens on the Jersey Palisades, ovens that could provide bread for thousands of troops. Not a single loaf was ever baked, but Rochambeau's ovens were like sorcery—watching huge metal caves with fiery mouths rise above the Hudson, right across from their Manhattan headquarters, the king's men could almost feel the specter of an invading army.

Alas, I had other specters on my mind. We'd moved our headquarters to a farmhouse near the French, and Washington seemed lost in the dream of war. He was plotting the route of his army—a sea voyage on land—since he had to find some "sea" where he could conceal his men from British eyes. And the more Washington hid in his war room, the bolder Malcolm Treat and his cohorts grew.

Why did I vex him so? He must have wished in his heart of hearts that he were Washington's love child, not I. 'T was most unreasonable. He looked upon me with utter malice—as if I had appropriated *his* eye patch and *his* general. I had become, for him, the Divil.

There was so much turmoil inside headquarters, Treat could move against me at will. One of his lads from the secret service tried to lure me into the woods with thc promise that Clara was waiting—I was sorely tempted to go. And once, while I was in the parlor, a pigsticker flew right past my ear. Champe must have crouched in some closet, familiarizing himself with my footsteps.

I was a little safer at night when I lived in the same bed with the commander in chief. We would lie together in the dark, near a dying candle. And while Sparks snored on his cot nearby with great stentorian grunts, Washington broke his silence and interrogated me like some manor lord. "Dost thou love thy mother, boy?"

"Yes, Excellency."

"And wilt thou promise never to abandon her?"

"I cannot promise, sir, but I will try."

I dared not mention my own misfortune while he was so abominably tired. And what could I have said? That his spymaster, Malcolm Treat, who had conspired with Rochambeau to create such monstrous ovens and had lured Clinton's spies into countless death traps, was insane on a single subject—Johnny One-Eye? Treat had contributed to Washington's war. I had not. I remained silent, while Washington stared at the candle's last little tail of smoke.

"I have wronged ye," he said. "I ought to have taken you hunting—at least once in your life. I ought to have thrown you in a crick."

"But I might have drowned."

"My bird dogs would have saved you," he said. "I ought to have tended to your tuition—instructed you in the art of skinning a rabbit. I gave you very little."

"But wherever I am, and in whatever straits, I will imagine what it would have been like to hunt with you."

"I have no love of imaginings, John. And so I do not imagine."

"How could you, Sir? You have a whole country to consider."

I could not sleep. My brains swelled with the sadness of my lost tuition. I tried to dream of skinning a rabbit. I failed. And I thought of the Old Man, who seemed so awkward he could not decide what to do with his enormous hands and feet. His feelings, his intimacy, all his vital lines were never on the surface. He was someone who did not like to show. He would have been pitiful inside a playhouse. But he could stroll into British Manhattan, redcoats all around, play vingt-et-un with Sir William Howe and win.

Sir William could not measure my general—saw nothing beneath the eyes. And Washington would never have gone to see Gert on Holy Ground without gambling his own life. Gert was his America—not the America of Martha and Mount Vernon—but of a certain bawdiness that seemed to elude him, of imagination he seemed to fear. He could not have conducted a war without such imagination, conjuring up a people and an army with the force of his mind.

I did start to dream—I plunged into the Housatonic with Washington's chestnut mare. 'T was delightful to fall through a bridge. I was never so certain of myself. I rode on that sorrel's back with the water up to my chin, the currents ripping away at the saddlebags. I clutched her reins with both hands, and when the reins unraveled with the violence of the water, I clutched her neck—it was the only thing in the world that could compare with Clara.

Fifty-Eight

A FACE PULLED ME FROM THE HOUSATONIC, ruined my sleep. Then I recognized him with his reddish hair and azure eyes. He did not have a manly figure. His shoulders were much too slim. But he had a certain puissance in the way he moved—like a leopard light on it feet. He'd come with coffee and little cakes. He was wearing a powder horn and a white plume in his hat—Sparks and the commander in chief were already gone.

"Rise up," Ham said. "I have stolen you from the Old Man and suborned you to my battalion. Johnny, I have seized all your rights. You will ride with me."

Alec was my rescuer angel—with Malcolm Treat around, I might not have lived out the month.

"I repeat," he said. "You will ride with me and have the rank of honorary lieutenant."

"Ham—beg pardon, Colonel Hamilton. I do not wish to have a rank."

"Honorary, I insist, rather than acting lieutenant, since our government cannot afford to pay you. You will not be issued a uniform, but you may wear your green sash."

"*Your* green sash, sir."

"For God's sake, we're not in the field—call me Alec. And 'tis now officially your green sash," he said.

"But I have no right. I have never been an aide-de-camp."

"I consulted His Excellency. You did from time to time perform the duties of an aide. John, you will wear the sash!"

I MARCHED TO PEEKSKILL with Hamilton's New Yorkers—a rigmarole of rags and blue coats, men with muskets and cartridge boxes, canteens and haversacks, men hatless or in leather caps, with clay pipes in their pockets, with salt horns and the simplest shoes.

I was hatless, like half the army. I wore a velvet coat Sparks had given me, leather britches, a white blouse, long stockings, a neckcloth, and my green sash. The other Yorkers were mindful of my sash. They saluted, called me "'Tenant Stocking, sir." But I was not much given to officers, preferring to march like a wolf, the way I'd marched with Arnold under the walls of Quebec.

I did wear a hanger, but declined Hamilton's offer of a horse. I marched on foot with all the lads. Hamilton knew better than favor me. He was our colonel, and the men did adore him, tho' some members of Congress called him a rapscallion because he had helped raise up the First Rhode Islanders, a regiment that was mostly colored, scaring slaveholders half to death.

We went along the river, with muffled drumbeats, crossing the Hudson in barges and small boats that had been waiting for us at King's Ferry, Ham and his officers riding their mounts onto a single raft, right near the end of August.

I was not looking to adventure my life into a moment of glory.

But I felt strong among these men as we shoved across the river, without much wonder at who we were—mechanics or farmers and free blacks, undivided on our little boats, except that I had a singular advantage. Our destination—Yorktown—was unknown to them. I could understand Washington's reticence to inform his own troops. He had to hit Cornwallis with the fist of surprise.

WE WAITED ON A TINY BLUFF until other battalions crossed, men as ragged as we—horses drowned, cannons sank, boats smashed against the reefs, their passengers bobbing in the currents until some other boat plucked them out of the water.

Then a battalion of Rhode Islanders crossed in a single great barge—a boatload of black men in tricorns. Their officers were all white, but it seemed of little consequence. These Rhode Islanders ruled themselves. The officers looked like dwarfs with red faces against a background of tall, dark men with little clay pipes and backs straight as a board.

Unlike the rest of us, they were not the least bit bedraggled. They wore blue leggings, coats with silver buttons that glittered against the sun and would have driven an enemy insane on the battlefield. They all had bayonets of the bluest sort of metal and would scratch themselves and pick their teeth with such instruments.

And who were these warriors? Fishermen from Newport; hunters, whalers, and foundry workers; some were even slaves. But they'd responded to Washington's call to arms against the king. They didn't own property or have a seat in Congress—most of them had never seen Philadelphia. But they would have gone to the Divil for their "little chief," even if he was a planter with a hundred slaves. He was also a gen'ral who sat on a horse, and was at least as tall as they were.

I pitied the king's men, pitied Cornwallis, who would have to struggle against such warriors. We marched beside them in the dust for sixteen days, dust that settled in our ears, formed strange little masks around our eyes. We paraded on Market Street in Philadelphia, with Rochambeau and his whitecoats just behind us, not a speck of dust on them. Their fifes and drums made splendid song. But no one really watched the whitecoats. Philadelphians were beguiled by tall black soldiers in a whirlwind of dust.

We marched in more dust to Head of Elk, where we climbed onto French barges that brought us down the Chesapeake, past the lights of little tidewater towns—folks wondering at so many black men in a barge, black men with blue bayonets.

We landed near some swamp and marched to Williamsburg—the meeting point for our assault—after having wandered over a month. A city of tents rose up around Williamsburg, like scores of soldiers strangulating an entire town. We were right near the Continentals' command tent. I'd come here to fight, but my heart seized up when I saw a man in an eye patch come out of that tent.

"'Lo, John," said Malcolm Treat as if we were classmates at King's. But I was not perusing him now. I'd heard a laugh from inside the command tent, bold and provocative, with a ring I could not forget. A tall woman galloped out of the tent, so tall she had to tilt her head. She wore a pannier, and much powder and paint. She clutched Treat's arm, but she must have felt her Johnny boring into her. She looked up and her doxied eyes flickered once—'t was neither shame nor regret, but a recognition, silent and sad.

"Clara darlin'," Treat said, "ain't you gonna say hello to your fiancé?"

But my belovèd dragged Treat away from the tent.

Fifty-Nine

WE MARCHED TO YORKTOWN THE VERY NEXT morning, the 28th of September as it were, through woods thick with briars that scratched my face. I licked at my own blood, welcomed the taste. The air had turned crisp of a sudden; we'd entered some kind of autumn—the ground no longer steamed under our marching shoes—but I cared not about the seasons. I might have gone mad in these woods, near a tobacco farm ravaged by the British and their raiders. I could have hid among dead tobacco leaves, buried myself in tidewater, stayed with the frogs. I knew Clara couldn't have signaled me in some open manner whilst she was with Treat. Was she dealing in silver bullets again?

We were an army despite our riven uniforms and ragged ways, and Washington rode up front on the same sorrel that had crashed through the bridge in Connecticut, or perhaps some ghost of that horse. The Rhode Islanders were right behind him. And there was a certain splendor seeing Washington on his sorrel, followed by a bevy of black men.

WE SETTLED IN A GOOD MILE from Cornwallis' cannons, Washington and Rochambeau in separate headquarters and separate camps. But there was constant traffic between the two camps, French officers galloping hither and thither with their aides.

Cornwallis had used a thousand blacks to build ten outer forts, each with moats and a shield of sharp sticks, to protect the heart of his citadel. Yorktown itself sat on a bluff, giving Cornwallis the advantage of higher ground. Washington would have massacred us all had he risked a frontal attack on Cornwallis' bluff. Neither he nor his generals was familiar with sieges and trench warfare. But Rochambeau's engineers had delivered a hundred sieges—the siege of Yorktown now belonged to them.

They and their sappers only worked at night, building trenches in the dark, protecting them with mounds of earth and twigs that fooled Cornwallis, at least for a little while. And during the day there was much bruit in Washington's command tent. I would have gladly kept away. I did not want to meet Clara and whatever officer she would parade with next. But Hamilton kidnapped me right out of my tent.

"You shall be my secretary," he said.

And as we traveled across our own broad camp with great vigor, General Lafayette broke into our stride—he and Hamilton hugged and kissed. Lafayette had recently recovered from the marsh fever he contracted in the Carolinas and was exceedingly gaunt. He no longer had to bother himself with Benedict Arnold and other raiders—Clinton's bulldog was back in New York, sitting on his haunches, a general with a mansion and no men.

We'd entered the perimeter of Washington's command post—sentries saluted us and stared at my green sash. I could have been a Chinese admiral in their eyes. I was with General Lafayette.

I followed him and Hamilton into headquarters, a tent as large and noisy as some Persian bazaar I had read about in a book of travels. There were five conversations at once, five cliques, five cabals petitioning the commander in chief—colonels from the Royal Deux-Ponts, the largest of the French regiments at Yorktown; Rochambeau's engineers; Lafayette's aides; Washington's own engineers; and his secret service.

The Royal Deux-Ponts would not even look at Lafayette. He'd arrived in America with some madcap notion of liberty and had seduced the rebel Congress into declaring him a general. He couldn't have been a captain in their own regiment. But it was Lafayette and not the Royal Deux-Ponts who held Washington's ear. Yet he still had to compete with the other cabals. I could not listen to all that commerce, could only concentrate on Clara. She was with Malcolm Treat, wearing her powder and paint.

For a moment all conversation stopped as Washington regarded me with one of his subdued smiles. And every whirling face inside the tent regarded me at the same instant, even Clara. Then Washington looked away, and the furor started all over again. I stood near Hamilton. He and Lafayette were talking about some insane dash up Cornwallis' cliff. I did not listen.

I had to stitch together why Clara was the lone woman in the tent. And like some prince of spies I soon gathered that Major Treat had been sending her through enemy lines.

Seems Cornwallis' citadel suffered a shortage of food, and Cornwallis was pondering how to reduce the size of his garrison. He'd settled on the most expendable items—the black soldiers and slaves who had built his ten forts. He'd promised them freedom, their own little heritage in Yorktown, but he had no further use of them now. Besides, an epidemic of smallpox was raging through the colored barracks, an old ramshackle barn. As the tale deepened, other conversations died.

"Excellency," Treat said, "their epidemic may soon be ours."

Washington interrupted him. "Major, we must listen to Clara—Clara was within the walls, not we."

Fool that I am, it took me the better part of an hour to comprehend that her paint was but a disguise. Ye gods, it was not her beauty alone that held the eyes of the Royal Deux-Ponts and the rebel chiefs. She had as much turbulence on her face as any of these men. And she had one great advantage—she knew how to enchant; they, it seems, did not.

The little major and I kept measuring each other with all the slanted precision of one-eyed men—he was convinced that John the Divil had walked into Washington's tent with the sole purpose of stealing Clara away. But Clara wasn't considering him or John the Divil.

Clara bowed to the commander in chief. She was the tallest person in the tent save Washington himself. "Excellency, I hear say that Cornwallis had his Britishers infect the Africans with smallpox so that he might catapult them over the ramparts—"

"And bring our army to ruin with the same disease," Hamilton said.

Washington's cheeks mottled with rage. "I thought the man indolent in his defense of Yorktown, but there is evil behind that indolence."

"Couldn't we help the men in the barn?" Clara pleaded. "Couldn't we bring 'em blankets and sweet water?"

"Ah, show we are Samaritans," said Malcolm Treat. "Mistress Clara, we are not a hospital ward."

"Yet I fear that by not helping them we may harm our own cause," Washington said.

"They are of small worth to us," insisted Treat; having Clara under the same canvas roof with John the Divil had maddened him. He mocked her in front of the commander in chief. "Sir, shall we send Clara through with a blanket brigade?"

"Would that I knew how. Then I'd be worthy of Rochambeau's engineers—Mr. Treat, could we not persuade some citizens within the walls to help these afflicted men?"

"Excellency," said Hamilton, "allow me to find my own route to that barn."

"Mr. Hamilton, we cannot spare you."

"But you can spare me," Clara said. "I could summon nurses within the walls—be my own nurse."

Treat was about to gnaw at her. "Impossible," he said with a twitch. "Lord Cornwallis will capture Clara."

"*Mon Dieu*," said one of the Royal Deux-Ponts, patting his brow with a perfumed handkerchief. "We should make better use of Clara. Have her sleep with one or two of Cornwallis' aides. What a *trésor* she will bring back to us!"

I did not like this Royal Deux-Pont and his perfumed handkerchief. Hence, I wandered into the fray.

"Excellency, if you do not help Cornwallis' black soldiers, you will bring havoc to your own troops."

"How so?" said Treat, his nostrils flaring.

"The Rhode Islanders might rebel should they get wind of our intransigence, our unwillingness to help those wretched men."

"Hang the Rhode Islanders!" shouted Treat. "I'll put them all in irons."

And while Washington and his commanders looked at Treat, Clara vanished from the tent without the littlest nod to me.

Sixty

SEEMS CORNWALLIS' CITADEL HAD SWALLOWED up Clara. I wanted to break through the walls and carry her home on my back. But I was a lad without a reasonable plan. And while I pondered, French engineering parties dug all night, closer and closer to Cornwallis' ten little fortresses in two parallel lines. 'T was a marvel to behold—the miracle of trench warfare. Our own fortifications grew out of the trenches like earth-and-metal flowers that were finally in range of the citadel itself. We fired at the British without mercy until Cornwallis ran from his headquarters in town and hid near the harbor.

He had to abandon three of his outermost fortresses, whilst we dragged the heaviest cannons up to our own little forts.

And then, amidst all this nocturnal movement, there was much hurly-burly in the woods near our camp. Cornwallis had begun to expel infected Negroes from his parlous paradise—drove them like cattle through the open rump of a particular fortress.

These men now wandered in the woods. Our own lads panicked, crawling deep inside their tents. Others ran to the woods with their rifles, but they could not get near the Negroes. A phalanx of Rhode Islanders was standing between them and the woods. Said Rhode Islanders didn't menace the riflemen—simply smiled and sent them back to their tents.

But they did not prevent me from going through. I saw black men with blisters on their mouths, others with scars that had turned their faces white; some had eyes so raw and red you could not locate the eyeball; still others ran in circles. I did not know what to do.

Then a voice beckoned from within the woods.

"Johnny One-Eye, you gonna help me or stand there forever?"

Clara appeared from behind a tree with blankets and pails of water, a candle tied to her forehead, canteens hanging from her military belt; she had her natural freckles rather than paint. She wasn't wearing a pannier. She had the britches of a man.

"And you dasn't pester me with questions, ye hear?"

I had said not a word.

"They're contagious, John. And you're not to get too close. But you can give them blankets, and feed them water with a wet rag."

"Clara," I said, sobbing now, "you'll get sick if—"

"Didn't ye promise not to blabber? I had the smallpox in Dominica, survived an epidemic. My mama nursed me through—I can angel them as much as I want. You cannot."

She gave me the blankets, the pails, and wet rags.

"Found a woman who lives right on the river, paid her to care for them. Mr. Washington lent me the money, and it wasn't from the paymaster—it's his winnings at vingt-et-un with Gen'ral Rochambeau. And I have to give these men instructions on how to get to the river lady. But you must keep their mouths wet, or they'll die. And you must give them the blankets until you run out of blankets, ye hear? And put your neckcloth over your mouth."

I drank in her sweat that was wondrous as any aroma.

"I missed you like the Divil," she said. "But Malcolm Treat wouldn't let me near ye."

She tied her candle to my forehead and I started distributing blankets and wetting the mouths of the Negroes with my rags. "Master," they kept asking, "what is your name?"

"Johnny One-Eye," I said, right through my neckcloth. "And I'm nobody's master."

Some of them shivered and fell in front of my eyes. 'T was Clara who picked them up, led them deeper into the woods. I could understand Rochambeau's engineers, but not a war that would deliver black soldiers and slaves unto pestilence.

Two lights started to blink and move along like some invisible monster—then this monster became all too visible. Major Treat and Sergeant Champe had arrived with enormous lanterns.

"Well," Champe said, the pistol in his hand shining like some magnificent silver article. "If it ain't ol' One-Eye with the boogers."

"Shut up," Treat said, swinging his lantern wildly to capture a wider swath of the woods—Clara walked right into the lantern light.

Champe was appalled. "That ain't her, Major. That's Clara's apparition."

"Shut up," Treat said. He was calculating in his mind whether to kill me. There was only a forest of black men as witnesses—and Clara.

"'Lo, darlin'," he said, "where did Johnny get all the blankets?"

"From George Washington's private treasury," she said.

"Clara's tricking us," Champe said. "Major, that is surely so."

Clara did not wait for Treat to aim at my heart with his own pistol. She whirled about and stepped in front of me.

"You still love this odious boy," the major said. "Clara, I shall count to three."

Clara clasped me by the britches, and I could not move—I did not want her to die.

"*One*," Treat said. "*Two*—Clara dear, it ain't no jest."

He couldn't survive without getting rid of his own Divil. And he was willing to fire right through Clara's flesh. But he never did count to *three*. Suddenly, Treat shoved his pistol into a pocket, plucked off his neckcloth, and placed it over his mouth. Then he picked up a water pail and began to wet the mouths of the infected men with much ado. Treat's transformation made sense once I discovered two Rhode Islanders standing with their rifles at the very edge of the lantern light, their faces obscured.

"How go ye, 'Tenant Stocking?" a voice shot out of that obscurity.

"Well as can be in wartime," I said with the deepest of shivers, for I desired the Rhode Islanders to enfilade Treat, but I would only have compromised Clara, prevented her from aiding those poor black souls stricken with the smallpox.

We worked together—Champe, Treat, Clara, and myself—like some independent army, until the woods cleared of these black souls.

Clara touched my hand, then slid away and trudged back to headquarters with Treat, Champe just behind them. I could have raged at the moon, but I saw none to rage at. Clara was, I could now see, much more of a soldier than I. Damn my own reticence, my own inclination toward folly—I was always at the edge of things.

The Rhode Islanders had already gone, and I marched out of the woods all alone.

Sixty-One

THE COMMANDER IN CHIEF WAS FOREVER ON his horse, riding hither and beyond, scrutinizing trenches his own engineers would not have been able to build.

'T was Washington who accompanied the French engineers into the foulest weather. And at dusk on the 11th of October, as the sappers prepared to dig, these engineers realized that they could not complete their system of trenches. Two of Cornwallis' little forts, known as Redoubts Nine and Ten, jutted out too far, and it would have been much too dangerous to dig.

Washington ordered his cannoneers to subject Redoubts Nine and Ten to a relentless barrage of fire. And on the afternoon of the 13th, Hamilton's own sergeant major went about camp selecting lads for some kind of secret mission. I was proud as the Divil to be among the chosen.

We were moved to a much smaller camp, where I met parts of my own New York battalion. I saw Rhode Islanders; I saw Royal Deux-Ponts. I saw Hamilton and Lafayette and a little string of aides. But there were no marching orders. Nothing was said. The Rhode Islanders puffed on their pipes, dreaming up maneuvers mingled with tobacco. The Royal Deux-Ponts batted a dried pumpkin with their heads; so skilled were they at it that the pumpkin never touched the ground.

And then the commander in chief arrived at our camp on his chestnut mare. He did not climb down to greet Hamilton or Lafayette. Our three little armies encompassed him—Rhode Islanders, Yorkers, and Royal Deux-Ponts sans pumpkin. We had not scaled a single wall so far, had not seen the enemy's eyes. Hamilton had not led a single charge. But Washington told us from his saddle that we had to capture Redoubts Nine and Ten, else we could not win the war. Cornwallis had reinforced the redoubts—they were manned with muskets and mined with sharpened sticks to discourage and repel even the hardiest of attackers.

"Clinton's armada is sailing from New York. We must take Cornwallis before that armada arrives in the Chesapeake."

Washington spoke with his usual reserve—yet 't was his very difficulty, his unmusical voice, that left so large an impression—the silences between his sentences seemed to reveal a prodigy of feeling. He had not remained with us more than fifteen minutes. But in some primitive fashion, he already inhabited our insides, tightened our bowels.

THE ROYAL DEUX-PONTS were meant to attack Redoubt Nine with their own war engines—bayonets and hooked ladders, heavy axes and little explosive bombs—while Rhode Islanders and Yorkers in ragged uniforms would attack Number Ten, with Hamilton leading the charge. I was wrong about Ham. He had not really thrived as Washington's aide-de-camp, had been more like a brilliant somnambulist. I had never seen such a glow upon him, the glow of a warrior angel.

He met with every single one of his boys, knew every name. He shook our hands, shared a pipe with the Rhode Islanders. He hugged me and kissed my cheek in front of the boys.

I barked at him with much affection. "Colonel Hamilton, you never did require a secretary. You have always been your own."

"Forgive me, John. You have uncovered our little fraud. But I wanted you with us. You'll wear the green sash—'t will be our banner."

We'd spent the night in our own little encampment. I did not dream of war. I'd dreamt of Gert and the nuns. But in my dream, Clara was not inside the nunnery. And my own mother would not reveal Clara's whereabouts. But I knew, of course—Clara was at Yorktown.

We did not eat much in the morning; near sundown we crawled into the trenches, with Redoubt Ten but a quarter mile away. I wasn't thinking of the Royal Deux-Ponts and their own mission. I thought of Washington on his mare—a general who offered so few signs of his feelings save a slight quiver in the cheek.

Promptly, at seven o'clock, Washington's cannoneers fired six shells into the night—six booms—that defied nature for a few moments and lit the sky with a sense of false daylight. We'd been ordered not to fire a single shot of our own lest we lose that element of surprise. We would charge the redoubt with unloaded muskets, greet the Brits and the Hessians with our bayonets.

Hamilton was the first to clamber out of the trenches with the Rhode Islanders, and the rest of us followed behind. We ran over the pocked ground, filled with craters and other signs of exploded shells. I near fell into a hole, but I stabbed my hanger into the earth and it propelled me forward.

The Hessians lit that no-man's-land with cannon bursts; what they discovered in the light would doom them, make the Hessians scream with fear, "the Moors, the Moors." They had never been assaulted by such a mottled army. They fired upon us with their muskets, hurled grenades, all the while bemoaning our Moors. We'd arrived at their little field of sharpened sticks in front of the fort. But it had been ripped asunder by previous bombardments. And the Rhode Islanders hacked at whatever sticks were still in place, hacked at them with hatchets and with their hands.

Beyond this field was a great ditch—meant nothing to the Rhode Islanders, who built a bridge with their own bodies, leaning low and collecting together, so that we could climb right over their backs. And whilst they stood there, they let out war cries that could have impaired the flow of any man's blood.

Hamilton jumped right into the redoubt from a Rhode Islander's back. Seems Cornwallis had his own "Moors"—the faces of his soldiers were blackened with grease and gunpowder. They struggled against our bayonets. I could not bring myself to hate these men. But I went at them with my hanger. I did not count the dead. I could hear the Rhode Islanders' war cry—its ferocious melody calmed my own blood.

The odor of excrement overwhelmed me for an instant—the Hessians had fouled their britches. They could not have dreamt to meet Moors at Yorktown.

The fighting was like a curious minuet in the dark, soldiers digging with bayonets under the clay walls of Redoubt Ten; different partners rose and fell 'til redcoats and Hessians walked through the dust and smoke with white handkerchiefs waving in the air.

'T WAS A MUCH LONGER MARCH back to my own tent, without the Rhode Islanders' chant in my ears. I longed to scream at the Hessians, "Disperse, ye lubbers! Run home!" Yet the home of these unfortunate men was their very next war.

I could not sleep. I heard a noise in the dark, the rustle of cloth. "Answer," I howled, "who goes?" And then, of a sudden, a freckled face hovered over me, licking my eyelids—'t was Clara in all her flesh, without an article of clothes. But she would not allow me to take off my stinking britches.

"Johnny," she whispered, "there's no time. Treat is coming to kill ye."

"A bagatelle," I told her. "I'll survive Malcolm Treat—'tis better than a miracle to find you without your clothes."

"You have to leave this instant."

"I have blood on me, Hessian blood."

"That ain't much of a bother," she said. "You're going to Canada."

"And live among Loyalists? Why the Divil would I go there?"

"Canada's the one place where Treat can't find you and the British won't bother to look—Johnny, 'tis no accident I'm at Yorktown. Gert kept hearing intelligence from agents passing through the nunnery, how Treat wanted to hire them to do ye harm."

"I am surrounded by secret agents."

"Posh," she said, "I'm a nun who carries silver bullets from time to time."

It pained me, lads, forced me to reconsider Anne Harding, and wonder if the whole world was filled with prison ships and female agents with their infernal silver bullets.

"Clara, I'll face Treat, kill him if I can."

"You dasn't," she said. "Mr. Washington cannot do without him. He sent me here."

"Washington? I will not believe it."

"He says there's no one to replace that reptile, no one with his daring."

"Then if I am to be sacrificed, Clara, you have brought me a wondrous bullet."

I could not even change my britches or wash the blood off me at the well near our latrine. I cursed this little military exercise of running from Treat and losing Clara at the very same moment, like a horse that kicked you twice in the head.

Clara had already worked out my route. I would ride downriver in a barge, catch a whaleboat to Newport, where a victualler would carry me into Canadian waters.

I watched Clara's shoulders move as she got into her clothes, desperate as I was to commit each dimple to memory. She gave me a parcel from Gert. I opened it, thinking to find some souvenir, or a very long letter at the least—it was packed with London pounds.

"But where's the letter that goes with the money?"

"Johnny, Gert couldn't write. Suppose the letter fell into enemy hands? I had to hide that parcel under my pannier—don't you dare frown. Gert's penmanship is rotten. And she didn't want you to catch her mistakes."

"I would have adored her mistakes."

"Hurry," she said. "Time is against us, Mr. One-Eye."

We had much difficulty sneaking out of camp. Malcolm Treat and his lads skulked about with lanterns, swords under their capes—lads loyal to Treat alone. We couldn't have lasted another minute in my tent. And I feared we'd never find an avenue into the forest.

They cawed at us in contempt. "Where are ye, Johnny boy? Come on home to your Maker."

I could feel the foul wind of their bodies, taste their murderous whiskey breath. I near banged into Treat himself, but Clara clutched my hand and led me into a wisp of darkness that even the most conscientious of assassins couldn't conquer with their incessant lantern swings. We found some little crack, the one flaw in their infernal focus of light. We still wouldn't have gotten through had the assassin nearest us not been a drunken sod who ranged his lantern a little too high.

Clara would not cross the woods and accompany me down to the river. She had to deflect Treat.

"Clara, I'll come back to haunt your bed."

"You'll stay put in Canada until you're called back—you killed Tobias. You can't return to York Island. And Treat will hunt you down everywhere else. When Mr. Washington has no need of him, then Gert and me will help you kill him. I'll kill him myself, drown him in a pool of sulfur."

"But if I think of you, Clara, think of you while I'm gone, will you think of me back? I'll feel it in my head."

"All the way from Canada?"

"Further even—I'd feel it far as Siam."

She looked at me as if I'd insulted her. "Then you won't miss me much, will ye? Because you'll have my thoughts. They'll be like pages in a book—oh, Johnny, go on down to the river. If I palaver much longer, I'll run to Siam with you, and I dasn't."

She held me in her arms, rocked me the way a very tall little girl might rock her favorite doll, and then she abandoned that doll and ran back into all the hullabaloo with great big galloping legs.

DOWN BY THE RIVER I saw six burly men. They were standing near a gondola, but these were not simple ferriers. They had the look of assassins. And I thought to myself—the little major has a longer reach than Washington himself. But I had my hanger, and least I could do was send one of the assassins into hell.

Yet 't was more insidious than I could have imagined. Even without the semblance of a moon, I noticed what they wore—they were members of Washington's Life Guard, with their gold buttons and other regalia. Ye gods, Major Treat must have owned the farmer from A to Z.

"You filthy yobs," I screamed, brandishing my hanger. "I'll fight ye five or six at a time."

They chortled, laughed in my face, plucked the hanger out of my hand, and hurled me into the gondola. I rolled over, right on my arse. A man sat next to me, wearing a long cloak. I could not mistake the red, red hair of the Marquis de Lafayette.

He smiled, kissed me on the cheek.

"*Petit*," he said, "I am so sorry, but the Chief could not come to bid you bon voyage! He would have sent Ham, but you see, Ham is too impetuous, and would not have agreed to this exile. It was my own idea. To lose you, *petit*, until the war will wind down. And we can survive without the major's services. He will not harm you in Canada. You have my word of honor, *petit*, my parole."

"But General, sir, I could hide in Little Africa."

"And endanger whoever is near you? He will burn Little Africa to the ground—no, Canada is best. Adieu, *petit*."

Lafayette climbed out of the gondola and left me to the Life Guard, whose members rowed me across the river. I shivered in my bloody britches, lonelier than the loneliest dog.

PETIT. AS IF I WERE HIS DWARF, his homunculus, his manikin. *Petit*. He knew how to wound a lad, this Lafayette did. His six yobs delivered me to a barge, where I lay for a week, living on crumbs of bread and cheese, and a drop of Madeira that might have come from Washington's own war tent. My new ferriers were waiting for some squall to pass. The wind rocked my wooden cradle, and I thought we'd sink right into the Chesapeake. A multitude of frogs landed in my lap—an inauspicious sign, if ever there was one.

I must have been transferred to a schooner while I slept. I found myself in my own private cabin, like some kind of duke, riding along the Atlantic coast, but this duke was not allowed beyond his own door.

I would sit in my cabin and recall the clutch of Clara's hand as we escaped that insidious lantern light of Malcolm Treat and his little band—'t was worth a hundred calvaries, a hundred campaigns. We were like children running from wolves with pale human eyes.

The winter cold would seep through my cabin window. I watched the snow capture entire towns near the coast, transform some steeple into a great white hump. The schooner's captain tried to steal my legacy of London pounds, but I must have looked ferocious with Hessian blood all over my breeches. Finally he left me alone.

Anno Domini 1782

GENTLE JACK

New Windsor

May 1782

He was playing vingt-et-un every single night. It had been his one addiction of the war, fed him whenever he failed to sleep. He could not field an army without his colored troops. Yet what could he promise them? A pension they would never collect? It saddened him that 't was all a subterfuge. And such contradictions troubled the commander in chief.

He remained attached to Hercules, his mulatto cook, who always rode on top of his carriage at Mount Vernon and would battle with Washington's overseers like a British boxing champion. He could never punish Hercules. And the paradox was that he would not even consider bringing Hercules to headquarters as his military chef and risk losing him at the end of the war. He counted on Hercules, depended on him.

And amid his own gloom, a letter arrived from one of his colonels, Lewis Nicola, begging him to become king of these United States lest the country fall into chaos. A king would bear more heft than a commander in chief, a king would be welcomed and congratulated by his officers, a king would comfort them. But Wash-

ington was appalled that such ideas existed in his army, ideas that could only lead to the greatest mischief—he had not sat on a saddle for six years with boils on his buttocks so that he could install a king's crown over the United States.

But then he was overcome by the Tempter's own thoughts—if he did wear a crown, he could dub Hercules royal chef-for-life, with a stipend that would also declare Hercules the first colored knight in the kingdom of America—a slave, a knight, and a chef.

Such an imbroglio drove out his insomnia, and he slept like a babe.

But he woke in the morning to the rottenest news. His orderly, Sparks, took ill. Sparks didn't have Hercules' flair. Sparks never rode at the top of his carriage, never cooked a soufflé, never wore a chef's fluffy white hat. But Sparks had no life apart from Washington, tho' he was a freed man, and Hercules was not. Washington couldn't have survived the hellish winters without Sparks, who shared the same room or tent with the commander in chief, often the same cup of wine. And Sparks never had to be polite. He wouldn't accept wages from the commander in chief.

"Does the army pay you, gen'ral? Then why should it pay me?"

"I am a farmer of means. Should I burden a bankrupt nation with my own salary? Better to buy leggings for my men."

"Can't your orderly contribute to the same fund?"

"Damn you, Sparks, but you are a most obstinate fellow."

"No more obstinate than you, gen'ral."

But Sparks had fallen down the stairs after fixing breakfast. It might have been a bout of apoplexy, or carelessness, or weakening eyesight. The commander carried him up to his own bed, tried to feed him broth, but Sparks never regained consciousness, never opened his eyes. And Washington buried him in the little boneyard behind headquarters that did not have a separate plot for Negroes. He could not scribble a letter to Sparks' next of kin, or even say if Sparks had had children or a wife. He was woefully ignorant of his orderly's personal effects and affairs.

He found a large tobacco tin under Sparks' cot. But there was no tobacco inside, just a little purse with one gold coin and a silver dagger polished to perfection. Pinned to the purse was a little note in Sparks' own hand:

For G. Washington, Upon My Demise

And Washington shivered at the knowledge that he, and he alone, was Sparks' next of kin.

Sixty-Two

I LANDED A FEW DAYS AFTER CHRISTMAS IN A dot between wilderness and water—they called it Fundy, the Bay of Fundy. It had been the site of an old French fort—St. Jean—on the north shore of the bay. There was a British garrison on a hill overlooking the water, but Fort Howe, as it was known, kept to itself and did not mingle with the minuscule community of Saint John, or with Lower Cove, a haven for smugglers and brigands right on the wharves, where I came to rest. Such brigands felt safe here, since 't was truly the end of the world—forests and water, and not a coffee-house in sight.

These cutthroats could ply their trade elsewhere and then return to our cove. Despite their many crimes, they were punctilious students of history, devoted to each relic of the revolution.

I wondered if my mum had sent her own silver bullet to Saint John. The brigands knew about my days and nights on board the *Jersey*, about my adventures at Yorktown—'t was the brigands who told me how the "Frenchies" had captured Redoubt Nine, albeit several of their own men had been impaled on the sharp sticks of a cheval-de-frise. They considered Hamilton and Johnny One-Eye as the essential heroes of Redoubt Ten.

And they screwed up their own eyes with much suspicion.

"Why are you in this godforsaken woods?"

I could not tell them that the American command had picked one mad major and his secret service over Johnny One-Eye. They would not have understood George Washington's serpentine ways.

"Lads," I said, "you're right about Ham. He charged into the Hessians with all his might. But I was one of the last to climb into the redoubt. None of us could have done much climbing without the Moors."

The brigands did not believe me. "Colored boys won the battle of Yorktown? It beggars the mind."

Cornwallis had surrendered Yorktown soon after we took Redoubts Nine and Ten, according to the brigands. But the Moors had already disappeared from America's imagination. And no matter what I said, I could not convince the brigands that there ever was or had ever been a black regiment from Rhode Island.

But they would not rest until I showed them my green sash. "Might we touch it, John?"

These brigands were patriots to the last man, full of worship for anything that touched upon Washington, even my sash.

They elected me their leader, with rights to my own tavern on the wharves. I called it "Little Manhattan," because as much as I admired the Bay of Fundy and the freedom of its wharves, I was lonesome for *my* island, with its own wharves, with Holy Ground.

I had to cast about for news of Benedict Arnold. After Yorktown there was little reason for Arnold to remain in America. He sailed to England with his family at the end of 1781, sailed on separate ships, I learned—Arnold cloistered in a man-o'-war in case the

Americans tried to capture him, and Peggy in a merchantman with no other passengers but her maid. The king awarded Peggy Shippen a lifelong pension of five hundred London pounds a year—'t was more than her beauty that had charmed the king. George III, *my* patron at college, was rewarding her prowess as a spy.

Peggy had become a great success at court, we were told. The queen strolled in the gardens of Windsor with her, gave Peggy another small pension out of her own purse. She would have been the sensation of London without her Ben. He bought a carriage and fell into debt. He was reviled when he and Peggy went to the opera. Loyalists living in London walked the other way when they encountered Arnold on the street.

While I could glean the latest news of London Town, I learnt almost nothing of New York. I hired Canadian victuallers to visit Holy Ground. They could tell me precious little about Clara and Gert. They were not even allowed into the nunnery—'t was either a disused British brothel or some kind of barracks and officers' hotel, they told me. I wanted to send Clara and Gert a packet of London pounds, but I did not know how to deliver it. I had to depend on the ingenuity of the victuallers. These men were able to bribe a young British officer, who did deliver the pounds to Gert. I waited months and months. And then the victuallers brought me back a note from my mother—'t was brutally brief.

> *My Dearest Johnny. You must not be in touch again. And you must not return. The redcoats will arrest you at our door. And you must not send me money. It throws suspicion upon us.*
>
> *Know that Clara and I love you. We talk of you every night.*

The note was unsigned, and I wondered if it had a censor's touch. But I did recognize Clara's childish scrawl—she must have become Gertrude's secretary.

SOON ALL THE COVE was called Little Manhattan, and by some strange default, or act of God, I became its squire. My brigands could neither read nor write, so Squire John had to serve as the bloody landlord of Lower Cove.

But something suspicious happened. My best yobs were getting beaten up within the boundaries of Little Manhattan, and not a living soul would claim responsibility. Then the most senior of my lieutenants was kidnapped, and no ransom asked—'t didn't feel like the tactics of some other brigand. This felt more like an Indian fighter. I kept hearing whispers: "The Regulator, the Regulator."

The Regulators, I knew, had been a wild band in North Carolina, as far as twenty or thirty years ago. They fought against the corruption of the Crown. They stole back horses that had been stolen from them. They kidnapped tax collectors. They burnt the barns of British sympathizers. They massacred Indians sympathetic to the Crown. They panicked the whole countryside, rode into villages and swiped every singe emblem of George III. But the redcoats went into battle, overwhelmed the Regulators, and executed their leaders right on the battlefield. Other Regulators were rounded up; some ran off to Ohio and still others were hanged. But no one could tell what happened to their general, "Gentle Jack," a ruthless and mysterious man. The Crown might have corrupted Jack, bought his services, or killed him. And I didn't like it at all when his name was bandied about Little Manhattan. Lads couldn't hide their hysteria from me.

The Regulators, the Regulators.

Why would Gentle Jack come to the end of the world? Had the Crown run him off every other cove? Still, I was careful as a king.

I traveled abroad with boys just as burly as Washington's own Life Guard. But I could not have imagined the sheer brutality of the Regulators. They struck one night, burnt a boardinghouse, a home for enfeebled pirates. The Regulators brought them into the parlor and flayed them alive with their scalping knives, and left their carcasses to crackle in the fire.

The stench of these burning bodies wafted across our cove with a storm of ashes. I ran down to the harbor with my brigands and scuttled Jack's little fleet. I would not burn his ships or the few lads hc left on board. I was not a scavenger or an arsonist, like the Regulators. We hammered into their hulls, 'til the ships sank in shallow water, their masts like strange leaning turrets. Now Jack had no armada.

But I hadn't counted on his ingenuity, his diabolic will to win. He'd have cut the throats of half my Life Guard if he could. Then one afternoon the Regulators visited me whilst I lay abed above the tavern. They wore black kerchiefs and the clothes of different climes—silks and fur cloaks; they clutched torches in their hands and looked at me in a most peculiar fashion.

"Lads," the surliest of them said, "summon the captain, if ye please?"

"I dare not," said another of these ruthless men. "He'll murder us, he will."

"Then we'll just have to set Squire John on fire and suffer the consequences."

But not one of these yobs approached me with his torch, and I did not know why.

I heard a rumble from the floor below, where the tavern was, and someone began to climb the stairs and shout, "Well, have you burnt his feet yet?"

And then he appeared—Gentle Jack or the ghost of him. Now I understood why the Regulators were so alarmed. Jack wore *my* face—older perhaps and gray about the ears, and minus an eye patch, but he was still my double. The Regulators watched him like a band of hawks, searching for the least sign of weakness, I suppose. His lip trembled but an instant, and it must have doomed him. He stopped asking these yobs to set my feet on fire. They smiled among themselves. They'd caught their captain unawares. He hadn't expected to find a curious replica of himself in Saint John. He ordered them out of my bedchamber with their torches.

He wore silks and furs, like his crew, but he also had a long red scarf.

"Jesus," he said, "I'm parched. Will ye not offer me a glass of wine?"

I kept a flask of Madeira close to my bed. I poured some into a goblet. But he would not drink 'til I drank with him.

"Are you daft?" he asked. "Or just deaf and dumb? Do ye not recognize your own da?"

"I don't understand."

"I sire only cretins," he said. "Jason Jennings at your service, beknownst as Gentle Jack because of my magnanimity to cripples, cretins, and blacks . . . lemme look at ye. Fess up, isn't your mum a certain Stella of Barbados?"

"No, sir."

He touched his forehead with a rather long finger. "Not my Stella? But a wench with blond hair—I cannot recollect her name. Thin as a wisp. Rosalind, or . . ."

"Sir," says I, emboldened all of a sudden, since he'd kill me no matter what I said. "You have small reason to discuss my parentage. Our resemblance is but a freak accident. I could not possibly be related to you."

I'd plucked his interest. "And why is that, pray tell?"

"Because no relation of mine would ever carve up enfeebled pirates."

"And if ye know my business, how else could I have frightened an entire town?"

"By dueling with my brigands," says I.

"Dueling, ye say?"

"Yes, in a sporting manner."

He began to cackle. 'T was most unbecoming—a hyena in a red scarf.

"Are we Regulators or Christian knights? Tell me your mum's name."

"I would not sully it, sir, in your presence."

He moved to slap my face, but seemed inexplicably deterred.

"And if I promised to do penance . . . and not mutilate a single soul for the next six months?"

"How could I ever believe a wholesale liar such as yourself? But I will tell you this much. My mother's surname is the same as your own."

"Sonny, I have made more than one Mrs. Jennings in my lifetime."

And why did I suspect that my mother's Christian name—the mere mention of it—would wound the fellow?

"She is none other than Gertrude of Holy Ground," says I.

And I could scarce believe it. This cruel man started to cry. It was piteous to see. A pirate, a murderer of men, bawling like some infant out of the cradle.

"Are ye Gert's?" he asked, wiping his eyes with his own red scarf. "Then I am indeed your da. Is her hair still the reddest in the land?"

He commenced to hug me, and I did not resist for some reason. He had carnage on his person—in the ruts of his face, in the folds of his boots—but his love of Gert still attached him to me. Nonetheless, I had great difficulty accepting him as my da. Perhaps I had brooded too long on the farmer, the same man who had condemned me to this wilderness through no fault of my own. Wasn't Washington also a Regulator? Wouldn't he have sacrificed Manhattan, burnt it to the ground, to save his army of men without shoes?

But I shouldn't have speculated so long while Gentle Jack was in my bedchamber. He had his own extravagant ideas about filial obligations. He'd pulled a dirk out of his sleeve and held its point against my throat.

"Best be quick," he told me. "Did my Gertrude ever love another man?"

I could appraise this Jack, even whilst I was a pinprick away from permanent slumber: he'd just as soon slaughter his own son as any stranger. And perhaps I was as willful as he was.

"Mr. Jack Jennings, she has adored *one* man to the very edge of distraction these past twenty-five years."

"Speak his name, or I'll pin ye to the wall."

And that's when his Regulators returned, each with a cutlass in one hand, a torch in the other. They were pleased as the Divil to catch their captain at my throat. "Ain't that divine, Jack? Finish him and we'll leave this pestilential place."

"You are interruptin' my interrogation," Jack said. "And it is of the most personal nature."

"But we can assist you," said his subaltern, the surly one. "I could burn out his brains."

And when the subaltern thrust his torch tantalizingly close to my scalp, Jack dug the dirk between this same subaltern's eyes. Lord-a-mercy, my head was near on fire. I howled with pain—'t was almost like being crowned with hellishly hot thorns. But in saving me, Jack had wrecked his own chances. The Regulators attacked him with their cutlasses, furious that he'd killed his own subaltern with a dirk. They stabbed him before he could pull out his cutlass, but he still began leaving cadavers all over my bedchamber. He drove the living and the half dead down the stairs.

My brigands must have been hiding somewhere. Once they noticed that fortune was now in their favor, they reappeared and hacked all the wounded Regulators to pieces. Their nostrils quivered when they pulled close to me. The smell of my singed scalp was truly unbearable.

"Squire," they asked, "shall we escort Gentle Jack to the hanging tree?"

"Ye gods, will you get him a doctor?"

But we had no doctors in Saint John, except at the fort. And I didn't have much faith in an army surgeon. I had my lads haul the cadavers down the stairs while I ripped apart the bedclothes and stoppered Jack's wounds as best I could. I dared not move him. He lay on my floor with a pillow behind his head. He was still lucid in spite of all the blood he'd lost.

"Squire John," he said with a cough, "will ye tell a dyin' man who the rascal was that replaced me in your mum's affection?"

"George Washington, the commander in chief."

The brow of his bloodless face was all in a wrinkle. "Him who fancies fat widows? He stole my Gert?"

"Sir," says I, "since my mother did not so much as mention your existence, I must assume that you abandoned her."

"And gallant George did not? He has remained with his Martha, unless I err . . . and your humble servant has a price on his head. But I'd bet my life I laid eyes on her before gallant George ever did. Her dada was a local gunsmith in tidewater country, a squire like yerself. And your mum was a volunteer nurse in one of the king's hospitals . . . unless I confuse her with another wench. But I cannot disremember a face full of freckles and how she tended to Jack the Regulator in a hospital of redcoats."

"Were you wounded, sir?"

"'T was an ignominious wound. In the arse. I'd been burning barns, creating havoc amongst all the king's loyal squires, and a redcoat comes out of nowhere with his musket and massacres my bum. I'd have met my Maker if Gert had not administered to me, swearin' to the hospital that I was some representative of the Crown. And one morning, while she was doin' up my bandages, I could resist her freckles no longer and I declared my love. I had the cheek to kiss her with redcoats all around . . . and we were married a month later—in '56 or '57, if I can still recollect."

"And what happened next?" I asked, curious as the Divil.

He coughed and spat a gob of blood. "There was no next. The king was on my trail. Merry Jack had to kiss your mum goodbye."

"But you might have come back for her."

"I'd wandered too far. Yet I am glad I have found ye. I won't dissemble now. I've met five—no, six—six of my other sons. And I did not have one moment of pride."

"And how, sir, am I different?"

"Are ye still a cretin? You gave me Gertrude again."

This was the last remark he uttered that made sense. He continued to gurgle blood while he held my hand. I could not love a murderer, even if he called himself my dad. But I buried him in Saint John, hired a few Indian maidens to chant Christian songs as we delivered him into the ground.

I was sorely confused. He'd arrived out of nowhere, a Regulator, and could have started an incendiary in Saint John that might have burnt us all and given Manhattan's Great Fire the appearance of a most minor catastrophe. Instead, he'd saved my life and plundered his own. Had he been searching for his son in some purblind way? If I hadn't come to this pirates' cove, would I ever have found him? Perhaps it was Divine Will that had sent a changeling called Johnny One-Eye to Canada. Was I a child of Providence, or a child of chance?

Sixty-Three

EVEN AS A CHILD OF CHANCE, I STILL HAD FAITH in Washington, believing all the while that he would redeem a lad who had never harmed him, and that I would be led out of this wilderness. I imagined him coming to Lower Cove, drinking beer from a pannikin, as we called our dented tin cups. I waited through the summer with little else on my mind, and suddenly I felt the unfairness of it all. I had a rage in me I could not quell. It worsened as winter approached. I plunged into the foulest of moods. All human company was anathema to me.

I would not get out of bed. I had meat pies brought upstairs with my grog. And things got worse in Saint John. Without a squire or local king, the town had fallen into disrepair.

The brigands broke down my door.

"Lads," I said, "has George Washington come to our cove?"

"No, Squire John, not yet."

"Then why are you molesting me?"

"Because you are a hermit living in a hermitage. Your own tavern has run out of beer and ale."

"But I have my daily grog."

"Squire John, you are drinking spit from the bottom of the barrel."

"'Tis a mere detail," I said, tossing my pannikin at them.

They returned in an hour with wondrous wrinkles upon their pates.

"John, I do believe the general has arrived. He wears a tricorn, hides the better part of him in a cape."

"Washington here? Is his head a little too small for his hat?"

"Would seem so," said my ablest brigand. "With an enormous beak of a nose, as far as I can tell."

"That's Washington," I said.

They uncovered a clean neckcloth, and I went downstairs in that piece of silk and a nightshirt. Silence reigned as I appeared. The pirates raised their pannikins. Lord knows what they were drinking!

"To your health, squire."

My heart was thumping. I kept looking at the stranger in the tricorn, tho' I could not see much of him in the tavern's meager candlelight.

"Excellency, might I welcome you to Saint John?"

He said nothing, nothing at all. I looked again. He did not have Washington's pale complection. This was a dark and dour fellow, no taller than myself. He demanded a pannikin of ale. My lieutenants tried to tell him there was nothing to drink but spit and blood.

"And who's the publican here?" asked this ferocious stranger.

"I am," I volunteered.

He unfurled his cape to reveal the pistols and the hanger that lived near the well of his britches. I was too lazy and too forlorn to have my own yobs make a mess of him. But why was he so willing to fight a house full of pirates sworn to me?

Then I caught him in profile and could scarce believe my eyes. He resembled a bird of prey, and even with the hat masking most of him, I recognized his dark demean—I'd seen him last coming out of the shitter a good two years ago, with Sergeant Champe waiting to deliver him to the hanging tree in Weehawken.

"May I ask the publican his name?" says he.

I knocked the hat off his head, but he had no fear.

"You abuse me, publican."

"I do, sir. And don't I have the right? I served under you, starved in the woods, ate my own stockings." I had chewed on those wormy things. "General Arnold, do you not recognize your late secretary?"

The pirates pricked their ears at the mention of Arnold. They would have torn him to pieces had I but signaled once. They'd been expecting the commander in chief.

Arnold looked at me out of his own bitter gloom.

"Publican, you should not give a name to a man that has not introduced himself." He looked again. "Scribbler, is that you?"

We fell into each other's arms. The pirates were amazed. But I didn't answer them. I still loved the filthy traitor.

ARNOLD RELAYED TO ME that he could not thrive in a London where both the populace and people of quality spurned him as a parvenu. So he'd come to make his fortune in the West Indies and the wilds of Canada, like some phantom trader who was still in the service of the Crown. Ye gods, how he had fallen! All his ventures had failed. He'd offered himself up to command some small fleet at the edge of the empire, but the admiralty would not have him. And so he sailed the seas with his rotten cargo—rancid banana oil, coffee beans alive with ants—that he planned to deliver to desperate, starving towns. But he had enough sense not to unload his coffee beans on us, else my lads would have made him swallow every ant.

"How's the missus?" I asked.

"Peggy sups with the queen, rides in a carriage I can ill afford, but I am loath to deny her the littlest thing. She has been the best of wives, Johnny, the best of wives."

Perhaps she was, and I had been unjust to call her Salome and Satan's strumpet. Arnold might have tilted to the British on his own. Perhaps he needed a wife such as Peggy Shippen. The warrior who had tried to take Quebec could not be this sorry man. He had much stubble about the chin, and his eagle eyes were listless in Saint John. He could have been part of the derelict cargo he was carrying.

I had to unload my own cargo, all the bile deep inside myself. "General," says I, "Mr. Washington has sentenced me to the wilderness. I have become an affliction for him."

I expected Arnold to excoriate Washington's little cabal and commiserate with its victim—me. But Arnold's eyes seemed sharper of a sudden.

"Johnny, the commander in chief is not a precipitous man. What could ye have possibly done to merit the Bay of Fundy?"

"Nothing. I fell afoul of his intelligence chief. You must have met him—a certain major."

"Malcolm Treat. And what did ye do to earn his wrath?"

"Exist, is all. He had an immediate and most irrational antipathy toward me."

"But that is what armies are all about—immediate antipathies. And to satisfy Malcolm Treat, the commander rid himself of you. I would have done the same thing."

"Then you are a monster, and not the Arnold I once knew."

"Johnny, I would have drowned you in the Dead River had my

chief of intelligence been against ye—you are a novice in the art of war."

"But Malcolm Treat is a crazy man."

"All the more reason to put a protective cloak around him."

"General, you never would have drowned me."

"I most certainly would. With my own hands, and I would have suffered not one sleepless night over it . . ."

"And," says I with a pith of cruelty, "should I emulate George Washington and send assassins after you?"

Arnold scraped his stubble with the palm of his hand. "I miss the Old Man. How was he last you saw him?"

"High on his sorrel, at Yorktown," I said.

"Would it astonish ye to hear that I love him? What wounds me most is that I will have to live out my life without recapturing his grace."

There was a wildness in Arnold, a reckless folly that had taken him to the precipice, to the very edge of humankind.

"General, how could you ever have thought you'd find a place among the Brits?"

"But I have found a place," he said. "Not on dry land. I can only breathe on board a ship."

We kissed for the last time, and he went off into the cold with his cargo of ants.

I HAD LEARNT VERY LITTLE about America from Benedict Arnold. But news began to trickle in from certain traders and victuallers who plied the Atlantic seaboard that winter of '82. Washington and his army crouched on both sides of the Hudson. The war had been taken away from them. Peace commissioners met in Paris, but they commissioned naught, not even the simplest end to hostilities. Instead of warfare, there was much barking and biting in the southland. A bit of mutiny here and there, the abduction of some colonel, with British spies moving in and out of American camps. But it mattered very little. Save for Manhattan, the Brits had nowhere to hide. American raiders set fire to their arsenals, attacked their supply trains, until the British evacuated their last two southern outposts before the end of the year.

And I had to wonder what part Washington's intelligence chief had played in driving the Brits out of Charleston and Savannah. Had Malcolm Treat and his agents skulked into Savannah, prepared an uprising, plucked out the eyes of redcoats stationed along Charleston's seawall? It gave me pleasure to imagine this mischief, to believe that I had been sacrificed and bruited about for some cause, that Treat's cunning was so absolute, his actions would determine the fate of the war. Without such imaginings I might have gone mad.

Anno Domini 1783

CLARA

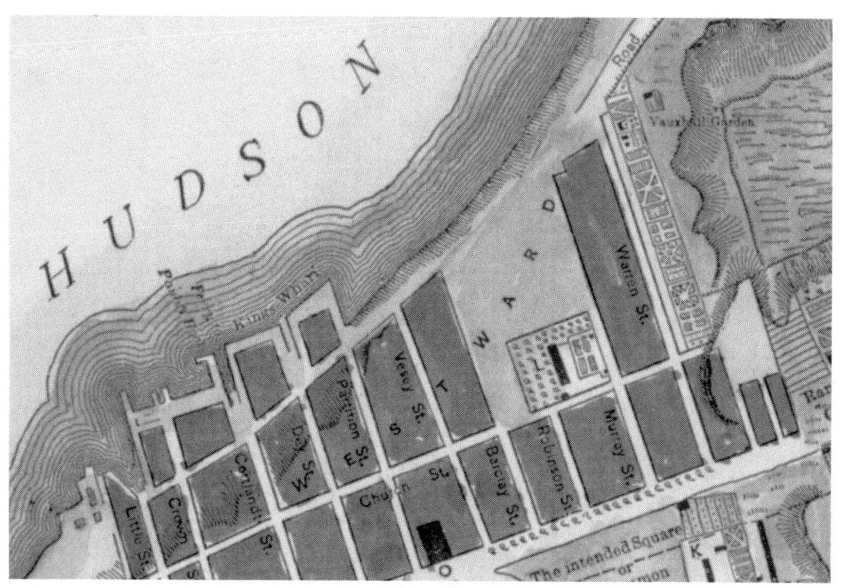

Newburgh
March 1783

It had become a dog of a life for the commander in chief. He disrelished the very Madeira he drank. Nothing could please him. Rochambeau had sailed away from the Chesapeake with all his whitecoats in January, and Washington could not harass the British in Manhattan without French military engineers and the French fleet. His own army had begun to unravel. 'T was near to mutiny—with officers circulating petitions against the commander in chief and the new country itself, a country that could afford to pay them not a farthing. Washington was moved by the eloquence of their petitions. Yet he longed to rescue these officers from the civil horror into which they would soon plunge.

He summoned a meeting of officers at a primitive town hall his own carpenters had built, tho' he did not plan to attend. He would have an aide read his words. Yet he did appear at the meeting in his winter cloak, and aroused much wonder when he clambered onto a stage that shook with the force of him.

The country they hoped to abandon, he said, was their own. Override reason with rhetoric, and speech itself might be "taken away, and, dumb and silent, we may be led, like sheep, to the slaughter."

The officers listened in silence, their faces still flushed with anger, as if Washington himself was the country's own python. Then he took a piece of paper from his pocket—a letter he hoped to read. But he lost his momentum, seemed frozen for an instant. He could not decipher the words in front of his eyes. The officers were startled, suddenly attentive. He fumbled for a pair of spectacles. They had never seen the commander in chief with spectacles bestride his nose. He bowed. "Gentlemen, you must pardon me. I have grown gray in your service and now feel myself growing blind."

All the arguments were gone, all the rancor. Some of the officers wept. They did not even listen to the letter, could not have recited a single word. A pair of spectacles, a bit of tin and ground glass, had brought them back into the fold.

Sixty-Four

I MISSED MY FAMILY OF NUNS. THE OLD YEAR had passed, and I heard not a syllable from Holy Ground. Robinson Street might just as well have been on the moon. There was constant banter about peace and war in gazettes that reached us from London Town. The king had been adamant for years about protecting his children of the thirteen American colonies—he swore again and again that he would never countenance our independence. But Yorktown, it seems, had changed the king's complection. He no longer talked of us as his children, according to the gazettes. King George was ready to cast off his colonies, convinced that Americans would go to the Divil. But he wouldn't abandon the Loyalists. He offered acreage and credits or cash to his former subjects who agreed to settle in the far country of Canada.

I was still a landlord, in spite of my disregard for lucre. I began buying up houses in Upper Cove, a world away from my wharves. I knew that these pretentious merchants, lawyers, divines, and government officials wouldn't want to mingle with lowlife pirates.

But I could not risk having them devour Upper Cove and then coming to prey upon us, to steal our land *and* our autonomy. And so, like some insatiable child, I bought whatever houses I could find.

A "SPRING FLEET" OF THIRTY-TWO SHIPS left New York Harbor at the end of April, with twenty-four hundred souls. These Loyalists settled in Upper Cove and soon assembled their own Common Council. Then in August a boat full of free blacks—its men had served as stevedores in Loyalist brigades—also arrived in Saint John, but the new white settlers wouldn't allow them near Upper Cove and its society of citizens and "freemen." The blacks came to live with us in Little Manhattan.

The Loyalist aristocracy even had its own slave market in Upper Cove, where it would auction men, women, and children. I burnt that market down with my own hands. The Loyalists put up another market and hired guards. I had them kidnapped. They put up a whipping post and scratched laws about who ought to be whipped. I let them have their trappings—a sheriff, a poorhouse, a legitimate jail, even a public whip, a brute of a man.

A colored woman was convicted by the Common Council's own little court, convicted of larceny—she stole five loaves of bread from a Loyalist baker—and received seventeen lashes at the whipping post and was burnt on the lip and on her hand by the brute. I happened upon this spectacle with my brigands and shook like a man with the palsy. I wrapped my cape around my fist, grabbed the hot iron, and branded the brute—burnt his arms, his face, his legs. The brute went howling into the streets and never appeared again.

The Common Council could have appealed to the redcoats on the hill at Fort Howe, but its members had already lived in a Manhattan of martial law and didn't want redcoats prowling Saint John.

So the council came to me. "This must stop, Squire John, or we'll never have a town."

"Then you must not brand black or white women for stealing a few loaves of bread—I will make restitution for every loaf."

And I turned my back on the Common Council. I hungered for news, but there was no regular packet between York Island and Saint John, no packet at all. And I wouldn't ask bloody Loyalists about Clara and my mum.

The Treaty of Paris had been signed in September, we would learn after a month, but the British continued to sit in Manhattan. I waited for some signal from Gert, another note in Clara's own scrawl. In the London gazettes I discovered that the Crown was scheduled to leave Manhattan the last week of November—but still no sign from Clara.

And then an envelope arrived right at my door, with a ribbon and the seal of the Continental Army. I shivered to open it—'t was not a letter at all, but an invitation to a banquet on the 4th of December, a farewell party from the commander in chief to his officers. First I thought I was the victim of some fancy folderol. I'd been the least bit of an officer, an honorary lieutenant, without pay, who'd taken part in one little skirmish at Yorktown. But the signature was genuine—*G. Washington, Esquire, General and Commander in Chief of the Forces of the United States of America.*

I didn't bother to sell my belongings as a proper landlord should have done. I packed a velvet suit and my green sash, carried enough specie and gold to last me six months, and boarded the next victualler to Manhattan.

THE ISLAND SEEMED FORLORN. I could not locate a single tree. Buildings jutted out like black teeth. The Crown must have seized all the wood. Manhattan had still not recovered from the Great Fire. It slept for seven years. A little boat met us in the harbor—soldiers of the new United States serving as customs inspectors. My name wasn't on the manifest since our ship was not permitted to carry human cargo. Not even my sash would save me. I'd be sent back to Canada.

The inspectors poked through my belongings, uncovered my invitation to Washington's farewell, saw his signature, and apologized like chastised children. They themselves rowed me ashore.

I could scarce believe the desolation. Noisome vapors rose from the mud and brackish water near the docks. I found offal everywhere, pile upon pile of rubbish—the streets themselves were like rumpled pastures where cows roamed with bells attached to their tails. Men roamed beside them, soldiers of every persuasion, redcoats and Royal Deux-Ponts and Hessians who had somehow been left behind.

I walked one enormous beggar's lane from Little Dock Street to Holy Ground. Giving out coins in my own wanton manner, I rewarded the petulant smile of a little girl or the unabashed greed of a frail old man.

I saw no commerce on Robinson Street, not one American soldier. Some new citizens' committee must have condemned brothels as a strictly British affair. I did find some women in homespun milling about, as if they were end-of-war spies. They frowned when I entered the Queen's Yard, or the spurious shadow that was left of it.

The place was all ashamble. The nuns' closets had been ransacked. Clara's was a pile of feathers and broken sticks. I shuddered at the thought of Gert's own plight. But I did not pull away from whatever carnage I might find in Mum's bedchamber. Had she been dragged from her house, sent to Wallabout with Clara, and now Washington himself could not retrieve them?

I entered without a knock. I was all agog—not a mirror was

out of line. The silver posters of her bed had not been pilfered. Mum's pillows were in their proper place. The queen's boudoir had not changed since my childhood. And Gert wasn't locked inside some prison ship. She was lying there on her comforter, looking at me.

She wore a peignoir of the finest silk or satin, silk that could not hide the starkness of her skin and bones. I could have carried her about like a bird. But her voice was far from frail.

"Is that my Johnny? I cannot see you."

She would not wear a lorgnette or another eyeglass. The whole world was fuzzy ten feet from her bed. I sat down beside her, rife with emotion, yet Gertrude and I had seldom sat in such proximity.

Mum had a jar of marmalade on her lap, and the two of us poked into the jar with our fingers.

"What infernal wind has gone through this house?"

"A human hurricane," she said.

"Were the ransackers British or our own?"

"Johnny dear, there's always rabble when one army leaves and another comes marching in."

"You and Clara could have traveled to Saint John. I'd have rebuilt Holy Ground on my own wharves—but where is Clara?"

She dug a finger into the marmalade and filled her mouth with the stuff.

"Child, Clara is gone."

"Mother, gone is much too grand a word. How can I find her?"

"Johnny, she does not want to be found."

I would not listen. "But if she's lost or in trouble, I will troll every street. I will burrow into the earth, bring in my brigands. I have brigands, ye know. I have settled on a line of endeavor—your honorable son is a pirate who lives on land. Mum, I have enough treasure to take care of you and Clara for the rest of our lives."

"Clara is living with another man."

I was nauseous and dizzy from all the marmalade. We had swilled half the jar without the blessing of a spoon. "Tell me his name."

"I am not at liberty to do so," said me own mum.

I was like a rogue elephant driven to despair—worse, a human about to prey on another.

"Mum, that Regulator, Mr. Jack Jennings, died in my lap—methinks ye knew the man."

She tossed the jar of marmalade at my head—it banged against my skull.

"Viper, say what you want to say, that your own mother made a mockery of your life with her monstrous lies—Jack wasn't much of a Regulator when I married him, tho' he had burnt a lot of barns. He was a pirate, as you are. And the handsomest man in Tidewater country. He was also the Divil. I saw him murder nine men in a room. That's when I fled, with only you in my arms."

"But why did you invent the fable that George Washington was my dada?"

"'T was Washington's wish."

I was trembling now. "Mother, I am lost."

"He loved you. And he wanted to protect you."

"As a shit-in-the-pants rather than the rightful son of Gentle Jack?"

"Jack meant nothing to me," Gert said.

"But you must have loved him—even for a little while."

"Yes. As much as you can love a pirate."

"I'm a pirate," says I.

"But you're my son. I have no choice."

Pirates and generals, pah! I had to peruse my past with a different candle. "I am older than you say I am, but by how many years?"

"Two," she said.

"And you hid me from Washington, did you not? He appears

at the inn where you work, him a soldier back from the Indian wars, engaged to Martha Custis, and he falls in love with your flaming hair—Washington told me so."

Her anger was gone. "You talked to him about *me*?"

"At his headquarters in New Windsor. He did most of the talking."

"You should not have listened," she said. Mum was not a skeleton now; the color had come back to her cheeks. "And I should never have struck you with the marmalade."

She began to cry.

"'T was twenty-five years ago, a full twenty-five. And I the runaway wife of Jack Jennings, suddenly a tavern girl with a child on her hands. Yes, I hid you from him. I was frightened that he would think ill of me and fall out of love with my red hair. But he was cleverer than I. He saw you in the tavern, recognized your own red hair."

"Mother, I protest. That is the baldest of lies. I have never been the least bit carroty."

"But you did have one reddish curl—as a baby."

I was vanquished again. I would never fathom all the divagations, not even the least red curl, in mum's past and in mine. I hugged her, held mum in my arms.

"Johnny," she said from beneath my shoulder, "promise me you will not search for Clara—should she desire it so, she will search for you."

I did not promise.

"Mother, I worry about seeing you all alone in this ruin."

"I am not alone," said she. "Mr. Washington has placed a guard in the house."

"I saw no such guard."

"You were not meant to see him. Besides, I will have my own pirate for company until he returns to Canada."

But Mum's pirate had only one plan—to find Clara.

Sixty-Five

PIRATE JOHN KNEW WHAT WAS KILLING GERT—the prospect of a life without the commander in chief. Revolution had reconnected them both, pulled him from his own cloister at Mount Vernon into the hurly-burly of a war without real perimeters or rigid lines. He had to carry a whole new nation around with him on the rump of his horse. And he had to seek some kind of sanity—call it my mother's red hair—amid all the confusion and morass. Retreating, running from place to place with his prodigious camp bed, he would summon up a woman whose scalp and freckles had once been on fire. Soon he had to see those freckles for himself. His secret refuge would become a bordello in British New York—this bordello and its mistress were his one true headquarters.

And suppose a penniless farmer, sick with dysentery from the Indian wars, did stop at a country inn and dandle me on his knee twenty-five years ago. That still didn't make him my dada. He was a man of great emotion under his dour demean. And he took comfort in sharing his bed at New Windsor with Gertrude's child.

How perverse that I'd been much closer to his bed than my mum would ever be. And how sad that Gert would probably never see him again. The farmer was going home to Mount Vernon. He had little need of a brothel that had been a house of refuge for himself and his spies. And he could not even visit Gert now that a band of patriotic women watched Holy Ground like malignant hawks.

And hawks could certainly not help me find my Clara. I didn't have one friend in the ruins of Manhattan save Prince Paul, my old comrade in arms from the Black Brigade. But I couldn't hire a sedan chair to haul me into Little Africa, even with my promises of silver. Sedan chairs did not travel into Out Ward day or night.

And so I walked. Ye gods, had I been gone so long? I could not find Little Africa—or at least with Africans inside its boundaries. It had the same old hovels, the same lampless streets, but these hovels were inhabited by other refugees—artisans and mechanics who sat idle with their wives and broods of children. There was little work to be had in this ghostly village of Manhattan the Brits had just abandoned.

The Crown had emptied Little Africa, housed blacks in barns, thus giving redcoats room for their own camp followers and whatever artisans they happened to need.

No one knew where the barns were, or had ever heard of an African prince named Paul. And I had to trudge back across the Negroes Burial Ground, through the old Indian barrier, and onto the late Queen Street—some committee had already rechristened it as Pearl, with little markings on the streetlamps.

SUDDENLY THERE WERE soldiers on my trail. I could not imagine what crime I had committed—hadn't been in Manhattan long enough for much larceny. Then I recognized Washington's Life

Guard and their banner, CONQUER OR DIE, with the emblem of an eagle in the corner. They'd been scouring the broken streets for a one-eyed man in a velvet suit. Gertrude must have sent a note to the commander in chief about her pirate son.

The Life Guard escorted me to Washington's temporary Manhattan headquarters on Broadway—the commander in chief and his staff were now occupying the same little mansion where Benedict Arnold and his Peggy had stayed in New York. I could not help but feel 't was a deliberate ploy to wipe out Arnold's traces, one by one.

The vestibule was packed with supplicants, yet I did not have long to wait. A minute after the Life Guard declared I was on the premises, Washington strode out of his office. His back was stooped. He'd aged more than I could ever have imagined—there were deep lines along his mouth. His eyes had little luster. He did not smile or say hello.

He touched the tricorn that seemed so small and out of place on his gigantic crown of reddish gray hair and rasped, "Come with me."

WE WERE A SMALL PARTY OF MEN—the commander in chief, two aides, one Manhattan commissioner, and myself. Washington overwhelmed us with his size, stooped as he was, his tricorn rising above our own little assembly. He did not require a horse in Manhattan, yet he seemed a bit irregular on the ground, as if he could not survey the landscape without a chestnut mare.

He must have known the presence he had. People watched us from every window of the island, from the remains of their porches, from the dead earth of their little gardens, from tents at the side of some road, staring at us with disbelief. He had not run after fame from a war tent in the middle of nowhere, from a dark bridge collapsing under his feet, from a cramped bedchamber overlooking the Hudson, or a field of soldiers with filth on their faces. But in spite of his long silences, his discomfort with speech, he had become America's irresistible man—a king in a tricorn rather than a gold hat.

Yet he would not be our king. It wasn't only because of his distaste for the tyranny that all kings bred. Perhaps he understood that a king was but an exalted jester, a clown put in place to amuse the people while he whipped them and stole from the public treasure. And Washington was not here to amuse or steal.

I began to notice the landmarks of our journey. He visited men who had posed as Loyalists during the war to shield their identity as Washington's agents. So successful was this disguise that the populace abused these men once the redcoats were gone. And Washington had to repair the damage. He did not make a public display. He entered the shop of a Tory tailor on Partition Street, and the mob that accumulated behind him looked in awe. He would not bring the tailor out to greet this mob.

I watched him kiss the tailor and present him with a bag of gold pieces. And I was startled when he turned to me with half a smile. "'Tis not a bribe, John. Tailor Montague risked life and limb to protect our liberty. I will not have men shun him."

We pressed on, visited an apothecary on Nassau Street and a bookman on Golden Hill Street who had been the Crown's own printer in the colonies. There was always a kiss, a hug, and that little bag of gold. We chatted with the bookman for twenty minutes over a dish of tea. This bookman became a hero of our time the moment we left his shop.

"It astonishes," Washington said, "how people turn on you, then rush to kiss your hand."

"His Excellency," I said, "we are all jesters, are we not?"

"Still, even jesters should deport themselves better."

We continued to chat as if the other men in our party were but silent witnesses. The grim lines were gone from his face.

"Johnny, I haven't got a bag of gold pieces to give you."

"But I do not merit any gold, sir."

"I talk now of Malcolm Treat. I protected him, and abandoned you. Treat was brazen, willing to thrust himself into the mouths of lions. We had lads right inside Clinton's quarters thanks to Mad Mal—I'm afraid your Clara will never forgive me."

My eyepatch quivered, but I did not interrupt.

"I am to blame," Washington said. "I had her send you away and could not answer why I punished you rather than Mal, why I let his madness go unbounded—I had need of the madman."

"Excellency, I would suffer Saint John all over again were I to learn where my Clara is."

He did not enlighten me, and it took another moment to realize we had come to Holy Ground.

NO ONE HAD WARNED GERTRUDE that the commander in chief would be stopping at the nunnery. She did not have time to paint her eyes or preen in front of a mirror. She had to greet Washington and his men in her peignoir—I did not count, of course. I was but her whelp, who could see her disrobed every day of the week.

Washington's jaws began to clench. He was filled with emotion, and perhaps that is why he had brought along his little assembly—to prevent him from breaking down.

He was not aloof. He sat beside her.

"Child, thou art so pale."

He could have been back at that country inn with Gertrude twenty-five years ago.

I had never seen my mother purr.

"Johnny, be a dear and find some French biscuits and marmalade for Mr. Washington and his friends."

I didn't have an inkling where to look. But Washington rescued me.

"Gertrude, 'tis a formal occasion, not fit for marmalade."

She purred even harder.

"Formal, General? What could be so formal that it might redress my marmalade?"

He removed a piece of purple cloth in the shape of a heart and pressed it lightly to her own heart with a gold pin—the cloth was all braided in silver.

"General, I have seen no such wonder in all my life."

"Only two others wear it, two as brave as thee."

"Don't forget my nuns," she said, rising enough to examine herself in all her multiple mirrors.

He smiled and seized my mother's shoulders with much affection.

"Then might I impress Gertrude Jennings to wear the Purple Heart for them all? Would that Clara could see it!"

"Later," Mum said. "Not while she is lost to us."

He turned from her to wipe his eyes and asked me to walk with him through the carcass of the Queen's Yard. He was trembling, yet would not lean upon his aides. He clasped my hand for a moment—'t was a mite easier now for a lad to measure his love for Gertrude, tho' perhaps it could not be measured, this one great incaution in the life of a very cautious man.

We stopped outside the front door. The mob was waiting—my mother had become immortal of a sudden. And they looked upon me, the whoreson of Robinson Street, as if I'd sprung whole-born out from under an angel's wing. But 't was Washington's kiss that mattered, not their emulation.

"Child," he said, "your Clara is with the castrato."

And he plunged into the wreckage of Robinson Street with all the mystery of that remark.

Sixty-Six

THERE WAS NOTHING IN THE WORLD MORE DANgerous than an artiste. Pirates paled in comparison. Regulators too. I had seen his image pressed to a wall on my marches through Manhattan.

IL GRAN FELTRINELLI,
Angel of Bologna,
CURRENTLY AT THE JOHN STREET THEATRE,
CASTRATO EXTRAORDINAIRE

He seemed to have a small head on a very large body. He wore a little cap, a kind of metal skirt, had greatly muscled calves, and a scimitar hanging from a sword belt—how could I have dreamt of Clara with a castrato, or any other artiste? But once I knew about the Angel of Bologna and his John Street address, Gertrude was suddenly eager to discuss Clara.

We sat on her bed licking marmalade off our fingers, a silken handkerchief over the Purple Heart. She would not soil it, would not take it off. Clara, it seems, was estranged from my mother's affections for the first time in their lives. She did not have Gertrude's fortitude, Gertrude's steadfastness about the war. She could not obey a command she did not believe in. She was the best silver bullet Washington had ever had—no less bold than Mad Mal, and with more daring.

She'd slip into an enemy camp, seduce some aide of a significant general—I did not relish hearing this—and return with that general's marching orders. But she was unpredictable, her own wildcat, who would not always hurry home with the "bullets" she was carrying. She might stop to feed a wounded woman among the camp followers, share a pipe with African stevedores, bandage up some raving man in the hospital tent.

But then she was told by Gert and Washington himself to "seduce" me into quitting the battlefield at Yorktown and hiding from Mad Mal. Clara had a simpler solution. She offered to strangle Malcolm Treat in his camp cot. But Washington couldn't spare him—a chief of intelligence who would sit in the dark and string secret agents together like a bunch of rag dolls.

Clara did get me to quit Yorktown, but that was her very last silver bullet. She herself quit Washington's camp, slipped back into Manhattan, and fell into the foulest of moods. She would not eat or converse for days. She would smoke her pipe and play with the dolls she had brought with her from Dominica.

Gertrude guarded her silences, did not interfere with Clara. The nuns had precious little to do. The Queen's Yard was now off-limits to British officers and to everybody else. And then Gert asked her to carry one final bullet for the commander in chief. Washington had dire need of information from Charleston, the last British stronghold in the south.

Clara refused. Mad Mal appeared, having come into British Manhattan dressed as a kind of rag doll. He threatened and cajoled, said he would chop off Clara's teats with a tomahawk.

Clara laughed in his face. He leapt at her, and she thrashed him, would have flayed him with her own fingernails had the nuns not climbed on her back and called for the queen.

"Mother," Clara begged, her nose bleeding not from the little major but from the very force of her exertion, "either kill him or kill me."

Mad Mal had to lie abed for days, shivering while the nuns held him in their arms. And Clara vanished from the nunnery with her shoes, her dolls, and her pipe—eleven months ago, December last.

She must have felt that Mum had chosen Mad Mal over her, *and* the man behind Mal—George Washington. Clara's war was always personal and abrupt. She could not lie or cheat for some larger good. And both Gert and the farmer had forced her to cajole. Seems Gert was shrewd about everything but Clara's convictions.

"I will never, never forgive that selfish girl," Mum told me. But 't was evident in every corner of her scrunched face that she missed Clara beyond comprehension—wasn't only George Washington that was helping her waste away.

At first Mum had thought Clara was living down by the docks. She had the nuns search everywhere. Finally they discovered her outside the John Street Theatre with a strange man in a little cap a child might wear. He was taller than Clara, tall as the commander in chief—Feltrinelli, master castrato, who could make the hearts of both men and women miss half a beat. He sang arias from Handel in so high a pitch that even the Divil would have wept to hear it.

Gertrude sent an emissary of nuns to John Street. The nuns came back. Clara, they said, did not have a single matter to discuss with the queen of Holy Ground. Gertrude sent them out again. This time only half the nuns bothered to come back. And Gertrude had to shiver at her own revelation—the nuns were siding with Clara. And within a week they all crept away with their shoes and panniers and pipes. Clara had become their new abbess and queen.

"Johnny," Gertrude said, with the Purple Heart pinned to her chest. "I think to die—I am some forlorn thing without my Clara."

"Mum, I will drag her back by her curly hair."

"No," Gertrude said. "I swore I would not involve you in this intrigue."

"But loving you both, I already am involved."

I TRAVELED TO JOHN STREET, passing seven cows, a runaway horse, and a rodent as long as a man's arm. The theatre sat in much debris. John Street was like an obstacle course with spent cannons, loose wagon gear, and torn tents. 'Tis a wonder any lad could find his way within. But I did, and there was not a particle of chaos or debris inside the playhouse, with its chandeliers and pitched balconies and plush seats. And the Angel of Bologna had his own assistants, it seems—Gertrude's nuns, now Clara's. They sat in "paradise," the mountainous peak of the uppermost balcony. I could see the telltale coals of fire in their pipes, but not their faces.

I sat down, and shortly the theatre began to fill. No one had bothered asking me to buy a subscription, and I'm not convinced there was one to buy. But within an hour we all sat in such close proximity I had half a dozen knees next to mine.

I had never met such a variety of rabble. Sailors, strumpets, and beggars, mingled with Hessian deserters and their newfound wives, several itinerant merchants and foreign noblemen stranded in Manhattan. There was also, I soon discovered, a whole gallery of madmen and melancholics that did not miss a single performance of John Street's male soprano, who had the reputation of curing melancholy princes and kings.

I watched his sinfonia assemble in the pit—five ragged men with two horns, two violas, and a harpsichord. They practiced on their instruments like charter members of a children's asylum delivering its own lamentable noise. I saw little future in it. Then the curtain rose and all the lamentation stopped. Feltrinelli stood on stage alone. He did have a metal skirt and an infant's cap. And without the slightest introduction, or the scampering of some hired clown, the Angel of Bologna burst into song, his rib cage pumping like a bellows.

I was woefully confused, a man singing with all the sweetness of a woman and the strength and coloratura of a male demon. He went through an entire opera of Handel, singing and reciting every part—shepherd, nymph, or Cyclops.

'T was the tale of Galatea, a tall and beautiful nymph, who is in love with Acis, a Sicilian shepherd boy. But Polyphemus, a brooding one-eyed giant, hungers for Galatea.

"I rage—I melt—I burn!" bemoans the Cyclops. He longs for his own shepherd's pipe, so he can breathe "Sweet Galatea's beauty." Yet he knows 't will be hard to tame a nymph "fierce as storms that bluster." He invites all the "wildings" to a feast—all the wild goats of Sicily—and Galatea. But the nymph will not have him. "Go, monster . . . I loathe the host, I loathe the feast."

The brute despairs and kills Acis with a boulder. But Galatea uses all her art as a nymph to turn Acis' own gushing blood into a fountain that will sing to her from the rocks.

Now I understood the costume that Feltrinelli paraded in. The slippers that he wore were a shepherd's shoes, the tiny cap was Galatea's, and the metal skirt and scimitar belonged to Polyphemus, as if he could isolate or combine all three characters at will, like some prodigious machine.

Yet he was no musical engine. His ability to range from Galatea's soft lament to Polyphemus' deep-throated cries was not akin to magic. All his voices seemed to fly from the profound sadness of his own monstrosity—the crippling of his sex at eight or nine would grant him a godlike unbroken voice and also a terrifying "mannishness" that would soon turn his entire body into an enormous male organ.

Feltrinelli was a false woman in a fierce man. He could have charmed a serpent out of its skin with a single note and cured every melancholic in Manhattan. I could not take my eyes off him. I was lost in his multiplicity. I imagined myself as Polyphemus, condemned to a life without Galatea.

When the curtain lowered, I discovered Feltrinelli's enterprise. He did not believe in subscription lists. He jumped off the stage with a wire basket to collect his fee and moved with said basket from aisle to aisle—every man and woman contributed to his welfare. God save the yob who did not.

And while he collected, the nuns came down from "paradise" with wire baskets of their own. And they would not let me clasp them in my arms. They yelped like skittish colts when they saw me and disappeared faster than the Divil. I cared not with whom they conspired. I sat in my seat until the theatre emptied and I was left in that plush velvet void.

Feltrinelli descended into the theatre's bowels with his wire basket. I waited. And the castrato emerged from a little trap door in the pit—took six or seven strides with his magnificent calves and stopped at my seat, wearing his metal skirt.

"Cavaliere John," he said in a voice no less deep than mine. "Clara loves you, but you must not come here again."

I didn't carry a dagger in my sleeve, like Gentle Jack. But even if I did, how could I dirk a castrato who bore me no ill will? Yet I had to hold my ground.

"Signore, I cannot leave the premises 'til I speak with Clara."

"She will not speak," said the castrato.

"Then perhaps you might desire her to do so."

The nuns had crept up behind him, clung to his metal skirt—now 't was clear to me that they had never really belonged to Gertrude. More than half the nuns were of mixed blood; superstitious creatures, they could have been casting about for their very own messiah—an octoroon with blond hair—and might have belonged to Clara from the day she arrived on Robinson Street with her rag dolls. Clara had been the sound of their own silence, stubborn and inchoate as they themselves were. Clara had puffed on a pipe with them. Gertrude did not. And 't was as natural as song itself that they would have followed Clara to John Street once there was a battle between their two mums.

Then I heard Clara's voice rebound off the castrato's back.

"Johnny One-Eye, I will not deal with ye 'til you promise to break all ties with that witch you call a mother."

I'd have promised her half the world and all my holdings on Saint John, but I would not deny Gert.

"Zounds, I will answer no woman whose visage I cannot see."

"I'm too ashamed," she said. "I dishonored you—and myself. I should never have obeyed Washington and his witch. I should have drowned them in my spittle, and done worse to you, Johnny One-Eye. Because you should have kidnapped me at Yorktown, drugged me, socked me in the face, and dragged me off to Canada as your concubine."

"Dearest," I said. "I do not have the means within me to sock you."

"But the occasion called for it."

"Hang the occasion! You must come closer. The seats here are too pitched. I am plagued with vertigo."

She stepped out from behind Feltrinelli and the nuns, her

freckled face gleaming under the chandeliers. Mighty God Himself could not have made another such Galatea.

I fell back into my seat and started to cry.

"Forgive me, Clara. 'Tis your loveliness. I cannot bear it. I have suffered so without your face."

She held her freckles close to me, like some act of war.

"Now will you promise unto God to untie yourself from your witch of a mother?"

"Clara, I cannot. I have come to reconcile both of you . . . and drag you back to Holy Ground by your hair."

I was a fool to provoke her—perhaps I wanted to *feel* her anger. She leapt on top of me, straddled my velvet chair, began to flail at my arms and face. I licked my own blood, and the sheer presence of Clara stirred me while the blows landed. I could have lived with that. But then she stopped. Her body stiffened against mine and went all ashiver.

The nuns watched us in their own silent rapture, as if Galatea had been reborn in front of their eyes, the tallest of tall nymphs, with a one-eyed pirate as her puny Cyclops, who could not even steal her from a man in a metal skirt.

The castrato plucked her away from me with his long beautiful hands, and she sat crooked against his shoulder, the entire length of her, like a collapsed child.

And the rub of it was that I had never been more jealous. He stroked her hair, sang Polyphemus' song—*"I rage—I melt—I burn!"*—and the sound of it ended her agitation. The Angel of Bologna seemed to have a most tender streak.

He carried her into the theatre's dizzying decline, with the nuns still clutching his metal skirt.

Sixty-Seven

'T WAS EARLY IN DECEMBER, AND I HAD BEEN ON York Island but a week, having missed the British departure by a hair—they had marched from the Bowery to Bowling Green on the tempestuous morning of November the 25th, climbed aboard their battleships in brilliant scarlet coats, as if America had been but an afterthought and meant nothing, nothing at all. And the lads who arrived in their place, arrived in rags, like some amateur army—thus my mother told me.

At the head of this motley crew was the commander in chief astride his chestnut mare. The populace was transfixed—not an eye wandered far from Washington as he rode down Broadway, without the rat-a-tat of a single drum. There had never been such silence, not in seven years, as if no one could believe the Brits were really gone—until Washington passed in his war cape, his tricorn bobbing higher than the tallest lamplighter could ever reach with his pole.

Did Gert hope that Washington would glance at her? He had not yet given her a Purple Heart, and she had not seen him, not touched his face, in three and a half years.

She was standing behind a barrier, at the very edge of Robinson Street as it spilled onto Broadway, standing without her nuns, who might have captured his attention. But he did not turn to look at Holy Ground. Gert would swear that his jaw did ripple once.

AND NOW, NINE OR TEN DAYS LATER, you could not find another general in Manhattan—officers, weary of war, were running home to the hinterlands—and Washington had to survive with a skeletal family; his lads ran to Fraunces' Tavern at the corner of the old canal and the newly named Pearl Street, to discuss the general's farewell banquet with "Black Sam" Fraunces, who hailed from Barbados and had been the Continental Army's official caterer.

General Clinton had often sat at Sam's center table—he served the best roasts, pies, and puddings in America. But Sam had also smuggled food aboard the prison ships and foiled several plots to poison Washington's peas. And now he was preparing the last lunch the commander in chief would have in Manhattan before he returned to Virginia and a life without camp cots and war tents.

Meanwhile, Washington remained on our island. He'd stop and sit with a mechanic near the docks, always with a mob around him, hungry for another glimpse of the great general—his battles, won or lost, had passed into myth. His retreats were now seen as victories in waiting, every skirmish a vital piece of the grand design. No matter how often he tripped, made mistakes—this was part of some vast puzzle of war.

I had passed him on our broken streets, had watched as mothers and babies kissed his hand; sailors and artisans got down on their knees to this tall man in the tiny hat. But I was preoccupied with my own little drama on John Street—neither the nuns nor anyone else molested me at the theatre door. I held to my seat under the chandeliers.

The Angel of Bologna would stop and sit for a few moments while loping about the theatre with his wire basket.

"Cavaliere," he said, "I have pleaded your case. But she insists. You had your chance to steal her, she says. Still, she cries every night. And that is an excellent sign."

Consoling as he was, he did not invite me to visit his dressing closet.

So I sat, and one night I saw that something was amiss—people were greatly agitated, as if yet another conflagration had decided to visit us. But I could not smell any smoke or glimpse a fiery curtain. Then a soldier clumped up the stairs, much out of breath, and informed me that Mr. Washington was waiting near the orchestra pit. I hurried down to meet him.

"Johnny," he said, his nose a trifle red. "I have a little unfinished business. Come with me."

And I followed him through unlit corridors where we both had to duck our heads, and into a maze that finally led to the castrato's dressing closet. He knocked once; the door opened a crack—I could see one of Feltrinelli's gray eyes—and Washington said, "Sir, will you have the kindness to inform Mistress Clara that General Washington seeks ten minutes of her time."

THE CASTRATO'S DRESSING CLOSET had become a sanctuary for the nuns' hatboxes and shoes—such articles being piled to the ceiling on uncertain shelves that leaned like towers. I still could not grasp Feltrinelli's hold over the nuns, including Clara. I was aware that some castratos had a strange sexual prowess, and that irate husbands of curious and emboldened wives often considered them as predatory creatures. And that is why Feltrinelli had come to Manhattan—he'd scandalized every major European village, even the minor ones, and had nowhere else to go.

But Clara did not cling to his metal skirts.

She was much confused by the general's visit, her freckles rising up with a raw and red color.

"Gen'ral, 'tis unseemly of you to come and plead Johnny's cause."

"Clara, the cause I plead is none but my own."

That had already disarmed her. "Do sit down, Mr. Washington. We aren't cannibals here."

But sit he would not. He went down on one knee. Clara put her hands over her eyes.

"Mistress," he said, "you must look at me."

"I do not have the power, sir, not whilst you kneel."

"You must look at me."

She peeked at him from betwixt her fingers.

"Mistress Clara, you have been reckless in my behalf. You have risked your life more times than I care to remember. Not one other person has been bolder than thee. Yet I did misuse ye, child."

"Excellency," Clara said, "ye did not. I am a brazen girl."

"Child, I misused thee. I did not honor your judgment. I forced you to be my own instrument in sending Johnny away. And thus robbed you of your power—to believe in the agency of what you were doing. I am adamant, Clara. You must forgive me."

"Gen'ral," she said, removing the mask of her own hands. "I can't even consider it 'til you get off your damn knee."

Washington rose up like a reeling behemoth and Clara fell into his arms with such force, I feared he would topple.

"Gen'ral," Clara said from within his shoulder, "where is Mad Mal, if I may be so bold to ask?"

"In the safety of an asylum," Washington said. And then he

kissed her eyes and announced that he had urgent business elsewhere.

I longed to remain awhile with Clara, but she looked right past me, as if I were a piece of dust in some unknown galaxy.

THE VERY NEXT MORNING, a little before noon, I strolled down to Black Sam's in my green sash. I walked under the fanlight and entered the Long Room, where British officers had sampled Sam's best pudding but a few weeks ago. The floors were waxed and the tables set with decanters of wine, great platters of bread, cutlets and cold meats, and endless pies. I was startled at how few officers there were at the farewell—less than ten, and I did not recognize a one. But I did recognize Sam, who stood near the wall in a white wig and black coat. He did not have to present himself with the finicky smile of a publican. Sam did not have to smile at all. I introduced myself to him as the late Lieutenant Stocking, home from Saint John.

"Mr. Sam, I have been away from our island. Might I ask you what has happened to Little Africa?"

He seemed genuinely puzzled. "Which Little Africa?"

"The streets in Out Ward where the Negroes once dwelled."

He laughed, and I espied one gold tooth.

"Lieutenant, the Little Africa you mention did not exist for me. It had no such name—just a jumble of streets north of the Burial Ground."

"And the people who dwelled there?"

"Some died in the war, I am sad to say. Others ran from men who tried to reclaim them. Others lost out in some greedy land grab."

"They just vanished, Mr. Sam?"

"Appears so—but vanishin' means they might have a better chance of staying alive."

Sam didn't have much time to speculate on a lost population. He had other guests. And I could not seem to enter into the little crop of officers that had come to Washington's farewell before going on furlough—perhaps 't was because I had no semblance of a uniform other than my green sash. But one captain of dragoons did shake my hand.

"How I envy you," he warbled.

I wondered if riding on a horse so long had rendered him insane.

"Lieutenant Stocking, I would give my right arm to have taken part in the capture of Redoubt Ten."

Another soldier drifted into Sam's, his uniform all askew, but with the same green sash as mine. This soldier also wore an eye patch—'t was none other than Mad Mal. Had he wandered out of his asylum? He could not even butter a slice of bread, his hand shivered so. And I realized soon enough that Malcolm Treat was his own asylum.

I would not badger him—my war with Treat was over. But he visited me, his mouth crammed with bread and butter.

"I saw ye," he said. "I saw ye at the thee-ayter on John Street."

I could not bear to watch him fumble. I wiped his mouth with a napkin.

"The nuns captured me, Johnny, trapped me between the aisles. There I am, lyin' prostrate, with the nuns spitting at me, attacking my face, on account of Clara, and behold, Clara comes—your Clara. She must have read my perilous condition, must have pitied poor Mal. She rocked me in her arms. Johnny, I have been Gawd-awful. But I am glad I did not kill ye."

He lapsed into silence and returned to the luncheon table.

A current seemed to wash over us, like some cold wind prior to a storm. Every soldier stood at attention—except Malcolm

Treat—as Washington entered the room. We stood apart from him, but Mad Mal clung to the general, like a clown to his king.

Where in hell was Ham? He should have been at Washington's side, wearing *my* green sash. Ham had a congressman's swagger, I was told, but he could have come up from Annapolis or wherever Congress was meeting at the moment—it was run out of Philadelphia by a gang of rebellious troops. Yet Washington did not search the Long Room for Alexander Hamilton. And I wondered if he had invited Hamilton at all. Perhaps he never felt comfortable under the awesome fire of Ham's azure eyes. Or perhaps he missed Ham so much, the clarity and excitement Ham could bring to every encounter, that he sought a much more anonymous peace and quiet here at Sam's, during his last hour as commander in chief.

The Old Man put some food on his plate, but he could not eat. He set the plate down and asked that wine be served. Sam himself poured from a decanter, filled each glass; then Washington filled a glass for Sam. His hand shook as he poured.

We raised our glasses, and Washington addressed us in a voice that seemed like a train of silence with a few syllables. With a heart full of gratitude, he said, he must take leave of us now.

He could barely sip the wine—the emotion locked inside Washington during seven years of war must have devoured him.

"I cannot—I cannot come to each of you but shall feel obligated if each of you will come to me and take me by the hand."

Mad Mal went to him first, and 't was not a shaking of hands, but some kind of embrace. And now I recognized Major Treat's worth to Washington. His very madness must have served as a respite for the commander in chief. Methinks Washington had much need of a clown.

He embraced the others. I was last in line. I did not dream of calling him "dada," but what are dreams at a farewell luncheon party?

"Father," I said, "I shall miss thee."

He held me in his arms and kissed me right between the eyes—that kiss landed like a silver bullet.

"And I shall more than miss ye, Johnny One-Eye, but that will not prevent me from ripping your heart out should you ever abandon Gertrude and Clara."

Ah, what a commander in chief! To curse and kiss in the very same breath.

And he walked out of Black Sam's, abandoning all of us, even his clown.

BUT WE DID NOT ABANDON HIM. We scuttled behind the commander in chief, some of us still clutching our wineglasses. His Life Guard had assembled, while half the populace of Manhattan stood outside Black Sam's like startled, shivering birds; children reached out to touch him, their mothers all agog. But he was still too torn with emotion to deliver even the faintest of smiles. I stood beside him now, saw the spasms in his cheek, this measured man who was suddenly at the very border of control. He stopped. I thought he would swoon, but he whispered in my ear as I clutched his hand.

"Johnny, where the Divil am I?"

"In Manhattan, Excellency. Near Whitehall."

He was a farmer returning to his farm. Perhaps I espied the end of a certain possibility—of boldness itself—a life without his redhead, without Gert.

"Child, will you walk with me a while?"

We proceeded to Whitehall Slip, where a barge was waiting, all decked in garlands, like some floating arbor. But I lost the clasp of his hand as we approached the barge. His Life Guard had bumped me out of the way. They helped him aboard, and while a gaggle of men, women, and children mobbed the ferry slip, I wept like a little boy. I feared I would not see him again as I watched the children wave goodbye to the commander in chief, most of them clutching garlands. But his eyes and theirs never did meet.

"Adieu," shouted several of his officers, who did not accompany him. But he was far away, in some territory inside himself—dreaming of his redhead, I'd like to imagine.

The barge pulled away from Whitehall the moment he was seated and vanished into the mist, tho' we could still hear the crash of oars for a very long time.

Sixty-Eight

I SHIVER TO REVEAL WHAT HAPPENED NEXT. 'T was almost as if Washington or some remnant of him—substance and shadow—remained with us. I wonder now if his appearance at the castrato's dressing closet had been staged for my benefit alone. All I can tell you is that the shoe closet at the Queen's Yard began to fill with shoes a shelf at a time, like some supernatural symmetry.

Then articles of clothing appeared in the nuns' own closets—a hat, a kidskin glove, a bodice braided in gold thread. Gertrude suspicioned Clara, said the house was possessed of demons Clara had sent all the way from Dominica. I could not agree. Demons would fill a house with dread, not nuns' shoes.

My logic was soon borne out. The nuns themselves arrived in our garden with hatboxes, porters carrying their trunks and storage chests. They immediately moved into their closets without uttering a word to Queen Gertrude or myself. They did not demonstrate the least curiosity about Mum's Purple Heart. They would sit in the parlor and smoke their pipes. Gert was bitter about it. I was not.

The nuns were waiting for their very own queen. And she appeared the next morning, with Feltrinelli at her side. Clara's woolly blond hair was coiffed to heaven—she broke off the branches of our wilted apple tree with her headdress. The waist of her emerald-colored gown was so pinched 't was a miracle she could breathe at all. She hadn't decorated herself to win over any yob or pirate. She'd come to battle with the other queen of Holy Ground, to defeat Gert with the sheer wonder of the way she looked.

She raged against my mother for her "cold-bloodedness," as Clara might have called it, her willingness to sacrifice her own son to "the stupid dance of war," to sacrifice the nunnery, Clara, and herself for Washington's sake. But truth is, Clara could not live without the nunnery, and there was no nunnery without Gert. She loved my mother and loathed her with equal vehemence, and the confusion had agitated Clara to such degree there wasn't even the littlest chance of parlaying with her.

She walked into Gert's boudoir, lowering her headdress like some engine of war. But Gertrude wasn't unprepared. She sat on her bed, her own red hair puffed out, the Purple Heart pinned to a magnificent velvet robe, her eyes painted a most subtle blue—she looked like a wild flower in a sea of pillows.

We were all assembled now—Clara, the castrato, the nuns, even the one Life Guard Washington had given Gert to protect us from pillagers. I sat on a gilded chair, smoking a pipe Clara had left behind. She knocked the pipe from my mouth with its burning timbers—rather have violence than nothing, nothing at all.

But Gert had to bear the brunt of Clara's attack.

"Mother, what in God's name is that little rag you wear upon your chest?"

'T was a fatal blow. Gertrude started to sob, and her eyes bled that blue paint.

"You are pitiless, Clara. 'Tis a Purple Heart, given to me by the general. Only two others are permitted to wear it."

"Did the other two also send their boys to Canada?"

"I did what had to be done."

"Mother, should I tell you what it was like having to sleep in the same tent at Yorktown with Mad Mal?"

"I will not listen," Gertrude said.

"You most certainly will. 'T was like having a cold pea pod on your belly."

I knew not whether to laugh at that pea pod or cry at its proximity to Clara. But my darling continued her attack. "Pray, are all of Mr. Washington's Purple Hearts redheaded crows like yourself, Mum?"

"And you," Gert said, "with snot in your nose when I found you. I had to pick the lice out of your hair."

"And have I not repaid you a hundredfold lying on my back with strange men who ne'er even heard of a monthly wash? I had to scrub their balls—I'd call it yeoman's service."

I was in dangerous waters listening to Clara—I did not like her attention to such detail. Some yob's filthy genitals would haunt my dreams for the rest of my life.

Mum was at a decided disadvantage, ignorant as she was of Clara's strategies. Clara had discovered her war cries in the African quarters of Dominica. The slaves would constantly mimic their masters, have mock battles in which they'd shout and scream in the voices of their masters and mistresses, hurling insults like musket balls—they called it *fantaisie*, or fancy talk, in their creole.

Clara had told me about that *fantaisie* when we were children, and we'd have our own epic battles of words in my narrow bed. But Mum could never have mastered its cruel play.

I longed to break into their fight with my own *fantaisie*. But I waited, lads, like a crouching tiger. And then Clara, my poor lovely child with her pyramid of hair, deigned to attack Gertrude's one and only son—me.

"Mother," she said, "I hear that your Johnny once resided in Mr. Washington's britches, as his pet homunculus."

"That is a most bitter lie," Mum said.

"I believe he sucks on a biberon all day, like the infant he has always been and will always be."

And I leapt in. "Methinks you could use a biberon, Clara dear. It might serve you well the next time you have to wash a man's balls."

She did not take kindly to my *fantaisie*. Her face contorted. "I'll biberon you," she said, and lunged at me with her painted fingernails—that first rip felt like a razor right under my eye patch. I was about to swoon. And that's when my mother shrieked and plummeted off the bed. And Clara stopped flailing.

I'd lost the privilege of helping me own mum—Clara scooped her up and placed her on the pillows. The furor was gone from Clara's green eyes. Seeing my mother fall must have settled that confusion of loving and loathing, settled it like a kindly slap in the face. But who could ever be certain with Clara?

"Gertrude," she said, "you should order me from this house. I bring havoc. I always have."

"I love your havoc," Gertrude said. "I will not live my life in an empty house—sons abscond. Their shadows are so short. But daughters can fill a closet—"

"With havoc," Clara said. "And all the necessary little noises."

I was seething, mates. I watched them conspire like a pair of lady pirates. They kissed one another, cried in each other's arms.

"Clara dear," Gert said, "I have just decided. You will dwell in my bedchamber. 'T will be your headquarters."

Clara arched her eyebrows with a certain elegance. "I will not steal your closet, Mum. Never."

"But yours is much too small."

"'Tis infinity, Mum, if I feel it so—I should not have called you a redheaded crow, nor mocked your medal."

"I am a redheaded crow," Gert insisted. "And Mr. Washington said that this Purple Heart was as much yours as mine. Did he not say so, John?"

I was wrong about me mum—she had as much force as Clara's *fantaisie*.

Sixty-Nine

CLARA AND I LIVED LIKE ENEMIES IN THE SAME house—seems I was not included in her rapprochement with mum. She ne'er said a word to me. But I could not fathom her relations with the castrato, who flaunted himself with the nuns. I'll wager he slept with every one.

His tenure at the playhouse was now complete—it had other occupants, a troupe of jugglers that recited Shakespeare while tossing cannonballs and stuffed parrots into the theatre's little sky. I did not bother to investigate its fare. I would sit with Feltrinelli between his trips to the nuns' closets. He was a most singular fellow, quite eager to recount his adventures with Clara. He'd first met her while strolling on the docks. She had just fled Holy Ground with her hatboxes—had run from Gertrude. Feltrinelli could not recall the exact date. His own calendar was occupied with Polyphemus and Galatea. She, who could have become the concubine of half a dozen nabobs or British generals, decided to rot away on the docks.

The Angel of Bologna was moved by her audacity. He brought her to his dressing closet. He smiled, figured he would seduce her with a song. The Cyclops always worked best, so he plied her with Polyphemus' saddest songs. And when he embarked on the pleasant little road of kissing Clara, he had a rude surprise. She asked him to pay for the kiss.

Whatever manly arts he had were shattered—he, Il Gran Feltrinelli, who cured kings of melancholia while sleeping with their wives, had never once paid for a woman.

He felt like a fool, but he argued his case to Clara—mutilation, he said, had turned him into a marvel, a "geldling," as he called himself, with his own sexual trumpet that could perform for hours.

Clara was penniless, without a home, and yet she laughed. "Maestro, you still have to pay me ten London pounds—'tis my fixed fee to look at a geldling or any other creature who hath no balls."

"Could you not fall in love?" the geldling asked with a meekness that was unusual for him. "Would love not lower your fee?"

"But I already am in love—with a one-eyed rascal, and for him, yes, I might lower the fee."

He couldn't even adopt Clara—Clara was the one who adopted him. Her household of nuns arrived on John Street, two at a time, and the geldling was suddenly blessed with a family, while Clara's own one-eyed rascal was not included.

And then the prodigal daughter returned to Holy Ground with her entire brood.

I COULD NOT GET NEAR CLARA'S DOOR. Whenever I approached, she would hurl a shoe at me. And one day, as Christmas neared, she fell into a deep melancholia without apparent cause. She could not leave her closet. Gertrude would call upon her, queen to queen, but Clara's condition did not improve.

Gertrude brought in doctors and metaphysicians who wanted to bleed the girl—have worms and beetles sit on her belly—but she would not succumb to their tricks. Feltrinelli sang to her the whole of Handel's *Saul*, but Clara seemed to suffer through the mad peregrinations surrounding this melancholy king. The more he sang, the sadder she grew.

The nuns prepared poultices and potions of molasses and sage tea. But Clara would neither wear the poultices nor drink the concoctions of tea. And these same nuns, who had been ignoring me, who wouldn't even share a pipe, suddenly had need of Gentle John.

They took me by the hand, like elves in a fairy tale, led me into Clara's closet, and locked this lad inside. How to explain my fright? I was alone at last with my tall nymph, my Galatea, who had such strangeness in her green eyes. Gertrude or the nuns must have covered her shoulders with a shawl. And she sat on her quilts without a nod of recognition.

Ye gods, the freckles had fled from her face!

"Clara, I wouldn't be here had the nuns not captured me and—"

I had to halt as she gazed upon my own miserable mien.

"Johnny, One-Eye, must you be an imbecile? I have been waiting for ye."

"'Tis a most peculiar wait. To toss a shoe at me the minute I approach."

"But you claim to be a pirate—more, a seasoned man of the world. Yet you cannot surmount a shoe? You might have tossed it back in my face."

"Darling," I said, "if you torture me like this, I will surely cry."

"I have plenty of criers. And I have no need of one now—I am turning into stone and I cannot stop it."

"How may I help? Speak! And I'll challenge the Divil."

"Fie!" she said. "I could challenge the Divil all by myself. I am laden with remorse—over you. Mr. Washington can come prancing on one knee. But he cannot acquit my own sin. I tricked ye into leaving the battlefield at Yorktown. I crept into your tent like some wanton girl employed by the Continental Army. 'T was the witch in me that did it, not Clara."

"Perfect," I said, trying to reason like a philosopher at College Hall. "Then I will exorcise the witch. Burn her to death."

The dullness went out of her eyes. "Burn the witch, Johnny, and you might burn Clara."

"Better still. I'll be done with both of ye."

Now she even laughed.

"The maestro's singin' makes me deaf. I miss your fairy tales."

I climbed onto her bed like a barking dog. I charged into her with my skull.

"Clara, once upon a time there lived a very tall witch, so tall that she could ne'er enter a house with her very own head."

"Pray then, what did she do?"

"Twist it right off at the stem, and reconstitute it once she was inside."

"You must not harm her," Clara said. "Methinks I like the witch."

"Harm her?" I said. "I will paddle her bum 'til it is raw. I will ravish her in hot oil."

Delight, pure delight, exploded upon her face.

"If you boil her, John, I shall never leave you, not in ten thousand years."

We kissed like children on a rampage. We chewed at each other's mouth with such monstrous labor, I worried we would shed all our teeth, tear the roof right off my mother's castle, and never come to Christmas.

Seventy

WHAT MARVELOUS COIN THE HOUSE OF GERTRUDE suddenly had—it rose right out of the ruins. And not because of any nun's business, but because of Washington's public visit to Holy Ground, and my mother's Purple Heart. Madame was now the sage of Robinson Street.

Daughters of Liberty, dressed in homespun and calico, waited in line to sit with Gert and have China tea with a woman they had scorned throughout the revolution. The Committee of Mechanics, Grocers, Retailers, and Innholders, which had captured most of the seats on the new Common Council, sent their own representative to meet with Gert—said representative was not against reopening Robinson Street, were it done in an orderly and quiet manner, without nuns of any kind parading on the porches in their undergarments. The committee itself would become a silent partner in the operation.

But after conferring with Clara and the nuns, Madame refused this offer to rebuild as a brothel. The nuns had grown too fat and were disinclined to have some yob in their closet. They preferred to remain part of Feltrinelli's private harem.

Madame saw little future in any Manhattan "street of shame." 'T would not be compatible with her Purple Heart, and she disliked silent partners. No, she would turn the Queen's Yard into some grand salon and millinery shop. Gert was shrewd enough to gamble that once all the fervor died down these new American nabobs would want to clothe their revolutionary wives in the best European fashion. And should one such nabob catch the fancy of a particular nun, who was Madame to oppose the contours and contortions of love?

This was all odious to Clara, who had risen out of her melancholy. She despised any mercantile exchange with a committee of grasping mechanics and grocers, despised having innholders in the house. But 't was also a convenient cover. In fact, the Queen's Yard remained a house of spies. But the warfare had changed considerably. There weren't redcoated combatants, or British generals in Broadway mansions. We were a different breed of warriors now, tho' Clara let me cling to the illusion that I was her own personal pirate.

She had been shielding African slaves throughout the war, hiding them in barns along the Hudson, so the Brits could not press them into service as cooks and common mules in one of their Caribbean colonies—but neither Clara nor Gertrude had bothered to tell Gentle John. We lads fight our little wars, while women circle around us, like falconers with their own invisible falcons.

'T was not the British who had dismantled Little Africa, tho' they believed in their little myth. Clara and the denizens of Little Africa understood that blacks would be slaughtered one day by some vicious drunken gang taking revenge on a "Negro rising" that had never happened.

She had tried to smuggle some African slaves aboard the *Lady's Adventure*, the *Mars*, the *Hesperus*, and other British ships that carried Loyalists to Canada this past spring, but her own plans misfired. The captains of these vessels couldn't protect runaways who were not listed in the "Book of Negroes," that invidious record of all freed blacks. And Clara's runaways were soon returned to their masters.

Never again would she trust any official route. And on New Year's Eve, while soldiers and civilians were preparing to unleash candle bombs and rockets in the harbor, Clara invited us to some mysterious party—perhaps another Ethiopian Ball at which she might again wear a mask. But she offered not a single detail. We drove along the road to Greenwich in Gertrude's new carriage, with the castrato himself at the reins, Clara and Gert inside with several nuns, who sat in tiers, and I myself on top of the carriage with another cargo of nuns.

We had no escort, no attachment of armed riders, and Cowboys still lurked at the perimeters of Manhattan. Clara would not permit me to carry a gun.

"Darling," I said, shouting into the wind, "our trip is full of danger and folly." I did not even know our destination.

Her headdress appeared outside the carriage door like some tapered blond pole. "God will provide."

I cared not for her sudden interest in the Great Provider. I have found it a sad but necessary truth that in most instances the Provider does not provide. But I couldn't argue with wind in my mouth.

And then, on a lonely fork in the road, near the King's Bridge, at the very northern limit of Manhattan, we did confront a band of highwaymen—five lads on spotted horses, long hats over their eyes.

"Stand and deliver," barked one of the highwayman, with a pistol in either hand.

I crouched above the coachman's seat, while Feltrinelli raised his horsewhip.

"Deliver or die," said the same lad, as he shot the whip out of Feltrinelli's fist. And that's when Clara descended from the carriage.

"I'll deliver you all to the Divil," she rasped, knocking the highwayman out of his saddle. He groveled on the ground, hat still on his head.

"Forgive us, Your Highness, but we did not recognize ye in the dark."

"Damn you," she shouted, knocking off the highwayman's hat, "you were commissioned to protect this road, not rob people."

The other four removed their hats—I had to lower my lantern or I would have failed to recognize that these highwayman were all black.

And now we had our escort, as Clara's Cowboys rode behind our bus.

WE ARRIVED AT AN ABANDONED BREWERY on the Hudson, just below Westchester. We did not leave our bus abroad, but rode it into the brewery, which was of a prodigious size—vast as the Fields as far as I could tell. 'T was filled with monstrous wooden tubs that smelled of malt, yet this cave above the ground had fewer than twenty inhabitants, the last men and women of Little Africa, who had to live among wooden tubs until Clara could ferry them to some faraway land where slaveholders did not exist.

I did not see my old compatriot, Prince Paul. Clara couldn't seem to account for him, said he might have died in battle. But no one could say whether he had been fighting against the redcoats or against us. Perhaps he'd escaped to some other far country and might reappear at a kinder period.

But I did recognize someone else—Black Sam of Fraunces' Tavern, and he wasn't in a publican's coat. He wore a scarf of many colors, like some Joseph in the land of Egypt. And I had to wonder how many of Washington's former agents were involved in ferrying Negroes out of York Island. We were in a most pernicious war. The Cowboys of Westchester, it seems, had gone into the profession of "bird catchers"—viz., the lucrative field of capturing runaways and returning them to their masters. But there were only black Cowboys in the barn tonight.

We all drank Madeira from dented tin cans. I did not pose questions to Sam. Let him have his treble life—innholder, spy, and ferryman for slaves.

We could hear the salute of cannons in the harbor, hear the whistle of candle bombs. Yet we still had a dozen minutes 'til '84. And there was no celebration on all the island that was as sweet *and* bitter as ours, inside this old brewery at Manhattan's edge. The castrato enchanted us, sang from Handel's *Samson.* How could we not have wept over the blinded brute, Samson in chains before the prison-house in Gaza, whilst the Philistines celebrate his defeat? Yet as wondrous as Feltrinelli was in all his voices, 't was Delilah's that held us in thrall.

"Sun, moon, and stars are dark to me!" Samson says. And then Delilah, his betrayer-wife, bursts upon the scene with her "odorous perfume." The blinded brute catches Delilah's scent, calls her a hyena and a whore. She does not sway. "I know thy warbling charms," she says. She wants to touch his hand. He promises to tear her limb from limb. She burns with "doubled raptures" but is condemned never to go near him again.

And all of us—slaves and nuns, pirates and princesses, innkeepers and colored Cowboys—might have read our own fate in Samson's bondage, but were still subdued by Delilah's songs. Perhaps 't was Feltrinelli's art, or my own primitive wish to hurtle headlong into a tale of love, no matter how desperate. I was "love's prisoner," like Samson himself.

I began to brood over this vast echo chamber where the sounds of Delilah rocketed off ceiling and walls. And I pondered whether the commander in chief had been involved in building this secret barrack. Had he visited the brewery whilst he was in Manhattan, meeting with this same band of angels?

"Mother," I asked a minute before the New Year, "has Mr. Washington ever been near this fork in the road?"

The other queen answered. Queen Clara was suddenly formal with me, formal as a mask. "Thou art a dunce, Johnny One-Eye. The slave quarters at Mount Vernon stretches half a mile. Why would Mr. Washington succor Manhattan runaways?"

"Out of some natural affection," I said.

"Yes, he hath much of that," my mother said, clutching her Purple Heart—and I knew in my bones that Washington had been here, in this curious cavern. 'T was his last secret mission of the war, to look after these Manhattan runaways, who had been caught in a most dire whirlwind.

And as the cannons boomed at midnight—to mark our first year of peace—Clara kissed me on the mouth.

"The gen'ral's left us some particles of himself, Johnny. Ain't that enough?"

She kissed Gertrude, all the nuns, Black Sam, the colored Cowboys, and the brewery slaves. And as she moved from face to face, dancing on the toes of her slippers like some fierce Delilah born of song, I realized one little thing.

The Divil himself would have to kill me before I'd ever leave Clara again.

Hercules

AN ENDING

Mount Vernon

November 1799

He had become a wild man. He would not dress for dinner. He wore an old ribbon round his neck—not even his body servant knew from whence it came. "'Tis against the Divil," was all he would say. He would finger that particle of frayed silk oft with a tear in his eye. He battled his estate manager, even had to whip a man. Martha was ailing and seldom went abroad. But Washington would ride about his farm immediately upon a breakfast of strong tea and spend the morning and early afternoon on his own acreage.

His enemies claimed that years in office had robbed him of his vigor—that he was a slavering fool with a mouth of hippopotamus ivory teeth. But the general had more vigor now than half a century ago, when Virginia wags had dubbed him "the stallion of the Potomac."

Would that he'd had a stallion's blinding want! But he did have a want in him that measured slow, like a fist or canker under the heart. He would ride along the broken boundaries of his farm and feel that fist begin to press. He was not a man who mourned what might have been. He was a farmer who assisted in the birth of foals and did not shy away from horse blood on his hands.

But of a sudden he had a dream that pursued him across his waking hours so that he had little rest. A pair of angels perched on his bedpost. He could recognize one angel by its blond curls—Mistress Clara, whom he had not seen in sixteen years.

The second angel was a much deeper puzzle. It seemed to have no face—not a feature he could discern, not a mark. Was it man or woman, light-skinned or dark? It set him to worry 'til he reasoned that such a formless face was a paradox with features that he himself might fill in. Was it Hercules, his mulatto cook, who had vanished from Philadelphia but two years ago? With Clara's help, he presumed.

'Tis Hercules who had saved his presidence. He'd come up north with Hercules in the spring of '89. Martha did not accompany him. She was gloomy about the prospect of living in a metropolis, where noise itself was a form of debris. And Hercules gave him a wild root to suck on during the journey.

'T was Hercules who prepared his meals at the presidential mansion on Cherry Street, Hercules who sipped Madeira with him after those maddening levees, where he had to sit with scoundrels who wanted a piece of his hide, Hercules who behaved as his scout. He kept hoping that Gertrude might appear on Cherry Street. And when she did not, he sent Hercules to spy on Holy Ground. Hercules came back with a mournful look. "Excellency, Madame is dead."

His hand shivered while he drank Madeira. He canceled his next two levees. Why had the nuns not notified him of her illness?

"Excellency," Hercules said like some ambassador to Holy Ground, "Madame has been lying in her grave these past four years."

Gertrude had suffered for six months with a hideous tumor upon her chest. He cursed Clara and Johnny One-Eye for a full ten minutes 'til he realized that he alone was at fault. He'd buried himself at Mount Vernon, locked away in the daily rhetoric of his farm, lived with horses rather than men.

Could he offer condolences four years after the fact? Ten times he equipped his chariot for the narrow ride between Cherry Street and Holy Ground, with Hercules himself in the coachman's box, and ten times did he annul the voyage. There were affairs of state, urgent letters he had to write, etc., etc.—'t was the excuse of a scoundrel and a poltroon. He could not confront Gertrude's family of nuns, could not revisit the remains of his own past. But he did visit Gertrude's grave after months of machinations. That's how long it took Hercules to find the site. She was buried in the backyard of a free school for colored children in the Out Ward. Clara herself was now mistress of the school, Johnny its headmaster. He immediately deposed an anonymous gift to the free school, without his signature or seal of the United States.

'T was ten years ago. And now he understood why the two angels had visited him—the second one, with its unfinished face, was his own unfinished affairs. Washington was a man who needed families during peace and war—and his war families pressed against his mind: Hamilton and the other young aides who broke through his melancholy; and Clara, Gert, and Johnny One-Eye, who were like his own secret face. That's why these angels haunted him so, as if he'd had a second, unlived life that he himself had denied, and was now denying him, like some marvelous sweetwater well at which he would never drink.

Yet the angels had not deserted him. He would harangue the one with blond curls.

"Clara, why did ye steal my Hercules? I have prepared a will—freeing Hercules upon my death."

And the angel answered, "Excellency, Hercules believed he did not have to wait for a will."

'Tis reasonable, he thought, but he still began to cry.

"Ye gods, where are you, Johnny One-Eye?"

And whilst he had such conversations in his saddle, his farmhands would look at the Old Man wearing a frayed ribbon round his neck and wonder if this here gen'ral had ever been bossman of the Continentals. A portion of him lay with his redhead in that boneyard behind the free school for coloreds. A commander in chief ought to know—a battlefield was just a boneyard wearing a disguise. He'd flee Mount Vernon if he could take his angels and live with them under a war tent.

Peacetime was but a sweet deception, a winter without black drummer boys—there was no end to revolution.

Author's Note

I HAVE BEEN WRITING *Johnny One-Eye* ever since I was nine, a street kid in the South Bronx. It was there that I learned about George Washington, the father of our country, who seemed much more benevolent and forceful than my own father, and who had become by some curious sleight-of-hand the patron saint of our borough. I clung to all the myths surrounding George: his devotion to Martha, his wealthy, diminutive wife; his steadfastness as he crossed the Delaware on Christmas night, 1776, and caught the Hessians by the seat of their pants; his agony at Valley Forge as his solders marched without shoes and left a bloody trail in the snow.

Still, Washington did not seem to have a voice of his own. He was a brooding giant, given to long silences, and had to depend on his wartime amanuensis, Alexander Hamilton, to write his letters and lend a certain song to his thoughts. Hamilton also had a sway over me, since he was the favorite son of my Alma Mater, King's (later Columbia) College; it was at Columbia that I first discovered Jonathan Swift, and realized that the world was a poor substitute for my own little library, wherein I could find Lemuel Gulliver lying on the ground with Lilliputians in his hair and chortle with nervous terror and delight.

I much preferred the eighteenth century, with its measured music and comic nightmare, to the psychological minefield of modern times, where some poor Gulliver in the land of six-inch men would be looked upon as a gigantic codpiece, akin to Kafka's cockroach, and analyzed to death. And within *my* eighteenth century, I could play with the ghosts of Washington, Hamilton, and Benedict Arnold, the bravest warrior of the Revolution until he danced with the Devil at West Point and sold himself to the British.

And so I began to write about Arnold, hoping to turn his betrayal into some kind of demonic quest, not to aggrandize him or explain away his skulking around behind Washington's back, but to seek out his music, his voice, with all its sulfur, its vanity, its greed. I could not find this music no matter how many books I read. After he bolted from West Point, leaving his wife and infant son behind, there was little but bluster in every stance he took.

But the more I read about Washington, the more I liked. He was, it seems, an alarmingly moral man, a farmer who had to transform himself into a guerrilla fighter and live without the least ambition or sense of personal gain for seven years. He was the last man on the last boat when his army retreated from Brooklyn Heights during the Battle of Long Island, one of the worst debacles of the war.

He often stumbled, made mistakes, was reckless on his white charger, riding right into enemy fire. He'd been in love with Sally Fairfax, a freckle-faced flirt, when he was a much younger man. He swooned over this wife of a neighbor, wrote her letters that he begged her to burn. I seized upon this bit of indiscretion, and it would serve as an instrument to crack open his secretive nature. Washington did have a "voice" and a welter of feelings under his dour demean. And I created a counterpart to Sally, *another* freckle face, Mrs. Gertrude Jennings, who emerges as the redheaded queen of Manhattan's most spectacular bordello. Her illegitimate son, Johnny One-Eye, is in love with Clara, the most coveted harlot of Gertrude's house. Johnny, Gertrude, and Clara—all fictional—become Washington's wartime "family" and continue to haunt him for the rest of his life.

Occupied by the British during seven years of war, riven by a fire that nearly ruined it, Manhattan was indeed a maelstrom of poverty and wealth, where British officers dined on blancmange while the rest of the population scrounged for scraps of food. Across the East River, on Wallabout Bay, was a fleet of rotting ships where the British stored their prisoners; the most notorious of these ships was the *Jersey*.

Manhattan did have a red-light district called Holy Ground (on Robinson Street, which no longer exists), where Britain's commander in chief, General Sir William Howe, passed a good portion of the time. He did have a concubine, Mrs. Loring, whose husband Joshua served as chief commissary of the prison ships. Benedict Arnold did have a beautiful young wife, Peggy Shippen, who may well have been the most successful British "sleeper" of the war.

Other characters are wholly invented, including Sir William's servant, Mortimer, and Washington's orderly, Sparks, though I like to imagine that both Mortimer and Sparks did have their own historical counterparts. Yet it troubled me to learn how hidden African-Americans were during the Revolution. There was a lot of sound and fury about those slaves who joined the British side as sappers and stevedores, but much less is known about black Americans who composed one-quarter of the Continental Army by the end of the war. Some were sappers and cooks, others fought beside white troops, and still others had their own regiment, the First Rhode Islanders, chosen to take part in one of the very last skirmishes of the war. This was soon forgotten, or at least left out of our history books.

But Johnny One-Eye is both our narrator and "remembrancer" of the Revolution. He grew up on Robinson Street among a little nation of prostitutes, half of whom were black. When he's dumped into a potato bin by Washington's spymaster, Malcolm Treat (another fictional character), he comes out with black dust on his face and is called "Son of Ham."

He is no Son of Ham. He's a double agent wandering across the landscape, a picaro who befriends "Black Dick" Howe, commander of the British fleet, saves the life of Benedict Arnold, and tells children's tales to George Washington, while reimagining the Revolution with his own "Divilish" rhythms and the infernal logic of an eighteenth-century child.

—Jerome Charyn
Paris, March 15, 2007

About the Author

Jerome Charyn's most recent novel, *The Green Lantern*, was a finalist for the PEN/Faulkner Award in fiction. His work has been translated into seventeen languages, including Polish, Finnish, Korean, and Greek. A former Guggenheim Fellow, he lives in New York and Paris, where he teaches film theory at the American University.